Must Like Dogs

Skye Blaine

Must Like Dogs is a work of fiction.

ISBN: 978-0-9779483-8-3

Author's websites and contact information:
www.skyeblaine.com
www.theheartofthematter-dailyreminders.org
skye@skyeblaine.com

Published by:
Berkana Publications
Sebastopol CA 95472 USA

Cover image: the beautiful Nessa, provided by Jane Steinbeisser
Book layout: Berkana Publications

Printed in the United States of America

Dedicated to all the dogs who have graced my life: Baron, Arthur, Nisa, Kyle, Jesse, Seer, Dancer, Emma, Maggie, Salaam, and Bodhi.

Baron CDX, a German shepherd, was sweet, highly intelligent, and very obedient.

Arthur, a rescue and shaggy dog, sported big black and white patches. He came with the name Bonzo, but we renamed him to provide dignity.

Nisa came from my friend Shelby. Nisa was reputed to be golden retriever, dingo, and herding dog, but I'm convinced she was a mixture of golden retriever and smooth collie. She rode in the car with her head on my shoulder, and remained a precious companion for ten years.

Kyle, my first Irish wolfhound, chose me when he was ten days old by crawling in my lap. He was bred by Carol Gabriel. A sweet, goofy boy, he died of osteosarcoma at age five. A crushing loss.

Jesse, a herding dog mix, was Kyle's best friend. We were blessed with her alert, smart presence for thirteen years.

Seer, a whippet as large as a greyhound, came to live with us at age eleven. He was a refined and poised gentleman. A friend asked, "But where is his smoking jacket?"

Dancer, an Irish wolfhound, came from Carol Gabriel as a young adult. She welcomed Emma the puppy with love.

Emma, a smooth collie, patrolled for wildlife and told us when anything with fur showed up. She was independent and clever.

Maggie, a Scottish deerhound, came from Judy Shaw. Both elegant and silly, Maggie fulfilled my request for a "soulful" dog.

Salaam, a rescue Saluki from Dubai. She arrived with undiscovered kidney cancer, and we lost her after three weeks.

Bodhi, an elder California Saluki. He's subtle, elegant, and an easy companion—unless he sees a jackrabbit or cat!

All eleven dogs have been remarkable and gentle companions, but the six sighthounds own my doggie heart.

Acknowledgements

Boudewijn Boom: my sweet husband, for his steady support and endless proof-reading. He applies his thorough persistance to this work.

My dedicated weekly critique group: who went through the manuscript multiple times: Patrice "PH" Garrett, Beth Matthews, and Marie Judson-Rosier. They continue to hold my hand and light my way. Thank you!

Jane Steinbeisser: for the compelling cover photo of Nessa. It's the first photo I was sent when I put out the call.

Laura McHale Holland: for her editing and inspiration. Her website is: https://www.lauramchaleholland.com/

Katie Watts: for her encouragement and detailed line edits.

Charlotte Tressler: for catching even more word and phrase repetitions, and noticing inconsistencies.

Tegan Blaine: my niece, for permission to share the details of her harrowing twin birth experience.

My beta readers: Jennifer Anderman, Suzette Wright, Denise Jessup, Boudewijn Boom.

An annonymous cardiologist: for his wisdom, experience, and generosity. You know who you are.

Anais Ryken, Marie Huertas, and Dan Henroid: they all work at UCSF and provided information about the layout of the building in 2010.

Kathleen O'Brien, Attorney at Law: answered questions on adult adoption in Oregon.

Constance Miles: for her wise input from her midwife's perspective on the birth.

Joni de Saint Phalle: at South Eugene High School who researched dates the school semester began in January, 2010.

Chloë Bradley: for assistance with millennial slang.

I'm sure I've missed some kind soul who assisted me along the way. Contact me, and in the next printing, I'll happily make the correction.

Chapter One

December 2009

Rowan woke, stretched, and glanced out the window. Christmas dawn, and big fat flakes sailed past like kites. Usually a white holiday delighted her, but she dreaded today. A knot of tension lumped in her belly and, unable to get back to sleep, she slipped out of bed. The gleaming hardwood floors in the ranch house here at Bender's Ridge were heated—cozy for bare feet on frigid winter mornings.

She walked to the window and squinted. The snow came too thickly to tell the depth, so she tiptoed to the front of the house, turned on the porch light, and peered outside. The white stuff at the ranch was clean and kind of crunchy, unlike the dirty, slushy street snow in Eugene. It was hard not to live at Bender's Ridge all the time, but Mossy and Mom said the schools were better in Eugene. At least they got to come to Sisters almost every weekend during the school year. Sometimes it was a little gnarly driving in a blizzard but, generally, chains got them through.

Zephyr danced at her feet and Rowan patted her giant dog, smoothing the tufts of hair that stood up on her head. "Anxious to get outside, huh?"

The dog nosed her and sat, eyes fixed on her face.

Rowan opened the door. Zephyr streaked out to do her business, poking deep holes in the drifts on the deck, leaping and cavorting in the front circle. At least four inches had already accumulated on the valley floor, which meant more on the mountain tops.

Zephyr trotted back to the house, shaking hard before coming inside. Rowan wiped all four paws, making sure to work the towel between the pads of each foot. Then she kneaded her wiry coat from nose to tail tip.

She remembered the winter in Eugene after they adopted Zeph. During a hard rain, Rowan thought she'd dried her properly, but when Zephyr bounded up the stairs, the long hairs on her belly were covered with sloppy mud which she deposited on the beige living room carpet. They'd had to hire carpet cleaners, and she'd worked off the hefty sum. It was worth taking the time to do it right.

Rowan chewed her thumbnail, still annoyed at her mom for the comment she'd made two days before. She had been outside with Zephyr, working on their hide-and-seek game—and honing their telepathy skills—but with play because, otherwise, dogs get bored. She'd forgotten to fold the laundry, and her mom hollered, "Please get in here and make yourself useful." Mom always acted as though her practice with dogs had no value. Rowan knew it was her life's work, unfolding and expanding every day, and to have her mom repeatedly dismiss it smarted. Most days she brushed off her feelings, but something about her mom's words this time ate at her.

She shook off her distress. Zephy by her side, they padded down the hall to peek in the library at the back of the house, but she signaled not to cross the threshold. Each year, following his family's ritual, Mossy—her dad who adopted her—tied a wide red-ribbon swag across the doorway. No entering until after the family shared a special breakfast.

She flicked the switch near the door and thrilled as little lights illuminated the tall, freshly cut cedar. She sniffed the wintry scent. The tree held many handmade ornaments including some she'd made in grade school. She always acted like they were childish, but she secretly warmed at seeing them.

Would this Christmas be awful? She was fed up with her mom's attitude about her telepathy gifts. *I can't handle another day of her either ignoring my truth or scorning it.*

Her parents must have been up late, because presents were piled under the tree that hadn't been there the evening before. She loved the tradition they had: gifts opened slowly, one at a time. Even the dogs got surprises. Each year, Mossy assigned the job of handing out the packages, another tradition from his family. Last year, Mom held the post. This year was her turn. She surveyed her favorite room—bookcases lined the walls, even under the corner window with its two-foot-wide marble ledge. After Mossy opened the ribbon gateway, he'd light the fire.

Rowan snapped off the switch and motioned to Zephy. They walked to the bedroom, and the dog leapt on the bed. Rowan nudged her over to have enough room, snuggled under the down comforter—she always called it a "downy"—and smiled as she felt Zeph's muzzle settle in the curve of her hip.

When Zephyr came to live with them five years ago, Rowan had searched for a word to describe how she communicated with her. Initially, they sent mental pictures to each other. She'd found a word-roots book—her mom's from college—and yanked it from the shelf. *Wow—I didn't know this kind of book existed.* She started by flipping through her thesaurus for words that had to do with thinking, and found "pensive." Loving the feel of it in her mouth, she turned to her mom's book. There, she learned about the French verb *penser*, to think, and from Latin, *pensare*, to ponder. After considering these, she invented a verb, "to pense." It still tickled her.

She didn't understand how it happened, but a couple of years ago, Zephyr's communication—which first had only been images, then images and feelings, and later included even smells—began flowing in as words in addition to pictures. She knew Zeph wasn't thinking in language, but that's how Rowan received the messages. She discovered she could send thoughts back instead of only images like she used to. Zephy understood them. Somehow, the telepathic translation worked. They still shared pictures and feelings, but didn't depend only on them. A close relationship with a dog was the best gift of all.

The tension was still thick with Mom—she hadn't been able to let go of her mother's attitude and comment. She hoped she could hold her temper and the day would go all right.

The kitchen buzzed with activity and laughter, her mom and dad busy working at the counters, dogs waiting expectantly for handouts.

Mom was finishing the Brown Betty, a recipe handed down through the Graham generations. She sat at the counter crumbling topping over the apples. The scents of cinnamon, nutmeg, cloves, lemon, and brown sugar filled the air. They wouldn't eat the dessert until Christmas dinner—late in the afternoon—but her mom loved to have the aroma from the bubbling dish flavor the holiday morning. Zeph stood by Carolina's side, patiently waiting for another apple slice. But then the giant dog nosed Mom's stomach. Not hard—Zephy was remarkably gentle. Rowan noticed how her nostrils whiffled, taking in information. She seemed intense. What was she picking up? She'd pense her later; there was too much going on.

Mom finished the topping, wiped her hands on a dishtowel, then turned to stroke Zephyr's ears and give the dog one last apple slice. With a kind murmur, she handed another to Moss's dog, Jazz.

"Hey Row, would you start the bacon?" Moss asked. "You make it the best of all of us. So crisp. Does everyone want scrambled eggs, croissants, and hot chocolate?"

"No cocoa for me," Carolina said. "I'd like a mocha, please."

"Me too," Rowan chimed in. Back in May, on her fifteenth birthday, her parents had finally agreed she could drink coffee. She loved the taste as much as the luscious smell.

She fished the organic bacon from the fridge. When they craved what Mossy couldn't bring home with his bow, they shopped at Long's Meats in Eugene. There they bought grass-fed beef and healthier bacon.

"I'll make mochas after I put the croissants in the toaster oven," Moss said. "Lina, can you prepare the eggs?" He pointed to a nearby basket filled with tan, white, and green eggs. "I collected those this morning. The light I installed so they'll lay in winter works beautifully."

"Thank you. They're gorgeous. And you washed them, too." Carolina gave him a squeeze.

Rowan carefully laid the strips of bacon in the largest frying pan. She turned them often, making sure they browned evenly, and pressed down on bubbles to make the slices go flat so the puffy parts didn't stay greasy and uncooked. She giggled to herself. Neither Mom nor Mossy had patience for any part of this job.

Moss hummed "Deck the Halls." Carolina added the words. Rowan joined in and all three sang as they cooked.

Her mom whisked eggs in a copper bowl. *Sha-boom sha-boom. Sha-boom sha-boom.*

Rowan loved the unique rhythm. "Who taught you that?"

"Before you were born, your daddo took me to Mont Saint Michel on our honeymoon. He saved a long time to make the trip happen. La Mère Poulard, a restaurant there, whips eggs this special way for their world-famous omelets. I prefer scrambled but think their method makes a difference—it adds more air. It's a kind of four-beat rhythm."

"Cool. How come Mossy didn't take you somewhere like that when you two got married?"

"Because he wanted to be here at Bender's Ridge where you're happiest and could feel included."

"*Really?*" Surprised Mossy would do that for her, the tag-along-kid, Rowan wheeled around to look for him. He was setting the table in the dining room. Peering in, she noticed he'd gotten silver candlesticks from the china cabinet. She watched him light new beeswax candles. A few minutes later, the honey scent filtered into the kitchen.

Carolina pulled the warm croissants from the oven and scooped fluffy scrambled eggs into a bowl. Rowan gathered her bacon from the paper towels where the strips had drained, and they carried the serving dishes to the table. Moss went back to the kitchen and returned holding a tray filled with mochas, hot chocolate, and cherry jam. All the mugs had whipped-cream dollops.

Zephyr lies at the margin of the room where people eat. She knows not to come in; asking for food at meals brings frowns and stern words. Jazz presses against her.

Her humans finish eating and walk to the tree-room. Kibble Man unties the leash blocking the door, and they go in. A tree comes inside during cold-and-snow-time. Remembering previous tree-days, she licks her mustache, anticipating treats. Pack Mama sits on the couch with Kibble Man, and Zephyr lies at her feet.

When everyone was settled and Moss put a match to the fire, Rowan sat cross-legged by the tree and picked up the first package, almost two feet long and four inches wide—but light. She opened the card. It was for Mossy from her mom. She pensed Zephyr: *want to deliver this to Kibble Man?*

Her dog rose and, taking the gift with a soft mouth, dropped it in Mossy's lap.

Carolina stiffened and frowned.

Rowan heaved a breath, cocked her head at her mom, and shook it. *She can't acknowledge the obvious.*

Lina knew she was making mistakes with her daughter, but memories of her own mother, decked out in long skirts and beads, still haunted—her high school classmates had made mean fun. Rowan was so like her, not in the way she dressed, but in her connection with the unseen.

Moss glanced at Rowan, surprise showing on his face at her boldness pensing in front of her mom, and then read the card out loud. "For Moss—my hunter-gatherer—from Lina." He made a curious what-is-this expression, jiggling the gift. It made no sound Rowan could hear, but Zephy and Jazz pricked their ears. Moss unwrapped the gift and tilted the box for all to see: four sleek arrows. Smiling, he lifted one out and, running his hand along its shaft, whistled. "Gorgeous. These are the arrows I've been admiring. Thanks, sweetie."

Rowan picked up the next present—for Jazz. She handed it to Zephyr. *This is for your pack mate.* She dropped it in front of the greyhound mix, and lay directly by her, watching carefully.

Carolina's mouth drew down into a flat line.

Ha, Rowan thought. Mom noticed. She'll have to deal with it. I'm done protecting her from the truth, hiding my connection with Zephy—ridiculous. No more.

Jazz watched Moss, waiting for his signal.

"She's never going to forget her early training from her first owner," Rowan said. "It's sad, all those dumb 'free' commands she waits for."

"Yeah," Moss said. "I've given up trying to change her. Harsh owners cause real damage." He turned to his dog. "Go ahead, girl, it's yours. Free gift." Jazz nibbled the gift open and nosed the paper away. Inside lay a new royal-blue octopus toy.

"Now Jazz has a Wubby as well," Rowan said. "Thank heavens—she's always stealing Zephy's. Good gift, Mom."

Carolina looked flabbergasted at the compliment. "Why, thank you."

Jazz sniffed the toy, then collected it between her front paws and rested her chin on the knob of its head. When Zephyr tried to nose it, Jazz wrinkled her lips and showed her teeth. Message clear, Zeph backed away.

Rowan fished under the tree and pulled out the two packages she'd been looking for. It wasn't fair to make the dogs wait. She read the card out loud: "For Zephy and Jazz, from Carolina and Row." She placed a gift between each dog's front legs. Zephyr set a paw on top of her package and ripped it open. Inside lay two enormous homemade dog biscuits shaped like Milk Bones, each a foot long. Jazz waited for Moss's approval, not tearing into her package until his signal.

"Free food," he said. "Go for it." It took Jazz a couple of minutes to dismantle the wrapping.

"Now wait, girls," Rowan said. Expectantly, the dogs looked up. She broke off pieces. They chewed contentedly, and she put the rest on the piano.

She opened and read the card on the next gift. "For Rowan, from Mossy. In support of your connection with animals." She felt the shape—definitely a book. It was such a relief Mossy understood and supported her. Opening it, she discovered an old volume, *Kinship With All Life*. "Oh my gawd, you found it," she crowed.

When Rowan glanced up, her mother was frowning at Moss—the "why are you encouraging her" look she knew well. *For heaven's sake, my parents have their own private telepathy, too—doesn't Mom realize? Is it so different from what I have with Zephy?* She whirled on her mom. "I take after Grammie—and remember, *you* made me. The way I am is not my fault. Geez. Get over it."

Moss squinched his face, dropped his hands between his knees, and tapped his thumbs together. Jazz immediately rose, bumped his leg, and leaned into him. He stroked her ears.

"Let's not do this now, not on Christmas," Carolina muttered.

"Yes, right now. There's never a good time for you." Rowan planted her fists against her ribs. "If you want a relationship with me, you've got to open your mind to what I love." She teared up, and her voice came out choked. "Otherwise, you won't know me. You already kind of don't. Is that what you want?"

Carolina folded her arms and looked away. Seeing her response, Rowan clenched the book to her heart, pushed off the chair, and stormed from the room.

Chapter Two

In the Christmas room, Carolina and Moss stared at each other. He rubbed his fingers up and down his forehead. Carolina snapped, "Why do you support her in this?"

"Because it's her calling," he said. "No one could, or should, separate me from writing, correct? Whether you like it or not, no one could or should separate Rowan from her gift of telepathy. Especially not you. This barrier you've constructed is tearing her up. Surely you can see it; you're her mother, for God's sake." He hitched to standing, and paced, limping a little. His prosthesis bothered him this morning. "I'm one-hundred percent on Rowan's side. She's not asking you to love her passion—she's begging you to simply accept how and who she is. She can't turn it off."

"I'm terrified her friends will laugh at her."

"Why?"

"Kids teased me because my mother was weird—she wasn't like other moms with bridge and book clubs. Every other word was about astrology or tarot. She even dressed strangely."

"But your mother has great friends, too—buddies who share her interests. So what if some people make fun? It's their own limitations, and Row certainly knows that. She's already more cautious than her grandmother—haven't you noticed? She has a good dash of you too, my love. She's sensible, and far better balanced than her grammie." He waited, then said, "Any chance you can apologize, start a peace talk with her, and salvage Christmas?"

She sat for a few minutes, head in hands. Moss stayed quiet. He'd done all he could. Now this was Lina's work.

When she stood, Zeph rose too. Together, they slowly plodded toward Rowan's room. Moss saw her grab some of Zephyr's neck fur.

Carolina hesitated outside her daughter's door, shifting from one foot to the other. Zephyr waited patiently. Confused and tense, Carolina couldn't parse what she could possibly say to mend this. Moss had never groused at her this way before, not in their four married years. He was right—she'd done real damage; mothers know these things. Regret clawed her heart, but resistance clogged her resolve even more. Kids had not only teased, but bullied her because of her mom's behavior. She'd never shared that with Rowan. Perhaps it was a way in. Her daughter had suffered through middle school; she knew how harsh it could be. With a glimmer of hope, she knocked.

"Go away. You're only here because Mossy sent you."

The bitter tone sliced through her. "Give me a chance," she called. "I want to share some details with you I've never told him."

Seconds, and then a minute, ticked by. Carolina tried again. "Please?"

"Why bother? It's—"

Carolina knew Rowan was searching her ever-growing vocabulary.

"It's *entrenched*. You won't change."

"You can't be sure. I've had an epiphany." She didn't think Row knew the word, and waited, hope rising again. For them, new words were often a doorway.

Finally, after a long pause, "Epiphany?"

"Insight. I've had a fresh insight."

Another pause. She imagined Row scribbling down the new addition on her word list.

"This better be good." Dragging footsteps, a huffing sigh. Finally, the door opened. Her daughter's swollen face crushed her.

"I'm so sorry," Carolina whispered.

"You should be."

"May Zephyr and I come in? I love you."

"No, you don't, not unconditionally. You don't love the core of what makes me, me. Yeah, come on in." She patted Zeph.

"Sweetie, here's why I've had trouble accepting this part of you." She sat on the edge of the bed. "One day in eighth grade, a church-going kid spat 'My mom says you're witch's spawn' in my ear when she passed me in the corridor. Another girl—one of the mean ones—overheard. For months, all I got was 'witch's spawn.' They tripped me in the hallways and on the playground. One time, I fell, smacked a bench, and broke my nose. Kids stopped sitting with me at lunch, even the girl I believed was my best friend. For a while, I had no one. It hurt worse because I already distrusted Grammie's new-age stuff. It was the year I turned against religion *and* the paranormal."

"Rough."

"That's only part of it. They made my life miserable. Cruel. You know how teenage girls can be."

"I see it at school." Her face softened a little bit. "It's why Maggie's so important to me. She understands. Well, and Mossy, of course. Mommo, you'll let her come again this summer, right? With Bender? I can't imagine vacation without her."

Carolina hesitated. She was relieved to hear Rowan's toddler name for her again; it often signaled intimacy between them. "Well ... sure. She's a great kid and a wonderful cousin. I suppose if we have to go to Eugene, Glady could come stay with you two."

"Yeah! I love discussing books with her, new stuff coming into the library that she wants to tell me about."

A chunk of silence fell between them. Finally, their eyes met. "After you finish the book Moss gave you, could I read it?"

Rowan brightened a little. "Sure."

"I can't promise I'll finish it. But I'll give it an honest shot." Carolina opened her arms, and Rowan came to her. Always wanting connection, Zephyr nosed between them.

On their way back to the Christmas room, Carolina put her arm around Rowan and said, "I'll make mistakes, fail even. But sweetheart, now I'm really trying. When I blow it, tell me. I can't lose my relationship with you. Not ever. It'd kill me." She leaned over and whispered in her daughter's ear. "What do you think? Can we pick up our Christmas celebration? Can you face more presents?"

When they re-entered the library, Moss was reading, Jazz at his feet. He glanced up, eyebrows raised.

"I'm sorry I lost it." Row stared at the floor. "Mom and I began a kind of truce. She's even asked to read *Kinship with All Life* when I'm done. I know this'll probably come up over and over, but it's a start. Can we try opening gifts again?"

He tilted his head. "Well, that's a relief. It's a darn scary household when the womenfolk aren't speaking." He pushed off the couch to an awkward stand and gathered the mugs onto the tray. "Our coffees are cold. I'll remake them before we start opening again." He leaned the tray on his hip and flashed Carolina a thumbs up on the way out the door.

Rowan glanced up and smiled when he returned with their mochas. She sipped hers with appreciation, then began handing out the rest of their presents one by one. With wrapping paper strewn around her, she thought they were done.

"Row," Carolina asked, "Would you please get the envelope stuck in the tree? It's for you, and it's time to open it. It's more … like a promissory note than a present, exactly." She took Mossy's hand.

What's up? Rowan wondered. She slid her finger under the glued edge and pulled the card out. It had dogs on the front—their cards usually did. Inside was written, "You're going to have a baby brother or sister next summer. We're due July 17th."

It took her a moment to process the information. "You're pregnant? This *is* a huge present! I'll get the sibling I've always wanted." She hugged them both.

Later, in her room with Zephy's head on her thigh, she let herself sink into thoughts and feelings. Here she was, fifteen-and-a-half, and finally going to have a sib, of all things. They'd been hoping since they got married, but it hadn't happened. Until now. It was weird and yucky to think about her parents, you know, doing it, but she was happy about the result. She'd been lonely as an only child.

At thirty-nine, her mom was having a *baby*. No, she'd be forty by the time she gave birth. *Wow. What age was she when she had me?* "Twenty-four," she muttered after counting back—her mom was considered a young mother then, but now she was at the end of the line. Time was strange. Mom didn't look old. She was slim and fit, and her hair wasn't even graying. Mossy, only two years older, had silver salted through his black curls. He grumbled the war did it to him, but it looked distinguished.

She was happy for them, but worried, too. Losing her daddo at seven had been awful. Pregnancy could be dangerous. What if something happened to her mom? She and Mossy might both come apart. She got up and paced. If the worst happened, at least they'd have each other. Since he'd adopted her, they *were* truly family.

Rowan tried to imagine them with the addition of a baby. Was it a brother or sister? Which did she want? Then she remembered—she needed to pense Zeph. She sat back on the bed. *When you nosed Pack Mama's belly in the kitchen, what did you notice?*

A picture of nursing puppies flooded Rowan's mind, and the words came: *It's a litter.* Zephyr turned to her, staring, then sent the same message again. Rowan pensed back, acknowledging she understood.

Could her mom be having twins? No way. She stood up. But then, Zeph had never been wrong. *Five* people and two dogs in the kitchen next Christmas? The thought of that creative chaos made her giggle. She couldn't wait to share this with Mossy, and felt a twang of disappointment her mom wasn't more open to interspecies telepathy. It made her mad, even though it seemed like they had reached a fresh beginning. What mother didn't want to fully know her own daughter? It meant Mom missed a huge chunk of who she was, of what was most important to her.

Suddenly, fright knotted her belly. Litters were usually *more* than two. Geez, could her mom be having triplets? She wanted to pense Zeph to get a clearer answer, but didn't know how to frame the question. She didn't think her dog counted, at least not like people did. How could she communicate this? After considering for a moment, she sent Zeph a picture of two puppies, then a picture of three, with the sense of a question. The reply came promptly. *Two.* Rowan sighed with relief. Her family already had two sets of twin cousins. She asked, *Can you hear them?*

Yes came the response.

She pensed back, *Can you smell them? Do they smell different?*

The answer: *Pack Mama has different smells.*

She yearned for a dog's nose—they knew much more about their world through scent. She felt like one of her limbs had been amputated—a limb Zephy had. Lucky dog.

Rowan couldn't wait to tell Moss about the twins.

She leaned against the pillows again, and a disappointing thought popped into her mind. Mossy's niece Maggie and her Doberman, Bender, had come to the ranch every summer for the last three years. The baby was due July seventeenth, her mom said. Rowan remembered *she'd* been born two weeks early; this baby could come at the beginning of the month. Her mom had said yes to Maggie's visit when she'd asked before—she hadn't wanted to spoil the secret. Would she change her mind and decide they couldn't come? Her cousin was ready to practice pensing with Bender and needed encouragement. This summer, Rowan had been planning to introduce her to the experience of the "big field"—the field of awareness prior to thought she'd discovered when she woke up from the coma after the rollover accident four years ago. It would help Maggie connect with Bender in a deeper way. She needed to convince the grownups they *must* come this vacation.

She gently knuckled Zeph's ears and played with her long eyebrows. The dog groaned with pleasure.

The next morning, Rowan found Mossy in the kitchen making mochas. "Where's Mom?"

"Sleeping in. Pregnancy makes women tired."

"Zephy told me something last night. Something big."

He tilted his head, waiting.

"She says Mom's having twins."

Moss's mouth dropped open. He stared at her. "What? Oh my heavens, I bet she's right, too. Lordy, what are we in for now?"

Rowan nodded. "I thought you should know."

An hour later, Moss went in to check on Carolina. She was pulling on jeans. "Can I make you breakfast?"

"Yes, please. And a mocha."

He sat with her while she ate. They talked about what had happened Christmas morning.

"You know," he said, "There's stuff Zeph has communicated to Row she hasn't shared with you."

Carolina stared at him. "Like what?"

"Not mine to—"

"You'd better, and right now. I won't let on."

"Are you sure you want to know? Be careful what you ask for; it's something provable."

"Now I'm even more curious."

He shook his head. "And ready to make fun and discount it too, I suppose."

She looked at her hands, working her fingers. "It's so unconscious on my part."

"It's time to make it conscious—and stop."

"Okay. I promise. I'll practice. Out with it."

Moss fell quiet. Finally, he whispered, "Zeph says we're having twins."

She slapped her thigh. "Ridiculous."

"Perfect example. Not a successful practice attempt. Each time, your attitude undermines Rowan. This'll be proven or disproved at your next appointment. What if Zeph turns out to be correct?"

"Huh." Carolina pursed her lips. "Oh my God, what if it's true? Holy shit."

"I'll bet she is."

She stared at him, eyes wide. "This is weird, but Zeph's been lying at my feet, not following Rowan so often."

Chapter Three

Zephyr hears the rooster crow, stands and stretches, her chest almost scraping the ground. She goes to the bed, sniffs her girl—still asleep—and trots off to find Jazz. Every dawn, they patrol the fenced portion of the big land, taking in rich scents, going after vermin. Occasionally a deer jumps inside, and it's the most fun—giving reckless chase. She's not interested in catching it. Running is what she loves most.

Jazz is still snoring in Pack Mama and Kibble Man's sleeping room. Zeph nudges her. The other dog wakes with a squeaky yawn and jumps up to follow, always ready for early morning adventure. They bound out the extra-large dog door, Zephyr in the lead, and head toward the barn. Now the chickens are squawking. The dogs' strides lengthen until they're galloping full out, determined to frighten away what's bothering the birds. A raccoon scurries for the garden fence, claws up it and, growling and hissing, hangs on top of a post taunting them. Zeph barks, loud and deep. Jazz joins in.

The volleys awakened Moss. Muttering, he swung to sitting and pulled on a thigh sock, then his prosthesis. Carolina stirred. He leaned over and whispered, "Go back to sleep, sweetheart. The dogs have treed something. I'll take care of it." She murmured "thank you," rolled to her other side, and tugged the duvet over her shoulder. He yanked on jeans and a sweatshirt and fumbled in the hallway for his boots and parka.

His breath made frosty puffs when he stepped onto the porch. Rubbing his arms to warm up, he hitched toward the noise. The damn 'coon again. The dogs had trapped and terrified the thing. When the raccoon saw him, it scuttled down the inside of the garden fence and hurried along one of the paths. The critter knew the way to safety; the dogs lit out after this guy regularly.

"Come on, girls," he said, snapping his fingers. "Great job, but Lordy, what a racket on a Sunday morning. You'll startle us all awake, and it's only eight. This is our one morning of the week to sleep in. How about breakfast, and back to bed?" They stayed trained on their prey until the raccoon finally waddled out of sight. Moss sang out "breakfast" again, and the dogs, tongues lolling, followed him.

After he fed both beasties, Moss limped back to their room and unlegged. He gazed at his beautiful wife, her hands outside the covers, protectively cupping the baby even as she slept. It had taken almost four years to get pregnant—they'd been about to give up trying. Carolina was soon to be forty, and he, forty-two—older parents, for sure. But they'd be solid, loving guardians of this little being.

Lina was having an ultrasound in a few weeks in Bend; their local doc didn't have the equipment. If it turned out they were having two babies, well, then Zeph and Rowan's communication was the real deal, which he'd always suspected. He slipped quietly back into bed and snuggled around his wife, filled with gratitude and the wild mystery of it all. *Twins? Wonderful—but oh shit. Chaotic.*

Later, in the afternoon, Zephyr presses her nose between her paws and puzzles over the sounds of Pack Mama's litter she can hear when she gets very close. Two sets of beats, one different from the other. Does her girl need to know?

The next day, back in Eugene—after Rowan left for school—Moss asked Carolina to come into his office. "Sweetie, I'd like us to build a writing studio here. Check this out: Smiling Wood Yurts has kits." He showed her a photo on his laptop of an octagonal wooden structure with a peaked roof ending in a central, circular skylight. "I think a twenty footer would be perfect—it could go behind the house, there—" he pointed out the window to a flat location. "I can get the quiet I need when I'm working. It's 350 square feet, big enough for a Murphy bed we can open without impacting the writing area, and has a bathroom, too. After our baby's born, if you desperately need a quiet night's sleep, or if one of us is coughing or restless, we'll have a separate little retreat space. What do you think?"

She gazed at the screen and clicked on a couple of photos. "They're handsome, but look awfully expensive—how much would it cost?"

"All tricked out, probably $40,000."

Carolina's eyes widened, and her fingers jumped to her mouth.

Moss smiled at her. "Will you ever get used to having money—you know, deep in your bones comfortable with it?"

She flushed. "After four years, you'd think I'd have adjusted."

He reached out and smoothed her brow. "Sweetheart, everything of mine is yours."

She fell silent for a moment. "Thanks. I know I'm stubborn. How about this? It's time we put you on the title of this house. You included me on the ranch property."

He pushed his chair back and frowned at her. "Only if you'll finally let me reimburse you for half the value. We could get it appraised, and have a real estate agent look at comps, too."

She squinched her face. "It feels uncomfortable, you giving me money. You already paid off my debts and Zeph's bills."

"That was years ago, because it was nuts paying interest," he said. Please consider it. This is a win-win for our family. The property value will increase, and we'll have an additional structure that'll help us out after the baby comes." He looked out the window for a moment. "Here's an idea—we set up a 'health-and-well-being fund' with the money I give you for the property, and it's yours to spend any way you choose."

She brightened. "Great idea. Then I won't feel guilty making a purchase for me."

"There's never any reason for you to."

Two weeks later, after Sunday lunch, Rowan, Moss, and Carolina sat at the Bender's Ridge table eating the crisp Moss made with cold-cellar-stored apples from their own tree.

"But I want to see an ultrasound of the baby," Rowan said. "Pleeease? I need to be included."

Moss and Carolina glanced at each other.

"Don't do your silent communication thing," Rowan groused. "It's only fair. Tomorrow's Martin Luther King Day, so I'll only miss school on Tuesday."

"Okay," Carolina said. "But not during the actual exam, just the ultrasound."

"Repulsive. I'll stay in the waiting room while she examines you."

"All right, come along," Moss said. "We'll eat somewhere in Bend."

"Let's go to Spork," Carolina said. "I'm craving kimchi. And their Thai Beef Salad."

"Again?" Rowan asked. "We went there the last *two* times. I'm hungry for a burger and fries."

Carolina frowned. "Doesn't the pregnant mama with weird food preferences get to choose?"

Moss ruffled Rowan's hair. "Too bad, kiddo. Pregnancy wins this one. You'll understand when you have kids."

"Not happening." Rowan said. "Never." She stomped back to her room.

"We're leaving at eight-thirty," Carolina called after her. Then she turned to Moss. "Are we going to survive a fifteen-year-old *and* a baby?"

Rowan stood pressed next to Moss in the examining room, trying to stay out of the doctor's way. Carolina stretched out on the table and bared her belly.

"You're showing a bit more than I'd expect at twelve weeks. Could you be mistaken about the date of your last period?" Dr. Jamison squirted a splat of gel and rubbed it around her mom's stomach.

"I'm pretty sure," Carolina said.

"Okay, I'm looking for your baby now." The doctor moved the wand around, watching the monitor. "There, a heartbeat." She slowly slid the tip along Carolina's belly. "Oh my—a second heartbeat." She searched for another moment, and Rowan realized she was making sure there weren't three.

Dr. Jamison turned from the monitor and met Carolina's gaze. "My dear, you're having twins. No wonder you're showing more than expected. Congratulations."

"You're joking, right?" Carolina sputtered. "Holy shit."

The doctor shook her head. "It's twins. No doubt. Look for yourself."

Rowan craned to get a better view. *Zephy was right.* She didn't say anything, but leaned in closer, grabbing Mossy's hand, giving it a little squeeze. She tuned in to Zephyr, and sent her a picture of a litter of two, along with a flood of joy and awe all jumbled up. She felt Zephy's return psychic tail wag of acknowledgment.

"Oh boy," said Moss. "Good Lord." He squeezed Rowan's hand back, then let it go, and reached for Carolina's. "Sweetheart—this is an extra blessing."

"I'm terrified," Carolina whispered. "I'll be forty before they're born."

"They aren't identical, though. These are fraternal twins. See?" The doctor pointed to the screen in two places. "They each have their own placenta."

Rowan stared at the monitor, taking in what Dr. Jamison said. She watched the hearts beat—so fast—inside little bodies with large heads. *Those grow into actual full-sized babies?*

Moss paced the room muttering to himself, "We'll be fine, not to worry. Everything will be all right."

Carolina turned to the doctor. "Can I handle this? At my age?"

"You're in great shape. You'll do fine. We'll watch you closely."

"But I wanted a midwife to help me deliver. At home. Oh Lordy, I want to be *home*. I hate hospitals."

The doctor frowned, thinking. "Well. There are some very big ifs. If both babies are head down, the rest of your pregnancy goes smoothly, and your blood pressure remains normal—possibly. I'd prefer you have an O.B. present to step in if necessary. Certainly not out in the boonies in Sisters. In Eugene, possibly—Riverbend has a great birth center you could think about; they make it feel like home. After all, your health and your babies are paramount, right? I'll send my report and images to your Eugene doc." She handed Moss a printout of the ultrasound. "You two need to consider your options carefully. I'd like to get another ultrasound at twenty weeks."

"We have plenty of time," Moss said, softly, staring at the picture. "One little step, then another." He leaned down and grazed Carolina's lips.

She wrapped her arms around him. "Thank you," she whispered.

They walked into Spork and found seats in the corner. After they ordered, Carolina got up. "I have to pee again," she grumbled, and marched toward the ladies room. Rowan sighed with relief, and turned to her dad. "Now we can talk for a minute. Can you believe it? Zephy knew. Mom's having a litter."

Moss chuckled. "You and Zephyr are remarkable. How are you feeling about twins? It's a big change for you, too."

"Actually, I'm happy—Mom won't have time to focus on me. Those babies will keep her soooo busy." She giggled. "I bet Zeph will be a fabulous babysitter. Sitter of babies, I mean." She erupted in laughter.

Moss set his hands on Rowan's arms, and waited until she calmed down and met his gaze. "Lina's going to need your help, too. Help from all of us. A lot of it, and for a long time. Probably until the kids start school."

"Ri-i-ight." She drew out the word, her brow knit, as though thinking about the implications.

"But keep in mind," he went on, "when all of you are grown, you'll be glad you have siblings, even if they are sixteen years younger. Build those relationships now, and it'll pay off later, for the rest of your life. Siblings are special."

The server brought their food.

Carolina made her way back to the table. "You two look like you're in deep conversation. What about?"

"Brothers or sisters," Rowan said. "I think it's going to be cool. Mossy was talking about how much work it'll take."

"It's a huge change for all of us. Two babies. Every time I think about it I get the jitters. I'm salivating," Carolina went on. "I need more kimchi. I can't get enough of it."

Moss flagged down the waitress and ordered a second side dish before digging into his West African peanut curry. "What a great change from my own cooking. The cilantro's fantastic."

Rowan bit into her Korean barbecue short ribs. "This is tasty," she admitted. "But a burger next time, okay? With sweet potato fries."

Moss watched Carolina shoveling in bite after bite. "I'm going to learn to make kimchi," he said. "It can't be difficult. Cabbage, carrots, salt…." He fished around, sniffing the other ingredients. "A touch of garlic and ginger. Maybe some shrimp paste." He peered at it again. "Are these leeks? I see daikon, green onion. And whatever ferments it. I wonder if there's a little sugar in there? I'll research recipes."

Carolina glanced up, eyebrows raised. "Be still my heart. Thank you."

Back in Eugene, after Rowan and Zeph went to her room for the night, Moss made tea and stretched out on the couch. Carolina plunked herself between his legs and rested her head on his chest. He put his arms around her. Jazz lay at their feet.

"My God, Moss—Zephyr knew, and somehow told Rowan. In Dr. Jamison's office, it was all I could do to keep my chin off the floor when she said we're having twins."

"Dogs' senses are much stronger than ours. She can probably hear the babies, and maybe smell them, too," he said.

"You think? It's kind of spooky. You didn't tell Rowan you shared her secret, did you?"

"Nope. So you don't have to apologize for not trusting Zeph this time. Who knows, Rowan may spill the beans after the fact. She's getting bolder about revealing their communication. You might want to consider how you'll respond."

"I don't know how to handle it." Carolina twisted a fist in the palm of her other hand. "I guess my best tack is to ask questions. Try to be curious." She rubbed fingers up and down her forehead. "Geez. My daughter tests every single resistance I've clung to."

"That's what teens do."

"But she's been in my face since she first started talking. In every way, she's my opposite."

"She's your teacher," he said. "And I'm not sure she's as opposite as you make out."

"Maybe I haven't wanted to acknowledge it. I've been trying to make her wrong."

She turned into his arms again, and he cuddled her while she wept.

One evening in Eugene a couple of weeks later, Rowan waited until they were all in the living room. Rain sluiced against the windows. Jazz lay as close to the fireplace as she could without igniting. A few times, Row put her hand on the dog's coat. *Scorching hot! She should live in Phoenix, not rainy, dank Oregon.*

She didn't dare bring up stuff about Zephy's communication with her mom unless Mossy was around—he kind of mediated things. But she'd promised herself to share their telepathy regardless of Mommo's reaction. Zeph nosed her, sensing tension. *I'm okay, but be ready for a grumpy Pack Mama*, Rowan pensed.

First, she went to the kitchen and made everyone chamomile tea. She carried the mugs on a tray, along with goodies she'd baked this afternoon—a recipe she found on the internet for super chocolaty cookies made with egg whites instead of fat. They'd turned out crunchy on the outside, moist inside. Both dog noses lifted, knitting the new scents. "Nope, not for you," she said. "Chocolate. *Bad* for dogs."

They both folded their ears and dipped their heads.

"Sorry, I shouldn't have said 'bad.' I wouldn't forget you—I brought your biscuits."

Now their ears perked forward. She set the tray on the coffee table and gave the girls their treats. As the canines crunched—Jazz, delicately picking; Zeph, ripping into hers—Rowan handed out mugs and passed around the cookies.

"Wow," her mom said, after her first bite. "These are fantastic. Be sure to put the recipe in the wooden box. It's a keeper."

Moss nodded. "Yummy."

"Thanks. So—" Rowan's heart rate zipped up, and she took a breath to steady herself. "I'm glad you're sitting down." She stood up and leaned against the back of the chair. "I need to tell you something about my communication with Zeph."

Her mother tensed, and turned to look at Moss. He gave an encouraging nod.

"Zephy told me about the twins before your appointment in Bend."

She stopped in front of Carolina, worried about what was coming next, but her mother's voice was calm. "How exactly did she communicate to you?"

Rowan thought carefully before she spoke. "She sent me a picture of a litter of puppies. I got scared there might be triplets, so I tried to figure out a way she could tell me how many. I sent her an image of two, then three. She clearly indicated you were having two."

"With another picture?"

Rowan nodded.

"Impressive."

She didn't get tense—a first ever. Rowan studied her mom through lowered lashes, still expecting a delayed reaction. *It's enough for now. Maybe I won't ever be able to tell her about the penses translating into words.* Puzzled and surprised, she glanced at Mossy, hoping to get his attention—but his gaze was focused on Carolina. Rowan shrugged and passed the cookies again. He took a second one, but her mom sighed and passed them back. "I guess one's my limit," she said, patting her expanding girth. "As it is, I'll get larger than a blow-up beach ball. I need to eat plenty of calories, but they need to be high-value food."

"I think I did okay, don't you?" Carolina asked Moss after Rowan went downstairs to do homework.

He smoothed her frown wrinkles with his thumb. "You did great. How'd it feel?"

"Kind of scary." Her voice quavered. "Like I gave up a chunk of territory."

"You did. And you'll feel lighter, once you get used to managing a smaller country. Consider this: instead of resisting Rowan's skill, how about inviting it? You know Zeph is a great judge of character; she chose Rowan. She'd most likely know if people were hiding something or extra nervous. When we interview babysitters, let's have Row and Zephyr there."

"Whoa. It's a big step."

"Not so big. We all have to get along with this person. Wouldn't you want all the help we can get choosing someone? Think about it."

Carolina pondered his comment before nodding. "This 'inviting' is like 'toasting the complications,' when you and I clinked glasses years ago?"

"Exactly."

"That's when I knew," she said.

"Knew what?"

She saw he remembered the moment as vividly as she did, but wanted to hear her say it. "Knew I was falling in love with you. The thought I had then was, 'He doesn't shrink from the hard stuff.'"

"If we hide from the difficult moments, we stop living the life we've been handed. Right? Here's one of those times, sweetheart."

Carolina blinked hard at the floor before meeting his gaze. "Wowza. Free fall again."

Chapter Four

One Saturday morning, Rowan wandered into the Bender's Ridge kitchen. Mossy was chopping cabbage. "What are you making?" she asked. "The house smells weird all the way back to my room."

"You've probably caught a whiff of the garlic and ginger—maybe the cabbage, too. I'm working on my first batch of kimchi." He glanced up. "Oh, I know what the smell is. I put in a little bit of shrimp paste. Want to help? I need more carrots for color. Could you get me two more from the cold cellar? No, get five or six so we have some in the fridge."

"Sure. It's spooky down there. What's this stuff?" She pointed at long, fat white roots on the counter.

"Daikon. White radish, originally from Asia. I grew these, though."

"How'd you learn to make kimchi?"

"I took an online workshop one day while you were at school. It's pretty easy, and it'll surprise your mom. Check over there—you can read the recipe."

"I'll go get carrots first." Rowan pulled on her winter parka and, taking Zephyr, trotted out to the underground food storage. Its door angled forty-five degrees from the ground and led to wooden stairs. She opened the creaky door and flipped on the light, then stamped her feet to scare away weird critters. She'd never told Mossy about the terrifying spider. She'd looked up, and right above her head, it hung like it was lying in wait. The thing was over three inches including its hideous legs.

She signaled for Zeph to stay and tiptoed down. The below-ground room was lined with shelves—apples, potatoes, carrots, winter squash, beets and more, neatly stored and labeled. Heart pounding, she fished a bunch of carrots out of a straw-lined box, and bolted for the door.

"You're out of breath," he said, as she reentered the kitchen.

"It's creepy." She scrubbed the carrots.

He put down his knife. "Did something scare you?"

She hung her head. "Not today, last summer. A huge spider. I felt too silly to tell you."

"Whoa, I wouldn't like it, either. Let's go down there later and check the room, make sure there are no spiders or other creepy-crawlies. You need to feel safe; it's our winter food supply. We'll take the mini-vac, pull the boxes off the shelves, and check everywhere."

She grimaced. "That spider wouldn't fit in *any* mini-vac."

"Did it have extra long legs?" He handed her the vegetable peeler.

He believed her. It was one of the things she loved about him. "Yup. The thing was about three inches across. Horrible."

"I bet it's a giant house spider. They're originally from Europe. They usually create a web near a crack where they can run and hide. They're scaredy spiders and reluctant to bite." He raised his eyebrows. "Remember, like you, it's trying to live its life as best it can."

"If we find one, you wouldn't kill it?" She sliced the carrots into thin rounds.

"I'd try not to. We'll take a wide-mouthed jar and some thin cardboard and re-home it. They're harmless, and they eat insects. It'd be fine in the barn or chicken coop—although, a chicken might eat it."

Rowan shivered. "On this planet, everything seems to eat everything. Ever watch the National Geographic Channel?"

Back in Eugene the following Tuesday, after Moss finished writing late in the afternoon, he went to look for Rowan. He knocked on her door and peeked in the living room—she wasn't in either place, and Zephyr was missing too. He went to the garage, rubbing his thigh as he walked. Even though it was cold, sometimes she hid out. And there she was, hunkered down with her laptop.

"May I come in?" Zeph lay at her feet, but rose to greet him. He stroked her ears.

Rowan glanced up. "Sure."

He perched on the edge of a low workbench. "What're you up to?"

"Avoiding Mom. Doing research. Well, and writing, too."

"Now you've got me interested."

She zipped her fingers across her lips.

"Okay, I won't share with Lina."

"I'm researching people who teach about consciousness and also trying to write down my own experiences."

"You mean like professors? That wouldn't set your mom off."

"Nope. Spiritual teachers. See why you can't tell her?"

He nodded. "Got it. Found anyone interesting?"

"Yeah, this cool guy named Colin. Colin James." She turned the computer screen toward Moss. "He comes from the Buddhist tradition—but he's Scottish, older than you. He leads retreats outside of Portland. I really want to attend one."

"I'm not going to let my girl traipse off to see just anyone, you know." He winked at her. "I guess I'd better check him out."

"He's well known, and married, so probably not some weird predator. And he's written a book I'm dying to read: *The Light of Emptiness*." Rowan squinched her face. "Like Mom would let me go to a retreat of his."

"Be patient," he said, "and kind to your mom. It might get you what you want."

Rowan sighed. "Why is it weird and wrong to be interested in spirit? I'm out here with a space heater because I don't want her staring over my shoulder and making a scene. It's crazy I have to, and it makes me sad."

"She's trying."

"Right. 'Trying' is the operative word. Trying to open up to loving her own daughter the way she naturally is. Geez. You'd think I was gay or something."

"She'd be fine with that."

Rowan snorted. "Now I'm wishing I'm gay instead of a mystic."

"You're precocious."

She giggled. "Yeah, well, nothing new. I got called precocious by my dad before he died—I was six."

He belly-laughed. "Listen. If you ever want to share writing with me, regardless the topic, I'm interested, and a great listener."

"Thanks. When I'm ready—if I'm ever ready—you'll be the first."

He started toward the door, but she called him back. "Mossy? Check out YouTube. There's a video by Colin called 'A Shift in Perception.' If you have questions, come ask me. He's the real deal."

"I'll look him up. You know, you turn sixteen in May. I doubt we can throw a huge bash with all that's going on, but think about what would make the day special for you, okay?"

"It'd be special if Mom would let me go to a retreat."

"We'll work on her. You'd need a chaperone, though."

Moss returned to his computer after the family went to bed. He went straight to Google and searched for Colin James. After spending a chunk of time digging through endless internet pages—James was well-known—he found no disturbing stories. The man had come out of the Zen Buddhist tradition. There was nothing about him having affairs with students, or any cult activity. The guy seemed like a straight-up dude; it spoke to Rowan's maturity, too.

Next, Moss went to YouTube and searched for the clip she'd told him about. It was only ten minutes long; he put on headphones and clicked the start button. Sometimes he thought he understood what this guy was saying but, most of the time, it only brought up more questions. He jotted them down so he could ask Row, and noticed his hand shaking. It dawned on him he was nervous. What was he scared of? Rowan being wiser than he was?

He went to the kitchen and poured a glass of merlot, then returned to his office. Leaning back, he swirled a sip on his tongue and pondered the question—if he grokked his own fear, he might better understand Lina's position. Rowan was the old soul of the family. He was often startled by her perceptions and insights, so the trembling wasn't brought on by her perspicacity. Was it the unknown of what she was exploring? Mostly, he decided, it was because this could turn their family upside down. He knew that when one member of a family changes, like it or not, everyone does. That, he realized, frightened him. Well, he'd better get used to it. His daughter was a little mountain goat—determined and persistent. Most likely, they faced a topsy-turvy road ahead.

He opened Amazon to order *The Light of Emptiness*, then blew out a breath. Rowan's attraction to mysticism was the main thorn between Carolina and himself. He'd have to tell Lina and cope with whatever entangled discussion ensued. One thing was for sure: before he gave the book to his daughter, he'd read it himself.

Zephyr lies on the bed, muzzle resting on her girl's hip. She senses something is different; Rowan feels more peaceful than she has since leaf-falling-time. The change comes after seeing Kibble Man earlier, in the warmer part of the day. She nudges her girl, who whispers, "Mossy listened, Zeph. He seems curious and open when I talk about 'big field' stuff. It's such a relief—I need someone to share with besides you. Maggie's not quite ready. I think she'll get there, though."

She loves when Rowan talks to her this way. She only gets some of the words, but her girl penses her pictures and feelings, too. She knows the big field is where they reach each other without touching.

Two days later, Carolina glanced up from the sewing machine in her workroom when she heard the delivery truck pull up. She set down the sleeping bag repair she was working on and squinted against the glare. Moss must have ordered something, because she hadn't. He was working in the garage. She saw him limp out to greet the delivery man, and warmed, as she always did, seeing his engaging smile. The package was small and flat—most likely another book. Thank heavens he was building a bookcase. Living with two writers, she sometimes wondered if the house would collapse under the weight of so much paper. Rowan's interests were arcane—she couldn't find what she wanted at the local library. They'd been talking about giving her a book allowance each month. How much was fair? One book a month? More? Moss favored two, but imagine—between both of them, they'd be adding a shelf or more of books every year, year after year.

A cup of tea was in order. She pushed to standing and went to the kitchen.

Moss came in and set the package on the counter. "Hey. Ready to do dinner with me?" He washed his hands before turning back to her.

Carolina had already pulled leftovers from the fridge so they could see what else they needed.

"What'd you order?" She pointed to the package.

"A metaphysical book Rowan told me she wanted." He glanced at her sideways, as though anticipating a reaction. "I'll read it before passing it along."

"She's lucky you can support her in this; it's clear I can't. Thanks for being aware of what she's ingesting."

"Good job not resisting or judging. She wants to go to this guy's retreat—outside of Portland. I'm vetting him thoroughly."

Her body froze. *Yikes.* "A book is one thing. But going to some hide-away with a creep we don't even know? What if it's a cult?" She glared at Moss. "No way."

"Whoa, slow down. We're only looking into this—it's important to pay attention to her predilections. Of course we'll make the decision together."

Carolina crumpled and leaned against the kitchen counter. "Damn. Look at me—right back to rejecting what interests my daughter most. Will I ever be able to simply let her be? If I keep screwing this up, I could lose her. Soon enough, she'll be off to college, and then gone."

He came up behind, cupping his hands gently around her belly. She felt his lips near her ear. "Soon enough, there'll be two whippersnappers keeping us busy every single minute. Row's been behaving responsibly. You're not going to lose her."

"She's awfully lippy—but, you're right, she has been trustworthy, and mainly sensible; not like her grammie, as you tersely pointed out to me on Christmas."

He raised his eyebrows—she knew "tersely" had caught his attention. Well—he had snapped at her. Upon reflection, she'd deserved it—but sure hadn't forgotten the dressing down she'd received from her husband and daughter. It still stung.

Chapter Five

Monday, March 15th, after a quiet weekend at Bender's Ridge, Moss lugged duffels from the ranch house to the van; Carolina carried her knitting bag and purse. They were headed to Bend for the twenty-week ultrasound and planned to drive home to Eugene directly from the appointment. Moss whistled for Jazz, who bounded toward the car, tongue lolling, a bright expression on her long face. "I think she misses Zeph when we come without Rowan and the big girl," he remarked. "She's almost smiling."

"Jazz is lonely for her own kind," Carolina said. "I would be. She has nobody to run and play with when Zephyr isn't here."

"A few more hours and we'll be on our way home—everyone reunited." He swept Carolina into a hug. "Wow, you've popped. It's hard to get close to you now, with that baby load in front." He leaned back and, smiling, looked in her eyes. "You're so darn beautiful pregnant."

"Thanks, I need to hear you say it. I feel like a cow," she said, ruefully. "Where'd my karate-self go? My breasts are enormous, and we're only halfway there."

"Luscious, simply luscious." Holding her gaze, he ran his hand lightly across her full chest, grazing her nipples. Then he glanced at his watch. "No time. Darn. Oh, how I wish," he whispered.

Smiling, she lightly batted his hand away. "Whoa, Nellie. We have an agenda for the whole day. This'll have to wait."

"Yeah," he said. "Let's get going." He signaled for Jazz to jump into the back of the van. "'Whoa Nellie'—that's a new one. Where'd it come from?" Moss asked, settling in the driver's seat.

Carolina giggled. "It's one of my mom's silly expressions. Hasn't she ever used it around you?"

"Not yet. I'll be waiting for it. I guess she'll come out after the twins are born?"

Carolina sighed. "I don't think we could keep her away. And she'll want to know the exact birth minute of each baby for their astrological charts."

Like every appointment with Dr. Jamison, Carolina bared her belly and waited for the shock of cold gel. Her doctor chatted, reporting what she saw, turning the screen so they could see, and pointing at it to show them both. Suddenly, her hand stilled. She fell quiet.

A chill ran through Carolina. The doctor was focusing in a different way. Her light demeanor had vanished. "What is it?"

"Taking a closer look. Let me concentrate for a sec." She made minute adjustments in the wand's position. "Huh."

"'Huh' doesn't sound good." Carolina's voice squeaked. "Mossy, hold my hand, would you?"

After another minute, Dr. Jamison sat back on her rolling stool. "Okay," she said. "I want you to have a fetal echocardiogram at Doernbecher Children's Hospital in Portland. I could be wrong, but there's something unclear about the great vessels in one baby's heart, and a specialist should check it out. We don't want to miss anything."

Something might be wrong with my baby? Carolina felt her face blanch. She squeezed Moss's hand so hard he winced. Her heart thundered; air came in tiny sips.

He leaned down to reassure her, whispering in her ear, "Hang in there, sweetie. We don't have any real information yet."

"It may be nothing," the doctor went on. "I'll call to find out when you can be seen. Can you schedule now?" She rolled her stool over to the phone in the corner, ran her finger down a list of numbers posted on the wall, and dialed. She glanced toward Moss.

He nodded, and slipped his cell from a pocket. Carolina saw him pulling up their calendar in preparation. Wrapping her arms around her belly, she silently talked to her babies as she felt them shifting and poking inside. *We'll protect you. Whatever this is—if it's anything—we're right here. Every moment.*

Moss touched her arm. She jumped. "Hey, love, where'd you go?" he asked. "Is Thursday all right with you? They can fit us in at 1 p.m."

"I was talking to the babies. Thursday? They want to see us this week?" She looked up at him, frightened.

"Yes," he said, softly.

"Okay. Yeah, sure." A sinking sensation flooded her torso. She knew—knew in her cells—this would be a long haul. Whatever "it" was, Dr. Jamison wouldn't raise concern if there wasn't a reason.

Silence reigned in the car for the first ten miles. Jazz stuck her nose between the seats into Carolina's armpit. She stroked the dog's soft, folded ears.

They both broke the silence at the same time. "Sorry, you go first," Moss said.

"No, you, please."

"Whatever happens at Doernbecher, I want us to get a second opinion at University of California, San Francisco," he said. "Theo lives nearby and we can stay with him. Rowan would love seeing Maggie and Bender, and my brother has privileges at UCSF. It's one of the best cardio centers in the country." He smoothly guided the van around a highway curve.

"Even if they say nothing's wrong on Thursday?"

"Yep. Oregon isn't known for having a top-rated cardiac center."

Carolina bit her lip. "I don't know, Moss. If they think we're good, I'd like to believe it. Traveling doesn't appeal to me right now—and we already have to make the two-plus hour drive each way to Portland and back."

"Sweetie, this is important. Hoping for the best isn't enough for me. She said something doesn't look right. I want you to be seen by the best doctors there are."

She took a breath. "I don't want to catastrophize. I need to trust."

"But if it isn't, and they miss something? It could be more serious down the road." His voice grew more insistent. "I'm not comfortable taking chances. We need to be aligned here."

One of the babies shoved a heel into the hand she had resting on her belly. It felt like an upset kick. She swiveled and stared at Moss. "Are we fighting? The babies think so."

He didn't respond, and they remained quiet until entering the lava flow area near the top of the pass. "I need to use the bathroom," she said.

Moss gripped the steering wheel harder than usual. He didn't answer.

"Did you hear me?" she asked.

"Yup. We'll stop. I'm thinking. Trying to calm down."

We *are* fighting. She felt her resistance—both to arguing with her husband, and acknowledging anything could be wrong with either baby. Slowing her breath, she tried to consider what he'd said from his point of view.

When they got to the rest stop, he pulled into a parking spot and braked abruptly. Without saying anything, Carolina got out and marched up the path. So damn ungainly. She linked her hands under her belly to relieve the weight.

When she walked back down, Moss was standing, hands stuffed in his pockets, staring out at the lava field. Sharp rock everywhere, she thought, like us. She slipped her arm through his.

"I don't want it to be hard," he said, his voice gruff. "And for sure, I want to resolve this before we get back to Eugene. Home is my safe place. I can't be fighting there." He turned to her. Upset and worry carved his face.

"How about this," she said. "Let's cancel the appointment at Doernbecher. You call Theo, and we'll go to UCSF instead. Only one trip and the best specialists."

His eyes opened wide. "Good thinking. Deal. I'm phoning Pa, too—I want the Learjet and pilot sent out here. It'll make our trip down south much easier."

"No way. It's not right. It's *not* company business."

"Bessie wasn't bought by the company. Pa purchased the plane after his heart attack four years ago." He stroked her cheek. "Imagine—no lines. No security. No uncomfortable, tight seats, people packed in on either side. Real food. We travel when we want." He ran his fingers through her hair. "You can lie down on the flight. Row and the dogs can come. Think of it as family time off."

Carolina munched her lip for the second time. She was all right knowing the family fortune existed, but spending money on a private jet flying across country and then between states—for her? It felt wrong. A waste of resources. She hugged her belly, sighed, and swung away—her turn to stare at the lava field. She took a couple of long breaths. This was for the babies, not her. She'd married him. She knew how rich he was before signing on. "Shit. Okay," she finally whispered.

"Great. I'll phone Theo. He can make the appointment with the doc he thinks is best. Then I'll call Pa."

"Yeah." Everything was moving too fast. She turned back to him. A sudden thought took her down, and she grabbed Moss's arm. "What are we going to tell Rowan?" Anxiety rocketed through her.

"Geez, you scared me." He patted her hand. "The truth, sweetie. We're going to tell her the truth the moment we get home. She's old enough. She'd be resentful if we didn't. Don't you agree?"

"When you put it so clearly, yes. Moss, I'm scared."

He muttered, "Me too, sweetheart. Bottom-line-terrified."

From their neighbor Sue's house, Rowan saw the van pull up the driveway. She grabbed her backpack and raced with Zephy to the gate between the properties, fumbled with the latch, and ran to greet them. "I'm glad you're home."

Zephyr nosed Jazz hello and then buried her muzzle in Moss's crotch. He laughed, gave her a love pat, and pushed her nose away. "She's always pleased to see me," he said, smiling.

"Of course she is. You saved her by luring her to the ranch house after the car accident," Rowan said, hugging her mom. "How'd it go? How's the ranch? Did you get the ultrasound?"

"A lot of questions." She put her hand on her daughter's cheek. "Let's go inside. We want to talk with you, hear about your weekend, tell you about ours."

"What are we doing for dinner? I'm starved."

"Order in," Moss and Carolina said in unison. They glanced at each other and managed to laugh.

"Ta Ra Rin?" Carolina asked.

"Yes." This time Rowan and Moss spoke at the same time.

"Done," Carolina said. "I need Thai food."

"More cashew chicken, please," Rowan said. Mossy handed the container to her. "You guys are awful quiet. What's going on?" She grabbed the *sambal oelek* jar and spooned hot sauce onto her plate.

"Are we?" Carolina asked. "You've grown to like spicy condiments, haven't you? Let's finish up, make tea, and move to the living room. Tell me about your weekend. Did you do anything special?"

"Yeah. I love this stuff." She mixed some of the Indonesian hot sauce in with her chicken dish. "The weekend warmed up. Sue took us to the coast—to Beachside in Waldport. It was pretty chilly there, a stiff breeze. Zephy had to stay on leash, but at least she's allowed on the beach. She loves to bite the water. I ran her until I was beat. Then Seth took over."

"Jazz missed her," Moss said. "Look at them now."

Zephyr lay on her side, Jazz curled up next to her belly and between her legs, her muzzle on the giant dog's hip.

Rowan carried the dishes to the sink. Moss called, "Leave them for now. I'll help wash up later. Put the kettle on, okay?"

Finally, they settled in the living room—Moss in his recliner, Carolina in hers, and Rowan on the couch with the two dogs. "Something's up with you guys, I can tell."

She saw her mom look at Moss, who spiked his eyebrows. "Well sweetie," Carolina began, "Dr. Jamison thought she saw something on the ultrasound, so she's sending me to get a fetal echocardiogram—an ultrasound of our babies' hearts."

"What? How come? It sounds scary." Rowan frowned and looked from Mom to Mossy and back. "Are you worried?"

"Of course we are," Moss said. "But we don't have solid information yet, so I'm 'keeping the faith,' I guess you could say. The whole family, dogs included, will be going down to stay with Theo and Maggie. And Bender, of course. Theo's going to make the appointment at UCSF tomorrow. He'll try to make it for a Friday or Monday. That way, you don't have to miss much school."

"It'll be soon," her mom said. "Within two weeks. We're taking Pa's Learjet."

"Oh my God, we can take the dogs? And they'll travel in the compartment with us?"

"Right."

"Great news. I'll be super glad to see Maggie. Which baby?"

"We don't know. But I suppose we may find out the sexes now—for sure I want to be able to send reassurance." Carolina rested her hands protectively on her belly.

"Yeah, me, too. Every single day," Rowan said. "Will it be different from the appointment I went to?"

"I asked about it. Similar—gel, wand, computer screens—but it'll take a lot longer. Afterward, we'll need to sit down with the pediatric cardiologist who interprets the results." She blew out a breath and patted Rowan's knee. "You don't have to come. You can stay with the dogs at Theo's house. I'm assuming Maggie will be at school. Hey—maybe you could go to the Urban Center for the Arts with her and see what it's like."

"But I want to be there. These are my siblings."

"I'm not sure." Her mom made eye contact with Mossy. "We'll talk about it."

Their special language again—it's dang annoying, Rowan thought. She uses it, why can't she understand it's similar to how I communicate with Zeph?

Later, stretched out with Zephy on her bed, she pensed something might be wrong with one of the babies.

Zephyr shifted her position on the bed. *Different sound. Hear on tree-day.*

Christmas? You heard it then? Rowan stared in her dog's eyes. *So there is something wrong?*

Different.

She couldn't know if it's wrong or not, Rowan thought. *Tell me next time, okay?*

Zephyr plunked her head in her girl's lap. *Next time.*

Later, Carolina slid into bed with Moss and tugged the duvet under her chin.

"We have some unfinished business from this morning. Come here," Moss said. He crooked his arm and she nestled in.

Would she never get enough of this man? She trembled at his smoky voice. It thickened when he was thinking about making love. "Are we about to have make-up sex?"

He chuckled. "That's what this would be? Let's spoon. What with the beautiful baby load, we've gotta change up our style."

Lina rolled on her side and he curved behind. His erection pressed against her. She shivered with anticipation and, groaning, shifted to her back to find his mouth. The babies woke up, kicking and elbowing. She kissed him, planting his hand along with hers so he could feel the acrobatics.

"They're somersaulting," he said. He moved to her breasts, and leaned in to tongue her nipples—first one, then the other, circling each before taking it between his lips. Pleasure surfed through her.

"I've only gotten started here," he whispered, sliding his hand up and over the crown of her belly. He buried his fingers. She gasped at his touch. As her pleasure mounted, he murmured, "Shift to your side again, woman. I'll take it easy, but I'm comin' in." He teased—caressing, backing off, stroking again—driving her toward climax. When she could no longer form words and could only moan, he slipped inside. Then, barely moving—his hands still playing her body—lips on her ear, he whispered, "Come to me, Lina." And she did—a slow, exquisite roll up and over the top as he joined her.

Afterward, she snuggled with him, one hand on his heart. "Lordy, we've never quite been *there* before. What was that?"

"Love shining," he said softly, and pulled her closer.

Chapter Six

Ten days later, they drove to the Eugene airport, but not the main terminal. Instead, they went to the north end where the charter division operated, and met the Learjet pilot, William.

"Bessie's tuned and ready to go," William said. "Let's load up. The weather's clear all the way to the Bay Area. Today we'll be flying at 41,000 feet, but I'll keep the cabin altitude at 4,000, to be safe." He handed Carolina a small device. "And you, Ms. Graham, will wear this pulse oximeter—you and Moss can track your oxygen saturation. Again, to be safe. Clip it on your finger, and let the co-pilot know if it drops below ninety-eight percent."

Carolina stuttered a "thank you," and took the gadget. "Holy moly," she said to Moss. "Do you think of everything?"

"Not me—Pa. The plane's stocked with oxygen and equipment like this for when he flies. The man is nothing if not thorough. And William here," he shot a thumb at the pilot, "hired a co-pilot who's an EMT. His name is Kadeem."

William waved them up the steps, Rowan first. Carolina saw the dogs' noses twitching side to side as they entered the plane. No wonder—the interior smelled of real leather. The eight seats were upholstered in a light tan. A table lay folded against the side of the central space, which reeked of elegance and wealth. It made her queasy.

"Let's sit near the bathroom. You'll need it." Moss took her hand. "It's okay, love; we're doing the right thing."

She squeezed his arm, grateful that he sensed when feelings about his family wealth overcame her.

"Buckle up," William said. "We'll be taking off in a few minutes. Our flight duration is eighty minutes." He walked forward to the cockpit where the co-pilot was already belted in.

Rowan stashed the dog beds in the area between the six seats facing the cockpit and the two at the front that looked toward the tail. "This is plush," she said, gazing around. She patted one bed. "Zephy, settle." To Jazz, she said, "Dog bed down." Both girls lay obediently. Rowan gave them each a chew toy, a pat and gentle words, and went to sit close by in a backward-facing seat. She wondered how Jazz would take to flying. She'd pensed Zephy beforehand; she didn't expect any real problems with her. Neither dog, as far as she knew, had ever flown. At least they didn't have to be crammed in crates in a noisy cargo hold.

When the engines roared to life, Jazz sat up, flattening her ears. Zeph leaned over and nudged her pal, gave her a lick. The airplane left the ground, and Jazz pointed her nose to the ceiling and howled. Rowan reached out a comforting hand and kept it on the dog during the steep ascent. "Wow," she said, "this is real different from a commercial flight." It felt as if they were riding a streaking comet.

Once they reached cruising altitude, Kadeem left the cockpit and offered them beverages. Rowan stood, stretched, and got a bowl of water for each dog. Zephy didn't stir. Jazz lapped thirstily before collapsing in bed and gnawing her toy.

Theo picked them up at the airport—much easier than at a commercial terminal, Carolina thought. Moss had been right. No crowds at the baggage claim.

Rowan let the dogs jump into Theo's van before getting in.

"Maggie wanted to come," Theo said to her, "but with dogs, luggage, and four of us, I didn't think there'd be room." He stashed the final suitcase behind the third seat.

"It's okay," she said. "I'll see her soon enough."

Carolina nudged Moss. "Sit up front with your brother; you'll want to catch up."

"Thanks." He flashed her a smile, and gave her a hand up before climbing in the passenger seat.

Cars ground to a stop in late afternoon bumper-to-bumper traffic on Highway 280. "Usually this is a fifteen to twenty minute drive," Theo said. "There must be an accident. We'll be lucky to get home in fifty."

His Noe Valley home, a stately Victorian, sat at the highest point on the street. It was painted off-white with warm brown trim, had an enormous window at the entrance, and a bay window to the left. Carolina guessed there'd be spacious views of the city. Anticipation tickled her.

While they unloaded in front, Theo said, "I bought the property behind for guest quarters last year—where you'll stay—but we'll go through our place and across the yard. I've parked the red Prius over there for you to use. Key fob's on your kitchen counter." He grabbed luggage; Moss handled dog beds and bowls.

Maggie was waiting at the door, Bender by her side. "You're here." She hugged Rowan first. "Let the dogs go; it's safe. Bender'll show them where the dog door is. I'm sure they need to pee."

Theo dropped bags in the entryway. "I'll give you the tour," he said.

"Are you going to stay with me in my room?" Maggie asked.

Carolina nodded when Rowan shot her an inquiring look. "Sure. You and Zeph can sleep here. Do you think the dogs will mind being apart?"

"Not as long as their people are with them," Rowan said, following Maggie upstairs. A few minutes later, panting heavily, the three dogs charged back into the house. Bender and Zephyr galloped up the stairs; Jazz circled Moss.

The house smelled of basil, tomatoes, and garlic bread. Carolina noted crown molding and wainscoting and gorgeous hardwoods on the main floor. Walking up the staircase, she fingered the intricate newel posts. The guest bathroom had an original claw-foot bathtub. From the master bedroom, she found the views she'd hoped to catch a glimpse of—in the distance, the whole cityscape. Imagine, waking up to this every morning.

She sucked in a breath as they walked into the kitchen—it had been fully updated: white cabinets, granite counter tops, brushed stainless appliances, and a huge island with stools around it—elegant, well-laid out, and comfortable. But the home seemed to lack a woman's touch. What was missing?

She counted back; it had been eight years since Phoebe died. Carolina traced a hand down one of the counter tops and wondered if Theo would marry again. Maggie shouldn't have to fill the hostess role.

"I knocked out a wall here to make the kitchen twice as large," Theo said, pointing. "Maggie has a group of her friends over from time to time."

The window over the farm-style sink overlooked the back yard. Rhododendron and azalea bushes were alight with color—plush reds, yellows, vivid oranges. A Japanese maple hung protectively over a stone bench.

"It's all so peaceful," Carolina said. "How long have you been here now? I know you lived in Boston when your dad had the heart attack."

"I guess it's been three years. It's a real sanctuary for us right in the middle of the city; no horrible winters, and much more space for Bender, too. On the walk to your place you'll see the yard close up. You can get settled—dinner will be at seven. Maggie cooked tonight." Theo checked his watch. "Oh—only twenty minutes."

The men retrieved the luggage and the adults walked a curved paver path along the edge of the large grassy area. Jazz tore circles around the grass, dropped to the ground and rolled, scratching her back. Some parts of the yard were sunny, others sheltered. A blooming patch of lilies of the valley surrounded the base of the maple. Carolina stopped and pointed at their little scalloped caps. "These are my favorite. May we have a sprig or two for our room?"

Theo reached down, pinched off three, and handed them to her with a smile. "These are the first of the season. They don't last long—replenish them whenever you want. Bending must be getting harder," he added.

Carolina took a slow whiff, and smiled at Theo. "Sure is." She patted her belly. "I can't believe there are two in here, but ultrasounds don't lie." She felt her stomach rumble, and was glad dinnertime was close.

"I hope it goes well tomorrow. Bhavna Bhat is a brilliant pediatric cardiologist, and good with people, too. She went to Johns Hopkins with me—second in the class. I was about twentieth." He gave a sheepish grin. "I fell in love with Phoebe while in medical school. It took a huge toll on my grades." He waved them forward. "We need to get back to the main house to eat. Maggie worked hard."

"I'm relieved you chose the right person for us to see," Carolina said. "I'm scared."

Moss patted her hand. "We both are."

"Of course you're nervous. It's to be expected," Theo said.

The guest house had three bedrooms and was furnished in a similar style, a miniature of the larger home. After they stashed suitcases in the master bedroom suite on the first floor, they walked back through the garden for dinner.

"Oh my gawd, this lasagna is delicious," Rowan said, putting down her fork. "I'm not a very good cook yet. You're putting me to shame." She finished her last bite of salad and French bread.

Maggie giggled. "Thanks. It's kinda my one dish, along with my only dessert, which I'll serve next."

"I smelled chocolate," Row said. "Brownies?"

"Fudge pie, but there's no crust. I'm warning you all," she glanced around the table, "it's ugly no matter what I do, but tastes great. I used to help Mom make it. Do you want it á la mode?"

Everyone nodded except for Carolina. "No ice cream, please."

Theo cleared the table and returned with ice cream and scoop. Maggie brought the pie—a nondescript brown with strange, lighter globs in the uneven surface.

Rowan giggled. "It looks like a cow pie."

Maggie set the pie down and folded her arms across her chest. "No disrespect until you taste it." She cut four pieces and dolloped ice cream, sliced a slab for Carolina, and passed the plates around.

Row took a bite. The moist, rich dark chocolate flooded her mouth. "Yum," she breathed. "Cow pie. Teach me to make this, please."

"Ha, my homely pie stands proud—never met anyone who didn't love it."

After dinner, the girls lounged in Maggie's room. Bender climbed on the big bed; Zephyr dug at her travel one before flopping down. *Not like my nest at home*, she pensed to Rowan, who bent over and gave her a reassuring pat.

"Can we pick up where we left off last summer?" Maggie's eyes were bright with interest. "I really want to be able to communicate with Bender like you do with Zephy."

"Sure. How's the work with him going?"

"I haven't had a whole lot of success with pensing. I'm missing some important piece, I'm sure. You said something that's been bugging me. It niggles at night, even wakes me up. I wanted to wait until we were together before I asked."

"What'd I say?"

"You described the big field, behind thoughts. You said we'd work on it this summer; you had a way of introducing me, or something. But I think I've been there." Maggie's voice shook a little.

"Outstanding. But of course it's not 'there,' it's right here, all the time." Rowan held her palms flat in front of her.

"Yeah, but it feels like 'there.'"

"And?" Rowan asked.

Maggie nibbled her thumbnail. "Words are clumsy."

"You're right; they can't reveal the truth. They only point."

"'Reveal.' Wow. How'd you get so … I don't know, wise?"

"I'm not wise."

"About this stuff, you are. Anyhow, I started noticing the spaces between thoughts. Nothing's happening, exactly."

"Great. Tell me more," Rowan said.

"Awareness is there—no, here—but not a thing. I mean, I can't seem to touch it. It feels huge, endless, maybe, and not personal." She tucked a lock of hair behind her ear. "Am I on the right track? There's no one else I can talk to who would understand."

"Yeah, I have the same problem, a dearth of folks to talk to, except you, of course. It's my new word, 'dearth.' But later this year, I'm hoping to go to a retreat—and meet people with a deeper understanding than I have. Anyway, only you can say whether you're on to something, from your own experience."

"I'm on the right track. I know I am."

"It's changed my life already." Rowan said. "Like knowing I want to connect people with their dogs—teach them to pense, if they show promise. It feels like my life work."

"But we're only fifteen. How can we know what we want to do forever?"

"Why not?"

Maggie braided a strand of her hair. "Yeah, I guess. A retreat? What's it about?"

Rowan filled her in about Colin James, and what the web said about the week-long stays. "They're silent, though. It might drive me nuts, because I want to communicate about this stuff. I may need to find a different teacher; I have to be able to make friends. If we aren't allowed to talk, it changes everything."

"A week not talking? I don't think I could handle it. Especially if Bender couldn't go." Maggie stroked her dog.

"No dogs allowed. But think about it. I can pense Zephyr. I'd be breaking the rules in a subversive way."

"Is 'subversive' another new word of the week?" Maggie elbowed Rowan.

"Yeah, you know me." Rowan squinched her face and grinned.

"What does it mean?"

Rowan glanced up to see if Maggie was serious. "Subversive? Like … undermining the system."

"But you're not technically breaking the rules. You wouldn't be talking with anyone there. Dope."

"Right. I hadn't thought of that. I'll be able to do the silent week." Rowan sat cross-legged on the other twin bed. "Okay. Let's try this. Let your thoughts fall into the background and rest in the field. Let me know when you're ready."

Maggie closed her eyes. After a moment, she nodded.

"Now. Imagine an envelope with a stamp on it. You're going to ask Bender to get off the bed and lie on the floor by sending him a picture—no, more like a little video. Your request, the video, is the stamp, but send it on a huge blast of love. The blast is the envelope."

Maggie frowned with concentration.

"Relax. You can do this."

"The love is huger than what I'm asking him to do?"

"Right. After all, Bender probably doesn't want to get down off this cozy bed onto the hard floor."

"Not like an obedience command."

"Correct. Pensing is never a command. It's *always* a request."

"Right. Okay," Maggie said.

For a moment, nothing happened. Then, with a startled expression, Bender jumped off and settled near Zephyr, but kept his head up, focused on Maggie.

Maggie's eyes flew open, and she stared bug-eyed at Rowan. "He did it," she whispered. "The first time ever. I've been trying all winter."

Rowan clapped her hands. "Praise him! Lots of praise."

Maggie dropped to the floor next to her dog. "What a good boy," she crowed, rubbing his ears. "We did well."

"Okay, now ask him to get back on the bed. Remember the big shot of love. It's like the airplane the request rides on. And never telling, always requesting. You're equals."

Maggie focused for a long moment, sighed and shook her head. "It's not working."

"I think your expectation is getting in the way. Take a long, slow breath and relax your mind. It's like thoughts still go on, but they're fainter and in the background." Rowan watched Maggie flex her shoulders up and down to relax them, and take a cleansing inhale.

A few seconds went by.

Bender leaped back on the bed, lay down, and crossed his paws. Maggie immediately praised him. Rowan sensed the dog was smiling.

Chapter Seven

Wandering the maze of UCSF hallways, Moss swarmed with memories of his long hospital stay in Germany. His body trembled at the familiar smell of cleaning products and the overlay of misery—few smiles in these hallways, only tension straining already drawn faces. This *was* a major medical center. More complicated cases were seen here. *Like us.* Taking a breath, he followed Carolina into a windowless room filled with computer monitors and a range of other mysterious equipment, most of which seemed discarded or, at the very least, in storage. He was glad Rowan decided to go to school with Maggie instead of coming with them.

At the back of the room, the technician asked Carolina to get on a gurney. Moss gave her a hand as she stepped on the stool. The normal routine—baring her belly, cool gel, wand. But this ultrasound took forty-five minutes, four times longer than previous ones. The technician said little, only noted marks and measurements on the screen, occasionally asking Carolina to shift one direction or another. The whoosh of blood and heart beats were the main sounds in the room. Moss squinted and concentrated but couldn't make out anything he understood.

After she wiped her belly and dressed, they were sent to wait in Bhavna Bhat's office. Without speaking, they played with their hands—interlacing their fingers, hooking only their baby ones. Moss cleared his throat; the sound echoed.

"Will she ever get here?" Carolina finally whispered. "My heart is pounding."

"Mine, too." He squeezed her hand. "We're the pair."

Ten minutes later, Moss heard a soft knock on the door, and Dr. Bhat came in and introduced herself. "Sorry for the delay," she said, in a soft Indian accent. "I was held up with another patient—often the case around here. Parents have lots of questions, as they should."

Moss stood to shake her hand and had to look way down. She can't be over five feet one, he thought. Her black hair, threaded with gray, was knotted in a bun.

She rolled to her computer, pulled their babies' images up on the screen, and waded through them in silence. After a few minutes, she swiveled her chair toward them. "Your son's heart looks completely normal. But your daughter does have a congenital heart defect." She rotated her computer screen for them to see. "This is called *truncus arteriosus*."

Carolina's hands jumped to cover her belly. "A boy and a girl? Wow. Our little girl has something seriously wrong with her heart? You're sure?" she asked. "I didn't actually believe our obstetrician."

"I'm afraid so. I'm sorry if you hadn't wanted to know the sex of your babies." With a small pointer, Dr. Bhat touched the screen. "Her pulmonary and aortic valves didn't separate. In a normal heart, the blood flow goes body-heart-lungs-heart-body. But in TA, the blood doesn't follow this path. There is only one vessel leaving the heart instead of two. The body doesn't oxygenate properly. Also, she has a ventricular septal defect—a hole between the ventricles—a common finding in this malformation. But there is good news: her aortic valve has three leaflets or cusps, which points to a more successful repair."

Moss found his voice. "We're in for surgery?"

"Yes. Open-heart surgery. Hopefully we can wait until she's two months old. Since twins often come early, and I understand you live in Oregon, I'd like you two to stay nearby starting at thirty-four weeks, and through recovery after your daughter's procedure."

Carolina turned to Moss, her eyes round moons. "Move our lives—and Rowan's—here for months? How can we make it work?"

"Hey sweetheart, we'll dig into this tonight. We clearly have a bunch of footwork to figure out."

Carolina asked, "How many of these repairs has the surgeon performed?"

"A very good question. A couple hundred. This CHD—it's short for 'congenital heart defect'—is found in one in ten-thousand births. There are around three hundred cases a year in the US. People come from all over the world to our pediatric cardiac center. We're big on acronyms here. Over time, you'll learn them."

"What about risks?" she asked. Moss felt Carolina grab his hand again, gripping hard.

"This is a serious procedure. However, consider these children don't live into adulthood without repair. Countrywide, over ninety percent come through the initial surgery. Dr. Tamaka's survival rate is over ninety-five percent. Most patients will need more intervention as they grow. Your daughter will require lifelong monitoring—all our patients do. But the odds are very good for a favorable outcome."

"What does 'favorable outcome' mean, exactly? Can she lead a normal life? Play sports?" Carolina asked.

"Recreational sports, most likely. Competitive sports, probably not."

"Will she be able to bear children?"

"Time, and the success of her repair, will tell. Hopefully."

"You mentioned additional interventions?" Carolina's voice shook. Moss could tell she was close to crying.

"They may have arrhythmias, pulmonary hypertension—high blood pressure in the lungs—or leaky heart valves. We turn the truncal artery into the aorta, but we have to use man-made material for the pulmonary artery. It won't grow with your daughter, so it will need to be replaced at some point."

Carolina covered her eyes with her hands, and wiped the corners. She looked up. "Did I cause this? Is it because I'm an older mother?"

Dr. Bhat shook her head. "We have no correlation with age. Please don't blame yourself. These things occur, and sadly, it happened to your family. By the way, something else I noticed: you have a fibroid on the outside of your uterus."

They talked for another forty-five minutes. "Please," Dr. Bhat said. "Many more questions will come up—make a list, and I'm available to answer them. Call my office."

Late in the afternoon back at Theo's, Carolina and Moss lay down on the bed holding each other close.

"They're going to slash her open," Carolina whispered. "Our tiny baby—she won't have any idea what's happening to her, except it hurts awfully. And she won't understand when we tell her it'll get better. Strange place, terrible pain, weird machine noises—how will she—and we—survive all this?"

"Kids are resilient. She'll get through this surrounded by our love." Moss sighed. "And us—we have each other, thank God. Now the footwork: I bet we can stay here. We'll ask Theo tonight. You need to put your work on pause anyway. You can barely sit close enough to the sewing machine."

"Disappointing my customers—yikes. But you're right. We'll need to include Rowan in this conversation," she said. "She may have strong opinions about being uprooted. The surgery could fall right when school starts. Let's stay in a bed and breakfast and not put the burden on Theo. I hate the thought of imposing. It doesn't seem fair, Moss."

He pulled away and stared at her. "Theo's going to *offer*. We're family. Rowan's grades are solid; she might be able to attend school with Maggie," he said. "And once I get set up, I can write anywhere quiet. We can do this." He smoothed the back of his fingers along her cheek. "Rowan and Maggie and the dogs would be thrilled to have more time together."

"But Theo's household will go from two—well, three including Bender—to seven including us and our dogs, and adding the babies, nine? It's an awful lot." she said.

"We're in a separate house. We could do our cooking here. For him, he'll have family who're neighbors instead of five hundred miles north."

"How about we share what we learned today, and see if he offers? I'd feel much better if he comes forward."

Moss chewed the inside of his cheek. "I'd rather be upfront and ask him. He's mature. If it doesn't work for him, he'll say so. We have a solid relationship."

Carolina stared out the window.

"Trust me on this one, all right? I know my brother."

She sighed. "Okay, I guess. Back to our babies. I think we need to name them. We can't keep calling our little girl 'our baby.' I'm undone by the thought of her facing life with a disfiguring scar. I imagine it is, anyway. I forgot to ask. If this affected our boy, at least there'd be the possibility of chest hair to cover it." She knotted her fingers into the curls on his chest.

Moss cuddled her closer. "Me, too. But remember, that scar will enable her to live."

After dinner, Moss, Carolina, Theo, Maggie, and Rowan gathered in Theo's living room. Rowan noticed Zephyr staring out the window at a clear nighttime sky. *It's different from the ranch—the big land—isn't it,* she pensed her dog.

So much hard ground. Like day at night.

Those are the sidewalks and street lights. Come, settle near Bender and Jazz. We all need to talk about the litter.

Zephyr left the window and flopped near the other dogs, groaning as she pressed her muzzle between her front paws.

"What happened today?" Rowan glanced from Mossy to her mom. "If we're having a family meeting, it can't be good news."

Her parents locked gazes.

"Right. It's not," her mom said. "We found out we're having one of each—exciting—but our little girl has a serious problem, a congenital heart defect called *truncus arteriosus*. She has to be born here at UCSF, and they want to do open heart surgery when she's two months old." Carolina pinched the bridge of her nose near her eyes. "If they can wait. It depends on how she does."

She's trying not to cry. Rowan moved to sit next to her, taking her hand.

Moss picked up the thread. “The doctors want us to come back to San Francisco for an extended period starting at thirty-four weeks of pregnancy. How would you feel about our renting the guest house? We could be here as long as four or five months, so we'd bring Zephyr and Jazz, too.”

“Ma and Pa are coming in early September,” Maggie said. “They usually stay where you are, but we have space here for them. Right, Dad?”

“I can't think of a finer use for the guest house.” Theo's voice was husky. “It's yours for the duration, and I won't take rent.” He swallowed hard. “Oh guys, I'm sorry. This is a real blow. It's going to take a while for you to absorb it all.”

“It sure is,” Carolina muttered.

“How did Bhavna handle telling you?”

“She's both kind and smart, and said we could call with questions any time. I appreciated her,” Carolina said. “Weird to like someone who delivers the kind of bad news that keeps on giving. Apparently, our little girl will have to be followed carefully and need more surgery as she grows. We're in for the long haul.” She swiped at the moisture on her cheeks. “Sorry folks, but this is the last time I'm going to apologize. Get used to it. I cry.”

“You have every reason to,” Moss said. “We both do.”

Maggie piped up. “Does Rowan get to go to my school? With me? Please?”

“If it's all right with you, we'd like to look into it,” Moss said. “Since it's a private school, it'd be a great fit for her. They might even have a creative writing program.”

Maggie stood up and did a happy dance, arm-punching the air. “They'll *love* her.”

“Whoa, hold up,” Rowan said. “I hadn't thought about junior year somewhere else than Eugene. I won't know anyone. I want to stay with *my* class, at home. Maybe I could live with Sue?”

“No, please come here,” Maggie said. “You'd know me, but I'm in a different track; we won't have many overlapping classes. There are lots of creative folk. They're kinda different. Focused. Together. Cool.”

“Row,” Moss said. “I want us all together as a family. It's important. You need to connect with the babies, too, and we need to bond as a larger family.”

Rowan frowned and went silent. She stood and walked to the window, staring outside. Zephyr went to her and bumped her hand. The girl patted her, but her whole attention was elsewhere.

Carolina started to speak, but Moss silenced her with a hand. "Wait," he whispered. "Give her a few minutes."

Rowan finally knelt on the floor, cupping Zeph's head in her hands. *Are you okay coming to live here with Maggie and Bender? City life is different. We wouldn't get to be at the big land for a long time.*

Zeph tongue-swiped her face. *A pack wants to be together. The litter needs us.*

Rowan went back to the window for a minute before turning to her parents. "Mossy, could you and Mom take me to see the school again? Maybe I could talk to someone, a counselor or something?"

"I need to rest tomorrow, if you don't mind," Carolina said. "We had a long day with a lot of walking. My body says 'stop.' Moss, are you all right taking her without me?"

"Sure. If they have questions only you can answer, I'll have them call. Keep the phone nearby?"

Carolina nodded. "Okay, but you'll do fine. You know Row at least as well as I do."

"If I hate it, I don't want to have to go there," Rowan said. She jutted her chin out and stared at them both.

"Of course," Moss and her mom said in unison.

"Take a writing sample," Maggie offered. "It'll impress them."

"I brought my laptop. You think they'll want to see one?"

"Yes. Your writing is fantastic. Let's go print it." Maggie got up and beckoned to Rowan.

Later, Carolina and Moss snuggled in bed. "Okay," she said. "Names. What are your suggestions?"

"Well, how about you pick the name for our baby girl, and I'll pick for our boy?" Moss suggested.

"Seems fair, as long as we each have veto power, too."

"Okay, sure. You go first," he said.

"I want to name her Francesca. It's been my favorite name forever."

Moss mouthed it and grimaced. "Sorry, veto. I think Francesca Westbury is a tongue twister. Do you have a second choice?"

Carolina looked crestfallen. "Rafe didn't like it, either, so Rowan got to be Rowan, my second choice. Of course it fits her much better than Francesca would have." She sighed. "Okay, Andrea, after your cousin. Our girl is going to need courage, too—the name means that, right?"

His eyes widened. "Yes. I love it. I'm still haunted by her final call from the World Trade Center. This'll honor her name."

She stroked his chest. "Exactly. One down. Now, what have you chosen for our boy?"

"Ashton."

"I figured as much. It's all right; I don't love it, but do like it. Not 'Ashy.' Kids get saddled with nicknames like those. Ash is fine, but not Junior. Never."

"He'd be Ashton Westbury the fourth, not Junior."

"I thought they'd both be Graham-Westbury?"

He sighed. "Hyphenated names are a pain in the butt because institutions don't know how to file the paperwork. How about we give him Graham as a middle name, but don't hyphenate it?"

"All right. Let's sleep on this because it's a big decision. Will your mom be all right with not using her name?"

"Ma's always disliked Alice. I'm sure she'll be relieved we don't choose it. What about yours?"

"Shirley? I warned her years ago I would never call a girl Shirley. I'm happy with Andrea," she said, firmly. "I also want to decide what the babies will call us."

"Since their grandparents are Ma and Pa, what about Mama and Papa?"

Carolina considered this. "I'd like them to call you 'Da' to honor your part-Scottish heritage. It's a common moniker for 'Dad' over there. We can be 'Da' and 'Mama.'"

"I like it."

The next morning, they stood at the double sinks in the bathroom each with a toothbrush in hand. "How'd our choices sit overnight?" Moss asked, after spitting toothpaste into the sink.

"They're perfect." She wiped her mouth and picked up a hairbrush. "Although I wonder what it would be like to be named after Ashton Westbury. It's a well-known moniker. It could be a burden." She glanced at him in the mirror, frowning.

"Westbury's recognizable more than Ashton because of Westbury Financial. But it's an honorable name; I'm not aware of any family scandals. I've managed fine—get stared at occasionally, but nothing more." He walked to the window in the bedroom and back. "I'd like you to consider using my last name instead of Graham. I think it'll be easier for the kidlets. It may be traditional, but I want them to carry my name."

Her eyes widened. "I don't know. I love Graham. Besides, it's what Rowan uses. It's a way she honors Rafe."

"But it's not your maiden name; it's his last name. I'd rather we have the same. I know Row wants to keep Graham, and that's fine."

"Why haven't you mentioned what last name I use? You never said a word before we got married."

"Honestly? I was afraid you'd bolt."

She grimaced. "I might have."

He took her hand. "Let's go sit in the bedroom to continue this … heated discussion." They settled into the reading chairs by the window.

"I can feel your resistance," he went on.

"Yeah." She worked her thumb into the palm of her other hand. "Busted."

"But why? Are you ashamed of my family?"

"Not ashamed. Uncomfortable, though. All that wealth."

"Jesus, Carolina, you say 'wealth' like it's a dirty word." He pushed out of the chair and paced the room.

"You married someone who came from nothing, who grew up in a trailer park." Her voice had a sharp edge. "It makes me uncomfortable. It's the truth. You need to get over it."

"Whoa! Get over something I can't change? Get over what's providing us with the means to make this pregnancy and complications less difficult? Eases our whole life? I don't think so."

"I only meant my resistance; it may never go away. Sometimes I feel like I sold out to the one percent." She clapped her hand over her mouth.

"What?" Moss snapped. "A huge slam, and not until now? After I've adopted your daughter—whom I love—and now we're having twins? A little hard to undo it all." He fisted his hands on his hips. "I'd like you to take mine. Please."

"I'll sleep on it," she growled. "But I don't get why it's that important to you; your attitude seems macho. We know lots of families where the parents have different last names."

"I haven't asked much of you. This is important to me. I have to get ready to take Rowan to that school." He stomped from the room.

Close to midnight, Carolina dragged blankets and pillows to the couch. For the first time in their marriage, they weren't speaking—she didn't even know how the school visit with Rowan had gone.

She'd blown it with Moss, no doubt.

Scrunching her pillow into a variety of shapes didn't help her get to sleep. Nothing worked: she counted sheep, listed gratitudes, perseverated about her own stupid behavior. She lay with her hands on her belly feeling the babies move. A hard lump remained lodged in her chest. Finally, she pushed off the couch and went to the kitchen where she threw open cupboards and drawers searching for chamomile tea. Jazz followed, looking at her, inquiring. Carolina shook her head in disgust. Only caffeinated stuff.

Now what? Stare out the window at this strange city until the sun came up? She wanted to go *home*. She wished for life to go back to the way it had been, with Moss and Rowan and the dogs. Twins would be an impossible load. And now, baby Andrea—not made right—posed a lifetime of challenges. She ached for her little girl. Tonight, the responsibility made her feel underwater with rocks holding her down.

Jazz nudged her hand. "What?" she snapped. Seeing the wilted expression on the greyhound's face, she invited the dog in close. Jazz was only trying to be a comfort. Her whiskers feathered along Carolina's cheek and, at the soft touch, tears leaked down—slowly at first, then a waterfall. She tried to be quiet, but her crying escalated into wailing. Burying her head in a pillow helped ease the racket, as did Jazz pressing against her. The companionship helped, but the babies didn't like her crying hard—she kept getting smacked with what felt like a heel against her already bruised rib.

She didn't want to inadvertently wake Moss and have to face him. She felt mostly responsible. She'd reviewed their fight multitudes of times already—the worst was her comment about the one percent. How had it fallen out of her mouth? He didn't deserve it—he was an honorable man: kind, thoughtful, mature, intelligent, generous. Had she meant it about selling out? What was the deeper truth here?

Carolina bundled in a fleece throw and curled in a chair by the window, harder now with her big belly. If it took all night, she'd figure out what the hell was wrong with her. Was the damage irreparable? It felt like it. He might even leave her for this—if their places were reversed, if Moss had made the same comment to her, she'd have probably packed a bag and left. The urge rose up to fly into the bedroom, take him in her arms and beg forgiveness, but it wasn't time yet. She had to know what her misunderstanding was.

Hours went by and still she sat, feeling the depth of her contention and trying to parse it. The babies settled down and seemed to go to sleep. When the barest rim of light colored the skyline, understanding opened. She hadn't sold out; she'd fallen deeply in love with a man who, by chance, was part of the one percent. It wasn't Moss's fault Ash had been wildly successful. Falling in love had been such a good thing for her.

And, it was done—the hard chunk in her chest dissolved, and she cried again, but this time in both relief and terror. Would Moss forgive her? Exhausted, with light increasing every moment, she rose stiffly from the chair and made a latte for him. Heart rattling in her chest, she tiptoed into the bedroom and stared at him sleeping. She set the latte down and knelt. "Sweetheart," she whispered. "I'm sorry. I've figured it out. This had nothing to do with you at all."

When he rolled over, seeing how broken and wretched he looked, she cried again. He didn't comfort her, but waited. Finally her sobs quieted as she explained what she'd come to see during the endless night. And she apologized again.

"My rage bled away during the night, but damn, your comment cut deep," he said. "Apology accepted, although it may take a while for the hurt to leave and trust to rebuild. You look awful. Did you sleep at all?"

She shook her head.

"Aww, geez, come here." He stuffed pillows behind his back and pushed up to sitting. She crept onto the bed and into his arms. Her weeping seemed unstoppable. Jazz jumped up and tried to worm her way into a lap, but no space was available. She curled up tight against them both.

"I need to know. Is this done for good?" he asked. "Or are we going to have to revisit it every few months or years? I couldn't stand it. Last night, I thought we might have broken us for good."

"Me, too," she whispered. "I figured you might leave me."

"I thought about it. I lay awake contemplating what it would be like."

"Holy moly," Carolina whispered.

"But," he went on, "the truth is, neither of us is going anywhere, ever. We're inextricably entwined. It seems obvious to me, and I hope it is to you, too."

She nodded. "It is. I'm sorry I didn't air this years ago. I guess it's taken me a long time to trust you could hear me, and I didn't want my words spoken out loud, either. They felt ungrateful. Small, even. You and your family have been nothing but kind, generous, and good to me." She paused. "Ashton and Andrea it is? With Graham as a middle name?"

He nodded.

"Moss, I'd love to know why your last name is this important to you, but I'll take Westbury and carry it with pride. I can encourage Rowan to change her name to Rowan Graham Westbury, like the babes ... like Ash and Andrea. Wow, the names feel weird on my tongue. It has to be her decision, though."

"I think we should let Rowan be. Let her come to us if she wants to change it." He took her face between his hands. "I'm not sure I can explain about the name stuff. But thank you. We got through it. This was *big*."

Chapter Eight

In mid-April, Carolina and Moss drove to Bender's Ridge for a three-day weekend—they had an appointment for her six-month checkup on Monday. Jazz slept in the back of the van.

"We haven't had this much time alone in a while," she said to Moss as they stopped in front of the ranch house.

"About time." Moss jumped down and came around to her side, helped her out, and smiled. "I need a few days only with you." Opening the slider for Jazz, he said, "Free dog."

He grabbed Carolina's backpack and slung it over his own shoulder. "You have to stop carrying heavy stuff."

"But Mossy, I need to—"

He cut her off. "Trust me, sweetie, once the babies come, you'll have far too much hauling to do. Babies, diaper bags, toys, who knows what. Your arms will always be full. Let me carry the load these last three months. I'll lay bets the doc says the same to you on Monday."

They walked to the front door. She swallowed hard. "You're right. Sheesh. I'm not used to your being so..." she squinted and searched for the right expression.

He stopped and raised an eyebrow. "Pushy?"

"Yes."

He grimaced. "Sorry. But in this situation, let me be your man. Self-reliance carried too far gets old."

She gulped.

He set the backpack on the deck and wrapped his arms around her. "Allow me to help," he said, more softly this time. "It's another way of letting me in."

She sighed against him. "Okay. I see your point." *I don't have to carry all this alone. Two babies are enough of a load.* Her body felt ungainly and thick—almost as big as when she'd delivered Rowan, and she had eight to twelve weeks to go. Her lithe frame had vanished. There'd be permanent changes; no denying this was the start of middle age. "I'm going to take a nap," she whispered, letting him go.

"Good. I'll bring in the groceries and get dinner going."

"Did you remember the kimchi?"

"You bet. One quart jar for now and five for the cold cellar."

Moss chopped an onion, garlic, chicken, yellow beet, and delicata squash, an assortment of vegetables, added homemade stock, and after the soup came to a boil, turned it low, and went to lie down with Lina. Jazz followed him and dug around before settling in her bed.

Carolina was curled on her side, dozing. After quietly dropping his clothes and unlegging, he slipped into bed and snuggled around her, fitting the surface of his knee into the bends of hers, his bare chest against her warm, smooth back. He traced a hand over her, resting it on her large belly, and was rewarded with a rolling bump—maybe an elbow or a foot. *Shocking, to feel life moving inside her. It must be crowded in there already.* She'd complained about feeling bulky, but to him, she radiated luscious health. Her breasts were taut, and he'd noticed this morning her nipples, now a deeper, richer chestnut, stood up most of the time. He moved his hand to stroke one, the lightest caress. His erection hardened against her backside. She let out a love rumble and rolled over toward him.

"Only us," she murmured. "No interruptions. Wow."

"It's different when we're truly alone, isn't it." He hesitated. "This far along with twins, are you sure it's okay?"

"It'd better be, because it's going to happen," she said. "But extra-gentle seems in order. No pounding on the door."

∽

Dr. Jamison, Moss, and Carolina discussed the results from UCSF. "This is what I thought I saw," she said. "It's important you got it confirmed, and at a top notch center, too." She examined Carolina before the ultrasound. "Your cervix is the slightest bit dilated. I'm sure it's from the pressure of the babies." She smoothed her gray hair back and narrowed her gaze at them. "By any chance did you two have intercourse within the last twenty-four hours?"

Carolina blushed. "Very gentle sex, yes."

"Sorry to break this to you, but seminal fluid has prostaglandins. They soften the cervix. Normally in pregnancy it's not a problem, but with twins—and this dilation—I wouldn't chance it. Fool around, of course. But it's best Carolina doesn't have orgasms, either. They stimulate uterine contractions."

"Shit," she said. "And he can? Not fair."

"You'll get through this; the time will go fast. And, more tough news. Time to stay in Eugene. If you dilate any more, off to San Francisco you go. No more commuting to the ranch on weekends. In other words, no long car rides. And you—" she focused on Carolina. "Bed rest. These babies need eight more weeks minimum. Preferably ten. Only get up to go to the bathroom. By the way, where's Rowan? She seemed interested."

"She had a school project due and she's with our Eugene neighbors." Carolina dropped her head into her hands and rubbed her fingers across her brow. "I don't have any control here, do I?" she whispered. "None at all. This is all just thundering on through. Holy shit."

"That's right," Moss and Dr. Jamison said in unison, then glanced at each other and chuckled.

She raised her head to both of them. "You're laughing at me? Give me a fucking break."

"Not 'laughing at,' sweetheart," Moss said. "Releasing tension. We're all powerless here." He ruffled her hair.

Dr. Jamison took off her stethoscope. "A final reminder: on the ride back to Eugene, your *last* long ride before these babies come, take a break in the middle and lie on your side in the back at least fifteen minutes to ease the weight and pressure. When you get home, go to bed. Moss unloads the car—you carry nothing, understand me? One other thing," she went on, "You're going to need help. A live-in person would be best." She folded her arms and looked back and forth between them. "Remember, families have been successfully bearing twins for millennia. You're not alone. There are twin parenting groups you can attend. All these concerns—they'll work themselves out."

As they walked out of the office, Moss said, "Do you want to look in Bend at strollers for twins, the tandem kind? We'll need one." He smacked his forehead. "No way. You're not walking around—we need to do this on the internet. In fact, I'll go get the car and pick you up here at the door."

"Stop," she snapped. "I'm not buying any of the stuff until the babies are here and healthy. Too much can go wrong. Not until I'm eight months."

"There's my sensible woman, back in gear again. How about this: we check Consumer Reports, reviews, and choose them, but not buy. I don't want to be stuck making decisions you surely want to be involved in. I'll write down the brands and model numbers, store them in my phone notes. As soon as we need the equipment, I'll pick it up." He rubbed his stubble. "By then, my office will be moved into the yurt. We'll have the space for a nanny to live with us."

"Whoa," Carolina said. "Having someone else in the house—I don't know."

"We're already going to have two new demanding beings sharing our home. Maybe it's the perfect time. Think about it—someone to share the exhaustion with us." He gave her a quirky smile. "We don't want to expect too much of Rowan. She deserves to be a teenager. She *needs* to be one."

After the appointment, they returned to Bender's Ridge to prepare for the ride to Eugene. Carolina was still fussing. "Bed rest? Good God, no. How will we manage?" She swung toward Moss. "I can't do this. You know me—I'll go bonkers. I already miss earning my share."

Moss huffed. "I know, sweetie, but we don't need the money—and certainly not when you should be lying down."

Carolina's eyes brimmed. "I'm darn emotional when I'm pregnant. I hate it. And your writing—when will you have time?" Carolina's voice was rising. "I can't stand being a burden."

"Love, you're never a burden. We'll work it out."

As they parked on the gravel, he rested a calming hand on her arm. "This is doctor's orders. I cook most of the time anyway, and you've had the wisdom not to vacuum in the last two months. You're already on leave from your business." He thought for a moment. "We'll ask Rowan to be in charge of laundry for now. Maybe she'd like to learn to cook, too. I can teach her."

Moss collected their belongings including Jazz's toys and loaded them while Carolina rested on the couch, waiting to leave. He conferred with Dakota, the veteran taking care of ranch work now, a last-minute transferal of tasks.

An hour later, they were ready. On Moss's command, Jazz jumped in the van's open slider and, squeaking a yawn, settled in her bed.

Carolina tried to belt herself in, but couldn't. "I must have expanded another inch while we were in the doctor's office. Shit. Mossy—will you snap this please? I can't reach the damn thing."

He laughed. "These babies are going to come out swearing. We're in big trouble now."

Jazz stood up and slurped Carolina's face, clearly an effort to calm her.

Lina patted her. "Aww, thanks. Dog bed down, sweet pea. It's safer for the ride." She looked at Moss. "I'll clean up my mouth. Why, I even snapped at you about your bad language in our first phone call, remember?"

He grunted in response, then started the van. Giving Dakota a wave goodbye, they drove out the dirt track and away from Bender's Ridge. The van's passenger seat reclined. They wouldn't have to make the fifteen-minute doctor-ordered stop in the middle of the trip.

Carolina craned her neck to look back. *Damn, I'll miss this place. Three endless months.* "It'll never be the same," she whispered. "The next time I'm here, we'll be swamped in baby-land."

He reached for her hand and squeezed it before returning his own to the steering wheel. "You're not sorry, are you?"

She considered his question. "No. Although twins—I didn't bargain for *two* babies. This could get tough."

"We have each other and Rowan," he said. "We'll weather whatever. You'll see. I'm a steady guy."

"It's not you I'm concerned about. It's the mix of all five of us, if both babies survive this craziness of having a mother of 'advanced maternal age.' That's what the Internet calls me—humiliating. Two infants *and* a teenager? Yikes."

Moss was glad to see she dozed for a while. At the top of the pass, surrounded by all the lava rock, he asked softly, "Need to pee?"

She yawned. "Too long a walk. Maybe Jazz needs to, though. I can't stop here without remembering the pee break with Rowan and the dogs just before the accident. Rowan and I were so carefree—chatting, making jokes."

"But I wouldn't have met you if the car wreck hadn't happened. I'm grateful every day."

She watched him. He took a breath and paused for a moment. *He's about to change the subject.* It tickled her she could read him.

"I want to talk about hiring someone to live in," he said. "We'll want those extra hands the doc talked about. I think we need the help now."

She dropped her head into her palms—for what, the third time today? "I know you're right, but let me get home and adjust to the idea of lying around eating bonbons." She snorted. "In any case, Rowan needs to be in on it."

"And Zephyr," he said, under his breath.

"Yes, Zephyr, too," she said, through clenched teeth. *Damn, I'll do anything to make it safer for the babes. Even that.*

Chapter Nine

Zephyr lifts her head. Our pack is close, she sends to Rowan. They're here sooners.

Her girl shuts her book and smiles. *Great—I've missed them. How do you know?*

The dog holds her human's gaze. *Zeph feels them with her ears.*

Rowan speaks out loud. "You feel them with your ears? I love it. I wonder if the pressure changes or something. It makes me mad I'll never know." She shifts to pensing. *Sometimes I want to crawl inside you. To understand how you know stuff. I want to "be" Zeph for a day.*

Zephyr rises from her spot nearby, leaps on the bed, and plunks her head in her girl's lap. She sends a picture of them entwined.

Rowan senses the words: *Zephyr and Rowan—always connected.*

When they arrived home, Carolina allowed Moss to settle her on the couch with chamomile tea.

"I'll leave Jazz with you, and pick up Rowan and the big girl. She's got that big project to carry. Think about if you want a bed that folds in different positions. That way, you can be out here in the middle of things."

She sniffed. "Not if it looks like a hospital bed. If you can find something else, maybe."

"I'll find one. Can we talk to Rowan about getting another set of hands around here?"

"Don't you think we can manage without? I hate the idea."

Moss sat down beside her and took her hand. "Lina, *I* need the help. I'll have to be in more than one place at once—I'm the only driver in the family as of now. And the more pregnant you get, the less willing I am for you to be alone in the house. Give me a break on this one, okay? We'll find someone quiet. No hovering allowed."

She realized he was frowning with worry and smoothed his brow. "I'm sorry," she whispered. "I've been self-involved, like this is only happening to me. I see your point." She gave him a kiss.

"I'm going to call Sue, and see if she can drop them off. This new routine starts now. Tomorrow I'm calling the contractor and getting the yurt finished as fast as possible. I don't mind paying overtime."

Carolina made a face, but nodded. She felt pissed off and crazy—but she'd follow instructions. The last thing she wanted was twins born too soon.

Moss phoned a couple of agencies and placed an ad in the weekend newspaper, both the print and online editions. As an afterthought, he decided to post it on Craigslist as well.

> *Live-in help needed with infant twins. Quiet presence and gentle nature required. Stability/steadiness important. No smoking or drugs. Long-term position starts prior to birth. Active, engaged family lives both Eugene/central Oregon ranch. Must like dogs.*

He reread it a few times, rewrote and deleted "must like dogs" more than once, until he settled on including it. After all, they were a fact of this family. First critter contact would start with the interview, and our dogs are bigger than most, he thought. He walked the printout down to Rowan to review.

Ten people responded to the ads. Moss talked to each one and handled the first cut—folks who obviously weren't a good fit: demanding, flighty, or didn't drive. Funny how much people revealed without realizing it. Four seemed worth meeting.

He arranged times in the following week to interview after Rowan got home from school, two people a day. They could gather in the living room where Lina would be set up—a circle, everyone participating. He figured a half hour each seemed about right; it might run longer if it felt great. He'd schedule the appointments an hour apart to allow for that. If any one of them, including dogs, rattled the interviewee or put them off, then they weren't a good fit.

He puzzled over one piece: he wanted Zephyr to weigh in early in the process. Whoever answered the door, and that would be a good job for Rowan and Zeph, could show the guest into the living room to meet Jazz and Carolina. They might get introduced and talk about the dogs while he made tea and brought in cookies. Zeph would have a chance to suss the person's energy. Maybe Row could be the notetaker, beginning with what Zeph pensed to her.

It seemed like a plan. He'd run it by all the girls later. *I'm glad one of these babies is a boy. With a wife, daughter, and two girl dogs, I'm surrounded.*

The adjustable bed arrived on Tuesday. Everyone seem pleased with its design—it didn't look like a hospital bed at all. Rowan and Moss moved the living room furniture around so the bed nestled near the window with a view of the yurt and the valley beyond.

"Come check out the peace eagles," Lina called. Moss came from the kitchen, and she pointed them out to him.

He stood by her, watching the birds float on thermals. "What a beautiful sight. They're immersed in their element, aren't they? Watching them must be a nice change from TV or reading."

"I'd go completely bonkers if I couldn't have a vista. Could you hang the bird feeders outside the window?" She pulled him in for a kiss. "And when do the interviews start?"

"Tomorrow afternoon. One at 3:30, another an hour later. And I'll do that—hang bird feeders. One for hummers, too."

"And the yurt?"

"They're finishing up today."

"I'm dying to see it."

"Yeah, but no walking out there. How about I carry you?"

"Do you have any idea how much I weigh now? I've gained thirty pounds. Take pictures for me." She looked wistful. "I want to see the bookcases, artwork, bed, your desk—all of it."

He nuzzled her cheek. "Okay. You're going to love it—the Murphy bed went in this morning. It's got a memory foam mattress, too."

"A wonderful bed, and we haven't made love on it? It'll be months until we can."

His voice went thick. "This is harder than I expected."

"Sheesh, me too. We passed six-and-a-half months—twenty-eight weeks. If I'll birth them by eight months or a little earlier, we're three-quarters of the way there." She hesitated. "Except, we'll have to wait a few weeks after they're born. And then we'll be interrupted by screaming infants. Oh Moss, what have we done?"

"It's overwhelming now, but we'll get in the swing of things." He rested his palm on her belly. The twins were wide awake and kicking. "I'll wait until you say it's okay. No pressure." He ran a finger along her jawline. "You lie here and do math?"

"Yup. Otherwise I'll go nuts with fantasies about touching you."

"Dr. J would be proud of us." He kissed her on the cheek. "I need to finish prepping dinner. Besides, this conversation? I'm hornier than hell." He started for the kitchen, and wheeled around. "*This* is why we're hiring someone. She can tend the babes, and we can head out to the yurt and play on the new, cushy Murphy bed."

"I get it," she muttered, but managed a smile. "You're right, again."

Chapter Ten

Rowan had never participated in a real interview. The day she'd met her cane teacher when she'd been blind, he'd provided lessons; it wasn't the same as an interview. The first candidate would arrive in half an hour. Nervous, she pensed Zephyr. *Give me lots of feedback, okay?*

The dog yawned widely, and crossed her paws. *The pack knows what's right.*

When the doorbell rang, Rowan ran to answer it.

Zeph strolled behind. *Relax, it's human, not mountain lion.*

Row stopped and stared. Had Zephy made a *joke*?

She pulled open the door. A heavyset woman—older than her mom—took one look at Zephyr and lurched backward. "Is this the Westbury household?" she said, frowning.

Rowan nodded.

"I'm Louisa. The ad said 'must like dogs,' and the man of the house said big, but this thing's a horse! She makes me nervous."

Rowan scowled. "Miniature horse, maybe. She's very friendly. Her name is Zephyr and I'm Rowan. Come in."

The woman lumbered after them. Bad hip? How could she run after a child? Rowan thought, and showed her to the living room. "This is my mom, Carolina. She's on bed rest. Mom, this is Louisa." The two shook hands, and Carolina invited her to sit down. Jazz settled near Moss's chair; Zephyr lay at Rowan's feet.

Zeph pensed a picture of an uneasy, overweight spaniel, lunging and snapping. Rowan sensed the words "fear biter," and had a hard time keeping giggles from spilling out. "I'll get my dad," she said, and trotted to the kitchen. "Mossy, this interviewing stuff is fun. But I'm not reporting what Zephy said yet. It might bias you."

"Wise girl. Write your notes before you come back in, though." He picked up the tray with cookies, cups, kettle, and a choice of teas, and carried it into the living room.

Rowan quickly jotted Zephy's contribution, and returned to the meeting. The interview only took twenty minutes.

After Louisa left, Moss asked Carolina, "What about you, love?"

"She's awfully stiff. I don't want to spend a lot of time with her. It's a 'no' from me."

"Rowan?"

"Nope," Rowan said. "She's too set in her ways. And she didn't respond well to Zephy. No wonder." She burst into gales of laughter. "Zeph called her a 'fear biter.'"

"She made me tense," Moss said. "Notice, we didn't even tell her about going to San Francisco for a few months. Unanimous. We move on."

Carolina nodded. "Row, let me see your notes."

Rowan handed them to her, and then watched her response carefully.

"You wrote these before we interviewed her? Zeph was right on." Carolina looked up from the paper and peered at the dog.

The next woman chewed and snapped gum throughout the conversation, earning a unanimous "no" as well.

After showing her out, they looked at each other. Rowan finally voiced the silent concern in the room. "What if we don't find anybody who's right?"

"Then we'll place another ad," Moss said. "The babies aren't due for more than two months. We have time."

The following day, Susannah was the first interviewee. After the introductions, she said, "I'm thirty, and a widow. I'm on my own now—no children and a whole lot of bills. I lost my husband six months ago, to cancer."

"I'm sorry," Carolina said. "We have loss in common. My first husband died of a virulent flu eight years ago."

Rowan watched them share a look.

"I had to sell my home. A live-in position would be ideal," Susannah went on.

"If you don't have children, do you have experience with them?" Moss asked.

"I was a nanny for a decade before I married."

"One of our babies has a congenital heart problem." he said. "Do you think you could handle it?"

"I'm sure I could."

"Of course we want to check references," Moss said.

Rowan noticed the woman hesitated before responding.

"I'll dig them out for you," she said. "It was a long time ago."

Susannah received two "maybe" votes and a strong "yes" from Carolina. They were puzzled by Zephyr's insight. She had pensed, *She's hiding a bone.*

"What do you think she means?" Carolina asked.

"I'm not sure," Rowan said. "But she's not telling us everything."

"Huh. Worrisome," Moss said. "I'll have my investigator, Dan, check into her. We need to know more." He went to make the call.

"I'm sure it's fine," Carolina said. "Zephyr can't be right about every single person. Susannah's the one for me."

A half hour later, the doorbell rang. Again, Rowan and Zephyr went to greet the latest applicant.

"Hi, I'm Teal Landis," the sandy-haired young man said. "Wow, what a gorgeous dog. Stately. And those eyes—they take in everything."

"They sure do," Rowan said.

Zeph wagged her tail in slow, wide arcs as she went up to the slender man. He patted her, and she snuffled him. *Not boy, not girl.* Another whiffle. *Girl and boy.*

Really? Rowan thought. She peered at him. His hair was buzzed about one-half inch, and he sported a trimmed goatee. Maybe twenty-three? He sure felt male.

They walked into the living room, and Rowan made introductions. Teal sat on the couch.

The family asked a variety of questions and he did as well. "Tell me about your country property," he said. "How often are you there?"

"Most weekends," Carolina replied. "Except I'm on bed rest until the twins are born, so we're in Eugene full time for now. I have to say, I hadn't considered hiring a man. Explain to me why you're interested in infants."

Zephyr crawled up on the couch, lay down, and dropped her head in Teal's lap.

"Nice," he said, stroking her neck. "She seems comfortable with me. I like her, too. To answer your question, I love babies, kids, and animals. We had quite the menagerie. I'm the oldest of six. I attended the births of the three youngest."

"You must have lots of experience with young children. One of our babies, the little girl, has a congenital heart defect. Do you think you could deal with it?"

Teal was quiet for a moment. "I'd want to get CPR training. I've learned we're all unique, and temporarily-abled. Maybe it's saying too much, but eventually something goes wrong for everyone."

"True," Rowan said. "CPR, what a smart idea."

"You're right. We should've thought of it," Carolina said. "We all need to get the training. Also, our family will be spending a few months in San Francisco to be near the UCSF med center. They have one of the best cardiac centers in the country. Would you be willing to travel with us?"

"Sure. San Francisco! Wow, I'd enjoy the city. Lots of culture there."

"Yes, that's true. Can you tell us more about your family?" Carolina asked.

"I grew up in the Oregon countryside, outside of Alfalfa, due east of Bend. We went to school in Redmond; the local one-room school house closed before I was born. My dad raises alfalfa—third generation—and runs some cattle. We kids learned a solid work ethic real young."

"What brought you to Eugene?" Moss asked.

"University of Oregon—graduated two years ago. I needed to get away. I'm pretty different from my family."

"Both Carolina and I went to the U of O as well. What was your major?"

"Creative writing. I figured if I got the job, when I had time off, I'd write."

Moss shook his head in amazement. "That was my major, too. I earned my Masters there. I'm an author."

"A lot of coincidences," Carolina said. Her voice was soft.

"I'd love to study further, but it takes money, and I don't have much. It took student loans to get me through college."

Rowan spoke up. "How are you different from your family? I am too."

"Yeah, but you're lucky. Your tribe obviously loves you." He went silent, and looked down, rubbing Zephyr's ears. When he raised his eyes, they glistened. "My parents are very … conservative. What I'm going to disclose may finish the interview," he said, "but it's important to be truthful. I'm trans. Transgender. I was born with the body of a girl—but it's not who I am. And they can't accept it."

Rowan pensed Zeph, *You were exactly right.*

After a long pause, Moss said, "I never would have known. You're so male. Nice goatee."

Teal smiled and stroked his beard. "Beards are big in my family. It took a few months to grow."

"You must have had a very challenging road," Carolina said.

"They won't even talk to me." He looked at each person in the room. "I'm sure this is a huge shock. You have the right to ask me anything; I need to be completely open."

"Have you had any of the operations?" Moss asked.

Teal hesitated, as though considering whether to reveal more information. "I got my chest flattened three years ago. And of course I'm on hormone therapy. Bottom surgery is stratospherically expensive. I'm saving. It'll be years, if ever."

"You're really brave." Rowan reached down to stroke Jazz. "How'd you choose your name? I love it."

"I didn't—I was given an androgynous one at birth. Kind of a weird joke, considering. But Teal's a family name."

"Your brothers and sisters? Mom and dad? They won't speak to you?" Rowan asked. "None of them?"

He shook his head. "I'm hoping my youngest sister, Isabelle, will come around when she's out on her own. She's only eleven now."

Zephyr resettled—now her head and front paws were in Teal's lap. He leaned down and planted a kiss on the knob on her crown. The dog wrinkled her lips.

"She's smiling?" Teal asked.

Rowan laughed. "Yes. But most everybody assumes she's mad when she shows her teeth. You know animals, all right."

They talked a while longer about salary, living accommodations, and time off.

"I have to go," Teal said. "I'm reading at Tsunami Bookstore tonight and have another interview Wednesday afternoon. I need work—badly."

"You're reading? That's great. We'll talk and decide by Thursday," Moss said. "What's a good time to phone you?"

"I write at night. You can call by 8:30 a.m.—I'll have some coffee on board by then." He hesitated and then said, "Of course I can change my writing schedule. I'm assuming you'd want early morning help." Teal shook all their hands, knelt down to pat Jazz, and tousled Zephyr's tufts. "Thanks," he said, when he stood up. "You're a great family."

"We appreciate your offer of flexibility," Moss said. "By the way, we do background checks."

"Of course, you should," Teal replied.

They said goodbye, and Rowan watched him walk to his car, Zeph by her side. *He's special,* she pensed.

Zeph leaned into her leg. *Be patient. Kibble Man and Pack Mama choose him.*

Over dinner, after the meal, and long into the evening, they discussed Susannah and Teal.

Carolina asked, "Zephyr identified Louisa as a fear-biter; Susannah as hiding a bone, whatever that means; and Teal as both boy and girl? And these insights came while meeting them at the door?" Rowan nodded.

"That's stunning. I liked Susannah, and want to give her a chance. She seems very motivated. She's my favorite."

Rowan frowned. "We'd better hear back from Mossy's investigator. If Zephy doesn't trust her—"

"But *I* do. She was friendly and quiet. I could get along with her," Carolina said. "I don't have anything against Teal, but I'd prefer a woman's company. Don't my wishes outweigh Zephyr's?" She looked to Moss for support.

He sighed. "Lina, we need to wait. I'm not willing to hire her without a clean report from Dan. He said he'd try to have some information by day after tomorrow."

The next day, Moss moved quietly through the house attending to Carolina, who snipped and fretted. Rowan avoided them and hung out with Jazz and Zephyr. *You were mistaken, Zephy. Mom went for the woman who's hiding something.*

Moss's cell rang just before dinner.

"Hey, Dan," he said, and then listened for a moment. "You're sure? Well, your report decides it. Thanks. I have another person for you to check out. I'll email you his information."

"What did he say?" Carolina asked.

Moss pursed his lips. "Susannah's using an alias. She worked as a nanny over a decade ago, but not since. Her husband walked in on her shaking their baby, and reported the incident to authorities. He divorced her and was awarded full custody. Lies of omission and commission, both—she hedged about having a child because she's not raising the girl, and she told us she was a widow."

"Oh my heavens," Carolina whispered. "Think about what might have happened because I assumed Zeph couldn't know." She patted the big dog. "Well," she said, swallowing hard. "I trust her instincts now. The way she put her head in Teal's lap—such an obvious sign of trust. He could benefit from a family, and we need his help. But I still want Dan to check him out. We can't be too careful."

"I'm delighted he's a writer," Moss said. "It'll be interesting to see how our relationship develops."

"He's great with the dogs," Rowan said. She pensed to Zeph, *I forgot to listen to the "be patient" part. You were right again.*

"I'll call Teal and let him know he's hired, pending Dan's report." Moss said. "Smart dog, Zeph."

"I'm so sorry I doubted you both. You *all*," Carolina said, glancing at Zephyr. "I feel like an idiot."

Chapter Eleven

Thursday morning, the investigator phoned Moss. "The kid's clean. No record of any kind. I sniffed around the university and talked to a couple of his previous professors, too. He's well-liked and a hard worker. Friendly. Kind to people who have challenges. Uh—he's different. Did he tell you?"

"Yes. He's transgender." They talked a few minutes longer. "Thanks for all your work. Send me a bill."

After Moss hung up, he called the family together. "I got a great report from Dan about Teal. Are we in agreement we can go with him? How about a two-week trial period?"

"Okay," Carolina said. "I liked him, but I'm sorry he's not a woman."

"Row?"

"Absolutely. He seemed easy-going and very friendly. And I know there's no problem with the dogs. They trust him."

Moss called Teal that afternoon. The young man answered on the first ring. "Hello?" His voice was anxious.

"Hi Teal, Moss Westbury here. We'd like to hire you. Are you still interested in the position?"

"Yes, sir."

"How about a two-week trial to get to know each other? See how it goes, for both sides? And please, no 'sir.'"

"Sounds good. I should call you Moss? And Carolina, and Rowan?"

"Please. We're casual. Would you like to start Monday morning?"

"I'm going to a retreat this weekend in California. I'll drive back Sunday afternoon and Monday morning. Is it okay if I come after lunch?"

"Sure."

"I'll bring a suitcase and my laptop. If it works out, I can move my other stuff after the two weeks? I don't have much."

"That sounds good."

"I'm grateful for the opportunity. I think I'll enjoy your family. And I sure hope we can talk about writing sometime." Teal cleared his throat. "I'm reading your first novel right now. It's great."

"Thank you. And I love conversations about craft. Rowan might want to join us—she writes too."

"Cool. Any dress code?"

"Clean blue jeans are fine. We're big on comfort around here. We'll talk more about family rhythms after you start."

"Clean jeans are about all I've got. Thanks for taking a chance on me. It's a relief to get this."

"Enjoy your retreat, Teal, and we'll see you Monday."

Moss went into the living room to cuddle with Carolina, who was taking a nap. As he sat on the bed to unleg, she rolled over to give him a kiss. "Did you reach him?"

"I did. He'll start Monday afternoon. He'll be at a retreat this weekend."

She traced a finger down his nose. "Rowan'll be interested. What kind of retreat, do you know?"

"I didn't want to pry. We'll find out soon enough. I suspect it's not Christian." He snuggled next to her.

She raised up on one elbow. "How come?"

"He hesitated when he said his family was 'conservative.' I figured he meant born-again."

"But we aren't sure. Let's not make assumptions."

"You're right; I know better."

Moss leaned over and kissed her, nibbling her lower lip. "Oh Geez. I'm hard as a rock. I have to get up. It's too difficult to lie here."

She breathed out slowly. "The twins dig when we're together. They're kicking like crazy." Her hand strayed over to feel him. "Wow."

He rested his fingers lightly on her belly. *Tempting*. The babies were active; it felt like they were doing somersaults. "I don't think so, sweetheart. It's too complicated for both of us. I get off and feel guilty; you don't get off, and I feel even worse. Soon enough. Besides, we're in the living room!"

"Shit. No more kids after this."

"Two is plenty, my love—double what we bargained for. Maybe I'll get a vasectomy. It sure would be nice not to have to think about contraception."

"I like that idea," she said.

Monday late morning, Carolina was propped up in bed in the living room reading *My Sister's Keeper* when the doorbell rang. "Come in," she sang out.

She heard Zephyr taking the stairs three at a time and bounding for the entry hall.

The door opened a crack. "It's Teal."

"Great—you're early. Come on in, if you can get past Zeph, that is."

Zephyr's tail made the same long, slow wag it had the first time they met. Teal walked in, rolling a battered weekender suitcase and carrying a worn laptop bag. He set them down so he could greet the dog, who was bumping his hip for attention. "I forgot how huge she is." He rubbed her ears and tousled her neck fur before walking over to Carolina.

"We all forget her size when we've been away from her for a while. Zeph, go get Rowan," Carolina said. The dog wheeled toward the stairs.

"Wow," he breathed. "Look at that."

"I know. I'm only starting to trust this side of her."

He pointed to the book on the bed. "Picoult sure can keep a story moving. And she picks current controversial issues."

Carolina met his gaze. "That's what I love. When Row comes up, she'll show you your bedroom. There's a small desk which we hope will work for writing."

"Thanks. I hope you didn't go to any trouble."

She smiled. "It was already there; everyone in this family writes except me." She heard dog and girl pounding up the stairs.

"You're here," Row said. "Look how happy Zephy is. She doesn't take to everyone."

"Where's Jazz?" Teal asked.

"Mossy's writing in the yurt and she stays close by him." Rowan picked up his computer gear. "Follow me. The room's not fancy, but you'll be comfortable."

Teal trailed behind, rolling his weekender. "Fancier than my old digs," he said.

Rowan walked into the room, set the computer on the desk, and turned to face him. "Where have you been living until now?"

She pointed to the luggage rack in the corner and he slung his suitcase onto it. "I've been crashing in my friend's garage. It's … basic, and freezing in winter. I couldn't afford anything nicer until I found a job."

"So, you need this to work out."

"More than you know. And for myriad reasons."

"I remember the first time I ever heard the word 'myriad.'"

"When?" He looked at her, head tilted.

"One summer, after a nasty car accident involving a deer, I spent eight weeks blind. My cane teacher—also blind—was a lawyer. He used 'myriad' and, since I'm a word freak, I asked him about it."

"You're a word freak?"

"Yep. Major. We all are." She sat down and bounced on his bed. "This is comfortable. It used to be mine."

He nodded. "I love words, too. When you find new ones, share them with me?"

Moss tapped on the door frame. "Anyone hungry? I'm making lunch—avocado and cheese sandwiches. Row, will you come help?"

"Okay. Teal, how many sandwiches do you want?"

"One's fine."

She cocked her head. "Did you even have breakfast?"

He looked at the floor and shook his head.

"We'll make you two. You're not starving with us."

"Punkin, you don't need to stand up for Teal. He's doing fine on his own."

She frowned at him. "I *wasn't*."

"Yes, you were, and this is important. Teal's going to have his own predilections, strengths, and weaknesses. We need to learn his. We're all human, with human failings—they're expected. He wouldn't be Teal without them."

"Predilections?"

"Tendencies," Moss said.

Rowan noticed the young man was watching them, wide-eyed.

"Please, eat as much as you want," Moss said. "Seconds, thirds. I remember being your age." He smiled at the young man. "You should know we grow much of our own food. We'll put you to work in the garden when we're back at Bender's Ridge this summer, if you'd like—when Carolina wants private time with the babies." He thought for a moment. "Let's talk over lunch—about your tasks, family rhythms, other stuff. Ten minutes until we eat. Row?"

Rowan carried the plates into the living room. She returned to the kitchen and poured a glass of milk for Teal. He looked up and smiled when she set it down in front of him. They ate on TV tables around Carolina's bed.

"How far along are you?" Teal asked, between bites.

"Twenty-nine and a half weeks," Carolina said. "It feels longer. We're hoping I get to thirty-six at least. Thirty-eight would be safer. But we have to be in San Francisco by thirty-four weeks. Doctor's orders. Twins are rarely carried to forty weeks—too much weight and pressure."

"That's why you're on full bed rest?"

Carolina nodded.

"What can I do for you before the babies come?"

"We were hoping you could help with cleaning, laundry, and fetch things when I need them. Shopping, too—of course, you can use our car. Drive Rowan places." She stretched. "I'm being very strict about this bed business. Do you cook at all? Moss is a wonderful chef, and he's been in charge of the kitchen, but occasionally he's gone for the day."

"I'm willing to learn. Mom kicked the kids out of the kitchen."

"We're big on organic vegetables," Moss said. "Also, I'm a bow hunter, and take a deer from our property each fall. I make a mean venison stew. We raise chickens, too."

Teal flushed and looked down at his tray. "I'm not sure I could kill a chicken."

Moss laughed out loud. "Not in your job description. Besides, we keep the chickens for eggs. We buy cut-up chicken at Long's Meats."

"Oh, good. I'm a wuss about harming animals."

Rowan piped up. "I'm a wuss, too."

Mid-afternoon, Rowan knocked on Teal's door.

"Yahoo," he called. "Come in."

"It's Row, with a question." She walked in, sat in the desk chair, and swiveled to face Teal, who was stretched out on the bed. Zephyr followed and curled in the corner. "You seemed surprised by our conversation before lunch," Row said. "How come?"

Teal got up and crouched near the dog, playing with her fur. "Your dad's very different from mine. I've never heard a family talk like this before—free and honest with each other."

"Did you like it, or did it freak you out?"

He got up and sat on the bed. "Oh, it's dynamite. It makes me feel … safer, I guess. Issues brought out in the open immediately—not stuffed away where they molder, like in my family."

"'Molder'—what a great word. Having to hide important stuff must have been hard. Then it's like there's no air to breathe."

"Exactly," he said.

Their eyes met.

Zephyr listens. There's lots of feeling in their human talk; she can almost understand them.

She sees inside. The girl-boy—a call name like "Kibble Man" or "Pack Mama" hasn't come for this new human yet—has no hidden bones, no meanness. There is hurt, but no infection. The wound heals. *This is a good person*, she sends to Rowan.

Her girl leans down and pats her. *Yes—and super kind.*

Puzzled, she puts her head between her paws. Can she share with this new human like she does with her girl? Will the girl-boy understand her?

"Your dog is unusual," Teal said. "Like different—spooky-different. When she looks at me with those eyes, her gaze goes in."

Rowan nodded. "Yeah. She's special." She wasn't sure whether to say more. Probably not yet; it didn't hurt to be too careful. She thought back to how long it took her to reveal their telepathic connection to Maggie—six months after they first met, not until Mossy and Mom got married. She and Maggie had been texting and emailing almost every day. Still, she'd been cautious.

"What's on for this afternoon?" Rowan asked.

"Going to Market of Choice for groceries and helping Moss cook dinner," Teal said. "And some laundry. I wanted to ask Carolina if she likes to be read to—I could keep her company sometimes. Do you know whether she'd enjoy it?"

"Well, she read to me every day when I was a kidlet. I don't know about the other way around. Ask. She's super practical and direct."

"And Moss?"

"He's more thoughtful and philosophical, more open to the unseen."

"I'm blown away by *Canceled*. What's he working on now?"

"I'm not sure. He wrote a memoir about his stint in Afghanistan called *Daymares*. His agent, Sarah, sold it to a big publisher, and it came out in November."

"I look forward to reading it," Teal said. "Time for me to get to work. My very first shift—hope I don't make any humiliating mistakes."

"Ask questions. I bet it'll go fine. Mossy's way cool."

"How come you call him 'Mossy'?"

"He's not my bio-dad. He adopted me four years ago. I asked him to."

"There's a story I want to hear," Teal said. "Later." He zipped his empty suitcase and slipped it under the bed.

That same afternoon, Moss had Teal drive him to the market in the van. He wanted to get a feel for his driving style and demonstrate how the family approached food shopping. When they walked in, he turned toward the fresh-vegetable department first. "Get only organic veggies and fruits. You'll notice I mainly shop the perimeter—the junk and processed foods are all in the middle aisles. I stay out of there, except for the bins. We're big on bulk foods, too." He turned to Teal. "You can add stuff from the center if you want; I'm not trying to control your eating habits."

Teal glanced at the list before reaching for organic broccoli. He selected four heads, considered what he'd chosen, assessing, and put two heads back. "Only four of us, not eight," he said, quietly. "I did a lot of shopping for my family before they kicked me out. It was one of my chores; my mother hated going to the grocery store, always having to haul bickering kids along. She was thrilled when I got my driver's license." He paused and fingered the bok choy. "Do you like this? It's one of my favorite vegetables."

"We do. In the summer I grow a fair amount of it."

He looked up at Moss. "May we get some today?"

"You bet." Moss said, "By the way, this family loves parsnips but none of us eat turnips."

"Other likes or dislikes?" Teal asked.

"I'm not crazy about coconut or collard greens. Carolina is wild for kimchi these days."

"What's that?"

"I guess you'd call it a side dish, maybe the Korean version of sauerkraut? A fermented food, made with carrots and cabbage, leeks, garlic—as Row would say, super healthy. I make it."

They wandered through the bins of fruits and Moss pointed out their favorites. He showed Teal how to test avocados without bruising them.

"We never got to have these at home. Too expensive, I guess, with all the kids."

Moss nodded. "Pick out four," he said. "Two ripe ones, and two that are harder. I'm grateful we're able to eat whatever we want. I don't take it for granted."

When they arrived home, Teal carried in the bags while Moss checked on Carolina. He returned to the kitchen to see how Teal was managing; the young man had unloaded the food onto the counter and was trying to figure out where to store the groceries. The pantry door was open. Teal grabbed some of the avocados and reached up to put them in the wire basket hanging from the ceiling. His sleeves pulled back, exposing horizontal scars—lots of them.

Moss stared at his forearms. "Teal?" His tone was low and concerned.

Moss didn't know what to say next, but Teal tugged his sleeves down. "Damn. I completely forgot. I was hoping we'd get to know each other before you found out."

"We're going to discuss this right now. We'll put the rest of the food away later. Let's go to the yurt where we can talk in private." Moss signaled for him to follow, and limped out the door. They made their way across the backyard in silence. Jazz trailed them.

When they stepped inside, Moss indicated two chairs where they could sit facing each other. Jazz leaned into Moss.

Before Teal sat, he asked, "Are you gonna fire me?"

"No, son, I'm not. But I'm obviously concerned. Please, roll up your sleeves; I want to have a good look."

Teal dropped his gaze and hesitated. After a moment, he shucked his outer long-sleeved shirt, and stood in his T-shirt, looking at the floor. He reached his hands toward Moss. Five inches on each arm were heavily scarred—welt upon welt upon welt—now ghost-white.

Moss took an audible breath.

Teal sat. "It's over." His voice cracked, and he hid his arms behind his back. "I did this years ago. My father caught me binding my chest flat with old ace bandages. He flipped—railed and screamed I was a sicko for trying to hide my breasts and, as long as I lived under his roof, I was to behave and dress like a girl. He even hollered I had to grow my hair and wear a bra." He made a derisive sound. "I was only fifteen; I wasn't ready to find a place and support myself. I desperately wanted to go to college. They shunned me, literally wouldn't talk to me. I think their church put them up to it. That's when I started cutting."

"I'd like to touch your arms now," Moss said, keeping his voice soft. "May I?"

Teal looked at him uncertainly. "How come?" But he slowly raised his arms again and offered them to Moss.

"I don't know exactly. Acknowledgment maybe, or welcoming." He ran his fingers gently over the scars until he'd touched each one. "Teal, I want you to talk with Rowan about this, and show her, too. Please explain the circumstances, and clarify how long ago it stopped. Tell Carolina, too, before they discover the scars on their own. Have you spent time in therapy?"

"Yeah, as a student at the U. Once you said you weren't going to fire me, I thought you'd never want me to expose them—I'd always have to wear long sleeves. I sure didn't anticipate this. Who *are* you?"

To Moss—when Teal raised his gaze, tears glistening, he looked like a young, tender, rejected boy. "I'm a man who's been to war, got a leg blown off, and came home with a significant case of PTSD," he said. "Trust me, I've seen blatant hostility, unfairness, judgment, and much worse. This—this place you've come to—is a household of healing. We're all a work in progress. Carolina and I heal each other; my love somehow heals Row's loss of her biological father, and now you'll be part of it, too."

"How did I ever deserve this?" the young man whispered. "How did this happen?"

"Zephyr saw who you really are. That's how," Moss said. "You were chosen by a dog who's wiser than most of us."

Chapter Twelve

Moss trailed Teal into the house, pausing on the way to the kitchen. He watched the young man go straight to Zephyr who was lying at Rowan's feet in the living room. Seeming respectful of their conversation, Teal moved quietly and knelt by the dog. He knuckled her ear, then mumbled something. Moss was pretty sure he heard, "You're the best. Thank you."

Teal joined Moss in the kitchen and they finished putting away the groceries. "I'll tend to the laundry first," the young man said, "and then you can put me to work preparing dinner."

Moss went to sit for a few minutes with Carolina and Rowan. He disclosed nothing about the cutting; it was up to Teal. "He's a safe driver, at least when I'm in the car, and he chose the vegetables and fruits carefully. He'll be fine. I'm going to make venison stew for dinner. All right by you?"

They nodded.

As Moss limped to the kitchen to start preparations, he thought, it's probably a relief for him to have his cutting history out in the open. The two of them had gotten past this unexpected hurdle. Now, Teal had to tell Carolina and Rowan, and both would need to process the information. He figured Row would be fine; he wasn't so sure about his wife.

As he pulled parsnips, onion, kale, carrots, celery, and venison from the refrigerator, he saw Teal through the partially open u-room door, folding clothes on top of the dryer, humming softly. I better tell him that's what we call the utility room, he thought.

A few minutes later, after conferring with Moss about sorting the women's clothing, Teal headed down the hallway to deliver stacks into different bedrooms. When he returned to the kitchen, he said, "You're gonna have to start at the beginning with this cooking stuff. Like I said, Mom didn't let us kids in the kitchen. Since I was the oldest, I had to keep the others out of there—I got knocked around if I didn't."

"If I gave you an onion, would you know how to chop it?" Moss tossed one to him.

Teal caught and held it gingerly. "I can handle an onion."

"Okay then." Moss pointed to the cutting boards and the magnetic knife rack. "We don't ever cut onions on the wooden boards because they absorb the flavor. Pick the white one, and the big chef's knife with the wide blade. It's on the magnetic holder."

After Teal cut the onion, he asked, "Do you want to leave them in rings?"

"You decide."

Teal nodded, and knifed the rings in half. Moss pointed to the pan with butter close to sizzling, and Teal scraped the onions into the pan. A moment later, he said, "Man, this smells good. With the part-time job I had, it was all I could do to buy the used books I needed for class, so I've eaten simple fare for years. This—this is real food."

Moss set down what he was doing and leaned on the counter. "I'm assuming at home you ate what you grew or raised. What did you eat once you started at the U?"

"Yeah, farm food at home. At the U, ramen. Lots of it—the cheapest food there is. It comes in three flavors, and a buddy of mine bought it for me at Costco. Twenty-four packages per box. I only ate out about once a week, and then at places like Taco Bell."

"It's pretty much farm cooking here. I suppose you won't miss ramen; you must be sick of it."

Teal chortled. "You have no idea."

"I won't make noodle soup anytime soon." He nudged Teal in the ribs. "But our food may taste bland because you've been eating a shitload of salt. Ramen's chock full of it."

"I never thought about sodium. On the other hand, I managed to eat on two to three dollars a day and, most important, I got my education. It was worth it."

"I admire your fortitude. And congratulations on getting your degree."

After chopping the carrots and celery Moss put in front of him, Teal set the knife down. "I want to get an MFA in writing, but there's no way I can afford it. Down the line, I thought it might be better to go to a different institution. Got an opinion?"

"A low-residency program might work for you; your vacation time could be spent at the twice-a-year residencies. Consider Antioch—I have a friend who went there. They have a diverse student body; lots of LGBTQ folks. If your writing meets their standards, you'd be welcome and probably feel right at home. Also, it's in Los Angeles, not on the East Coast where many programs are."

"Thanks. I'll check them out."

Moss noticed Teal watching, eyes squinted, as he sautéed the vegetables, braised the venison cubes, assembled the stew, and added a frozen cylinder of stock.

"What's the lump?" he asked.

"It's venison stock. I made a number of quarts from the bones of the last deer I took. They're stored in the freezer in the garage."

"Homemade? I'm impressed." Teal carried the cutting boards and utensils they'd used to the sink.

"Geez, I forgot the garlic." Moss looked at the clock. "It's five; you're off duty. I'll do it. We'll eat about six-thirty. Of course, you'll eat with us."

Teal hesitated. "I thought I might ask Carolina if she wants me to read to her. Would it be all right with you?"

"Go for it," Moss said.

Carolina lay curled on her side, watching the peace eagles sail the valley. She heard a soft tap, and sat to see who it was. "Hi, Teal. What's up?"

Teal glanced out the window. "Are those turkey vultures? They're so big."

"Yes, but we call them peace eagles because they don't kill. The name makes me like them so much better."

"Nice moniker." He hesitated. "Uh—do you enjoy being read to? I don't mean to overstep, but it seems like you could use a diversion."

She glanced at the clock. "This is your time off. Please, don't spend it on me. Get settled, read, write, go for a walk in the woods, nose around and get to know the place. But, yes, I do like someone reading to me. Moss does, occasionally. I'll take a rain check, okay?"

"Sure. By the way, does your family have a piano?"

"There's a baby grand at Bender's Ridge, yes, and an electric keyboard in a closet here somewhere. Ask Rowan; I bet she knows. Do you play?"

He blushed. "Yeah, at home, and some in college. It calms me down. If we find it, where can I practice?"

She chewed her finger, thinking. "Depends on the music. If you love rock, we'll have to figure it out. But softer stuff, in your room would be fine. Wait, I think we have earphones—then you could play whatever, anytime. Row's probably out in the front with Zephyr if you want to go ask."

When Zephyr took off across the field toward the house, Rowan turned to see where she was going and saw Teal. Her dog danced around his feet. She was still startled by how Zephy had taken to him. She called out, "Is it dinnertime yet?"

"No, it's a few minutes after five. Dinner's at 6:30. Your mom said there might be a keyboard and some headphones in a closet? Do you know where?" As he talked, he patted Zephyr.

"I think they're in the cabinet in the rec room downstairs. Are you a musician?"

"No, but I love music. Can you help me find them? I don't want to go prowling around; it feels weird, like I'm poking where I don't belong."

"Let's go look." She turned to him. "You're very sweet with her. You've had a dog, haven't you."

He blinked fast. "Sam, our smooth collie. When my parents kicked me out, they forbade me to take him."

They walked next to each other. "How unfair. Worse—cruel," Rowan said.

"Yeah, they were looking to hurt me, and sure succeeded. I was lonely already; they'd barely talked to me in years. He was my main companion before I left for college. I don't even know if he's still alive. That's the agonizing part."

"Oh, my. I can't imagine parents acting so mean." They approached the house, but Rowan stopped on the porch. "Mossy said something about you starting late today because you were at a retreat?"

"With a guy named Adyashanti."

Rowan bounced with excitement. "Cool. I've seen some of his videos. Check out vids by Colin James, too. I've been watching them on the net. Mom'll probably veto my idea to go to a retreat of his."

"Why? Why would she shut off your interest in such a positive direction?"

"To her, it's weird and negative. My grammie's big into all things unseen. When Mom was young, she got teased and bullied because of her mom's strangeness. It does kind of leak out of Gram all the time, but I love her. We're pretty similar. What did you think of Adya?"

"I like him. I got drawn to look beyond this crazy business called 'Teal,' what with being the way I am, and all." He sat down on the steps. "Maybe we'd better talk about this out here."

Rowan sat beside him.

He glanced at her before he went on. "I'm going to share something difficult, and show you, too. This might freak you out." He took a deep breath. "Around age fifteen, I was close to suicidal. I got into cutting." He hesitated, then slowly pulled up his sleeves one by one, exposing his forearms.

Her eyes widened. "Teal. Do my parents know about this?"

"Moss does. I still have to tell your mom."

"When you made the cuts, didn't it hurt a lot?"

"It's weird, but I've heard other people talk about this, too. When someone is suffering as much as I was, the pain of the cuts is more clarifying than anything. It brought me out of the suffering and into the present moment. But I want to be clear—cutting is not an answer. To anything. I guess at the time it was a symptom of my misery and loneliness."

She shook her head. “I got very depressed at one point. My dad had died of flu—it was so hard; we were close—then, a few years later, my best friend’s father was transferred to Indonesia for work, and their family left here for good. I went awfully blue. Finally, Mom suggested I get a dog. She always says, ‘We got Zephy instead of anti-depressants.’”

“That’s a lot of loss. Your mom made a sensible choice, though. I got spirituality. It saved my life. My folks bribed me and said if I stayed at home and lived as a girl through high school, they’d pay for the University of Oregon.” He looked down and played with his fingers. “After I left for college, I couldn’t stand it anymore. I started on hormones and came out as a man. When I returned to Alfalfa after my sophomore year and walked in the house, my mother didn’t recognize me. She looked frightened, seeing a strange guy. I said, ‘Mom, it’s Teal.’ She literally shoved me down the hall and onto the porch yelling, ‘You sicko queer, get out!’ and slammed the door in my face. I’ll never forget the expressions on the younger kids who were home at the time—shock and fear, mostly.

“I came back to Eugene. They stopped paying my tuition; what a scramble to finish college. In addition to processing all the grief, I ran up a fortune in loans.”

“Oh, Teal.” *What an awful predicament.* She looked at him with deeper understanding.

He stood up. “Enough about me. Can we look for the keyboard?”

They walked down the stairs, and Rowan opened a closet in the rec room. Not there. She went to a wall of cabinets and opened one. “On the top shelf. Can you reach? It looks like the headphones are sitting on top of it.”

“I’m not much taller than you, but I’ll try.” He managed to grasp the keyboard with both hands and gingerly lifted it down. “Fantastic. I’m thrilled to have this to use. And with the headset, you guys don’t have to listen.”

“But I want to. What kind of music do you like?”

“Classical. A little blues and country. New Age. It was my pastime in college. I haven’t played in the two years since I graduated—no keyboard. I’ll be real rusty.”

“As soon as you tune yourself up, I want to hear. I hope you’ll let me?”

He seemed undecided for a moment, and fingered his goatee. Then his face broke into a smile, and he said, "Of course. I'm a tease. Watch out—there's a lot to get to know."

Chapter Thirteen

Two days later, Carolina smoothed the bed covers, then tossed a pillow across the room. "Would you read to me, Teal?" she asked. "I'm bored, even tired of watching the peace eagles wheel over the valley."

"No wonder you're bored. Sure. But..." he hesitated. "There's something I need to tell you about first. Moss made me promise."

"What? I'm all ears."

He stood and paced the room.

She saw he was chewing the inside of his cheek. "Please, sit down." *What was this about? How bad could it be? I've gotten attached to him already—he's not leaving, is he?*

He sat on the edge of the chair near her bed. "You know how awful it got with my family—how they wouldn't talk to me? Any of them. And, I was forced to continue living as a girl through the rest of high school. We lived in the deep country, and my only companion was Sam, my dog."

"Yes, you mentioned it during the interview. I can't imagine treating a child of mine harshly, no matter what happened. I'm sorry."

"I started cutting." He rolled up his sleeves to expose his arms. "Moss saw my scars the first day when I was sticking fruit in the hanging baskets."

She gasped, and pressed her hands down on the duvet. "Teal, good grief." She stared at his arms. "How scary. But you must have stopped; these are old—thin white lines, hardly even raised anymore."

"Moss had quite a talk with me in the yurt. At first, I was afraid he'd fire me. I cut for about a year when I was fifteen. I dropped acid one day and saw through it all. Somehow, the actual pain when I cut mirrored my internal mess. I turned to writing, instead. It wasn't for public consumption, but it, along with spirituality, sure saved my life. I left for college at seventeen and got out of there. I got clear during therapy."

He looked up and held Carolina's gaze. "Moss made me talk to Rowan about this, to impress upon her how cutting doesn't solve anything. You don't need to worry about your girl. She's seems well-balanced and positive."

"She is. I'm not worried about her picking up a razor blade. And while I'm at it, she likes you. Be careful, Teal."

"Ma'am, I'm into men, not girls."

"I made an assumption; I'm sorry."

"No worries. Rowan's way beyond psychedelics, if you're concerned about that," Teal went on. "She already knows what most people learn from them."

"I'm not sure that eases my motherly concern. But maybe your writing from those years could help another teen."

"I suppose there probably is a memoir in me. My story could help someone. But I'm not ready. The whole tale ain't writ yet, if you know what I mean. I'm keeping a journal, and I'll have it to reflect back on, if and when I'm ready."

A phone jingled next to Carolina. "Oh, that's Moss's cell." Holding up a finger, she answered. "Hello? Moss is writing; may I take a message? Oh! Sarah, hi. Wait a moment, please." She put her hand over the phone. "Would you go get him? It's his agent."

Teal hurried out the door, and Carolina saw him signal through the yurt window. They both trotted across the yard. Moss smiled and ran a hand up Carolina's arm before taking the receiver from her.

"Hi, Sarah." He listened for a moment, his eyes growing bigger. "Oh, *fantastic*. Wait until I tell my family. Sure, we'll talk then." He clapped his hand over his mouth after hanging up the phone. "Big news. HarperCollins sent *Daymares* to be considered for the American Literary Society awards." He shook his head as though trying to clear it.

With a wide smile, Teal arm-pumped.

"I never believed in the book," Moss said. "It took years to write, a painful struggle every day."

"This is wonderful recognition. I'm so happy for you." Carolina tugged him in for a kiss. "I knew your book was great."

"Do you have a copy around here?" Teal asked. "I'm anxious to read it."

"I'll get you one—hang on," Moss said. He grabbed one from the yurt, came back, and handed it to Teal.

"How much is it?" Teal asked.

"Perk of working for the family. You get a copy," Moss replied.

"Thanks." Teal had already turned the hardbound book over and was reading the synopsis on the back. "Would you sign it for me?"

Moss took it from him and went to look for a pen.

"Before you start it," Carolina said. "You offered to read to me, and I said yes. So on to Jodi Picoult." She tossed Teal the novel.

Chapter Fourteen

May 7, 2010

Rowan awakened to a soft knock on her door, then voices singing "Happy Birthday." Oh my Gawd, I'm sixteen! She tucked the covers around her neck. "Come in," she called, "I'm decent."

Zephyr lay by her, head up, alert.

The door opened and Moss and Teal walked in, carrying a breakfast tray. "It's a little early," Moss said, "but it's a school day and we wanted to celebrate before you had to leave."

Her eyes lit up when she saw the beautifully decorated gingerbread cupcakes. She could smell them. "My favorite."

"And your mocha's coming next," Teal said.

"Awww, thanks. Let's go out to the living room so we can be with Mom, too."

Obediently, the men nodded and moved toward the door. Rowan threw on a robe and followed them, Zephyr at her heels.

"I'd love a hug," her mother said. "I'm having trouble wrapping my mind around your being sixteen, especially while I'm pregnant with twins. By the way, we rented *Hatchi: A Dog's Tale* to watch tonight."

"Cool. I haven't seen it yet. This is perfect—the small family party I wanted."

"I'm thirty-one weeks," Carolina announced at the breakfast table a week later. "In three weeks, we have to head to San Francisco, earlier if the birth seems imminent. It's time for each of us to pack a bag. You too, Teal." She smiled at him. "You're great—and permanently hired."

Rowan, Moss, and Teal all grinned widely.

"Rowan and I will gather supplies for the dogs," Moss said. "Bessie the Lear is here now, available the moment we need it. I'll put William on notice."

"If our bags are packed, we could leave for the airport within half an hour," Carolina said.

"Thanks for the permanent position. I love it with you guys. But—" Teal hesitated, and frowned. "Uh, I'd rather not pack yet. I won't have anything left to wear. I have some stuff back at the garage. It's…" he sighed. "Tacky."

"Moss can take you clothes shopping. Consider it your uniform," Carolina said.

"Let's do it." Moss turned to Teal. "We can go this afternoon and get it out of the way."

Teal shuffled his toe against the floor. "That's generous, but I'd be wearing the clothes for more than just work. I could pay you back $10 out of each week's check."

"Sure," Moss said.

Carolina shot him a heavy frown. He held a finger up low where Teal couldn't see it. It was their signal to talk later.

Moss raised his eyebrows. "Lina, are you having signs? It's too early."

"No, I would have told you. I'm planning ahead. We should be on call, ready to go, that's all."

"Agreed," Moss said. "I need to stay very close to home."

"Me, too," Rowan added.

"Carry our cell phones at all times," Teal said, turning to Carolina. "Especially you."

She nodded. "Sue has a key to the house; we can lock up and leave in a hurry. I can always phone her from the airport."

Moss paced the room, thinking. "If we forget anything important, William could bring Teal back to collect stuff for us."

"What *are* we forgetting?" Carolina asked. "What about Bender's Ridge?"

"Gladys stopped by and checked the place out. She said Dakota's doing a fine job. I don't think we have to worry. The chickens are thriving, and he seems to be on top of the fox stuff. We haven't lost a bird since he's been there."

ꝏ

"Where would you go to look for clothes?" Moss asked Teal when they pulled into Valley River Center.

"Penney's," he replied.

"Great, we'll start there. I noticed the laundry last week, and you could use some socks and briefs in addition to jeans and shirts. And a pair of slacks—to go out to eat with us when jeans aren't appropriate. Look, I said you could pay $10 a week—and I appreciate your offer—but frankly, it makes me uncomfortable. You're living on a shoestring. Let's get you set up, and then you can be on your own. It truly is your uniform. Okay?" Moss looked Teal up and down. His athletic shoes were frayed, and the sole looked loose. "Shoes, too."

Teal fiddled with his lip.

"I'm not trying to make you feel bad, but be realistic. You need the $10 a week more than I do."

Frowning, the young man nodded slowly. "Yup. Thank you."

"Okay, then."

Six-hundred-seventy-two dollars later, Moss and Teal returned to the car, shopping bags in hand.

When they got home, Teal took his bags to his room and Moss went to check in with Carolina. "We talked, and I told him not to pay us back. I think he's okay with it. I felt it was better to handle in private to allow him his pride."

"Right. Smart. Is he well supplied?"

"Almost seven hundred dollars' worth. Socks, T-shirts, underwear, four pairs of jeans, dress slacks when we go out to dinner, and a few shirts. A sport coat. A couple of sweater vests. Two pairs of shoes. He has some boots. Oh, and a winter coat, too. He's in good shape. I jotted down his sizes—figured you'd want to put them in your note program. When it's time to buy gifts, we'd have the information."

"Good on you. Great thinking."

Chapter Fifteen

Three weeks later, Carolina delivered Rowan to their neighbors. "You'll be all right at Sue's?" she asked, hugging Rowan goodbye. "It feels weird to be taking Zeph with us to San Francisco and leaving you behind."

"I'll be fine, and Zephy will be, too. She needs to go with you—you know she keeps nose and ears out for the babes. It's only eight days until the end of school. But you have to promise—call me if you have *any* signs of labor. I want to be part of it for sure."

"Of course! William will be on standby to come get you earlier if we need to. I have to admit, the jet's been such a blessing, even though it still makes me feel guilty."

"Get over it, Mom. It's one of the perks of being part of Mossy's family. Keep the gratefulness and dump the negativity."

Carolina sighed. *I mustn't let on about the terrible row I had with her dad when we were in San Francisco.* "You're right. Please don't mention my guilt to you know who."

"I won't see Mossy for eight days, and by then I'll have forgotten about it." She hugged her mom again. "Be safe, and take great care of Zephy, please. Teal will help with her. I packed everything she needs." She thought for a moment. "You know, except for when Zeph was lost after the accident, this is the longest we've been apart."

"You're being brave." Carolina gave her a sideways hug, made a clucking noise for Zephyr, and they headed to the van.

"This is what Zephy wants," Rowan called after her. "That's why I'm okay with it."

Moss stashed the last suitcase and helped ease Carolina into the van's front seat. Teal took the far back with the dogs in the center. Familiar with the routine, Jazz crashed in her bed, but Zephyr sat upright staring out the window at Rowan. Teal reached to stroke her. After one last, long look, she went to him and buried her head in his lap.

"It's okay, sweet girl. We'll see her soon, and then school will be done so she'll have more time with you." He knuckled her ear. She leaned against his hand and groaned.

Carolina reclined her seat, and Jazz moved to lie under the back of it, long nose sticking out.

"All tails in?" Moss asked.

"Wait," Teal said, and grabbed Zephyr's. "Okay, now you can close it." He turned to the dog. "Zeph, settle."

She peered at him reproachfully before curling up on the floor.

Once in the air-car, Zephyr gently nudges her pack mate, then collapses in her own bed. Jazz watches, then lies close by in hers. Zeph penses a picture of calm Jazz to Rowan and gets a return message of delight. They both remember Jazz's howling when flying the first time. She can feel her girl's longing to be with them. *Sooners*, she penses back. *Zeph needs to be with Pack Mama.*

Moss turned to Teal who was gawking at the interior of the plane, testing the tray table, checking how his seat adjusted. "You've flown before?"

"Nope. This is my first time."

"Well, hang on," Moss said. "Bessie takes off differently than commercial airlines. I'm sure you've seen large jets take off in movies or on TV. She streaks up, steep and fast. I always think of riding the back of fireworks during lift off."

"Thanks for warning me."

"William has logged thousands of hours flying these little guys. You can trust him."

"The dogs seem unconcerned, which gives me a bit of confidence."

Taxiing down the runway, Moss noticed Teal clutching the armrests. "Don't break your fingers there, son."

Teal looked down at his hands and gave a nervous laugh. "Right." He worked his fingers open and closed. Then, eyes brimming, he stared at Moss. "You called me 'son.' My own mother and father don't."

"Didn't plan it; it fell out of my mouth. I guess, intuitively, that's what this feels like—I'm twenty years older, so you could be. Do you mind?"

"No, sir. It … it feels good. Like I finally belong somewhere."

"Well, then." He smiled across the aisle. "You do. And please don't call me 'sir.'"

When the plane lifted off, Moss glanced at him again. His face had gone white, and his knuckles blanched, too. What if he hadn't prepared Teal at all, hadn't listened to his own quiet hunch? The boy was raised in a back-country rural environment, not a major metropolis. And with six kids in the family, Moss figured they didn't go much of anywhere. Too expensive for a farmer's family. "This part will be over soon."

Once the Lear leveled off, Teal seemed to relax and Moss saw him peering out the window.

Carolina took Moss's hand and squeezed it. "You're so good with him," she whispered.

"He's a great fit with our family. I hope he stays a long time," he said, in a low tone.

Theo met them again, and ferried the family to their new home for the next few months. Moss noticed Teal's gaze caught by the scenes of San Francisco as they made their way through neighborhoods and up steep hills. He hoped the young man wouldn't fall for an SF guy. *Geez, how unkind of me. He needs more love in his life, not less. But still, we need him too much right now.*

As soon as they were let out, Zephyr and Jazz raced to find Bender in the main house.

When Moss showed Teal his room, his eyes widened. A large space with a cherry writing desk in front of the window, the room looked out on a cityscape vista.

"You should have plenty of time to write before the babies come," Moss said.

Teal nodded gratefully. "Thanks. But I want to do more cooking, too. I don't want to lose the chops I've gained assisting you. I like the process, and the results, a lot."

"Great. Carolina enjoyed the last meal you made, the lamb stew with spinach? We all did. Tonight, Theo and Maggie are cooking. We're off the hook, but tomorrow, let's prepare dinner together."

"Sure. I have a couple of questions—different topic. Are you younger or older than Theo?"

"Younger. I'm the baby of the family."

"And Maggie's mom's story?"

"She died of breast cancer eight years ago."

"Too young to lose a mother. I'm curious her dad hasn't married again."

"Phoebe and Theo were a remarkable pair. Different—she was a ballet dancer, and he's a physician—but they complemented each other. Quite the love match. I don't think he's found anyone as special."

The three dogs bounded up the guesthouse stairs and into Teal's room. With four hands and three dogs, everyone got a pat.

"Your family seems to do love well," Teal said.

"We've been lucky. Or maybe cautious. I didn't marry until I was thirty-eight. Also, my parents are very happy. We have a great role model."

"What do you think a good relationship takes?"

"Hmm. Gotta think about it for a moment." He gazed out the window into the distance before looking back to Teal. "Kindness, and trusting the other is always doing their best." Moss smiled. "Ma taught me, and I think she's right."

"I'll remember. Will you call me when dinner's ready? I'm going to write for a little while. This beautiful desk beckons." Teal reached for his computer bag.

Moss nodded. The dogs followed him down the stairs.

A week later, Carolina and Moss went in for their first appointment with Dr. Sierra Jacobsen, whom Dr. Bhat chose for them. "She was a midwife before she became an obstetrician," Dr. Bhat had said, "although I don't tell most patients. Theo told me your daughter was born at home. I think Sierra'll be a great fit for your family. She's an excellent physician, but has fine people skills, too. I'd like to say all doctors do but, sadly, that's not the case."

They sat and sat in Dr. Jacobsen's waiting room. Moss kept glancing at his watch. "It's been an hour."

She swept into the room. "I apologize. I had emergency surgery this morning, and it was more complicated than expected. Come on into the examining room. Sierra Jacobson," she said. "Please call me Sierra. It always seems to me—barring cultural differences and considering how intimate birth is—we should be on a first-name basis."

They followed her. She did an ultrasound before the physical exam. Stripping off her gloves, she said, "You're looking great. How do you feel?"

"Enormous," Carolina said, huffing as she hauled herself off the table. "Ready to have these babies."

"I get it. Go ahead and get dressed, and meet me in my office." She pointed to a different door.

After they were settled across the desk, she said, "I've gone over your records carefully. You're thirty-five weeks now, and the babies are big enough. I'm no longer concerned about when they're born. In fact, we don't want your little girl to get much bigger because it would make labor harder on her. So—you are now off bed rest, Carolina, and you and Moss may have sex again. In fact, I encourage it. Lots of gentle intercourse. The prostaglandins in his semen will help soften and ready the cervix, and orgasms help, too."

Carolina's eyes widened. "Wow, I certainly didn't expect to be given *this* prescription. I thought there wouldn't be any sex until a few weeks after birth." She looked at Moss. His eyes had gone smoky and Carolina wrapped her fingers in his.

"Are we done here?" he asked.

"One more thing. Please let me know as soon as you go into labor or your water breaks. Dr. Bhat wants to check out Andrea the moment she's born. If she knows you're in labor, she'll stay close to her cell so I can text. Do you have any questions for me?"

"Yes," Carolina said. "We want our nanny, Teal, to be present at the birth, for strong bonding. He's been at three of his siblings' births, including twins. Our daughter, Rowan will be there, too."

"Teal's not a family member, correct?"

"Not literally, no."

"When you come to the hospital, introduce him as your son. Then, the rest of the staff will welcome him. I'd allow him anyway, but there's institutional protocol, as you can imagine. How old is Rowan?"

"Sixteen."

"Oh great, not too young." She smiled. "Now, off you go. Have fun."

"It's getting closer," Moss said to Teal over lunch. "The obstetrician, Sierra Jacobson, said they can come any time. But, to get you into the birth, we'll need to introduce you as our son so we don't run into any bureaucratic road blocks."

"Whoa. I might have said the wrong thing if you hadn't mentioned it. Row's coming when?" Teal asked.

"Two more days," Moss said. "I'll feel better when she's here."

Teal rubbed his chin. "Have her come first thing Saturday. Early. It's only thirty-six hours."

"I think you're right," Carolina said. "I'll let William know."

"May I have some time off this afternoon? I want to check out San Francisco."

"Sure. Take the Prius," Moss said. "The fob's in the basket by the back door. Be prepared for the very steep hills."

"You won't need it?"

"We're staying here," he said.

"Good. You won't have peace much longer. I'll be back by dinner," Teal said.

After he left, Moss and Carolina moved into the living room and sat on the couch.

Silence. Then they both starting talking at the same time.

Laughter and more silence.

"Being told to have sex is weird," Carolina said. "All the spontaneity is gone. I feel shy and self-conscious. You don't mind enormous me?"

He play-hit her arm. "You are gorgeous and sexy." Their gazes locked. "First of all, no pressure. If our energy doesn't rise, no biggie."

"Oh my God, do you actually question it? With the two of us? It *will* rise—or has." She glanced at his crotch and smiled.

Moss stood and reached out to help her up. "Is it strange being able to walk around freely again? You were in bed for almost two months."

"Yeah, and I love it. The babies are awfully heavy, though." She eased her hands under her belly. "The support belt helps some."

He cupped his palms over her hands to add his support, leaned in to brush her lips with his, then followed with a fuller kiss. "Oh my Lord, you taste good," he said. He turned and slowly kissed her ear.

She moaned and leaned into him. "You're yummy. More, oh more, please. I can't wait for your nimble fingers."

"Ah. Want to head to the bedroom?"

She nodded. "Too bad we can't go to our yurt and try out the Murphy bed. It'd feel more private."

He heard the Prius start. "We have privacy," he said. "Teal's off on an adventure."

"At least his room is on a different floor," she said, twining her fingers with his and walking toward the bedroom. "And not above ours, either."

"I'd like to undress you," he whispered in her ear.

"Yes, please."

He took his time. "Wow," he said, staring at his fully pregnant, naked wife. "You are gorgeous, and ripe." He cupped her breasts which felt twice as heavy as eight months ago.

"Thanks, but I'm over-ready to have these babies and work on getting my karate body back."

"Come," he said. "Lie down with me."

She eased down on the bed. "Did you bring your fabulous lubricant?"

"You bet." He grinned. "The first item I threw in my suitcase." He shucked his clothes and prosthesis, and grabbed the lube.

She giggled. "And we weren't even *having* sex when you packed it. I'd say you had hope incarnate."

"See what happened? It worked." He waggled the bottle in front of her.

"Yes." She turned on her side and he snuggled around her. Then his fingers found her nipples. "Tell me what you want in luscious detail. I'm yours."

Chapter Sixteen

The dogs asleep nearby, Carolina and Moss snuggled in bed. This was the third time they'd made love in the twenty-four hours since they were given the "prescription."

"What a relief to be able to connect with you this way again," Moss said. "We've always been good together."

She smiled. "Lucky us. We're sure yummy."

Moss stroked her cheek. "I like the name Ashton Graham Westbury, and want to keep it, but I've been thinking we could call him Graham. Ash is such a sibilant sound, and two Ashs in one room—when my folks come to visit—would be confusing."

"Graham." Carolina mouthed the word a couple of times. "Ooooh, yes. But do you think Pa will be disappointed?"

Moss shook his head. "I think he'd agree it's the best choice. Of course, the little four-year-old Graham will have a harder time learning to spell his name, but he'll get there."

Carolina laughed. "Try having *my* name. I remember my pride at having a first name with *eight* letters—all the fingers on one hand and three more on the other. The only way I learned was Mom taught me to sound it out first." She shifted toward the edge of the bed. "I have to pee. I've been having tons of Braxton-Hicks contractions this afternoon." She planted her feet on the ground, feeling to make certain they were both flat since she could no longer see them. Moss put his steadying hands on her hips. She'd taken two steps toward the lavatory when a rush of warm water cascaded down her legs. "My water just broke!" She stared at the puddle and grabbed a towel. "I'm in *labor*. Not Braxton-Hicks. Call Sierra, please."

"Shit—is this my fault? Did I cause this making love?"

Carolina looked at him. His face was contorted with guilt and worry. "Not your fault, sweetheart; you did nothing wrong and everything right. You were so, so gentle. It's time. Time for our babies to be born."

"Right." Moss took the towel from her and mopped the floor.

Carolina made her way into the bathroom and didn't see Moss leave. "Rowan," she called. "We've got to get Rowan here."

"Be there in a sec," he said. "Went for my cell." He came back a couple of minutes later. "I reached Sierra's service. They'll call her, and Dr. Bhat. Rowan's already on her way, remember? She'll be here..." he squinted at his watch. "Darn, I think I need reading glasses. She'll be here in half an hour. I'll let William know to put her in a taxi, Uber, whatever, for UCSF. We're going now, right?"

Carolina had a death grip on her knees as a full contraction took her over. She closed her eyes, concentrated, breathing in a measured way. When it eased, she glanced up at Moss. "Lordy. I forgot what these are like. Rowan's birth was so long ago. Intense. I've been repacking what I need to take. It's not in the suitcase yet; sorry, you have to finish." She reached out a hand for him. "Sweetie—our family's about to get *two* children bigger. I can't even imagine what this will be like. Call Teal, would you? We'll all go together. Let Maggie know she's in charge of Zeph and Jazz."

Moss was on his feet, setting the roller case on the bed and putting her things inside. "You can relax now. We've got this. Anything else you can think of?" But Carolina reached out her hand and grabbed his hard.

"Breathe," he said. "Concentrate on your focal point. You're doing great."

Once the contraction eased, he gave her a hug, and went to find Teal. There was no answer to his knock, so he tried again. Nothing. He opened the door a few inches and called out, "Teal! Babies coming."

"Hold on, tangled in my headset. What did you say?"

"Carolina's in labor. You need to come with us to the hospital now."

Teal's eyes got big. "I thought it'd be another week or so. I'll drive. I can drop you in front and handle the parking."

"Please. Bring what you need for eighteen hours or so."

"I have a backpack ready to go."

"Good," Moss said. "And please call Maggie and let her know she's in charge of the beasties. Carolina's almost ready. Rowan's arriving at the airport right about now. She'll go directly to the hospital. Thank God you suggested she come earlier." Moss waved and walked back down the stairs. His wife was in the throes of another contraction. He sat beside her, took her hand, and breathed with her.

When it eased, she said, "I want to go to the car now, before these get much stronger."

"Sure. This ready?" He gestured toward her roller bag. She nodded. He reached for the pack and case as Teal showed up.

The young man grabbed the bags. "I've got 'em. I reached Maggie—she's on the dogs, and called her dad. Theo'll meet you at the hospital's front door to grease your way through the bureaucracy. His words, she said." He strode toward the car.

Zephyr and Jazz milled around their feet. Moss spoke to Zeph. "Go find Bender and Maggie. Take Jazz with you. Good dog." Zephyr knew "go find" and Jazz and Bender's names. Sure enough, Zephyr nudged Jazz and they took off through the dog door and across the yard.

"Let's get you to the hospital, love," Moss said. "Take my arm."

They pulled into the UCSF Medical Center driveway and Moss went to get a wheelchair. Once Carolina maneuvered herself into it, Teal left for the parking lot. Moss had explained to him on the way that it was underground, with unusually steep and narrow turns. "I've scraped my car," he said. "Gotten lost down there, too, and wondered if I'd ever find my way out. Truly catacombs."

Theo waved as he exited the front door to greet them. "The big day. How are you doing?"

Carolina smiled up at him. "Great, thanks. Nervous."

"To be expected," Theo said. "You must remember being anxious right before Rowan was born?"

"Yeah, concern about how much it would hurt. This feels different. I'm older, I know more—which may not be helpful—and Andrea has a congenital heart defect. The stakes are much, much higher."

"You're right, of course." he said. "We're going directly to obstetrics. I already registered you."

"Another one's starting." She gripped the wheelchair's sidearms.

They got off the elevator on the fifteenth floor and made their way to the nurse's station. Teal, out of breath, caught up with them.

"Are you Carolina Westbury?" the nurse asked.

Carolina had not heard her new last name spoken out loud until now. "Sure am." She glanced covertly at Moss. A wide smile had spread across his face.

"Dr. Westbury notified us you were on the way." She pointed down the hall. "Sierra Jacobsen is your obstetrician, correct?"

Carolina nodded.

Rowan hurried up, her eyes bright with excitement. "Hi everybody. I wanted to make the airplane speed up, but William said, 'No way. I'm sticking with my flight plan.'" She bent down to hug her mom, and Carolina was touched by how gentle she was. "How are you, Mama? And how's my Zephy?"

"Both of us, very fine," Carolina said. "Maggie's in charge of the girls while we're here."

"Yes, Zephy showed me."

Rowan hugged Moss and Teal. "I've missed you all."

"I assume these are all immediate family members?" the nurse asked.

"Right," Moss responded. "Our kids. They'll be at the birth."

Carolina was impressed by how easily the white lie slid out of his mouth. He'd been practicing—envisioning the scene—like in a novel. It was against his nature to be anything but directly honest.

"So long as Dr. Jacobsen is all right with a crowd," the nurse replied.

"She is," Carolina said. "Everyone needs to bond with the twins from the get go. Otherwise, how will we survive?"

The nurse laughed out loud. "Twins *are* a handful. There's a gown on the bed waiting for you."

"I won't be using it. I brought my own," Carolina said. "A good-luck garment."

"Go ahead and get it on, and one of us'll come in and take your vitals, or Dr. J can do it when she arrives. I'm pretty sure she'll put you on a monitor, too. She'll be here soon."

Carolina sighed. "Here we go. It sure isn't the home birth I wanted so badly. Rowan was lucky."

Moss steered the wheelchair into the room and helped her ease onto the bed. "This was a decision based on Andrea's needs," he said. "We didn't have a choice."

"Right. That's how it's going to be from now on," Carolina snapped. "And here comes another damn contraction."

Moss glanced at Teal with a "holy crap, we're in for it" look. He grabbed her outstretched hand and breathed with her.

"Hey, love," he said after the contraction ended, "I know you're grumpy and scared, but let's make the best of this. These are our beautiful babes you're swearing about."

She stared at him. "Bottom line. I'm terrified," she whispered. Her eyes flooded with tears which she tried to dash away, but she surrendered and cried. Moss crawled on the bed from the other side, snugged himself around her back, and held her close.

Once her sobs subsided, he said, "We're in competent hands. Probably the best in the country."

"Are you really sure we'll be able to cope with twins? How are we going to pull it off?"

"One breath at a time," Moss said. It was a direct quote from his mindfulness teacher.

"I aim to be a big help," Teal said. "I adore babies."

"I'm in school and everything, but I can give a hand, too," Rowan said, "when I'm not being a raging teenager." She giggled. "And Zephy will help in her own way. She's a tremendous comfort."

"She is," Moss said. "Jazz, too. Kids, Lina needs to get changed, so could you step out? It may be her only moment of privacy in the next twenty-four hours."

"The vending machines," Rowan said to Teal. "Let's go find them now. We'll be needing them."

Sierra showed up a few minutes later. "Hey, you'll meet your beautiful babies soon. Moss, have you timed a contraction?"

He shook his head. "Not yet." He glanced at his watch. 7:10 p.m.

"This one's already started—time the next one," Carolina said, grimacing. "Here comes the hard part." She gave a long groan as the peak hit.

As soon as it subsided, Sierra moved in. "Let me check you right now." A minute later, she said, "Over four centimeters—the beginning of active labor."

"About what I expected," Carolina said. "They're getting a lot stronger."

"I want to listen to the babies' hearts, and yours too, while I'm at it. Are you still sure you don't want pain meds?"

"Positive. I birthed eight-pound Rowan without, and these babies are much smaller. With my sweetie encouraging me, I'll be fine. Besides, it's better for Andrea."

"You're right. Okay, quiet for a minute." Sierra listened to all three hearts. "Everybody sounds good," she said, taking her stethoscope off.

When the pain came, Moss glanced at his watch. "Five minutes since the last one," he said, kneeling by Carolina. He checked the time when it abated. "Fifty seconds long."

"Or an eternity, depending on how you look at it." Carolina ran her fingers through her hair, blew out a breath, and forced a smile.

"Now, a quick ultrasound. I want to see the position of the babies. We'll get you on the monitors once you're around seven centimeters." She lowered her voice. "The midwife in me wants you walking during early active labor. No point having you tied down with wires at this point."

"Monitors plural?" Moss asked.

"Two babies, tracking two heartbeats," Sierra said, moving the wand around. "And they're both head down. Great news."

"I had no idea birthing was this long and painful," Rowan whispered to Teal as they walked to the vending machines. "Why do people *have* kids if it's this hard?"

"We don't have to whisper out here." He chuckled. "Oh yeah, it's a mountain to climb. I watched my mom have twins and then, two years later, she had my youngest sister. She didn't handle it nearly as well as Carolina. Your mom is strong and centered. She doesn't whine or scream. She growls." Teal paused. "But babies? There's nothing like them. Wait until you smell the back of their necks. And the love ... they capture and reel us in."

"I'm not sure I want any. It seems like a huge distraction—like life has to completely reorient down the kidlet track and forget everything else. For *years*. Decades, even."

"Pretty much," he said. "I'm going to have to adopt if I want kids, or find a surrogate, I guess. Of course the first huge task is finding someone to love who'll love me back."

"It'll happen for you," Rowan said. "I know it. You're too—" she paused, looking for the right word. "You're too good not to have someone snap you up."

"Thank you," he said. "I haven't heard nice things much in my life, not since I came out. Your family is wonderful to me, but I'm still shell-shocked from being shut out by my people, not to mention bullying, being tripped in the hallways, and dissed in every other way imaginable at school. I suspect it's a lifelong wound. Like war. I think about your dad often. The compliment means a lot."

Munching on their snacks, they made their way back to the room. "Here's the deal," Teal said, stopping before he opened the door. "Two things can happen when someone experiences trauma. One, they take their rage and hurt out on others—usually the people closest to them, pushing them away—or two, they become inclusive, which draws people closer. As far as I can figure, the first leads people to addiction and possibly suicide, the second toward the possibility of a fulfilling life. Your dad's a great role model; he keeps me on the second track." He put his hand on the door handle.

"I'm staying out here for a couple of minutes. I need to..." she looked at the ground. They hadn't talked about this yet. "Zephy and I communicate. I'll tell you about it sometime. Even Mama can't deny it, although she sure wants to."

Teal took a breath and said, "I look forward to it." He opened the door.

Rowan pensed Zephyr. *Are you having fun with Jazz and Bender?*

Zeph sent back a picture of the three of them racing around the garden after balls Maggie pitched, their tongues hanging out. *Litter babies?*

Soon. Probably before sunrise. She sent Zephyr a virtual pat and kiss, and felt a bump in reply.

Chapter Seventeen

By the time Carolina reached seven centimeters, the labor pains were lasting seventy-five seconds with less than two minutes between. She couldn't talk much, just stayed focused on her opening cervix. As each contraction peaked, she rumbled deep in her throat. Someone sat with her at all times, mostly Moss. Sometimes, when it was Rowan or Teal, she was only aware of her need for the comforting sound of breath as companion to her own, and a hand to grab. Moss had to take breaks to snack and pee, she understood, but wished he could be by her side every moment.

Carolina had no sense of time passing, only unstoppable, intense rushes with almost no rest before the next one seized her. She talked to the babies, but wasn't sure if the thoughts were only in her mind or if she'd spoken out loud.

Sierra's voice. "We're moving you to the room where you'll deliver."

Endless waves of contractions rising, falling, rising again. "Is it morning yet?" It was hard to find her voice; it croaked, and seemed to come from across the room.

"It's 2:10 a.m. I'll check you again." Sierra's calm tone. "Over nine centimeters. Great going. Let me know the moment you have the urge to push, and I'll check one more time to verify you're fully dilated. Pant until I give the signal."

"Ice chips?" Moss's deep voice.

She nodded, and savored the bright, cold moisture.

An hour later, she still didn't feel the need to push, so Sierra rechecked her. "Nine-and-a-half," she said. "You're almost there. I'd like you to stand and hold on to the bar at the end of the bed. Right now, gravity is your best friend. Let me unhook the monitors."

Lordy, this one's a slamming tsunami. Carolina gripped Moss's hand so hard he yipped. "Sorry," she whispered, after the pain abated. "Help me, would you? I don't trust myself to stand without support."

Carolina leaned on Moss until her palms found the bar. The contraction was so powerful she wondered if her body was going to rip apart. Four contractions later, the powerful urge to push asserted. "Sierra!" She panted fast.

The obstetrician materialized by her side. "Checking now." A moment later, "Ten centimeters. Here's an arm. Back to bed; everyone can watch in the mirrors. Time to push your first one out. Moss, do you want to catch your baby?"

"No." Carolina's voice filled the room. "Stay right here."

After forty-five minutes of pushing, Ashton Graham Westbury, pink and wailing, slipped into Sierra's arms. "Graham looks good," she said. "Let me do a quick Apgar assessment, and then you can hold him." She wrapped him in a towel and carried him to the table nearby.

Rowan noted the time for Grandma Shirley.

A minute later, Sierra swaddled him in a thin flannel blanket and brought him over, eyes questioning who to hand him to.

Carolina smiled. "Moss first. Rowan and Teal? Come take a look. You can hold him right after I do."

"You've probably got fifteen to twenty minutes before contractions start again, so Carolina, you'll have time with him," Sierra said. "He scored nine on the Apgar out of ten. A strong boy. He weighs four pounds nine ounces." Sierra set him in Moss's quivering, waiting arms.

He stared down at the infant. "I have to sit down. Wow."

"Use the rocker," Sierra said.

Never taking his eyes off his son, Moss slowly lowered himself into the chair. "I'm terrified of dropping him."

"It's natural," Sierra said. "You'll get comfortable quickly."

Rowan and Teal stood on either side of him. "Weird. I'm not an only child anymore," she said. "I always wanted a brother or sister."

Teal touched a finger to Graham's damp curls. "Now I'm officially your nanny. You're finally here."

Moss pulled back the edge of the blanket. "Beautiful Graham. Hello, fella, I'm your da." He breathed in the baby's scent, rocked him for a few minutes, gave him a kiss on his head, and then handed the precious package to Carolina.

"Hi, sweetheart," she whispered to the baby. "Look at you. You're a ringer for your da. And you're going to take after your older sister." She smiled at Rowan, and checked Graham's tiny, but perfectly formed hands. "His fingernails are so small. I'd forgotten."

"Look," Teal said. "He's an ancient, little man when he wrinkles his forehead. Like a ninety-year-old."

"Mama, he's yawning." Rowan almost crowed with delight.

"Mama—you've never called me that before." Carolina tilted her head and stared at Rowan.

"You told me the babies are going to call you and Mossy 'Mama' and 'Da.' I don't want to confuse them."

"Sweet," Carolina said. "Considerate, thank you." She beamed, and handed him up to Rowan, who received him with a sharp intake of breath.

"He's smaller than I expected. Mossy," she said, "I totally get why it's scarifying to hold him." She tried a rocking motion, and Graham's eyes flew open. She locked gazes with him. Lifting him higher, she sniffed his neck. "Oh, my," she whispered. "Teal, you were right."

"About what?" Carolina asked.

"How baby's necks smell, and how they…" Rowan paused to recall exactly what he had said. "Capture and reel us in. Those were your words, Teal, right?"

He nodded. "Exactly."

Rowan rocked her little brother in her arms for a couple of minutes.

"May I hold him now? I mean, I'm his nanny and all. I need to fall in love, too."

Rowan gave him a good-natured frown and handed Graham over. Teal rested the baby on his arms in front of him. After smelling the infant's neck, he pressed his elbows together with Graham's head in his cupped palms, his baby feet only reaching halfway to his elbows. "Hi, handsome," he said. "You and I are going to get to know each other very, very well." He teared up, and kissed Graham's forehead.

"What's wrong?" Moss asked.

"It's about what's right," Teal responded. "This is fabulous."

"Wait until you have two to hold," Carolina quipped. "Both screaming."

Teal laughed. "Bring it on. I've done it before with my twin brothers."

After a few minutes, Teal relinquished him back to Rowan.

"Whoa, it's starting again." Carolina blew out a breath.

"Graham's placenta is coming," Sierra said. "I'm going to knead your belly while you push."

Half an hour later, the contractions picked up in earnest. Sierra texted Dr. Bhat that Andrea would be delivered within thirty minutes. They took up their posts: Moss by Carolina's side, Sierra stationed between Carolina's legs. Fascinated, Teal stood to Sierra's right. Rowan held Graham nearby.

Carolina mumbled, "Almost done, almost done. Come on, baby girl, we can do this."

A few contractions later, Sierra stepped away to the supply table. As she moved, Carolina gave a ferocious karate-strength push. The baby squirted out. Towel in hand, Sierra spun around as Teal, eyes wide, launched forward and caught Andrea. She didn't wail, but stared up at him with big, innocent eyes.

"My God!" Moss cried.

"Good Lord, what a save." Rowan hung on to Graham, glanced at the clock, and mouthed the time of Andrea's birth. Grammie would never forgive her if she got it wrong.

"Oh my heavens," Sierra said. "Thank God—good catch, Teal. It's never happened to me before, the moment I've gone to grab a towel." She reached for Andrea.

"Teal caught Andrea?" Perplexed, Carolina frowned.

"Sierra, toss me your phone and I'll text Dr. Bhat," Teal said.

"Why isn't she crying?" Moss asked, voice tense.

"She appears to be breathing fine," Sierra said, handing her cell to Teal. "She came out calm. It happens. I'll do the Apgar now." A moment later, "Seven out of ten. Four pounds one ounce. Quite a bit smaller than Graham. Decent for a CHD baby."

"May I hold Andrea? She's not an acronym." Carolina huffed. "I need to touch my little girl before you doctors wrest her away from me."

"I'm sorry." Sierra brought Andrea over, nestled the baby in her mother's arms. "Of course she's not an acronym. I'll listen to her heart while you hold her." She warmed the stethoscope between her hands before resting it on the infant's chest. "Kind of a lub-swoosh sound," she said. "But strong."

Afterward, Carolina handed her up to Moss. "Meet your daughter, Da."

Moss cuddled and talked to the baby before walking her over to where Rowan held Graham. "Why, they look alike," he said. "Shall we switch, so you can hold her?"

Rowan took her turn, and passed her on to Teal for the second time. "Hey, baby," he said. "Aren't you sweet? We're going to be good friends." After a couple of minutes, he took her back to Carolina.

A short while later, there was a soft knock on the door. "Come in," Sierra sang out. "Andrea awaits you."

Dr. Bhat walked in smiling and greeted everyone. "All right, then. I want to take a listen and do an echo. Where's my little charge?"

"I'm holding her," Carolina said, reluctantly handing over Andrea.

Whispering in the infant's ear, the cardiologist carried her over to the table. Andrea squeaked when the doctor bared her chest. The monitoring took close to fifteen minutes. She placed the stethoscope in thirteen or fourteen places, each time holding up a finger to quiet the room. When she was done, she handed Andrea back to Carolina and nodded slowly. "I can clearly hear the VSD—oh sorry, ventricular septal defect—there's a 'lub' and a wet whooshing sound instead of a 'dub'—blood traveling through the hole between the ventricles. As we would expect. Moss, do you want a turn?"

He nodded, and walked over to take the stethoscope. Dr. Bhat moved it to different locations. On the cardiologist's suggestion, Moss listened to Graham's heart. "Sobering," he said, handing the stethoscope back to the doc. "Their hearts sound quite different." He looked to see if Carolina wanted to listen, but Sierra was finishing delivery of the second placenta.

The cardiologist asked Teal to hold Andrea still while she performed the echo. "As we expected," she said, after a couple of minutes. "*Truncus Arteriosis.* I'd like to have Andrea in the NICU—Neonatal Intensive Care Unit—tonight, so we can keep a close watch on her. Chances are she'll need diuretics. Because of heart failure, these babies tend to retain liquid."

"Heart failure?" Carolina blurted. "She's in heart failure now?"

"What heart failure means is, due to the malformations, her heart can't pump as much oxygenated blood as her body needs. That's why she'll require open-heart surgery before too long."

"Oh. Lord, my heart's pounding. Guess I'd better get used to nasty surprises." Carolina wrapped her arms tightly around her body. "Graham and Andrea have always been together. Could he be with her tonight? In the same crib? It would make me feel better."

"Graham needs to be with you so you can nurse him," Sierra said.

The labor-and-delivery nurse slipped in near Carolina. "I'm kneading your belly to get your uterus to contract."

Carolina grimaced and nodded.

"We'll supplement Andrea to make sure she gets enough nourishment. She may not have the endurance to get all her milk from breastfeeding," Dr. Bhat said. "They'll give her bottles in the NICU—when you're there, of course you can. It takes less energy to get milk from a bottle than the breast. We hope you'll pump—she needs your colostrum." She took Andrea to Moss and set her in his arms. "I'm afraid Graham can't stay in the NICU—hospital protocol."

"Not fair," Rowan griped.

"May we visit her?" Carolina swiped a hand across her eyes.

"Yes, of course. We want you there. Babies do better when their parents stay close. It's on the seventh floor. The only time you'll have to step out is during nurse shift changes, 7:00 to 7:30 morning and evening."

"So how are we going to do this?" Carolina asked Sierra. "I need to be everywhere at once."

"Usually with twins, if a baby needs special help, a parent stays with each baby, and then you can switch. But you have Teal and Rowan as well. Teal could take Graham if you both want to be with Andrea at the same time, like when the doctors are examining her. Do you want to try breastfeeding Graham?"

Carolina nodded. "I had an easy time with Rowan; I'm hopeful it will go as well now. Sweetheart," she said to her older daughter, "will you please bring him here?"

The baby latched on and sucked vigorously. Carolina grimaced. "I forgot how sensitive nipples are right at the start." He nursed for a few minutes.

"Let's see how Andrea does," the cardiologist said. Moss and Carolina cautiously traded babies. Graham's head lolled against his da's collar bone.

Andrea rooted for the nipple, but didn't grab right on. Sierra tickled her cheek next to her mouth and, when she opened her lips, Carolina offered her breast. Her tiny babe nursed for a minute before falling asleep.

Dr. Bhat nodded. "Already tuckered out. She's going to require supplemental bottles. I'm going to take her down to the NICU now."

Carolina clung to Andrea for a moment. "Here goes, baby. I'm sorry." She wiped her cheeks and handed her to Dr. Bhat. Suddenly chilled, she tucked the covers around herself. She felt—strange.

Sierra squinted at her and pulled up the covers from the bottom end. "You're bleeding more than I'd like. Massaging your belly hasn't done the trick. I'm going to check for tears."

Rowan and Teal stood wide-eyed near the head of the bed.

As the obstetrician examined her, Carolina said, "Tender down there."

"Of course you are. No lacerations, that's good. Do you need to pee badly?"

She shook her head.

"I'm going to do bimanual compression to get this bleeding under control. Sorry, it's uncomfortable," Sierra said.

Moss quickly passed Graham to Teal and took Carolina's hand. She squeezed hard and gave a loud growl. "Geez Louise! Lordy, that hurts!"

"I know, sorry again, but I'm trying to prevent more invasive solutions. The blood loss may be due to the fibroid."

When the flow continued, Sierra gave her an injection of Pitocin but the bleeding wouldn't stop. She injected methergine. No change.

Sierra took Moss aside. "I'm taking her to a fresh operating room. We may have to open her up."

Carolina pulled herself to sitting and went white. "Faint," she whispered, and dropped back, unconscious.

Sierra pushed a red button on the bed remote. "Emergency, stat!" Her firm words unleashed orderly chaos. Nurses exploded into the room. A technician arrived with a gurney.

"Oh my God," Rowan cried, "Mommo, I still need you."

Shaking, Moss bent to kiss Carolina's forehead. "Hang in there, love. We'll all be waiting."

The technician wheeled her out of the room.

Graham woke up, wailing. Teal jiggled him.

"Moss," Sierra called, heading for the door, "Does Carolina want more children?"

White-faced, he answered, "No. We talked about it."

"If we can't stop the bleeding, we may have to do a hysterectomy. I'll work very hard not to. There are papers for you to sign—go to the nurses' station first. I'll find you in the waiting room. No guarantees here; we'll do our best." And she was gone.

Chapter Eighteen

"What do I do?" Rowan asked, wrapping her arms around herself. *Geez. Mommo did this same thing. Self-comfort, I guess.*

"Stay close to your father," the cardiologist said, pitching her voice above Graham's howls. "He needs you. Teal, the nurse will get Graham breast milk—we have frozen colostrum. Once they have the bottle ready, bring him back here. We don't know what room Carolina will end up in yet."

Teal cuddled the screaming baby against his shoulder, bouncing him gently. "Poor guy. He picked up all the shock and fear in the room."

Thank God he's experienced with infants, Rowan thought.

"Go there," Dr. Bhat said to Moss, holding Andrea close and pointing to a nurses' station, "for the required forms. I want to get her down to the NICU right now."

Rowan's heart fell watching her baby sister—teensy in the doctor's hands—move farther and farther away from them.

The family trailed out to the nurses' desk.

Teal spoke up. "Dr. Bhat said you'd get me some colostrum for Graham." He pointed to the infant in his arms.

A nurse produced a clipboard. Hands shaking, Moss signed the papers without reading. "Where's the chapel? And where do I go after? I didn't register what she said."

"Surgery's on four. We don't have a chapel, but there's a meditation room on the first floor."

Sensing how terrified her dad was, Rowan stared, wide-eyed. He had no religious affiliation, and in the years they'd known each other, she'd never seen him anything other than calm. She'd depended on *his* strength. Her insides curled. *Now he needs mine. Can I do this? I'm a kid.* Inhaling, she straightened up. *Apparently not any longer.* Turning to Teal, she said, "Will you be okay with Graham? I need to take Da to the meditation room."

"We're fine," Teal said. "Graham'll settle down when he gets a bottle and rocking chair. Once he's asleep, I'll take him to the regular nursery, check on Andrea, and come find you. We can all wait for good news together."

Lost in his inner landscape, Moss got disoriented twice. Rowan took his hand. "This way. I see the meditation sign above the door."

He cleared his throat, trying to wrest sound from the thick lump blocking it. "Leave me here. Go be with Teal."

Row stopped just at the door and put her hands on her hips. "Why, exactly? So you can be strong for me and then go cry alone? You're not getting rid of me." She opened the door and waved him in. "We're both worried sick, Da. We need to be together. Teal'll be fine for a bit."

He slid into a chair and slumped there. Sobs wracked him. "I'm more than worried sick—I'm terrified. The sight of all the blood? I've seen people die losing that much. Reactivated my PTSD." He tried to contain the sound, but wails erupted. "I'm a mess. I miss Jazz so much—she always comforts me when I get upset. And I shouldn't have told you what I've seen."

She sat down and pulled him close.

"I can't do this—parenting twins, and you—without Lina. I depend on her. She's steady and wise. I love her very much."

"No one doubts it," she said. "You two are disgustingly hot together." She clapped a hand over her mouth. "I'm sorry, inappropriate timing."

Moss yelped. The line came to him: a *laugh bound inside tears?* He shook his head. Even in the middle of a crisis, his wordsmith brain wouldn't turn off. Crazy-making. "I guess we deserve it, although I'd edit out the word 'disgustingly.' Nothing disgusting about it. I hope you are as lucky."

"I can hear Grammie say, 'Keep thinking good thoughts. Positive energy helps.' So that's our job—we can't focus on what we saw."

He groaned. "How does one unsee what's been seen?"

"We can still think good thoughts."

He sighed, then took a deep breath. "Right. You're absolutely right. Okay, let's imagine her strong, healthy, and nursing both babies."

After Teal fed Graham, he took him to the nursery. He spoke briefly with the nurse, explaining the situation, and waited until Graham lay asleep on his back before heading downstairs to find Andrea. After he identified himself at the NICU desk, the nurse handed him a gown.

"I need to wash my hands before I pick her up," he said. "Where's the sink?"

She smiled and pointed. "You're way ahead of most family members. One less worry for us."

After he dried his hands thoroughly, the nurse led him over to her crib. "She won't take the bottle from any of us. If she doesn't start nursing in the next hour, we'll have to put in an intravenous line. Usually, in a newborn's scalp. I hate doing it to the tiny ones."

Andrea was fussing, gnawing on her fist. "I'll feed her," Teal said. "She'll eat for me." He smiled. "I'm a bit of a baby whisperer."

"Apparently I'm not today," the nurse said. "I'll bring the bottle right away."

"Colostrum, right? Not formula."

She nodded and went into a different room. Five minutes later, she returned with the bottle. Teal tested the temperature on his inner wrist. "Okay, little girl."

She stared up at him, wide-eyed and blinking, with the cloudy, unfocused look newborns have.

"I know it's not politically correct, but you're a very pretty baby. Lots of babies are kinda silly looking. Bald and pointy." He slid one hand under her head while the other supported her body, and carefully lifted her. She squeaked with surprise. He hummed "Home on the Range" until they were settled in the rocker nearby, nestled her in the crook of his arm, and tickled her cheek. She turned her head, opened her mouth, and he slid the nipple in. She immediately sucked.

The nurse had come back. "Well, look at you. You *are* a baby whisperer. I'm watching to see if she needs a nipple with a larger hole so she doesn't have to work as hard."

"How can you tell?"

"I'm timing right now. After a few minutes, we'll see how much she's ingested."

He nodded and rocked slowly, his eyes never leaving Andrea. She was struggling, and the level wasn't dropping. "Too hard for her, I think."

"I'll get a different nipple and switch it out. Okay," she said, when she came back. "Let me have the bottle, please."

When he slipped the nipple out of her mouth, Andrea frowned, puckered, and howled. "Oh, baby," he whispered and, putting her against his chest, rubbed her back. "Have a little faith in me. We'll get this right."

A few minutes later, she latched on to the bottle and he could tell she was getting milk. "What a relief," he said. "You need to gain weight. Little meals very often, I figure."

"Exactly right," the nurse said. "About every hour and a half. I'll leave you two. Hopefully, the next time she'll allow one of the nurses to feed her, otherwise you'll be exhausted." She pointed out the call button.

"She has a twin brother; we're going to be exhausted no matter what. For quite a while."

"A twin? Good Lord, you can't be running between floors. Let me make a call. Her brother needs to be down here with her until their mom can take over."

"Her cardiologist said Graham couldn't—"

"Never mind what she said. It's ridiculous. And don't you dare go repeating what I just said. I'm the charge nurse in this NICU. I'll make it work."

He sighed. "It would help a lot, whether it's me, her da, or her sister, Rowan."

"Are they baby whisperers, too?" She smiled at him.

"I guess we'll find out. If not, I'm in big trouble."

∞

Rowan hugged her dad. "I'd be happy to call the grandparents and bring them up to speed. It's late enough where they live—they'll be up."

"Oh, please, yes. I don't want to talk to any of them yet. Not until I can keep my cool."

Teal opened the meditation room door. Rowan turned at the change in air pressure. "Perfect timing," she said. "How are the babies? I need to make phone calls. Will you hang with Moss?"

"They both took a bottle and crashed out. The charge nurse in the NICU said she'd make arrangements so Graham can be with Andrea, and I won't be running between floors. Damn, you could die waiting for those elevators. What a relief."

Moss glanced up. "Once I pull myself together, Rowan and I can take turns, too. Right Row?"

"You bet," she said, taking out her phone. "Although Teal will need to teach us how to feed them. How to hold them. Basically, everything. I'm going to the sitting area—be back in a few."

"Grammie?" Rowan said, when her grandmother answered the phone.

"Have the babies come? Are they okay? Do you have the times?"

"Yes, they're here, ate, and are asleep. But there were complications. Mom hemorrhaged."

A gasp on the other end. "Oh my. Let me sit down and catch my breath. What happened?"

"They're trying to stop the bleeding, but they may have to do a hysterectomy." Rowan rubbed her eyes.

"Aww, hon. But she'll be all right? May I have the doctor's name? Carolina mentioned her, but I don't remember, and I'll want to call her later. What did the doc say to you?" Her voice sounded tight and sped up. "Be sure to have Moss call me."

"There was an awful lot of blood. The doctor said they'd do their best; I guess there's a team working on her."

"I'll get a ticket and come immediately."

"Not yet. Let us get through this part, okay? Teal's taken on his nanny role."

"Are you sure? How's Moss? He must be worried half to death."

"He is, but coping okay." Trying to redirect her grandmother, she said, "Do you have paper and pen for the birth times?"

"Wait a second."

Rowan heard shuffling and a soft expletive.

"Okay, I'm ready."

"Graham was born at 3:42 a.m." She could hear her gram's pencil scratch. "Andrea came out at 4:19 a.m. June 17th, exactly one month early."

More pencil noises. "Good work, my special girl. Now, tell me—how are you?"

"Scared. Really, really scared. This is like my worst nightmare. It brings back losing Daddo."

"Sweetheart, of course it does. I'm scared too—anyone close would be. But she's at one of the best medical centers in the country."

"Yeah, I keep telling myself that. Okay, I have to go. I need to call Ma and Pa Westbury."

"Phone me the minute you get news about your mom, you hear?"

"I will," Rowan promised.

"Those twins are lucky. You'll be a wonderful big sister. Bye for now."

The phone call with Ma started out the same way. Rowan suggested they stay home, too.

"How's Moss holding up?" Alice asked.

"Shaken, but strong. You know Mossy."

"And how are those babes?"

"They're beautiful—both have the Westbury curls. Graham outweighs his sister by half a pound—she has some catching up to do. She's in the intensive care nursery so they can monitor her closely and possibly put her on medication. Her heart goes lub-swoosh instead of lub-dub, but Dr. Bhat, the cardiologist, said it's typical of TA babies."

Rowan heard a deep sigh on the other end.

"I'm sorry about this. Lifelong health concerns—it's a weight to carry, and you won't want to communicate worry to her."

"Yeah—I talked to Mom about when I was blind four years ago. I wanted to know how she handled it. She said the same thing—most of all, she wanted to be strong for me, didn't want me to worry."

"You have a terrific mom. She and Moss will figure out how to juggle all this. And Teal seems like a blessing."

"He's skillful—picks up those tiny babies like it's the most natural thing. Mossy and I have an awful lot to learn. We have no baby experience at all."

"You'll be pleasantly surprised. In two weeks you'll be old hands."

"We'd better be. Mama—if she comes through this—" her voice caught. She cleared her throat. "She'll be out of commission for quite a while."

After hanging up, she yearned for Zephyr, so she settled in a chair and closed her eyes. Immediately, she felt her dog's sweet presence.

Are you hurt? Zephyr asked.

My heart's aching. Otherwise, I'm fine, but I miss you.

How can you miss Zephyr? Zeph's right here.

I want to feel your fur, smell you, cuddle on the bed.

You come?

Not yet. Pack Mama's real sick. Remember when your leg was sewn up? Pack Mama needs to be sewn up, too.

My girl's hurting.

Too much blood, Zeph. Scary.

Her dog fell silent. Taking in the message, Rowan figured. Then she felt a blast of love.

I love you too, sweet dog. You are my everything. Laters.

Chapter Nineteen

Half an hour later, Moss went back to the surgical floor and, after squinting at the clock, strode to the nurses' station. "I'm Moss Westbury. My wife, Carolina, is in surgery. I'd like an update, please; it's been almost three hours."

"There isn't one yet, Mr. Westbury," the heavyset, red-haired nurse said.

"One of you can use the intercom and talk to the surgeon while she's working."

The two nurses gave each other a glance. Moss took note. "You can do this. We need news," he said, keeping his tone friendly, respectful, but firm. He pinned them with his gaze. "My older kids are worried sick."

"I'll go." It was the dyed blonde. "Sit in the waiting room and I'll come find you."

"I'm fine here," he replied, leaning on the counter.

"Whatever toots your horn." She frowned and walked away.

"I'm sorry; she has a terrible headache," the redhead said. "How are your babies doing?"

"They've both eaten and are napping. A little bit of peace while we catch our breath. Our..." he paused. He'd almost said "our nanny" but went on, "older son fed them both."

"Well, aren't you lucky. You brought the young man up right, I see."

Moss smiled, but didn't say anything.

The sullen nurse reappeared a few minutes later. "They're closing now and then your surgeon will speak with you."

"Oh, thank God. I appreciate your help." Moss turned to go find Rowan. Graham had been moved near to his sister on the seventh floor, and Teal was handling another round of feedings. *We'll have to start switching off—Teal can't keep doing this without rest. I'd better cat-nap. Twenty minutes and I'll be good to go.*

Rowan was stretched out on three waiting-room chairs; he decided not to wake her until Sierra showed up. Someone had gotten her a pillow. Then he noticed a second pillow stashed under her chair, and knew she'd found one for him. Taking care not to wake her, he reached for it.

Twenty-five minutes later, Dr. Jacobsen came into the waiting room. Moss leaned over and touched Rowan. "Doc's here." Rowan popped up, rubbing her face. They both stood to greet Sierra. There were dark circles under her eyes.

"Carolina's been moved to recovery. I have to say, it was touch and go for a while. Her blood pressure bottomed out at 40/20."

"Good Lord," Moss said. Rowan grabbed his arm.

"I barely avoided a hysterectomy. We inserted a tamponade balloon into her uterus—that stopped the bleeding. Her condition now is guarded. Her blood pressure has come up to 80/50. We expect it to rise even more when she gets another transfusion."

"How many has she had?"

"This will be her fifth, and she received plasma, too." Sierra passed a hand over her forehead.

"Isn't that an awful lot?" Rowan asked, swallowing hard.

"It is, yes. After recovery, she'll go directly to ICU. Once she's settled, you can visit. The next twenty-four hours are critical."

"May I sit with her in recovery?" Moss said. "It's important she knows I'm there."

"I doubt they'll allow it, but I'll check. How are your babies? I'll go see them now."

Rowan piped up. "Teal got Andrea to take a bottle—the nurses weren't able to. They're calling him the baby whisperer. The head NICU nurse worked magic and now Graham's there, too. When she heard Teal was racing between floors, she had a fit and figured it out somehow. Hospitals have such weird rules."

"Yes, they're bureaucratic," Sierra responded. "But they provide a safe, clean place to save lives." She stretched her hands high above her head. "If you don't mind, I'd like to go see them before you do? I'll be quick. Need a nap. I'll stick around the hospital, though, with my pager."

"Good—makes me feel better," Moss said. "Do you know why this hemorrhage happened?"

"She had a sizable fibroid on the outside of her uterus. It kept her womb from contracting properly—and clamping down is what prevents excessive bleeding. I removed the fibroid." She yawned. "Ready to go see your kids?"

They found Teal napping in the intensive care nursery's waiting area. Sierra came back from the NICU ten minutes later. "Both babies are asleep; they look good. Moss, you go on in."

He said to Rowan, "I won't be too long." He gowned, washed his hands, and stood between the little cribs staring first at Andrea, then Graham. "My children," he whispered, trying to process the enormity of love, concern, and responsibility he felt. He reached out and dusted his fingers through Andrea's curls and Graham's—so softly, neither baby stirred. "I'm going to send in your big sis." He turned to walk away, but swung back. "Oh, little ones, you're lucky babes. You've come to a wonderful family filled with love. Wait 'til you get to spend time with your mama. She's special."

"I'm heading back to the surgery waiting room," he said to Rowan. "I'll probably crash again. Can you take the next feeding shift? I'm leaving my number at the desk."

She nodded, gave him a hug, and opened the door to the NICU.

Graham opened his eyes while Rowan admired her brother and sister. "Hi, little bro," she said. A nurse hovered nearby. Rowan picked him up, trying to support his head in the right way. It felt awkward, but he didn't cry, so she carried him to the rocking chair and settled in. Within a few minutes he'd fallen asleep but, loving the feel of him in her arms, she kept the motion going. He made curious expressions even while dozing—lip puckers, raised brows, frowns.

Andrea squeaked a few minutes later. Rowan set Graham back in his crib and went to her. The nurse appeared and helped organize monitor wires. Andrea had been swaddled; it felt more like picking up a soft log than a baby.

"I'll get a bottle," the nurse said.

"Thanks."

Rowan had watched Sierra with her mom and imitated what they'd done to get her to take the breast, but now with the bottle, instead. Andrea's peeps turned to squeals.

"What am I doing wrong?" Rowan asked. "It's me, I know it." She stood, anxiously jiggling Andrea.

"Nothing," the nurse said. "We couldn't get her to take the bottle, either. Only your brother's been able to. He'll have hints."

"Well, she needs to eat. He's sleeping in the waiting room—could you wake him? I hate to, but we need him." She glanced around the room at all the cribs. "I don't want to put her down 'cause she'll scream and wake everybody. You'd have pandemonium."

"Sure." The nurse pushed open the door. A couple of minutes later, she showed up with Teal.

"Please tell me how I'm messing up," Rowan said.

"Let me watch you." Teal leaned in.

Rowan went through her moves—sat, cuddled her, stroked her cheek. Andrea's mouth remained firmly shut, but she'd quit screaming for the moment.

"You're tense, and she's picking up on it. Try taking a deep breath, blow it out, roll your shoulders a couple of times. The deal is, when they start hollering, people get upset, and the babies get more freaked out." He watched her for a minute. "That's better. Notice, she relaxed, too? Settle back in the rocker again—she'll be all right now."

Rowan hummed to Andrea. "Hey, little sister," she whispered. "Let's try again." When she tickled her cheek, the baby opened her little bud mouth and took the nipple. Everyone breathed a sigh of relief.

She pensed Zephyr images of the NICU and the babies, and waited for her response.

I want to sniff and lick them.

I bet you do. You'll know lots more about them when you get to. Tell me what you learn.

Come back to Zephyr sooners?

Not yet, I'm afraid. I haven't seen Pack Mama. They sewed her up, but it's still serious. Nudge Jazz and Bender for me. Maggie, too. Love and laters.

Sierra came out to the waiting room. "Sorry, Moss, the staff wouldn't budge. You'll have to wait until they take her to Intensive Care. It should only be another fifteen minutes or so." She handed him a sticky note. "Here's my pager number. I've got to lie down."

The minutes ticked by. He couldn't take his eyes off the clock; each second made a loud click. His palms hurt. He peered at them and realized he'd dug his nails so hard, there were little purple wounds. *Shit, I need to buck up. Now Andrea's here, the stress is going to keep coming.* To relieve the tension, he stretched his hands open wide and paced the waiting room.

After what seemed like an hour, a nurse approached him. "She's not fully awake yet, but we're moving her to ICU. Give us ten minutes to get her settled, then we'll come get you. Head over to the waiting room. We'll look for you there."

He plodded to yet another bland room with uncomfortable chairs. A half hour passed. *Something doesn't feel right.* He shook his head to clear it.

Fifteen minutes later, a stocky nurse came over. "You're Moss Westbury?"

He nodded.

"I'm Robert. Follow me. You can go in now, but first you need to—"

"Gown and thoroughly wash my hands. I know the drill. Point out where."

Robert swallowed a chuckle and held the door open.

Moss spent extra time massaging the antibacterial soap between his fingers, under his ring. He dried them thoroughly. *I'm stalling. Fucking terrified to see how she looks.*

"I'm as ready as I'll ever be," he told Robert, who nodded, and walked him to the far end of the room. An IV bag of blood hung on the pole, and drops slithered down the tubing toward Carolina's arm. When he focused on her, his hands shook. Her face looked bloodless, and she seemed shrunken. *Well shit, she's down two babies. Of course she looks small.* But he knew the reason was different. She didn't feel quite in her body although he didn't know how he knew. Pulling a chair close, he sat, took her hand, and pressed his lips to her knuckles. "I'm here, love."

She didn't move or make a sound.

"It's Mossy," he said.

Nothing.

His heart contracted and thudded in his chest. He pressed the call button.

The woman he'd seen behind the desk came right over.

"She's not responding at all. What's up?"

"Birthing, blood loss, shock, surgery. Your wife's been through a lot in the last eighteen hours."

"Yeah, but this doesn't feel right. I've seen guys blown up by IEDs and they at least reacted."

"You need to give her time. She still has a lot of anesthetic in her." She went back to her post.

Half an hour later, even though he talked to Carolina steadily, there was no change. He rang the call button again. The same nurse walked over.

"My daughter, Rowan, needs to see her mother, and I need to be with her when she does. She'll be scared. After Rowan goes, I'm pulling these curtains and slipping in bed with my wife. If she doesn't feel my skin against hers, she'll be dead by nightfall."

"I'm sorry, it's simply not allowed," the nurse snapped. Everything about her tightened.

"Are you going to stop me?" He straightened and glared at her. "You surely don't want her death on your hands—especially since I'll report you wouldn't honor my request. Call her obstetrician. She'll back me up."

The woman huffed, "I will. Right now." She turned and stomped away.

Moss went to get Rowan. "She's not awake yet."

She stared up at him, eyes wide.

"Be prepared. She's awfully pale. It'll take a while to get her color back." He put his hand on her in support as they walked into the ICU.

"Mommo?" Rowan choked out when she saw her. She stared at Moss. "Is she going to be all right?"

"We hope so," he said. "Sit with her for a moment. Let her know you love her."

Rowan dropped into a chair and held her hand. "You've got to get strong again, okay? The babies need you. We all do!" Tears streamed down her face. After hugging Moss, she fled for the waiting room.

Moss pulled the metal-ringed curtain along the piping until he and Carolina were closed in. He shucked pants, shirt, prosthesis, and sock from his good foot. He considered her position—all the attached tubes and wires—and got in the side with the least going on. He slid his arm under the pillow until he could touch her far shoulder, pressed his body all along hers—being careful not to bear any weight—and whispered in her ear. "I'm here with you, love. You need to wake up so we know you're all right."

He must have dozed, but startled awake when she twined her fingers in his. She still hadn't said anything, but she knew he was here. Relief welled up in him. She moaned. Almost a sob.

"Are you in pain? Do you need more drugs?"

She gave an imperceptible nod. Hands quivering again, he pushed the call button. A moment later, Robert spoke through the drape. "I have to come in and check the monitors. What does she need?"

"More pain medication. She was groaning, so I asked her. She nodded. We're decent; it's fine. Join the party."

Robert slipped through the curtain. "She has a self-monitoring system—she can give herself more medication, but can't overdose. We set it up even before they're ready to use it, and when we check on the patient, we give it to them if needed." He showed Moss how to operate it. "Listen," he said, when he turned to leave. "I get it, but you need to move back to the chair before shift change. You've got about three hours."

"Sure. Can you give me a heads up? I'll probably sleep." Moss depressed the button to dispense the medication.

"Happy to."

Two minutes later, he felt Carolina's body soften, as did the grimace on her face. "Sweetheart, can you say something to me? We'd all feel better if we heard you speak."

A long silence. His heart contracted.

In a rasp, "Babies?"

"You remember! Graham and Andrea are good." He softly kissed her cheek. "Rowan's fine, too. She was here with you for a few minutes."

"I hurt." Her voice was feeble. "Bad."

"You hemorrhaged, sweetheart. Sierra had to perform surgery."

"Fainted."

He could barely hear her voice. "Yeah," he said, but didn't disclose how low her blood pressure had fallen. Plenty of time for details later.

They both slept.

"Mossy?"

Carolina's voice sounded stronger and more awake.

"Yes, love?"

"So…" A long pause. "I'm in the hospital, but you're in *bed* with me?"

She almost sounds like herself! "I splintered the rules and enraged one female nurse. She sent the guy nurse after that."

Giving a faint giggle, she clutched her belly. "Can't laugh. Too painful."

Carolina went silent, and he looked to see if she was snoozing. Her eyes were closed. "I need to see the babies," she whispered.

"I'll work on it."

She fell asleep.

Chapter Twenty

"Time's up." Robert's voice came through the curtain. "Shift change in fifteen minutes."

"Okay, thanks." Moss sighed, and swung carefully out of bed so he didn't wake Carolina. He dressed and went downstairs to find Teal and Rowan.

"How's Mommo?" Rowan asked, with a catch in her breath.

Moss smoothed the frown from his daughter's face with his thumb. "Better. Her voice is stronger, and she even laughed, although it hurt. Then she nodded off again. Teal, why don't you drive Rowan back to the house, and both of you get some real sleep. I'll take the next feedings."

They both looked relieved.

"I need to see Zephy," Rowan said. "And Jazz, too. She probably doesn't understand where you went."

He smiled. "I bet Zeph told her. Be sure and talk to Theo and Maggie. I'll call the grandparents again, since we have some decent news."

"I need to clean up," Teal said. "When do you want me back here?"

"Take the night, both of you. I think I can handle it."

"Remember to relax when you feed Andrea," Teal said. "She won't eat if you're tense. Roll your shoulders, take a couple of deep, cleansing breaths. It worked for Rowan." He stood and stretched. "If she doesn't settle down, call me."

"He's right," Rowan said. "She took the bottle for me. And if I can work magic, surely you can." She dragged herself to standing. "I'm beat. And hungry. Teal, let's rustle up food at home. After that, sleep."

"Come here," Moss said, enveloping her in a hug.

"Love you, Da."

"It's strange to hear you call me Da instead of Mossy."

"I'll use them both. I'm practicing."

"You two were troupers. Teal, you're earning your keep, big time."

The young man beamed.

Rowan followed Teal out into the June sunshine. "Look at these people going about their lives. We've been locked up in an alternate reality for almost a full day."

"Yeah. Hospitals are strange places. So's this parking lot. Check it out."

They took the elevator down four floors.

"Spooky," she said. "It echoes."

"Let's hope we can find our way out of here. Moss said he's gotten lost in these catacombs."

Twenty minutes later, they pulled up in front of the guest house. Rowan fumbled with the door and raced inside. *Where's my girl?* she pensed. She heard thundering strides and nails clicking on the hardwood. Zephyr, tongue lolling with that wide doggy smile, pushed her nose into Rowan's crotch. Crooning with delight, Rowan milked her dog's ears.

Jazz peered from Rowan to the door and back.

"Looking for Mossy? I'm sorry, he won't be home until at least tomorrow." Her tone must have communicated, because Jazz's head drooped. She padded into the living room and settled on the rug with a deep sigh, blinked her limpid eyes, curled in a ball, and stuffed her nose under her back leg. Rowan made a mental note to insist Moss come and comfort her. It wouldn't be right to neglect his faithful dog. She went over to Jazz and knelt down, gave her some special love, and whispered to her.

She heard Teal rummaging in the kitchen and went in to talk about dinner. "I have to run over to the main house to update Maggie." She glanced at the clock. "I doubt if Uncle Theo is home from work yet. Got a food plan? If not, I can dig in the freezer."

"Grilled cheese," he said. "How many do you want? I'll fix a salad, as well. We need our vegetables."

"Two. Salad's a great idea. Let's make up for the stupid vending machine food. I'll bring some dill pickles from Maggie's—I don't think there are any here. Anything you want?"

"I found yellow mustard at the back of the fridge. See if they have bread-and-butter pickles, would you? They're my first choice."

"Will do. Okay if I ask if Maggie wants to come over to eat?"

"Sure."

Rowan called the dogs and scooted out the back door.

Zephyr and Jazz sped ahead, stretching their legs into a race, probably sprinting to find Bender. Rowan could tell Zeph didn't run full out, pacing herself so Jazz could keep up. *Sweet. She knows her friend is lonely.* The abundant Fuchsias were blooming—deep reds and purples, her favorite. She thought of the flowers as shy because they hung their heads. The dogs found Bender, and the three were now cavorting on the lawn. It seemed Jazz had perked up. Rowan stopped for a deep inhale of lavender before hurrying to the house.

"Maggie?" she called, walking into the kitchen.

"I'm up in the garret," Maggie yelled. "You seen Bender?"

"He's frolicking with the girls," Rowan said, mounting the final staircase.

"Great word, 'frolicking.' Everyone okay? I want an update." Maggie stopped what she was doing and sat cross-legged on the daybed, signaling Rowan to join her.

Rowan leaned over, hands on thighs, to catch her breath before sitting down near Maggie. "Mama's doing better. Mossy said she even tried to laugh, although it hurt bad." She teared up and stared at the bed cover. "She almost died. Her blood pressure dropped to forty over twenty before they stopped the bleeding. She's had..." Rowan paused to think. "...five blood transfusions and other stuff, too. I think they called it plasma."

Maggie's eyes went wide. "Scary."

"Yeah. Thank God for Mossy in my life. Being an orphan would be devastating." Rowan grabbed another breath. "But the babies seem to be doing okay. Andrea's fussy about eating; Graham seems to take it all in stride. They sure are cute. Little curly-haired Westburys."

"So they'll match Uncle Moss and you."

Rowan nodded. "Andrea's cardiologist did an echo to check her heart a few minutes after she was born. She's got what they thought—*truncus* whatever. It's sad and complicated."

The dogs burst into the room, tongues dripping, and flopped on the floor.

"Oh yeah, I completely forgot. Teal's making grilled cheese sandwiches and wants me to bring pickles back. You're invited. Do you have both dill and bread-and-butter?"

"We do." Maggie jumped up, grabbed Rowan's hand to help her off the bed, and started for the door. "Pop said he'd be late. I'd love to eat with you. Hurry. I'm starving."

"What will he do for dinner?" Rowan asked, as they pounded down the stairs, dogs in quick pursuit.

"Leftovers—more for him since I'm eating with you. He'll be fine. I'll leave a note on the kitchen counter."

The nurse helped Moss sort the monitoring wires the first time he picked up Andrea from her NICU crib, then went to get a bottle. Andrea's peeps boiled into screeches. He remembered Teal's advice—and success—and took a breath, flexed his shoulders. He sat in the rocker and snuggled her into the crook of his elbow. *Such a tiny thing. Her feet don't even reach my hand.* He encouraged her to grasp his finger—hers didn't fill up the space between his knuckles.

"Thanks," he said, when the nurse handed him the warmed milk.

Moss tried several times to get Andrea to take the nipple, but she twisted her face away. He squinted up at the nurse.

"I think you need to give her your full attention and talk to her. That's what your son did and it worked."

He nodded, and stroked his daughter's halo of black ringlets. "Hey punkin," he whispered, gazing into her eyes. "Here's yummy food. You need it." As soon as he looked at her with focus and intent, she took the nipple. "Well," he said, smiling down at her. "We know who's running this show. Princess Punkin herself."

"Oh my gawd." Rowan pointed a pickle at Maggie and Teal. "Here we are, loitering without parents anywhere in sight. Loitering's my new word." She bit into the tart spear.

"Yeah," Teal growled, forcing a frown. "I'm the grownup in this gathering. We have to clean up after ourselves. I've got to keep you young women on the straight and narrow and hang on to my job."

"We'll be good." Maggie giggled. "Check out the dogs." They were sitting in a line, noses pointed at the sandwiches. "No begging," she admonished. Bender promptly lay down. Zephyr and Jazz folded their ears and looked away from the food.

"Impressive," Teal said. "All of them, and only one command."

"They'd better," Rowan and Maggie said in unison. Staring at each other, they started to laugh. "Pinky swear," Rowan squealed, and the girls hooked baby fingers.

"I thought it was only my family." Teal shook his head, chortling.

"It's everywhere." Maggie took a bite of salad. "Pa and Ma use the same expression. They're a different generation, and all the way on the East Coast."

"Your grandparents? Go figure. I'm the last to know—probably because I grew up in the boonies." Teal flipped another sandwich in the skillet. "Either of you want more? I'm still hungry."

The girls shook their heads.

"I need room for mint chocolate chip ice cream," Rowan said. "It makes me think of Bender's Ridge. We eat a lot of it there. I miss the place."

"Me, too," Maggie said. "I guess we don't get to go this summer?"

"Maybe you two and the dogs could," Teal said, "if the librarian was willing to stay with you."

Rowan hooted. "Gladys. What a fine idea. I'll hit Da with it when he gets home. Or should I check with Glady first?"

"Why not?" Maggie asked. "Ducks in a row. Teal, I guess you're stuck here, since you're the nanny."

"Not stuck. It's what I want to do."

"How come?"

"First: I support myself, and I started out flat broke. Second: I'm crazy about babies. Third: this is a fabulous family to work for." He pointed his finger first at Maggie, then Rowan. "So don't ask me to do anything your parents wouldn't approve of. This job means *everything* to me." Teal cocked his head. "Fourth: on top of all that, Moss is a published author. I'm can learn from him."

"How'd you get so responsible?" Maggie asked.

"I got disowned. If I'm not responsible for me…." He shrugged, rubbing the toe of his shoe on the tile.

Chapter Twenty-one

The nurse pushed Carolina's wheelchair out of the ICU to a regular room. "Soon, you'll be able to see the babies," Moss said.

A wide smile spread across her face. "I may fall asleep waiting. I seem to sleep and sleep and sleep some more."

"Rest is what's healing you, love—give over to it. Won't go on forever."

She squeezed his hand. "Once I get settled, you and Teal can switch. It's time for you to go home, get a good night's rest. You've been catnapping for two-and-a-half days."

He stifled a yawn. "Yup, you're right. I hate to leave you all, but I'm beyond bushed. Before I go, I'd hoped to see you connect with the munchkins."

"Sierra said I can nurse now."

"Terrific news." He set the chair brakes, eased her up, and tucked her into bed. *At last, a private room. Most of the endless beeping, gone.*

The nurse bustled around, tending to regular duties—blood pressure, temperature, oxygen level, checking her incision.

"Remember," he said to Carolina, "Andrea will get most of her nourishment from the bottle. She has to work too hard at the breast. You're pumping for her; she's getting your milk now."

She grimaced. "It's sad she isn't strong enough to nurse. It's more bonding."

"You'll cuddle her plenty. We'll do our best to make her life as normal as possible. I figure it'll take daily adaptations, right?" He hugged her. "I'm calling

Teal now. He'll have to drive me back; I'm not safe behind the wheel—too exhausted. Then I'll check on getting the babies in here for a visit."

"I want them to sleep in the room with me." She smoothed the bed covers.

"I know. One step at a time. Soon enough, we'll be going home."

"But to San Francisco," she whispered. "Not Bender's Ridge. I miss it so much."

He sat on the edge of the bed carefully, trying not to make her wince. "Oh, yeah. Me, too."

"You need to be writing again."

He patted her hand. "Writing? What's that?"

Her eyes widened. "Don't say 'what's writing'. You frighten me. Writing is who you *are*."

He entwined his fingers with hers. "I'm also the father of gorgeous infant twins who have stolen my heart. Right now, you, and they, are my priority."

"Mossy—"

He pulled out his cell. "I'm calling my ride, then heading home to crash." He kissed her tenderly. "This conversation can keep."

They heard a soft knock. Teal stuck his head around the corner. "Hi, Carolina. Man, you look better. Figured I needed to ferry the big guy home and get back here for the next feeding." He kneaded Moss's shoulders. "You'll revive after a night in a cushy bed."

"Isn't your timing impeccable." Moss held up his phone. "Two secs, and your cell was going to ring. I wanted to see her with the babes, but I'm wasted."

"Sweetheart, go home," Carolina said. "Teal, how's Row?"

"She's fine. I fed the girls sandwiches and salad last night, omelets this morning. They're going to hang together today."

"You don't have to fix food for them, too," Carolina said. "We don't want you to burn out. Please don't overdo. This is no sprint."

"I was cooking for myself anyway. Not a problem." He grinned and flexed a muscle. "Young. Strong."

Moss chortled. "You like showing off."

"Yes, sir," Teal said, a glint in his eye.

"Look." Carolina's eyes went wide with disbelief. A nurse and Sierra made their way in, each pushing a tiny crib. "My babies." Sobs overtook her and, flinching, she pressed a pillow across her midriff.

Moss felt the depth of her discomfort in his own body. He remembered. Surgery hurt.

A moment later, she regained her composure and reached out. "I want Andrea first, please. I need to snuggle her. Could someone get her bottle?"

"I will," Teal said.

"Nope, please drive me home before I collapse," Moss replied. He said to the nurse, "Could you get the milk please?"

"Sure."

Both babies tuned up to cry. Sierra delivered Andrea to Carolina and helped settle the infant in the crook of her elbow. She picked up Graham and patted his back. "You go home, Teal. I can help now. Get Moss out of here."

Moss lolled against the seat, almost forgetting to latch his seatbelt. He gave a loud yawn and closed his eyes. "Are we going to survive this?"

"The first couple of years with twins are awful tough, but you'll find your footing. You survive until you thrive. At least it's what happened in my family. And you have me to help. Six hands are way better than four."

"Thank God for those," Moss murmured, and then he was out.

"How's Mommo?" Rowan asked, the moment her dad trudged in.

Jazz let out a doggy squeal and launched herself at him. He caught her, and knelt down to scratch her wriggling body. "Give me a minute and I'll tell you details. The short answer is your mom's doing better, and was reunited with your brother and sister a few minutes ago."

Jazz continued to make a sound Rowan had never heard before. *It's like she's talking—no, complaining about all the time he's been away.* "Poor thing. *Listen* to her. She didn't think you were ever coming back."

Moss was whispering into Jazz's ear, stroking her, soothing her.

Just right, Rowan thought.

Moss put a hand against the wall and levered himself up. Rowan was shocked to see how exhausted he was. "Make sure he doesn't fall on the way to bed, Teal." She hugged her dad. "Tell me everything later, after you sleep."

"Perfect." He sighed, and, leaning on Teal, limped toward the bedroom. Jazz followed right behind him.

Teal came back ten minutes later without Jazz. "That man is bone-weary. I made sure he got horizontal before I left the room—afraid he'd fall down, otherwise. Jazz clambered right up on the bed with him and stuck her head on his hip. Happy girl. Now, I should get back to the hospital."

"Can't you take five and update me on my mom? I can't wait until Mossy wakes up."

"Of course. Sorry I didn't think of it." Teal told her all he knew.

Carolina glanced up when she felt a hand on her arm.

"It's Teal. I'm back. Where are we with feedings?"

"Is Moss okay? Did you get him to go to bed?"

"Oh yeah. He would have fallen if I hadn't insisted he lie down. He's snoring. And the girls—human and dog—are doing well. I updated Rowan; she was worried about you."

"Of course she was. Maybe I can see her tomorrow—hope so. Both babies ate—Andrea took a bit of bottle; Graham nursed." She glanced at the clock. "She needs to eat again in about forty-five minutes."

"I'll take the feeding. How are you? Honestly?"

She tugged up the covers before speaking. "Endlessly tired. In some belly pain. Overwhelmed and wondering how we're going to manage."

Teal sat in the chair near the bed. "Abdominal surgery's tough. Give yourself a couple of weeks—you won't believe how much better you'll feel. But, it'll take far longer to get back that karate self you've told me about. Only take the babies when you're truly up to it. Moss and I can handle most feedings. You spend time with them when you have the juice."

She sighed. "Thanks. I yearn for life to find … a new normal, I guess, whatever it turns out to be. Sierra said I might be able to go home as early as two days from now. They want my hemoglobin to reach some level first." Her eyelids closed. "Can't remember exactly what she said."

"I'll check at the desk. No worries—I'm rested and ready to handle whatever."

She nodded and, a second later, fell asleep.

Chapter Twenty-two

Moss ferried Carolina, Teal, and the twins home three days later. Teal sat in the back between his little charges. Moss's hands ached from clenching the steering wheel in San Francisco's late-afternoon commute traffic. He tipped his head to both sides to relieve neck stress. *The weight of this baby responsibility—I have to learn to handle this better.* He glanced over and saw Carolina had closed her eyes, head pillowed on her folded jacket. "Getting home's going to be good for you," he said. "Hospitals can be difficult."

"I don't like them either," Carolina said, her voice a faint whisper, "but they saved my life. I'm grateful."

"Point taken." He patted her leg. "I hope you'll be happy with how we set up the cribs. For now, they aren't in our bedroom, because you need as much rest as you can get. We put them in Teal's room."

She was silent for a long time. He could tell she was wrestling with a plan arranged without her.

"Okay, for now," she said, sighing. "A couple of weeks, max."

"It may be a month or more, sweetheart. Whatever it takes."

The quiet thickened between them.

"I guess," she said, softly. "But maybe shorter. I'll get my chops back … karate girl, remember?"

Rowan got a pense from Zephyr, a picture of the soon-to-arrive car. *My twenty-minute early warning? Thanks.* Rowan texted Maggie and got to work pumping up the helium balloons.

Maggie and Bender blew in, breathing hard.

"Thanks for getting here quick. Could you take over filling these? I'll start tying the balloons where we talked about. Everything else is done."

"Even the banner?"

"Damn, forgot. Let me finish this and we can put it up." She nodded at Maggie, and went out the front door to tie two balloons to the mailbox. A gust caught them, almost ripping them away. She held the strings with both hands and made her way slowly to the box, tied them, and ran back to hang the banner with Maggie.

The Prius pulled up as they secured the ends of the "Welcome Home" message from the second-floor windows.

"Too close," she said. They raced downstairs and threw open the door.

Her mom saw them and blew a kiss. Moss hoisted one of the baby carriers and Teal grabbed the other. Carolina held on to Moss's other arm.

Maggie whispered to Rowan, "She looks so weak."

"Yeah, well—" Rowan tilted her head. "She almost died. Her color's pretty good now. Much better than after the twins came and she hemorrhaged. She looked bleached white. Scary." When her mom reached the front porch, Rowan hugged her—but very, very gently. "We're relieved you're home."

"You girls made it festive—it makes us feel welcome. Now I need to lie down."

"Dinner's in half an hour. Theo and Maggie cooked, and he's bringing it over," Rowan said.

"Splendid. Thanks, Maggie." She gave her niece a careful squeeze.

Moss and Teal had set the baby carriers at their feet, but now, after hugging everyone, carried them inside. The three dogs were waiting, noses busy scenting the air.

Rowan had made them sit and stay while the car unloaded. "They want to greet the babies. Okay by you, Mama?"

Carolina settled into the couch. "As long as you're overseeing them, sure. Please, no face-licking. I won't be concerned when they're older."

Zephyr waited calmly. Jazz quivered, barely able to keep her butt on the floor. Bender's tail stub wagged fast against the hardwood floor.

The girls called the dogs into the living room. Teal and Moss set the carriers on the sofa and extracted the infants from the straps and extra padding.

"They're awfully tiny," Maggie whispered, her voice filled with awe.

"And they've grown since birth. Graham more than Andrea," Moss said. "She is gaining, but much more slowly."

Moss called the dogs over one at a time to sniff and greet the twins. Zephyr walked to them first, looking from Andrea to Graham. Then she pressed her nose right against Graham's body and inhaled.

Rowan could see all the information Zeph took in, nostrils flaring. Her dog went to Andrea and repeated the examination. She pensed Rowan, *this pup sounds different.*

Yes. It's Andrea, the little girl.

Zeph sleeps near her.

Rowan's eyes prickled. *Their cribs are in Teal's room; you won't be with me.*

The pup's in the pack. Zeph needs to be close.

Rowan stroked her. *I know you do.* But her heart felt thick at the thought of not cuddling her at night. Oh my God, she thought. If Maggie and I go to Bender's Ridge, Zeph's not going to want to go with us.

Maggie let Jazz go second. "Immediate family members get priority," she said. "Bender's only a first cousin."

Rowan tried to smile.

Maggie stared at her. "What's up?" she whispered.

"I'll tell you later."

Jazz, more tentative, quivered as she nosed the babies.

"Do you think she's afraid?" Moss asked. "She's acting like it."

"Nope. She's unsure, though. She recognizes them as young things," Rowan said. "In dog culture, another dog has to be super careful around pups that aren't hers. She's probably anxious about getting attacked. By Mama."

Moss laughed.

When Maggie whistled, Bender trotted across the room and, at her hand signal, sat. "Gentle," she warned. "Easy does it."

He smelled their toes and legs, then lay on the floor nearby.

"Lots of great overseers," Rowan said, able to laugh now. "These babies have a houseful of caregivers."

"We need every one," Teal said. "Especially after they start walking. Sooner than any of us can imagine."

Moss's cell rang. "Hi Sarah. We just got home from the hospital with the twins, so if I get called, I'll need to run. What? I'm a finalist? That's a surprise! Thanks for letting me know. Carolina will be thrilled, and we need some good news around here."

Zephyr lies near Andrea with her nose pressed between her paws. *Humans need help. Zeph sleeps in the small pup's room and listens, tells Rowan if she gets worse. But my girl is sad.*

Carolina hauled herself up from the couch, and supporting her abdomen, made her way to the dining room when Theo arrived with dinner. It smelled sweet and spicy and rich. For the first time in more than a month, she had an appetite. At the end of her pregnancy, there hadn't been room to eat much. Now she needed to consume enough to make milk. Homemade soup was perfect.

Maggie carried a long loaf of seeded French bread. Rowan trotted to the kitchen, brought out the butter, and they all sat around the table. The twins reclined in their baby carriers between Teal and Carolina.

"You two," Carolina said, eying Theo and Maggie, "thanks so much for nourishing food—it's exactly what we needed."

Graham tuned up from fussing to hollering. Teal unbuckled him, and hoisted the infant against his chest. Patting his butt, he spoke in a soothing tone. "Babies always demand attention at mealtime. I have no idea why. Carolina, was it true of Rowan?"

"Sure was."

"Babe, you stay where you are and eat. I'll warm up a bottle," Moss said. "I'd better make two. Andrea's sure to wake up."

No sooner had Teal settled in the rocker with Graham than Andrea woke crying. Moss came back with the breast milk, handed one to Teal, and set the other near his chair. He picked Andrea up. "Oh my, she needs changing, and I need a lesson. Rowan, can you take Graham so Teal can teach me?"

"Please let me have him," Maggie said. "I'm dying to feed one of them." She plunked in the corner of the couch. Teal handed her baby and bottle and slipped into his room where the changing table was set up. Moss followed with Andrea.

Carolina could hear Andrea complaining, her cries changing to quavering howls. She pressed her arms against her chest. "My milk let down. Guess I have to get used to this." She rose from the table, a damp spot already staining her blouse. "Sorry to leave you alone, Theo—I have to go pump. We'll be back soon."

"Good Lord," he said. "I only had Maggie. Twins seem like four times the work of a single baby."

"Ya think?" Carolina said, her tone wry. "We're *so* in for it."

Moss slipped into bed with Carolina. She made sleepy puffing noises. He spooned around her from knee to shoulder hoping not to disturb her, but thrilling to her feel and scent. *Too damn close a call.*

"Oh, you're here with me," she whispered, her voice dozy-soft. "Lordy, I've missed this."

He groaned. "Yes ma'am. Me too. I was damn fucking scared, and you know I don't swear much. I'm still recovering."

She rolled over and eased toward him. The process took her thirty seconds.

He saw her grimace in the moonlight. "Still hurts, I know."

"Oh, yeah. Will for a while," she said. "Sierra said we have to wait *six* weeks. But where are those lips of yours? They'll heal me."

Her smile made his heart jump. He leaned over and gave her the lightest kisses, starting at her brow and making his way down the soft skin of her cheek to meet those lips he'd fallen in love with at first glance. She softened. "It's a hint of what the future holds, when you're healed up and the time is right," he said. "Now, back to sleep."

Zephyr stretches, shakes, goes out the dog door to the grass, and squats. Her nose works the salty tang of the big water coming with the fog. She stops in the kitchen to lap from her bowl, trots down the hall to her girl's nest, gives her a tongue swipe and nudge. Rowan giggles and sends a *thank you* back. Toenails tapping on the floor, Zeph heads back to the pups' room. She walks to Andrea and stands, listening. No change. She flops on the floor, rolls on her side, and sleeps.

Chapter Twenty-three

By the end of July, when the babies were six weeks old, the family had found a semblance of rhythm. Carolina needed sleep more than anything and, the sooner she healed, the faster their family could settle into the new normal she wanted. She was doing much better, up longer between naps, spending more daytime hours with the twins.

Teal handled most of the night shift but, when both babies woke hollering, Moss helped, staggering out of bed and giving a bottle to the other twin. This way, some nights, Carolina was able to sleep all the way through. Other times, she heard their cries and her milk let down, waking her. She took to stuffing gauze squares in her nursing bra so her nightgown didn't get soaked.

During the day, Carolina suckled Graham and gave Andrea snuggles and a chance at the breast but, at the first hint of struggling, had a bottle by the chair. It was uncomfortable to pump, but she was determined Andrea receive the same nutritious mama's milk Graham got.

Teal slept in the afternoons. Once a week, Moss, Rowan, and Maggie took over and insisted he have a full twenty-four hours off. "You need more breaks than this," Moss said. "Starting next week, we're scheduling them in."

"But I love my job," Teal retorted.

"We know you do. But sorry, not negotiable. Against the law, even." Moss cuffed him lightly on the arm. "More time to write."

"You've got a point there."

Zephyr remained on faithful duty near Andrea most of the time. Rowan was relieved her dog checked in often with a soft nudge or pense.

Would you go to Bender's Ridge with Maggie, Bender, and me? Rowan asked.

Zephyr needs to listen to the pup, her dog pensed back.

For her whole life? Rowan felt close to tears—begrudging this teensy, wailing, snippet of a baby girl stealing her attention.

Zephyr needs to listen now.

Right. The only possible answer, Rowan realized. Zephy lives in the eternal now. Dogs were luckier than people. Humans had to deal not only with nasty memories, but also nightmare futures. She sighed. *Yes, of course you do. You're so connected to her. But can't you sense her from a distance? Like when you're at home and we've been away, you know our car is getting close?*

Different.

Maybe not, Rowan thought. *When Andrea goes to the fix-it doctor, you and I will be here, at this house. Try to pense me about her then?*

Zephyr tries.

The next week, Carolina, Moss, and Andrea piled in the Prius to go see Dr. Bhat. Teal remained at the guest house, caring for Graham with strict instructions to text Rowan at Maggie's if he needed help. After all, it was his first time alone with one of the babies. Cell phone in her pocket, Row holed up with Zephyr, Maggie, and Bender in the garret at the main home where her cousin and dog practiced pensing.

"You're hoping Zeph can track Andrea's condition from here while she's at UCSF?" Maggie asked. "If she can, the four of us might get to go to Bender's Ridge?"

"Yup. We need privacy to work on pensing. My secret worry is whether distance will degrade—my new word—her ability to read Andrea's health. Remember after the car accident four years ago, I got helicoptered to the Portland hospital and Zephy was lost near Bender's Ridge? After I came out of the coma, she and I were in touch. We could feel each other over 150 miles. We weren't nearly as skilled at pensing as we are now, but she knew when I was sad; I knew when she got hurt by the cougar."

Maggie frowned and ground her fist into the pillow. "I get so jealous when you tell me stuff like this. It seems like I'm getting nowhere. Will Bender and I ever get good at communicating?"

Rowan walked over and hugged her cousin. "You two are doing great. Look at the progress you made when Bender jumped off and back on the bed, from your pense."

"I feel like we're in kindergarten," Maggie grumbled. "Okay, okay, go on; finish what you were telling me."

"This situation is different—Andrea doesn't pense," Rowan said. "She can't even think in words. I assume she has feelings and images, but we can't be sure. Can Zeph pick up on her from 500 miles away and communicate to me? Because otherwise, my stubborn dog won't go." She affectionately scratched the top of Zeph's head. "I have no idea what the answer is, and I don't think Zephy does either. Supposedly, the doctor is giving her some new medication today. It'll make a change to her heart—speed it up, slow it down, I don't know the details. But will Zephy notice? This is a *big* test." She checked her watch. "The doctor will give her the meds sometime in the next hour, I figure."

An hour and a half passed. Rowan gave Maggie a crestfallen look. "Guess not," she whispered. "Got a Plan B?"

"Maybe you need to leave Zeph here, and the three of us go to the ranch. You two are never truly separated. Will you at least consider it?"

Rowan pulled a face. "It's an awful big ask. I need to think on it. And talk to her, too." She tipped her head in her dog's direction.

Twenty minutes later, Zephyr abruptly sat up, ears pricked.

"Shit," Rowan grumbled. "They're probably on their way home. Guess it didn't work."

Suddenly, Zeph swiveled around and stared at Rowan. *The pup changes.*

Changes how? Good or bad?

Zephyr actually looked puzzled.

Forget the part about good or bad. Can you tell me about the change?

The dog walked to stand alone by the window.

"Look. She's *concentrating,*" Maggie said, eyes wide. "Like she's listening, or something."

A minute or two later, Zephyr came back and sat. *Pup's beat is faster.*

Rowan's own heart sped into overdrive. She rubbed her dog with affection. *Fantastic work.* She thought for a moment. *Does it feel like she's in the same room with you, like during dark hours?*

The same.

"Maggie, she *can* do it!" Row relayed the content of the penses to her cousin. "There's a chance we can go." She fist-pumped the air.

"We've got to convince both my dad *and* your folks," Maggie said, marching around the room. "Might not be easy."

Bender raised his head to watch her.

"I'd love to get out of here for a couple of weeks; the craziness is getting to me." Rowan flicked her hands to shake off the madness. "Endless screaming babies."

Maggie bent to stroke Bender from the knob on his head to the end of his tail-stub. "It'd be cool if it was only us four."

Rowan plunked on the window seat. "We can try, but my mom? Fat chance."

"Moss might talk her into it. You never know."

"Maggie and I are calling a family meeting. Everybody," Rowan said. They were eating Moss's clam chowder and French bread for dinner. The fog hadn't lifted all day and the thick, nourishing soup warded off the evening's chill.

"What have you girls cooked up now?" Carolina asked.

Rowan ignored the question and pulled out her phone to check the time. "Theo and Maggie can come tonight. Say 7:30? It won't take long." Her mom and Moss did the eye-connecting communication thing. It bugged her.

"Teal," Carolina asked, "can you field the twins if need be? I know Rowan wants you at the meeting, but we have to be able to hear."

"Sure, but it's usually their solid nap time after they scream bloody hooha during dinner." Jiggling Andrea, he smiled. "Row, can you nuke my soup for a minute to warm it up?" He nuzzled the baby's cheek. "See what you did? Made my soup cold. Powerful girl in a tiny body."

At 7:30, Theo, Maggie, and Bender walked in, Maggie dragging her dad by the hand. They settled in the living room.

"Let's hear it," Carolina said.

Rowan looked from Maggie to Theo, to Moss, to her mom. "It's been nuts around here. Maggie and I want to go to the ranch for four weeks—with our dogs, of course. The last three summers we've had two full months there together."

"Dad says he's got business at a hospital nearby," Maggie said, "and he's willing to drive us. It's only forty-five minutes more from Bender's Ridge to Redmond."

"Glad to," Theo said. "I have four days of consults. I was hoping to spend the first night at the ranch. I haven't been there since ... since Phoebe died."

Moss focused on his brother. "Eight years? You're welcome any time. I've said so more than once."

"I know. Too many memories until now. But I think I'm ready."

"I'm glad you want to," Moss said. "Row, how are you all planning to get home?"

"We haven't figured that out," she admitted.

"I see why you'd want to go," Carolina said. "But you certainly can't stay without supervision. Dakota's living in the barn—we don't know him other than superficially, and he's only twenty-five. If he were sixty-five, it might be different." She paused and frowned. "Wait a minute. Let's back up." Her words were clipped. "You're planning to take Zephyr away for *four* weeks? She's been keeping watch over Andrea—why, she barely leaves her side."

Rowan stared her mom down. "All of a sudden, you trust my dog's senses after dismissing them since the beginning? Yeah, yeah, I know you've made progress since Christmas. A smidgen. I won't get to be with her because *you* need her? I'm gobsmacked."

"Watch your attitude," her mom snapped. "And your language."

"Gobsmacked isn't a swear word," Rowan retorted. "It's Scottish slang and means 'astounded.' Sheesh."

"Whoa, let's all slow down," Moss said, in an even tone. "Everybody, take a breath, keep this civil." He looked at his daughter. "Your mom's concerned about Andrea's well-being, and Zephyr's presence eases her worry."

"Tell them about the test you conducted with Zephy today," Maggie whispered. "While they were at UCSF."

"Like they'll believe it," Rowan muttered.

"What'd you do?" Moss asked.

Rowan fiddled with her hands. "While you guys were with the cardiologist, I asked Zephy to tune in to Andrea and report changes. The time seemed too long, so when she did perk up, I figured it was because you were on the way home. But she pensed me, *Pup's beat is faster.* It was right at 3:25. I checked my phone."

Moss stared at her, then turned to Carolina. "Right around then, Dr. Bhat gave her medicine."

"But UCSF's only a few miles away," Carolina said. "At the ranch, you're *500* miles. It's..." Rowan saw her mom computing in her head. "over 150 times the distance."

"Zephy told me it felt like she was lying right by Andrea's crib. It's like—the connection isn't in time and space. I don't think distance has anything to do with it."

"You don't think." Carolina snorted. "And if you're not here, it puts a bigger load on Teal."

"Geez—you're grabbing for excuses. So now I'm your part-time nanny?" Rowan shook her head and chewed her lip, trying to get control of herself. "How about this? You ask Glady to stay with us at the ranch. We drive up with Uncle Theo, and if Zephy can't feel Andrea from there, we come back with him. I'm craving the freedom with Maggie and the beasties. Teal, could you handle it?"

"Sure," he said. "No prob. Moss helps out a lot, too."

Carolina walked to the window and stared out at the cityscape. "I have to sleep on this," she said.

The next morning, Carolina and Rowan walked into the guesthouse kitchen at the same time. "Want some coffee, sweetie?" she asked her daughter. "I'll make you a mocha. Can we can talk a bit while we drink them?"

Rowan's expression brightened. "Sure, thanks."

As her mother finished the espresso drinks, Andrea woke up with her familiar squeaky cry.

"I'll ask Teal to take this shift," Carolina said, "so we can have some time together. Give me five minutes to roust him."

She saw Rowan's sigh of relief, and went to warm a bottle of breast milk.

Teal showed up, buttoning his shirt.

Crooning, Carolina picked up her tiny daughter, snuggled her close, and handed her to Teal. "Thanks," she said. "Row and I need to talk."

"Good plan," he said.

Mother and daughter took the two recliners which looked out at the city view, and swiveled to face each other. "I think your suggestion of trying the four days is a great one. I know it's a big compromise, and I appreciate it." Carolina sipped her drink. "I sure wish this didn't have to be decaf, but hey—I'm grateful for what I *can* have."

"You only drink one mocha a day—very moderate intake. You're a great mom, you know."

Carolina pressed her hand to her own cheek. "Why thanks. High praise. So, hopefully, Zeph can work her magic from afar, and keep tabs on our little girl. Maybe I could tickle Andrea or something, and see if Zephyr picks up on it? Please call or text as soon as you know. I'll phone Gladys this morning, but I don't think she'll have a problem—she's grateful for any time she gets at the ranch. And if the four days go as well as you think they will, you and Maggie get your four weeks."

Rowan's eyes went wide. "Thanks. Wait until I tell her." She squinted at the wall clock. "I doubt she's up yet."

"With regular check-ins, please."

Rowan frowned. "It sounds like you're asking me to call multiple times a day? No way."

"I wasn't clear, sorry—I know you need your space—call or text only if Zephyr picks up something we need to know about Andrea's health. Although, I'd appreciate hearing from you at least every other day."

"I'm good with that."

Theo and Maggie walked in.

Carolina waved at them, but continued her conversation with Rowan. "This Dakota guy? I know nothing about his character. Please, keep your distance. Unfortunately, he's handsome."

The girls exchanged a glance.

"No going upstairs in the barn. *Ever.*" Carolina stared each of them down.

"But didn't Mossy know him overseas? Aren't they friends?" Rowan asked.

"Nope. He hired Dakota through a veterans' organization. The guy apparently has bad PTSD—worse than Moss's—so planting, watering, harvesting, and caring for the chickens are his therapy right now."

"Bad PTSD like what?" asked Maggie.

"Migraines, cowering at loud noises, nightmares, stammering," Carolina said. "Terrible self-esteem. Guilt. His list is longer than Moss's."

The girls shared another look.

Rowan turned back. "Uncle Theo, when are you leaving?"

"I'm planning to go Sunday," he said.

"We'll be ready," Rowan said, and grinned at Maggie.

Chapter Twenty-four

Early the following Sunday, Rowan and Maggie rolled suitcases to the van, and went back inside to grab the necessary dog supplies—beds, bowls, food, leashes. Theo had preloaded his hanging garment bag, backpack, and physician's case. Once Bender and Zephyr saw their gear inside the vehicle, their ears perked and they leapt in.

Maggie's eyes widened. "Dad, if you're bringing suits, you must be having awfully important meetings."

"I wanted to keep my white coats pressed, too. I've been invited to be part of a team that's going to separate conjoined twins—the babies live in Redmond, but the surgery will be done at UCSF—it's too complicated for a small medical center. I'll be monitoring the babies' vitals while the surgeons work their magic. These are the preliminaries—we'll meet the family, the twins, the docs who will oversee them in Oregon when they get back from UCSF."

"Where are they joined?" Rowan asked.

"At the belly. The girls only share a liver, which makes the odds in their favor. Livers can be split, and they regenerate—the only visceral organ that can. If we pull this off, they can look forward to normal lives." Theo started the car. "We've got a long drive, longer if we stop for a nice lunch in Shasta. Gladys said she'll cook us dinner. Hop in, buckle up, and I'll tell you more on the way."

Zephyr rests her head on Bender's hip. *The big land?* she penses Rowan.

Yes. We get to go back. You can run the raccoon out of the garden again. Pay attention to Andrea, too. We've come a long way; can you still feel her?

No change.

Good job. Her girl leans forward and knuckles her ears the way she loves most.

Zephyr leans into her hand. *Bender wants his girl closer.*

How do you know? Can you pense with him?

Different. Zephyr senses him.

Interesting. Rowan reaches into a bag and pulls out two biscuits. *We'll change places when we stop. Here's one for you, one for your buddy.*

Bender's nose lifts at the scent.

After the ten-hour drive, Theo pulled into the dusty gravel circle at Bender's Ridge. They burst from the car. The dogs galloped toward the barn; Theo, Rowan, and Maggie stretched their stiff limbs and carried gear to the house.

"Drop those bags," Gladys said, opening the door. Beaming, she swept Rowan and Maggie into her arms, one on either side. "Look at you two—taller than I am now." She kissed each girl on the cheek, then hugged Theo. "Welcome back. Lands sakes alive, I'm glad you came. It's been forever."

"Too long," he said, a frown creasing his forehead. "I was afraid to face my grief here, where Phoebe and I conceived Maggie."

Maggie's face flared in a blush. "Dad! TMI."

He looked at her and shook his head. "Oh lord, Maggie-girl. Give your pop a break. Those kinds of memories of your mom are important to me."

"Way too embarrassing," she muttered.

"You wait," he retorted, "until you have kids. Hey, I can smell Glady's yummy cooking, and I'm hungry and beat."

"I invited Dakota for dinner tonight," Gladys said. "This will be the only night, a courtesy since he lives on the property. You need to meet, and obviously he and the dogs have to familiarize themselves. But I'll be watching you both"—she raised her eyebrow and pinned her gaze first on Rowan, then Maggie—"make sure you keep your distance. He's ten years older. The barn is off limits. Flirting—off limits. Conversations with him in private—off limits. Cross the line? I'll rat you out and show you the door. No second chances. I've given him the same lecture. Do I make myself clear?"

"Yes, ma'am," Rowan said.

"Yikes," Maggie whispered.

"I'm waiting for a proper response from you, young lady." Gladys focused on Maggie.

"Yes, ma'am," Maggie said.

Gladys rang the gong and, a minute later, Dakota appeared at the barn door. Wide-eyed, he stopped while the two dogs gave him the once over. "Jesus, they're huge. They won't eat me, will they?" he hollered across the circle.

"Not if you have a kind heart," Rowan yelled back. "But if you don't, watch out. Let them get a good whiff." She saw him push Zephyr's nose away from his crotch.

"Good grief," Maggie whispered. The dogs frolicked around him. "The guy is drop-dead gorgeous."

"I forgot somethin'. Have to run back to my digs." Dakota went back toward the barn. "Just a sec."

"Don't take long," Gladys called. "Dinner's hot."

"*He's* what's hot," whispered Maggie.

"If you ruin this for us, I won't forget or forgive," Rowan said.

Maggie stomped ahead, picked up her bag, and pushed into the house, slamming the screen door.

Theo frowned, scratched his head, grabbed his backpack, and followed his daughter inside.

"You girls having a spat?" Gladys asked Rowan.

"Apparently. Our first in four years, other than the day we met. I found out later it was the fourth anniversary of her mom's death, and she was outraged she couldn't visit the grave."

"Ah," Gladys replied. "No wonder."

Rowan stuffed dog beds under one arm, kibble under the other, dropped them in the living room, and made one more trip for her roller bag and their bowls. The girls avoided looking at each other.

Dakota knocked and slipped inside a moment later. "I purchased a bottle of wine for the grownups, and fresh-pressed juice for the girls. A thank you for including me."

"Thoughtful, thanks," Theo said. "I'd love a glass. I'll get the corkscrew."

"First things first," Gladys ordered. She introduced the three of them to Dakota. "He's a big help around the place. Now come sit down."

"Hey, hello," he said to the two girls.

Had his gaze lingered on Maggie? Rowan wasn't sure.

"It's splendid here," the veteran said, once the food was passed around.

Rowan took a good look at him, trying to see him through Maggie's eyes. His blond hair, almost bleached white, was long, pulled back into a knot at the nape of his neck. Kind of severe. His steady chestnut eyes stripped down all they saw to its essence. It didn't feel creepy, though. His arms were well-muscled and deeply tanned. He didn't appeal to her—his heart felt closed. Why would he attract Maggie? she wondered. She dug into her food. "Glady, this is delicious. Thanks."

"Wonderful to have a warm meal after the long drive," Theo said. "By the way, I'm planning to take a walk in the morning, reacquaint myself. And go up on the ridge. I haven't been here in nine—no, ten—years."

"Since my sixth birthday," Maggie said in a flat tone. "Mom was too sick. You wouldn't come." She scowled at her father.

"You're right. I was grieving." he said.

"Too little, too late." Maggie pushed back her chair and stalked from the room. Bender trotted after her.

Theo grimaced, rubbed his forehead. "That rankles."

After they finished, Rowan filled a plate and, Zephyr at her knee, carried it to her cousin's room. Rowan knocked and opened the door, waiting for neither rebuke nor invitation.

Zephyr went to Bender and touched noses. Maggie patted them both and raised her head.

Rowan noted her swollen eyes. "Here's dinner," she said. "Want to talk?"

Maggie nodded.

Rowan decided to let her cousin start the conversation.

Maggie ate in silence and offered a soft thanks. "I'm totally drawn to Dakota," she breathed. "I don't know if I can stay away. But whatever, however, I'll be cagey. I won't get caught."

"Everyone always gets caught." Rowan stalked around the room, running her fingers through her hair. "You and I made an agreement with Gladys. Remember? Only two hours ago."

"Yeah, we did. I conveniently forgot ever since Dakota caught my eye over dinner. I swear, he saw me as a woman." She played with her thumbnail and let out a big sigh. "It's a first. I'll keep my distance, though. Somehow."

Rowan raised her eyebrow. "So, we're good?"

Maggie groaned. "Damn. Okay, I suppose."

Rowan trudged back to her room with Zephyr. She pressed her hand against her cheek and pensed her dog. *I forgot to ask—too involved with Maggie. Can you feel Andrea-pup?*

Zephyr feels her. No change.

I'm happy distance doesn't make sensing her harder. I'll call Pack Mama and let her know.

The next morning, Maggie announced after breakfast, "I'm going out to weed."

Theo tilted his head. "Since when did you develop an interest in garden maintenance? You never suggested helping out before."

She shrugged. "Guess I'm growing up. You're heading up Bender's Ridge, right?"

"Yes, and after the hike, I need to shower and leave for the hospital—we'd better say our goodbyes now. Remember to let me know if you're riding back with me. I'll leave early Friday morning."

"So far, so good. Shall I call you Thursday evening to confirm?" Rowan asked.

"Please. And make it after 8 p.m. I'm in consultations until then."

A couple of hours later, Maggie came back to the ranch kitchen loaded with produce. "Look what we picked. I love pea pods, and here's a load of them."

"We?" Rowan frowned and studied her cousin.

"Yeah, well, Dakota and me." She cast a sideways glance at Rowan.

"So did we have an agreement last night, or not? Weeding together? Not exactly keeping your distance, is it?"

Maggie shrugged. "Nothing happened. We weeded and talked."

"Gladys said no private conversations." Rowan planted her hands on her hips. "He doesn't seem warm. He feels hurt, guarded, on edge. You're clear, I hope, you can't fix him?"

"I don't know. Love can solve lots of problems."

Rowan stared at her, incredulous. "What's love got to do with this? You only met the dude."

"Well, it feels like love."

"Infatuation, maybe. Love? Unlikely. Love grows over time."

"You think you know all about it?" Maggie snarled.

Rowan put her hands up in the air, palms toward Maggie. "I don't. But I do know some stuff about … human nature, I guess."

"We're both sixteen. How come you think you grasp more than me?"

"I woke from the coma different. Changed. Understanding things I didn't know before the accident. Like the big field."

Maggie raised her eyebrows and nodded. "Well, true. But you've never had a relationship with a guy."

"Right. And I'm not ready, either."

"Maybe I am."

Rowan walked across the room and back. "All I can tell you is, he's in trouble. I'm not suggesting he's a bad person. I don't know. But war hurt him, and worse than Mossy. He's got a ton of stuff to figure out."

"Well, I've got a ton of stuff to figure out, too. We can do it together."

"What?" Rowan shook her head, unclear whether she was enraged, frustrated, or terrified for her friend. "You're deluded. And if you don't know what it means, look it up. Come on, Zephy, Maggie's not listening." On the way out, she slammed the kitchen door.

Bender whined, a low, moaning, melancholy sound. It tore at Rowan's heart. She went back to her room—Zephyr right behind—and flung herself on the bed, pounding her pillow. Her very best friend had strayed, and there was no one she could talk to about it.

Chapter Twenty-five

Zephyr knows something is wrong, but her girl isn't pensing. She's gone inside. Zeph crawls onto the bed and pushes her nose into Rowan's neck, snuffling in her scent. She nudges, and her girl rolls over, curls around, and holds on tight.

She's gone, Zephy. Maybe for years, maybe for good. She and Bender were beginning to get the hang of pensing, and now she's lost interest.

Zephyr is puzzled. *Not gone. She's in the making-food-room with Bender.*

I don't mean gone away. Stupid human stuff. All she can think of is that broken man. She's lost her mind.

Lost her mind?

You know, like when a male dog is near a female, ready to breed?

But she's female.

She's crazy with lust. All of her attention is on him.

Does she breed?

She'd better not. If she does, and Kibble Man finds out, we may not be able to come back.

The big land is home. Kibble Man comes back.

Rowan rubs her puffy eyes. *You're right, but Maggie and Bender may not be allowed to come. I wish I could tell someone.*

Zephyr penses her a picture of Gladys. *She helps.*

Gladys? Are you sure?

Zephyr keeps her gaze on her girl.

Won't she send us home?

She helps.

ꝏ

The following morning, Rowan, thinking she heard the front door close, peered out the window. Maggie and Bender looked like they were heading for the ridge, but was it a ploy to sneak into the barn? She dressed and padded to the kitchen. Seeing the coffee maker had already been used, Rowan knocked softly on Gladys' door.

"Come on in. I'm sipping my pick-me-up." Gladys plumped the pillows, leaned back against the headboard, and patted the bed. "What's on your mind?"

"How'd you know?"

"Can you think of another time you've come knocking on my bedroom door?"

"Oh. Right." Rowan sat. "We've got trouble. Maggie's about to do something stupid."

"Dakota?"

"Yup. She said she's in love with him; she'll be 'cagey.' Her exact word. When I pointed out she'd just met him, she got in my face. You have to stop her."

"Let me think on this." Gladys took some hair pins from the bedside table and, after combing her hair with her fingers, twisted her long gray tresses into a bun. "It's good you came to me." She sipped her coffee and pursed her lips. "I've gotten to know Dakota a little. The man's bright."

"And broken."

"You're right. But he admits it. Let's see where this goes before jumping to any conclusions."

Rowan stared at her. "What? You're not serious."

"I am—quite serious. Think about it. If I step in, Maggie will know you told on her, and you've lost a friend. Permanently, I suspect."

"It's better than her getting hurt."

"That's generous of you; however, I don't agree." Gladys got up and pulled on her flannel robe. "In the long term, your friendship is far more important. You have siblings now. She's an only child; she needs you."

Rowan opened her mouth to speak, but Gladys held up her hand. "Let it play out. I'll keep a watchful eye and step in if needed. You pay attention, too."

"She took off with Bender this morning. Maybe she went straight for the barn and Dakota. I don't know. I'm scared."

Through the kitchen window, Rowan saw Maggie and Bender trudge back, so she assumed they had gone for a long hike. She pressed her trembling hands against her thighs and realized relief was coursing through her. Apparently, her cousin hadn't acted on her stupid thoughts. Yet. Maybe she'd gotten through to her last night.

She was in the middle of baking oatmeal chocolate-chip cookies, and the scent wafted through the house. But Maggie didn't wander into the kitchen to ask for a taste like she usually did.

Zephyr got up to find Bender. They both heard Maggie's door slam. Zeph's ears pinned back and she lay down again, muzzle pressed between her paws. Rowan felt bad for her. Because she and Maggie were on the outs, did their dogs have to be, too? It seemed unfair. She slid the last batch into the oven, washed her hands, and went to soothe Zephyr. "I hope it will blow over," she whispered. "But honestly, I don't know. Maggie is super pissed." She stroked her Zephy's ears. "You know what? I'm pissed too. Our time at the ranch was supposed to be about getting stronger at pensing, not pining for some older guy. She's spoiling everything."

Zeph swiped Rowan's face.

Rowan giggled. *I love your comfort; you always know when I'm upset, even when I'm not pensing. You must be bummed too, what with Bender being off limits now. This sucks. Neither of us has a playmate.*

Zephyr shoved her nose under Rowan's elbow, thrusting it into the air.

She laughed out loud. *Yes, we have each other, but I know it's wonderful to run together. You must be missing it. Dogs need dogs, too.*

Zeph sat and looked at her. *Zephyr misses Bender and Jazz.*

In the afternoon, Rowan took a bucket and brush and went to clean the chicken cubbies, venting her rage and frustration on the encrusted dirt. It was hard work and took a while, but she always felt better for the birds when the job was done. After all, she wouldn't like a dirty house. She used a toothbrush in addition to the larger scrubbing one, and emptied and refilled the bucket four times. Zephyr lay outside the fence, watching.

Rowan heard something and peeked through a crack. Repeatedly looking over her shoulder, Maggie walked toward her. Rowan's heart thudded and she instinctively ducked, thwacking her head on the edge of a cubicle. But Maggie passed by the coop and into the barn. Swearing silently, Rowan sucked in a breath and rubbed her forehead. She could feel the lump growing.

"Need a break?" Gladys stood at the coop door. "Here's some lemonade. Take a moment."

"Thanks."

"Your kindness toward animals is beautiful. You do for the birds; I do for you."

Rowan heard Dakota's voice. Loud. "Jesus, what the fuck do you think you're up to?"

They strained to hear Maggie's response, but Rowan couldn't make out words. She could only hear her cousin's pleading tone.

"Don't ruin this for me!" His voice rose.

More of Maggie's beseeching she couldn't understand.

"You don't get it," Dakota snarled. He wasn't yelling, but the intensity carried. "Without this peace, this opportunity, I'm a *dead* man."

Wracking sobs.

"Back off! You're half my age, only a kid. Get the hell out. Don't come back."

A moment later, Rowan heard footsteps pounding down the barn stairs. Maggie fled across the circle and into the ranch house, banging the outside door. Bender didn't make it in and stood on the porch, looking deflated and bewildered.

"Well." Gladys said, softly. "I thought Dakota could handle himself. Probably Maggie will come to you for comfort."

Rowan stared at her, eyes wide. "You knew this would happen?"

Gladys nodded. "It's the very best way—no fallout on you. Or me. We can deal with her hurt feelings, but the alternative? It would have been far messier."

Zephyr loped over to join Bender on the porch. They touched noses, then lay down to wait.

"Do you think I should go to her?"

Gladys shook her head. "Not yet. It's best if she comes to you. If she doesn't show up for dinner, take her a plate like before." She picked up the lemonade glass. "I surely hope you two can have a few nice weeks here now. We should know by tomorrow."

"Tomorrow's when I have to tell Theo if we're staying or going home."

Gladys put a hand on Rowan. "Let's keep this to ourselves. I'm not informing her father, and I suggest you don't tell your parents, either. It's enough Maggie has to deal with the humiliation. It's plenty of punishment."

"You sure are wise. And you never even raised—" She clapped her hand over her mouth, hoping she hadn't hurt Glady's feelings.

"Oh girl, I had many of them, all the kids who came through the library week after week over the last twenty years. They raised *me* up in the ways and wiles of youngsters." She smiled and put an arm over Rowan's shoulder. "And I love every one of them. They're my children. You are, too."

Maggie didn't show up for dinner as Gladys had predicted. Rowan heard her let Bender in. After helping with clean up, she prepared a plate and carried it to Maggie's room. This time, she knocked. "Here's your dinner, couz."

Long silence. "Set it by the door."

"Come find me when you want."

No response.

Chapter Twenty-six

A soft rap pulled Rowan from the depths of sleep. She glanced at the clock. 2:25 a.m.

"Row? Can I come in?"

She knuckled her eyes and rolled to a sitting position. Zephyr woke and jumped off the bed. "Sure. I hope Bender is with you. Zephy's lonely."

The door opened, and the Doberman shot into the room. The two dogs sniffed and danced with delight.

"I hadn't realized how much they missed each other," Maggie said. "Now I feel terrible on top of awful." She dropped to her knees to hug the dogs.

"Don't be so hard on yourself. Do you want a cup of sleepy tea? Let's go make it." She threw her arm around Maggie and squeezed her as they walked to the kitchen.

"I've been such a dweeb."

"I can't disagree. But you're here now. Sit, and I'll brew us some." Rowan switched on the under-cabinet lights and busied herself getting out the bags and finding the teapot. When she looked at her cousin, she almost choked with shock. "What did you *do*?" Her hair had been shorn to a ragged inch. Obviously, she'd tackled it with scissors and misery. Rowan went to her and wrapped her in a hug. She felt Maggie shake and, soon enough, she broke into full-blown sobbing.

"I've b-b-been such a f-fool. H-he hates me. Now I c-can't even be his f-friend."

"Mags, it happens. We're kids. We do stupid things." Rowan poured the water.

"He y-yelled at me."

"I heard," Rowan admitted. "I was cleaning the chicken coop. Harsh, huh?"

"Yeah, but he was r-right. I p-put him at awful r-risk. All I could think about was m-myself." Maggie clamped her arms around herself. "How can I ever f-face him?"

"Let's pour tea, and I'll get scissors to neaten up your 'do. It'll be super cute. All you need is a little gel—I've got some you can try."

Maggie swiped her eyes dry. "Th-thanks. Look at our d-dogs, how happy they are to be reunited."

"It's been hard." She hugged Maggie again.

"I don't think I can stay here right now. Can we go home?" Her face was screwed into a picture of shame. "I can't face him. Not ever."

"I want to stay—we were going to work on pensing here. For starters, don't you think you owe him an apology?"

Maggie's eyes opened wide; her mouth circled into an O. "Apologize? I have to do *that*?"

Just before sunrise, Rowan was awakened by Zephyr punching her nose into her armpit, woofing. She sat bolt upright and pensed her dog. *Is something wrong?* Maggie had fallen asleep next to her; she signaled Zephy to follow her into another room.

Andrea pup. Different. Talk to Pack Mama.

Can it wait? It's not sunup yet.

Talk.

Hands shaking, Rowan went back into her room and felt for her cell. Where had she left it? What if something serious was happening? She trembled so badly she had to sit down and breathe for a moment, try and think where she'd used it last. *Kitchen. The kitchen island.* She scurried quietly as she could and flipped on the light. There. She pounced on it, typed in her password, and dialed. It rang a long time. She hung up and called again.

Six rings before her mom answered. "Rowan? Are you all right?"

"Yes. It's Andrea. Zephyr says there've been changes. You need to call her doctor immediately."

"Oh my God, I'll go check. The minute I know something, I'll phone."

"Okay, bye."

"Thank you. Pat the big girl for me." The call ended, and she could imagine her mother shaking Moss awake and racing for Teal's room.

Rowan knew she couldn't sleep anymore. After praising Zephy and pensing Pack Mama's thanks, she closed the kitchen door to reduce noise while she made a mocha. Although her hands were still shaking, the familiarity of the machine's rumble helped calm her. After she steamed the milk and dispensed the espresso, she poured it into her travel mug and pounded the bottom of the silver chocolate dispenser until a lovely dusting coated the foam. She threw on a coat and carried the drink onto the front porch. Zephyr stayed pressed to her side.

It was light enough to see, although it would be a long while before the sun crested the mountain. Tendrils of mist hung along the ground, clinging thickly around plants and other objects, an other-worldly sight—gorgeous—but not enough to stem anxiety prickling her belly. She repeatedly told herself there would be no news for hours. With a hand dangling to stroke Zephyr's head, she blew out a long breath and settled into the big field, her form of meditation. No repetitions, but moving into presence—the only place she felt truly safe. It wasn't like her life was threatened, but moment to moment, everything was always in flux. Except the big field. In the four years since she'd awakened from the coma, she'd come to depend upon the stability of resting here. Best of all, Zephy met her in this space. It never altered in any way. Always open, transparent, lucid, awake. Her home.

Rowan didn't get a call back until 11 a.m. Body quivering, she steadied her finger to press the green phone icon. "Mama?"

"It's Mossy. Lina's with Andrea. It took them a while, but they diagnosed an abdominal aneurysm—a serious thinning and swelling of a major vessel. They're preparing her for surgery now. If it bursts, she probably wouldn't survive."

"Our poor baby." Her mind swirled. "I'll come home with Theo tomorrow morning. So we can all be together? Da, why'd this happen?"

"Oh, Row, we have no idea. Bum genetic luck, I guess. What about Maggie and Bender? Will they stay at the ranch, or come back as well?"

"We'll all ride with him, get back around five, maybe earlier, if we leave very early."

Rowan could hear her dad thinking, weighing, considering. "Sure. Come home, sweetheart. We can use all the support we can get."

They left Sisters before dawn. The ride home felt interminable; smoke from a fire in Plumas County coated the valley which, on the best of days, was a monotone landscape. It was too foul to open a window or even have the car set to outside air.

Rowan's cell rang. "It's Mossy. Have Theo bring you directly to the hospital, please. Then he can take Zephyr and the rest back home after he drops you off."

"Okay, Da. We'll be there in a couple of hours." She hung up. "Something's wrong," she said. "He didn't sound right and wants you to drop me at the hospital first. Maggie, will you take Zephy and feed her with Bender?"

"Yeah, of course. What'd he say?"

"Nothing other than to come to the hospital. But there was something about the tone of his voice. Scary. I hate this." She pensed her dog so she'd understand what was happening.

The moment they came off the Bay Bridge into San Francisco, Rowan's stomach flip-flopped and didn't stop. Adult responsibilities sucked. She dreaded having to walk into the hospital and, again, realized how it must have been for her mom after the rollover accident.

While Carolina held Andrea in pediatric intensive care, Moss paced the waiting room. Teal sat nearby giving Graham a bottle. "Moss, come feed Graham. It's soothing and life-affirming."

"Thanks, but I'm too nervous." He peered at his watch. "Row's due any time. What the hell am I going tell her?"

"The truth," Teal said. "She's a strong girl. She'll deal."

Moss pinched his brow together with his fingers. "Yes, of course. It's me I'm concerned about. I don't want to lose it. The family needs me to be strong."

"And you are. No question." Teal stood and walked to Moss, settling Graham in his arms. "He's sleeping now. Look how gorgeous he is. *He* needs you."

Moss stared down at his son. His beautifully formed lips—so like Lina's—still made little nursing sounds. Teal was right. Graham had zoned out. Moss cuddled and rocked him, the motion now as familiar and comfortable as breathing.

Rowan stepped off the elevator twenty minutes later. "Da." Her voice had a little hitch in it.

She's damn intuitive. He handed Graham back to Teal, then wrapped his arms around her. "Sweetie, I'm glad to see you. Come, walk with me."

"It's bad, isn't it."

Moss nodded, and went to sit by the windows where it was quiet. He patted the chair near to him. "Your mom is with your sis." His voice choked. "Andrea's not strong enough, Row. She's dying. I wanted you to get to hold her." He swiveled away. His throat thick as wood, he forged on. "How come we love these little people the moment we lay eyes on them? It's a cruel trick."

Her tears fell steadily, spotting his hand she'd grabbed. "C-can't they do anything? Anything at all?"

He shook his head. "Her heart's failing, and she's not strong enough to undergo heart reconstruction. The surgery yesterday took everything out of her."

"P-poor little thing, st-struggling, only eight weeks old. How's M-mama? Geez, I-I'm s-stuttering."

He patted her. "She can't stop crying. I've never seen her like this."

"No, you haven't. B-but I have, when D-Daddo died. She still had to be strong for me, though. M-maybe it saved her?"

"We're supposed to protect these tiny humans. I'm struggling not to feel guilt—a horrible, powerless guilt. The doctors feel awful, too. Even though they don't say much, you can tell." He held his arms open and invited her in. She laid her head against his chest and wept. He stroked her hair, feeling the springy curls. His throat hurt, and swallowing—his instinctive response to the pain—made it worse. A chunk of unbearable grief, he thought. It's lodged there.

They walked back to Teal.

"Can I see Mama and Andrea now?"

He had to jerk himself out of his own misery to respond to her. "Of course. Come with me. They've given us a little private place."

"What about Teal? Doesn't he get to hold her?"

"I have already," Teal said. "Your folks always include me."

"They'd better. You've spent as much time with Andrea as any of us."

"Yeah, true." His cheeks were wet, too.

"Come with us, Teal," Moss said. "It's time we were all together."

Rowan dragged her feet. Mossy, and Teal holding Graham, followed behind. She saw her mother's uncombed hair first, then her eyes, swollen from weeping.

Carolina reached a hand up. "Oh, thank God. I was afraid you wouldn't make it. Switch places with me. You need to hold—" She couldn't say any more and, with shoulders shaking, stared down at her baby. "We made the doctors promise they wouldn't try to bring her back." She took a shuddering breath. "I couldn't survive their using shock paddles. They've already made it clear they can't save her. Why put her through it?" She gave Andrea to Rowan, then slowly levered herself out of the rocking chair. Row held her tiny sister close.

Her mom was quivering with exhaustion and anguish. "Take one of the rockers, sweetie. She loves the motion."

Rowan glanced at her dad. Mossy was right. Her mom didn't even seem aware of it, but drops poured down her face. "Mommo, this is awful." She sat carefully, never taking her eyes from Andrea. With her foot, she started rocking. She pulled the blanket back from the baby's little face. She was too pale, but her eyes were wide open and, staring up at Rowan, she broke into a slow smile. "Hi, sweet sister," Rowan whispered, her voice breaking. "You hung on 'til I got here."

Andrea peeped, a weaker sound than her squeaky cries at home.

"I love you, little babe." Drops fell on Andrea, who blinked fast. "Oooh, sorry," Row said, and carefully wiped them away with the bottom of her T-shirt.

"She recognized you," Carolina said, leaning back against Mossy, his arms supporting her.

"You think?" Rowan smiled back at her sister and trailed her finger down Andrea's cheek. "I'll remember this forever. Teal, has she smiled at you?"

"Made my day." His voice was gruff. Graham sucked vigorously on the end of Teal's baby finger before falling asleep.

Carolina reached out her arms. "I'd like to hold him. He hasn't had much of me these past couple of days." Teal transferred him carefully so he wouldn't wake up. She sagged into the second rocker and snuggled Graham in the crook of her arm. "He's out," she said. "Nothing sweeter than a sleeping baby." She reached a hand to Andrea, who grabbed her forefinger. "We're all connected," Carolina whispered, drops still sliding down her cheeks.

A few minutes later, Graham startled awake, caterwauling. At the same time, Rowan felt Zephyr's mournful howls. She peered down at Andrea, who'd gone lax in her lap. "Oh no!" She stared wide-eyed at Mossy. "Mama, Da—"

Her mother stared down at her finger. They all saw. Andrea had let go.

Chapter Twenty-seven

Carolina slogged around Theo's guest house. Her chest, a stone, could barely move air. Skin ached all over. Touching or being touched was out of the question, didn't belong in her bleak universe. She stared into the hall mirror at unwashed hair, sloppy pajamas; she fingered the bags under her eyes and looked away.

Graham wailed in the other room. She made no move, but heard Teal open the door and talk softly. It made no sense—she felt horribly guilty—but she resented Graham for being the one to live. He was out of sorts, too, fussy and whining. She knew he missed his sister, but was grieving so badly herself, she wasn't able to enfold or comfort him. Moss and Teal would have to fill her role. She couldn't be a mother, not now, not yet. Hopefully soon. Maybe never. She didn't know. The idea of nursing repelled her. She methodically pumped and froze her milk. Everyone in the house covertly watched and sidled around her—she noticed, and it irked. What did they want from her? *I'm a rotten shambles. Can't they see and leave me alone?*

Moss had made her accompany him to the funeral home to pick out an urn. She didn't care what the hell Andrea's ashes went in. He insisted. The baby urns were impossibly small and the very sight of them made her cry. Luckily, neither of them wanted the style with bas-relief angels the smarmy funeral man assumed they'd choose—their agreement, a single moment of grace in a vast field of misery. They settled on a small, elegant alabaster one. Immediately, Carolina turned on her heel and left. She sat in the car until Moss came out. They drove in silence.

After two weeks had passed, Moss sat her down. "It's time we go home to Bender's Ridge. There's no reason to remain here, no point overstaying. We need to be back in Oregon anyway because Rowan starts school soon. And—" he hesitated. "We need to bury Andrea's ashes. The little graveyard at the ranch is beautiful and peaceful."

"Fine," she muttered. Her surroundings didn't matter; she couldn't see anything but wasteland anyway.

"Sweetheart—" he said.

She heard the faintest pleading in his tone. "Don't," she snarled, more harshly than she intended. "Can't you see I'm in pieces?"

He steepled his fingers and pressed them to his mouth, his gaze fixed on her.

His eyes carried anguish too. She looked away. Would she ever be able to reach out? Grieve with him? Certainly not until she managed to help herself.

Rowan sat on the floor of her room trying to comfort Zephyr. *I'm sad too,* she pensed. *We did what we could. The rest was up to Andrea and the doctors. Pack Mama is grateful for the help you gave.*

Bad happens.

Yes, it did. But I think it helped Pack Mama understand how we talk with each other.

Zephyr plopped her head in Rowan's lap. *Rub ears?*

Of course. Rowan stroked and knuckled Zephy's beautiful ears. *Does this make you feel better?*

Comforts Zephyr. Go to the big land?

Yes, when the sun comes up. A long car drive.

Does Bender come?

Rowan shook her head. *No, only Jazz. Maggie and Bender stay here, where they live. Maggie has to go to school. They'll come visit, though. Maybe in the hot season. After a few sunrises we have to go to the other house so I can start school, too.*

Too long gone.

You have Jazz for company when I'm in class.

Zephyr misses Andrea pup.

Rowan sighed. *Everyone is hurting. We're a mess.*

A mess?

Sad. You know, wet faces, shaking shoulders. Rowan stroked Zephyr. *Come on, I'll make your dinner.*

Moss paced the living room, his eyes on the 2 a.m. San Francisco skyline. They were packed to leave early in the morning. He couldn't bear to lie in bed with Carolina, who had closed up, a wounded turtle since Andrea's death. He paused in front of the window and took a deep breath, trying to relieve the knot of grief lodged in his chest. He'd lost his wife—at least for now—in addition to his beautiful little girl. They needed to support Teal and Rowan, too. Their whole household was a sinkhole of unexpressed emotion. Even Zephyr was depressed. She wouldn't run with Jazz and Bender, but lay curled up tight near the couch or walked slowly to the yard to do her business.

He understood now, better than he cared to, how this kind of strain could rend a family. All it took was one person unwilling to bear another's grief, however it was expressed. One snipe too many, one comment that knifed too deep, and they could be torn apart for good. He couldn't, he wouldn't let that happen.

The seven of them piled in the van at 6:30 a.m.—Rowan and Teal in the back with Graham harnessed in his car seat; Moss driving, with Carolina in the passenger seat; Jazz and Zephyr curled in their beds. Andrea's urn was nestled on a pillow at Carolina's feet.

"Tell me we'll get through this," Rowan mouthed—even softer than a whisper—to Teal. "It's awful. I can't remember when Mossy and Mama have been this quiet."

He leaned in close and spoke in her ear. "I feel it, too. It's disconcerting. Give them time. It's like—" he stopped to think. "Like they have to figure out a new family configuration, minus one. My family went through this. When parents lose a child, the grief is crushing. Kids are supposed to outlive their parents."

"I dread putting her ashes in the ground."

"Yeah, it's final." He sighed and cracked his knuckles. "Oh, sorry. A nervous habit. Burial—it's important, though—a big part of letting go."

The late morning sun warmed the graveyard. It had taken a week to assemble everyone at Bender's Ridge: the grandparents, Pa and Ma, and Shirley; Theo and Maggie; Gladys and Dakota. Teal held Graham. Zephyr and Jazz lay in the shade nearby with Bender.

Rowan had fought to preside over the memorial. She wanted to offer this final gift to her baby sister. "I can do it," she said to Moss. "Wouldn't it be much better to have a family member than some stranger? Surely neither you nor Mama should take this on."

"Okay. Keep it simple," Carolina had said.

Graham fussed in Teal's arms. The new single-child stroller was parked nearby. Moss had quietly disposed of the double stroller and other twin paraphernalia; Carolina couldn't bear the sight. He'd talked to Rowan about it. If he'd put them on Craigslist, people would have asked why they were selling virtually new stuff and he didn't want to answer their questions. It reminded him of the apocryphal six-word story: "For sale: baby shoes, never worn." It had been easier to give the equipment to someone who needed it, and Gladys, who knew everyone in town, picked the recipient and took care of the handover. Bless Gladys.

Rowan walked to the little mound of soil and faced her extended family. "We're here to honor Andrea. We wanted her to outlive us all, but it turned out that wasn't possible." She'd printed out a couple of eight-by-ten color pictures of her little sister, and now she passed them around. She wanted everyone who hadn't gotten to meet her in person to see how cute she was. "Andrea had her own little personality. She peeped and squeaked instead of screaming, and loved when people talked to her. I'm very sad not to get to see her grow up. And I know Graham misses her even though he can't say so yet."

She stopped to dash away a tear. "I bought some bulbs—daffodils and hyacinths—to plant on her grave. I have three trowels. We can put them in the ground today." She asked Teal, "You knew her as well as anyone, do you want to say something?"

"She brightened my days." He took a slow breath. His voice was rough. "I'm going to miss her something awful."

Rowan handed each person five bulbs and gave Moss, Carolina, and Teal the trowels first. "Every spring they'll spread more and bloom for her, and we'll remember. Bless you, Andrea, and Godspeed."

"Thank you," Carolina whispered, hugging her daughter. "And the bulbs—" she had to stop, clear her throat. "What a wonderful thought. Now, you be sure and plant some, too. After I talk with people—they expect it—I'm going up the hill."

Rowan nodded, lip trembling.

After speaking with family she couldn't avoid, Carolina turned to see where Moss was. He stood, head tilted, looking at her with naked longing. She made a gesture, an acknowledgment and don't-follow-me, all in one, and trudged in the direction of Bender's Ridge.

Step by step, Carolina walked away from her daughters—one in the ground, one very much alive—her baby son, and Moss. She didn't know how to be with anyone, didn't know how to be with herself, either. She needed to escape from her own too-tight skin.

She stopped midway up the hill to catch her breath. The sun was out, but the day seemed gray, dull, thick. She looked back down the path and at the graveyard. Squinting, she noticed a figure. It was Moss—alone now, and very still—staring at the small mound. Something about the cant of his body made her fold over, and it was then she realized what set her off. He was weeping, too.

Carolina reached the top of Bender's Ridge. The sun was warm, but felt unpleasant on her face. *How can time keep rolling along? Shouldn't it stop, grant me some breathing room?* She was missing an important, a crucial body part, and yet the days inexorably carried on, taking her further and further away from Andrea. Already eighteen days, eighteen nights gone. She sat and wrapped her arms around her knees. *Moss and I—we have such different ways of grieving. He wants me close, wants to touch, talk. I can't bear the feel of anyone's hand, most of all his. What are we going to do? It's probably the end of us.* She felt nothing at the thought—no sadness or even regret—only leaden weight bearing down.

∞

Moss was left tending a large family crew, trying to make them feel comfortable while he was a hollowed-out gourd, scraped clean of anything he recognized. He ached for Carolina, but was furious, too. She wasn't responding like he'd anticipated from knowing her for over four years, and he didn't know how to reach out, bridge their differences. Everything he tried infuriated her. He hardly recognized the person she'd become. Where was his loving wife who adored cuddling and talking? *Why won't she share with me? I need it so badly.*

After feeding everyone lunch—with Rowan's and Teal's help—he poured a glass of merlot and slumped in an Adirondack chair outside. He didn't care he was drinking before 5 p.m. Carolina hadn't come back. Worry snaked through him.

He heard the front door close, quiet footsteps approaching. Ma, he thought. Shit.

But when she bent over him, rested a hand on his heart, he was glad for her company. She settled into the chair nearest him. He glanced over—she, too, held wine. So like her—she'd noticed he had a drink and wanted to keep him company, make him feel comfortable. No talking required. Silence reigned for a good twenty minutes.

She reached over and took his hand. "She's in trouble, isn't she?"

He nodded.

"It's like you were when you got back from Afghanistan. Shell-shocked. Frozen inside."

"Yeah."

"Are you scared?" She shook her head. "Dumb question. Of course you are."

His throat lumped up. It hurt to form words, and they came out sandpapery. "She's my everything. Was my everything. I don't know, Ma. Are we done for?" His throat lumped up. "I'm not scared. I'm terrified."

"It's way too early for talk like that." She patted his leg. "Are you taking anti-depressants? You should be."

"I'm still on a low dose, was thinking of going off before this happened. Guess I'd better not. I may need to up it."

"Good idea." She tipped her chin in the direction of the barn. "Here she comes. I hope you can encourage her to get evaluated. Soon. Please take good care of yourself." She stood up. "I'll go find your dad, leave you to it. Oh—Rowan did such a beautiful job presiding."

He watched Carolina trudge across the circle. She wasn't striding today.

"Hi," she said, not quite meeting his eyes.

"I go up there to clear my head, too." He reached up to her. "Come sit with me in the bedroom. In private."

She didn't take his proffered hand, but acknowledged him and followed behind. Moss shut the door after her. He didn't even try to touch her. He cleared his throat, striding back and forth before sitting across from her. "Sweetheart, I think you're profoundly depressed."

"Well, yeah. What else could I be? My infant daughter died."

"*Our* infant daughter," he said through clenched teeth. "Don't leave me out." He twiddled his thumbs around each other. "You need help to deal—"

"Therapy?" She broke in, her face a rictus of horror.

He gave a harsh chuckle. "Not therapy. I wouldn't suggest it to you. Medication. A little anti-depressant boost out of this heavy gray cloud."

"Heavy gray cloud?" She stared at him. "How can you know?"

"Lina, my love—I've suffered bouts of severe depression. I recognize it. It's a dark caul covering you. There's no shame in getting assistance."

She hung her hands between her knees, then erupted in a humorless snicker. "Oh God, I suppose I can try."

"I'll make an appointment with our doc in Eugene. For later this week."

She squirmed in her chair. "Can't it wait?"

"No," he said, softly. "I can't wait."

Chapter Twenty-eight

Moss hiked with Jazz to Bender's Ridge the morning after Andrea's burial to catch the sunrise. He lowered himself to sitting, stretched out his prosthesis, and folded his arms around his knee. *I feel horrible waking up alone in our bed. Can it possibly make Carolina feel better to sleep by herself?* He stared out at the familiar mountainscape.

Well, wait a minute—come to think.... He'd spent almost two years hiding out after coming home from Afghanistan. Even as loneliness overtook him, he simply couldn't be around people, make light conversation, or converse at all; rarely could stand being touched except by his fellow veteran Jesse because, since she shared war experience, she understood. *It must be equally bad for Carolina.* Could he possibly wait as long as she needed to come around? He rubbed his forehead, ran fingers through his hair. *Scary.*

No one had drummed fingers for him to pull out of depression after his fiancée, Sophie, dumped him. It would've been awful—someone foot-tapping impatiently while he tried to get it together. *Is that what I've been doing with Lina?* He pushed to standing, considering this revelation. Insights often came here on the Ridge. *I'm a big boy; I can wait.* But what about Graham? An infant needs his mama. Not having her could change his life forever—he might feel abandonment, depression, rage, even the sense he'd done something wrong by being the one to live. This was his real worry: baby Graham. While he waited for Lina to come around, he'd focus on his son.

Moss stretched his arms wide, inhaled a deep breath of the sharp, dry, late-summer air. The sun now warmed his face. Time to head back.

Banging and bustling in the kitchen woke Carolina. She yanked the pillow over her head. *I hate having them here. Can't they go home?* Every morning she awakened into a personal nightmare—another day to drag herself through with Graham, Moss, Rowan—even Teal—all wanting her. She cupped her face in her hands. She hadn't felt like crawling deep into the ground after Rafe died. Why now? It'd been awful, but she'd had to pull herself together for Rowan. Now, Row could more or less take care of herself.

What she was going through felt too intimate to share with anyone, even—especially—Moss. She knew she was supposed to be open, grieve with him, but how could she tell him she wanted to hole up and die? And what did it say about mothering Rowan? Had she loved little Andrea more than her older daughter? Immediately, she knew it wasn't true. Babies, though, were uncomplicated. Nurse, comfort, change them, talk to them. Teenagers—complex. She couldn't seem to get her rhythm with Row; instead, she was always stepping in messes of her own making. *Can't I love the girl as she is?*

She knew Moss was right about anti-depressants, although she hated admitting she was weak. *Hold on—I don't see him as weak. Why am I so hard on myself?*

Carolina rolled over and buried deeper under the downy—into the warmth. *If I hide long enough, I can make the world vanish.*

Rowan heard the jingle of the "food's-on" bell and, tucking T-shirt into jeans, headed for the dining room. She pulled up short. Wow—a whole brunch-like spread. Mossy and Teal pulled this together? Pa and Ma had already filled their plates with steaming scrambled eggs, bacon, English muffins. Grandma Shirley was digging a spoon into the grits bowl, trying to bat her scarf out of the way with her other hand. Rowan went to her, snagged the scarf ends, and tucked them into her grandmother's neckline at the back.

"Thanks, sweetie pie. I've always got something dangling."

"You wouldn't be you without your dangles and bangles and long skirts, now would you?" She kissed her grammie's cheek.

"Aww, sweet. Isn't your mom going to join us?"

"I doubt it." Rowan lowered her voice. "She's having a tough time with everyone here. Even these precious people. Losing Andrea has taken her down, way worse than when Daddo died."

Looking thoughtful, her grandmother knocked grits off the spoon onto her plate. "I should do a read—"

"No!" The forcefulness shocked even Rowan. Family members turned around to see what was going on.

Her grandmother drew back, startled.

"Sorry." Rowan heard the pleading in her own tone. "You know Mom. It'd make everything worse."

Her grandmother's eyes brimmed. "I want to help. I don't know another way."

"You being here is wonderful for Mossy and me. Graham and Teal, too. You're so sweet with our little guy. There's nothing anyone can do for Mom. Mossy's trying, but even he can't get through to her. She has to find her own way."

"You're such a wise one, little love."

"You haven't called me that in forever."

"You'll always be my little love."

Moss heard Graham tune up and was about to go get him, but Teal scooted in. Bless Teal. A few minutes later, he came back out, singing a soft ditty with Graham nestled in the crook of his arm. The little guy continued to fuss.

"He's been cranky ever since his sis died," Teal said. "I worry about him."

"You know the swing in the garden?" Rowan said. "I bet the motion will soothe him. One of us should give it a try."

"On my way," Teal called. "Hadn't thought of it."

Twenty minutes later, Moss walked out to check on them, Jazz at his side. Graham was sucking his thumb, staring up at Teal, who kept the swing moving. Calm.

"Look—her suggestion worked."

Teal smiled. "Sure 'nuf. Your daughter's intuitive. I listen up when she speaks."

Moss sat on the swing next to him and continued the rhythm, giving Teal a break. Ever-cautious Jazz settled nearby, out of smacking range of the swing. "She was aware at eleven when I met her. Now, she's a canny, wise soul in a teenage body."

Teal laughed out loud. "Yeah, not expected in teens. Can we get a swing like this for the Eugene house?"

"Sure. We'll put it under cover on the patio. Then we can swing in rainy weather, too. Any special features?"

"Room for at least two. As little squeaking as possible," Teal responded.

"Will do. On another subject, how are *you* coping? You spent so much time with Andrea."

"I miss her something terrible," Teal said. "But my selfish worry is, with only one baby, you might not need me anymore."

Moss hooted. "No chance. Haven't you figured it out? Carolina and I agree; you're a member of this clan as long as you want to be."

Relief softened Teal's anxious face. "That's good news."

"And you'll have a bit more time to write since, when he's asleep, there's no one else howling for attention." Moss's voice caught at the end. He tucked his head, twiddled thumbs between his knees.

"Here, hold your son. It helps." Teal nestled Graham into Moss's arms. "Shouldn't I use the extra time helping out around the house?"

Moss cozied the baby close. "No, you shouldn't take on more chores. Write. You've got talent."

"Thanks. Will you check with Carolina? I'm real worried about her."

"Me, too," Moss said. "I've pushed her to go on anti-depressants, made an appointment Friday in Eugene with her primary."

"Thank God," Teal said. "This little guy needs her."

"We all do."

Pack Mama's sick, Zephyr penses Rowan. She presses against her girl's feet. They're lying on Rowan's bed in Eugene.

Yes, she's sad-sick. Kibble Man tries to help. She sees the doctor later this week. And after three night-sleeps, I start school.

Long away time. Zephyr bumped her knee.

Afraid so. I wish you could come with me.

Kibble Man keeps Zephyr close when my girl is gone. Kibble Man throws the ball. Zephyr and Jazz run.

Rowan curls around her. *I know he watches out for you. It makes me happy.*

A few days later, Carolina and Moss sat in their doctor's waiting room. "Do I have to do this?" she whispered. "We could wait and see."

"We're past waiting and seeing, love. We did that already." He patted her thigh. "I don't think you realize the dimension of change. Knowing how far I fell down the rabbit hole, it's scary for me to watch. And, in my experience—remember, I've been through this—letting depression get too deeply embedded isn't a good idea. It's bad for Graham, too. I'd like to come in with you for a few minutes. I haven't seen her since my appointment six months ago."

She tilted her head, frowning. "How come?"

As he beamed love, he kept his response simple. "She may want my reflection."

Carolina huffed. "Yeah, okay, I guess. It makes sense. I can't see myself right now."

Half an hour passed. "Let's go," she said, standing up. "I'm sick of sitting here. This was a bad idea."

"Hold on." He walked up to the receptionist. "Awful long wait for Kathleen today. Any estimate?"

"Ten minutes or so."

He lowered his voice. "My wife's here for depression and she's about to bolt. Can you at least put us in an exam room?"

"Got it. Less than a minute."

A nurse opened the door and called them back.

In the tiny room, Carolina drummed her fingers on the armrest. The nurse took her temperature and blood pressure. Fifteen minutes later, Dr. Friedmann knocked and walked in.

"Sorry about the delay." She sat and looked directly at Carolina, who burst out crying.

"We lost our little girl. I can't get out of bed in the morning. I'm a mess." She hunched over in the chair. "I haven't cried much. It's like I'm frozen."

Kathleen reached out and touched her arm. "You've had a shocking loss. One way the body has of dealing is to shut down when feelings are overwhelming."

"Moss wants me to go on antidepressants. I don't know. Drugs don't seem like an answer. Shouldn't I be stronger?"

"Needing medication isn't a sign of weakness." Kathleen asked more questions, directing some to Carolina and others to Moss. "How's your son? Graham, right?"

"Real cranky," Carolina admitted. "It's hard for me to warm up to him since Andrea died."

"Another reason to consider medication. Infant trauma is a real thing—there's new research. He needs you." Kathleen reached for a prescription pad. "Let's try this. Antidepressants can have side effects. Over the years, I've come up with a tactic. I'll write you two prescriptions. Fill only one. If you have a bad reaction like sweating or nausea, call—I'll let you know if you should fill the second scrip, depending on your feedback. These two are in the same class of drugs, so you can stop the first and start the second the following day. Sometimes it takes four or five tries to find one you tolerate well. Oh—you can take these and breastfeed."

"Some good news," Carolina said.

"I'll leave now," Moss said, "and let you two have privacy."

Moss glanced over at Carolina on the way home. It hurt that she wept with their doctor, but not with him. He was her husband, for God's sake. Had he done something wrong? Shit, he'd tried in every way to reach out, support her. It felt like a slap in the face.

Chapter Twenty-nine

"Can peace of mind really be found in a pill?" Carolina fiddled with the bottle, turning it round and round on the way home from the pharmacy.

"It softened the sharp edges for me," Moss said. "The mindfulness stuff, learning to be here, now, in the present—and not stuck in war memories—was only possible once my chemistry came into better balance."

"Maybe, if this works, you could teach me about it," she said, softly.

"Sure." Moss kept his eyes on the road, but he wanted desperately to see her expression. He was surprised at her interest.

When they got home, Carolina went straight to the kitchen sink and filled a glass of water. She tipped a pill into her palm and stared at it. "Wow, they're tiny." She held his gaze as she swallowed it. "Oh, dear Lord, let this work."

By morning, Carolina was sweating profusely. "Do you think this will stop?" She pulled her drenched tee shirt away from her skin.

"Give it another twenty-four hours," Moss said. "If it doesn't stop, call the office. This is miserable. I'm sorry."

Kathleen switched her to the second prescription, which Carolina started early the following morning. By late afternoon, she hung over the toilet, retching. This time, Moss called a few minutes before the office closed.

"Take her off it," Kathleen advised. "Tell her to drink lots of water for seventy-two hours before starting the new prescription. I called it in to the pharmacy. I hope she has better luck with this one. But if not, there'll be a fourth one on file."

The following morning, Carolina clunked the third bottle down on the counter, filled a twelve-ounce glass of water. "I'm only willing to try five medications," she snapped. "The side effects are worse than depression. And now I have to glug down all this water before I can even start."

She groused and sniped through the next three days. "Okay, wish us all luck," she warned her family, staring down at the new oval beige pill. "This one's called Celexa."

Two days passed with no side effects, and Moss sighed in relief. Now, if only it eased her depression. The drug sheet said it might take six to eight weeks to mitigate the worst of her symptoms.

Two weeks in, he noticed she was sleeping better. A week after, he caught her smiling at Graham.

Pack Mama gets well, Zephyr penses Rowan.

Yeah, I noticed she's smiling some. She smooths her hand over the crown of her dog's head and down her back, feeling the knobs of her vertebrae.

The boy pup screams less. Better for Zephyr. Loud.

More peaceful around here, too. Okay, I've gotta study.

Walk now?

She focuses on her. They'd missed their walk yesterday. *Sure. Get your leash. And Jazz.*

Zephyr tears out of the room, slips at the corner, pedals to stay on her paws. Rowan chuckles. If only people had such simple delights.

Four weeks later, Carolina rolled over and glanced at the clock. 5:40 a.m. She felt decent this morning, and her sleep had not been rent with nightmares for a week now. Small successes. She listened for Graham. Not a peep. She figured Moss was already hard at work writing; the least she could do was make him a mocha and take it out to the yurt. Yawning and stretching, she pulled on sweats and padded out to the kitchen. She busied herself making his drink, but when the tart, pungent scent of freshly-ground coffee wafted up, she realized, for the first time in months, it smelled delicious. Two mochas were in order. She thought about it, and made hers decaf.

Before she put chocolate on top, she went to the front hall and slipped her feet into clogs for the trip outside. Going back to the kitchen, she dusted both mugs, and made for the yurt with them in hand.

Moss must have felt her coming, because she saw him glance up, eyebrows raised. He opened the door. "Well, hey! What kindness for a struggling writer. This is unexpected. Thanks."

She smiled and handed it to him. "You need to concentrate," she said.

"Hey—you brought your mocha. Please stay for a few minutes." Not wanting to be distracted, he snapped off his computer monitor and swiveled his chair.

She sat in the recliner nearby.

"Our baby boy isn't up yet?"

"Not a sound. Probably soon, though." She took a sip, reveled in the bold taste.

"You're drinking coffee?"

"Yep. First day it's smelled appealing in months." She fingered the rim. "No nightmares last night."

"More good news. It's a warrior's blessing, and you're a warrior for sure."

Carolina quirked a one-sided smile. "Want a good-morning hug?"

His eyes flew open wide. "You bet." He rose to meet her. She brought him in close.

"Oh my God," he choked out, followed by a heaving sob. "I'm sorry—I didn't intend to break down."

She ran her fingers through his curls. "You've been so patient with me. I know it's been terribly hard."

"Whatever it takes," he whispered, "to get you back."

"I want to start sleeping in our bedroom again," she said, softly. "We've got to take it slow, though."

His eyebrows whizzed up. "Yes, ma'am."

∞

As Moss limped toward the bedroom to undress and do stump care, he saw Carolina still nursing Graham in the living-room rocker. The sight of her, so open with their son, filled him with relief and delight. "See you in a bit," he said in a stage whisper, not wanting to disturb their boy.

"He's about to drop off. Another ten minutes," she said, softly.

"Where's Teal?"

"Writing, I think."

Moss gave a thumbs up.

He was still massaging cream into the stub of his leg when Lina came in. He glanced up and smiled. "Welcome home. Is sweet Graham asleep?"

"Yep. And thank God for little beige pills," she said, her tone wry. "They made this possible—sleeping in here again, being cuddly with our son."

"Depression truly is a form of hell. Spoken by one who knows. Thanks for taking my advice."

"Uh, you didn't give me a choice."

He steepled his hands and tapped his nose with his forefingers. "You're right. I hope you'll forgive me."

"Already done." She got into bed facing the outside.

He slipped in next to her. "I understand we aren't making love, but I sure would appreciate a snuggle."

"You know I'll cry," she confided, rolling over on her back.

"For as long as you need," he whispered. "C'mere." He slid an arm under her and invited her in. As soon as she moved close, the tears flowed. After a long while, they eased, and he asked, "Why more when we're together?"

"Because we made her together," she stuttered out, weeping again. She fisted his chest. "Will I ever get past this?"

He thought for a moment. "Life will keep coming at us; that's what life does. Will we ever stop missing her? No, of course not. I wouldn't want to. But the memory will soften, and we'll recall sweet stuff more than sadness. That's how it was with my grief after I lost Frank in Afghanistan. Different with our baby, though."

"I can't bear being vulnerable right now."

"Is that why sex seems out of the question? Too defenseless?"

"Yes. But I *will* get there."

They were quiet for a while. Carolina's head rested against his beating heart. "Sweetie, when are the American Literary Society awards presented?" she asked. "You need to go."

"What made you think of the awards? I got an email this morning. December fourth. You'll come with me? Actually, all of us should go. Teal and Rowan both write. There's a whole conference on craft. They'll eat it up."

Shifting against him, she said, "I'll come, of course. Maybe I can sit out some of it, and stay at the hotel with Graham. It'd free Teal to enjoy it and allow me to stay out of the fray."

"I'm glad you'll be with us," he said.

She went unusually still. Finally, after a couple of minutes, he asked, "What is it?"

"I have tell you something. Complete change of subject."

Her tremulous voice shook him. His heart rate shot up. "Okay, I'm listening."

"Remember when I told you about being raped?"

"I couldn't forget."

She pushed out of his arms and sat. "I," she stumbled, and cleared her throat. "I…" This time she got out of bed, grabbed her robe from the chair, pulled it on, and looked at him. "I got pregnant."

"What? You never told me. Why not?"

"No, I didn't." She walked back and forth. "I knew I couldn't raise a child conceived in violence. For one thing, I would never know who fathered the baby. I couldn't bear it."

He rolled to sitting, and perched on the edge of the bed. "And?"

"I went to get an abortion—figured it made the most sense. But," her voice trailed off.

He waited. Silence yawned between them.

"The women, they were all chatting in the waiting room. One was even eating a cookie. Not me. I was miserable, busy considering the ramifications of what I was about to do."

He knew this wasn't the time to speak.

"I walked out. I want women to have the choice. It turns out I couldn't do it."

Each time Carolina stopped talking, a new cavern opened in the room, unapproachable and dangerous.

"I figured I'd give the baby up for adoption. B-but..." Again, she stopped. The tension stretched between them. "At five and a half months—I was just showing—I lost the baby. S-stillbirth." She dashed away tears. "A little girl." Apparently unable to stand any longer, she folded onto the floor. "Th-they did an au-autopsy. Sh-she had a severe heart defect." Carolina raised her face. "The doctors said it had no specific cause, just b-bad luck. Eighteen years later, An-Andrea came. Since it happened again, it might have been me. M-my genes."

Moss stared at her. None of it dragged on him except she hadn't shared it. *Shit.* Rage and grief braided together, roiled through his torso. "Didn't you trust ... why didn't you tell me? Jesus, Carolina—I thought we were honest with each other; we could depend on it."

Andrea's diagnosis and death must have been doubly awful. He wanted to go to her, comfort her, but he couldn't. *What else is she hiding from me? Do all women hide the truth? Or only the women I get involved with?*

He snapped his fingers for Jazz—who leapt to her feet—grabbed his crutches, and left the room, smacking the door behind them. Jazz pressed her nose to his leg and stayed with him as he grabbed a jacket and stomped to the yurt. He slammed the door hard, with all the satisfaction of rage. He plunked down on the bed, face in his hands, and swore until the anger washed out of him.

He raised his head and saw Jazz cowering under his desk. "Oh pup," he said, his voice very soft, "I'm not mad at you. I'm so sorry." He crutched slowly to her and, murmuring little nothings, eased himself to the floor. Finally, she put her head in his lap. "I forgot. Damn thoughtless of me. You'll never forget your previous owner's mean treatment, will you?" He stroked her ears, brushed his lips across the top of her head. The tension drained out of her. "Come on, sweet pea." He pushed himself to standing and went to the bed, which he patted, inviting her up. She tilted her head, pondering him carefully to make sure it was all right. "Free dog," he whispered. She jumped up and, with a little groan, curled in a tight ball. He tucked her in with a couch throw.

Moss lay awake for a long time, his hand resting on Jazz, his heart a ponderous, angry weight. Sophie, before he went to Afghanistan, had lied to him—twice—and, like Carolina, lies of omission. When he'd confronted her about being covert, even underhanded, she hadn't seen any problem with her behavior at all. The interaction had left him feeling a little crazy, as though his need for truth wasn't valued. Then he'd gone into battle, and staying alive was all that mattered.

He thought of his wife lying alone in their bed, undoubtedly thrown by his reaction and anxious about what might unfold. *I can't even look at her right now.*

Carolina was scrambling eggs in the kitchen when Moss limped in the next morning.

"I'm going to the ranch for a few days," he said, his tone gruff. "Alone."

"Can't we talk about this now?"

Moss shook his head. "Sorry. I need time." He walked out the door.

Chapter Thirty

Carolina lurched against the door frame, dumbfounded, while Moss opened the 4Runner, invited Jazz in, and drove off. "He's leaving, damn him, without talking it through," she muttered through clenched teeth, not wanting to wake either Graham or Teal.

Weak-kneed, she clung to the wood.

Rowan stumbled into the room, dressed, but still rubbing her eyes. "Did I hear Mossy's car? He was supposed to take me to school. Where'd he go all in a hurry?"

Carolina struggled to keep her voice steady. "Bender's Ridge."

Her daughter's eyes widened. "Did you have a fight?"

"We'll get through it," she said, unsure if that was true. "Grab your books. I'll drive you to school."

Carolina had the comfort of Zephyr's companionship as she slogged through the day, tending to laundry, caring for Graham. No Teal, though. He had time off and went to meet with someone on campus. Moss felt far away, their lines of connection cut. She ached for his sweet presence. Why hadn't she ever told him about the pregnancy? Was it because she hadn't talked with him about the heart defect, or because she simply hadn't told him at all? She had no idea. But surely, there were events in his life he hadn't shared.

She tried to imagine what he was doing at the ranch, and figured his first stop would be the ridge. She saw him in his spot, back supported by his favorite tree, scanning the vast mountain vista. When Moss was upset, he hungered for the wide view. Disquiet spread through her. She pressed her hands against her thighs. What buttons had she inadvertently pressed?

Rowan sat in the classroom, unable to concentrate. Her mind was caught by her parents having a fight so intense her dad drove three hours to get away. She'd already lost one father. Mossy walking out rattled her. She was angry with him, and worried about her mother. She pensed Zephyr, *is Mom okay?*

Pack Mama cries, came back the answer.

Give her extra attention, please, Rowan pensed.

Zephyr here with Pack Mama.

Good. It's what she needs. Rowan tried to tune back into her American history teacher's monologue, but it was flat and uninteresting. She glanced at the wall clock. Only five more minutes. Then English, the one bright spot in this scary day.

Zephyr presses against Pack Mama, who is on the bed, weeping.

"Thanks for staying with me, big girl," Pack Mama whispers, curling closer around her. "What a comfort you are. I've got to pull myself together before Rowan gets home. Oh God, I pray Mossy comes back. I'm awfully scared. What have I done? I broke something, and I'm not even sure what. That's the worst part."

Zephyr gives the back of her neck a tongue swipe. She understands Mossy is Kibble Man, and Kibble Man is mad.

Moss leaned against the big leaf maple his grandfather had planted sixty-two years before. It survived and thrived because of the spring here on the ridge. He felt protected and nurtured by the majestic tree. Jazz lay near him, nose on his thigh, and once again, he sent quiet thanks to Francine, their vet who'd cornered him into re-homing her. Dog and man—they needed each other. He lifted his gaze to the freshly snow-capped mountains and sent his worries sailing out on his breath. The peaks were sturdy enough to handle it all. It had been wrong to leave without sitting down with Carolina—he hadn't pulled this kind of stunt in a long, long time—but he'd been so enraged, afraid something might fall out of his mouth he couldn't take back. She was too important to him.

She'd hidden such a big event in her life from him. *Have I done or said anything that's made me unworthy of her trust?* He had to ask the question, but he damn well knew the answer. He was an honorable man.

He bounced his fist against his forehead—he'd agreed to take Rowan to school. *Damn. How could I forget?* When he got within cell range, he needed to text Lina so she knew he'd arrived safely, and Row to apologize. He couldn't call, not yet. The last time he'd been this angry was when he had confronted Sophie nine years ago. Clearly, he had conflated her transgressions with what Carolina had divulged; he suspected his anger was about his ex-fiancée more than his wife. Still. They needed to get a few matters straight.

He stayed on the ridge for another hour, until his stomach started growling before hiking back to the house. He fiddled with the phone, tossing it from one hand to the other trying to get up his nerve before sending two quick texts.

He thawed stew in the microwave for lunch and sat in his recliner to eat. Damn quiet, he thought. He hadn't realized how his bigger family had added to the commotion in his life. At this moment, he missed them all—a visceral yearning, a kind of hunger—and was grateful for Jazz's company. He leaned down and ran a hand over her ribs. She thumped her tail in response. Five years ago, he couldn't bear to be around anyone and now he was missing a whole passel of them. *Change sure creeps in unawares.*

The next afternoon, while he puttered in the garden, the sensations started. Moss recognized them. First, faint tingling behind his eyes. Then, a series of quiet waves passed through him. Four times in the last nine years. He'd been planning to catch up with Dakota; they could meet tonight, instead. *This*, when *this* happened, came first. It had to. The eruptions were unstoppable—some memory had chosen today to make its appearance. He checked his watch. No time to hike to the ridge, process whatever showed up, and get back before nightfall. He might have attempted the return in the dark before he lost his leg. Not anymore. Rubbing his chin, he felt the rising stubble. Hair growth was unstoppable, too. After rescheduling with Dakota, he'd go sit on the swing.

Rowan arrived home from school, greeted a very happy Zephyr, and found her mom sitting in the living room, teaching Graham patty-cake.

"Look at how he's smiling at you. You played it with me, Mama. Seeing you now, I remember."

"I sure did, sweet pea. I bet these baby games are as old as time." She sang the song again to Graham, supporting him on her knee. "Patty-cake, patty-cake, baker's man, bake me a cake as fast as you can. Roll it, pat it, and mark it with a B, put it in the oven for baby and me." When she said "mark it with a B," she drew the letter on his chest. He gurgled and laughed. "They thrive on repetition," she added, "and never weary of the game."

"But don't you get sick and tired of it? Babies seem boring to me."

"See his giggles? Mothers yearn to hear those."

"I don't think I want to have kids."

Carolina gawked at her daughter. "Why?"

"I have different work. Seems to me, mothers spend a couple of decades focused on their children. They don't have time for much else."

Carolina tilted her head. "True, but it's rewarding. You remember smelling the babies' necks right after they were born? Love blossoms. You can't get enough." She pinned Rowan with her gaze. "I'd love grandkids, you know."

"Graham can give you grandbabies."

"Ever heard of the biological clock?"

Rowan squinted at her.

"When women are in their early thirties, their bodies often yearn for a baby. The clock starts ticking. Fertility begins to decline around thirty. By my age, a woman may never conceive."

"I doubt I'll change my mind." She pulled on her jacket. "Zephy and I are going to the woods."

"No. Wait. There's something I need to tell you."

Rowan swung around, and Zephyr skidded to a stop. "You know, you two scared me bad this morning. Are you and Mossy going to be okay?"

"I think so. I hope so."

She frowned at her mom. "Don't spoil everything. I love Da big time."

"I know, sweetheart. He's precious to me, too. Please, sit here with me. What I need to tell you is connected."

Rowan looked puzzled, but sat down. Zephyr settled at her feet.

"Moss has made it clear he wants no secrets between us. I've come to believe he's right, so I don't want to keep this from you, either. I think you're old enough. In fact, you need to hear it, possibly for your own safety and wellbeing."

Rowan put her fist against her heart. "What?"

"When I was a freshman in college, I used to study late at the library. One night, I was walking back to the dorm around eleven, right after the building closed." She stopped and took a deep breath. "Sweetheart, I got attacked."

Her daughter's eyes went huge. "No—you weren't!"

"Yes." She took Rowan's hand in both of hers. "Three men jumped out of the bushes, raped, and beat me. Ever notice this scar?" She parted her hair on the left side of her head.

The color drained from Row's face. "Oh, Mommo, how awful. You never told Mossy? Don't you two share everything?"

"I did tell Moss, the first weekend I went to be with him at Bender's Ridge. Remember? You stayed with Seth and Sue."

Rowan was sitting upright, stiff, her whole attention focused.

"He divulged his war experiences, and I explained about the attack."

"Why'd he leave mad today?"

"I never told him I got pregnant. Until this morning."

Horror shot across her face. "Not me!"

"Oh, no, of course not—this was five years earlier."

Her daughter's expression relaxed. "But what happened?"

"The baby came when I was only five months along—way too early to survive." Carolina swallowed hard. "She had a heart defect, too. Moss thought he had a right to know—he felt I'd broken trust."

"Do you agree?"

"That's what we need to work out."

Chapter Thirty-one

Moss pushed his foot to get the swing moving, leaning back to survey his garden. He'd broken his rule and let Jazz come in with him. She lay nearby. It was the end of harvest season; Dakota had done a good job, even with emails as the only oversight. The man might have a broken spirit, but his work showed fine quality. Dakota had been very pleased at his boss's satisfaction. Moss hoped this place brought healing to the veteran as it had to him.

He put his attention on his breath, and allowed sensations to return in tingling waves. Now he needed to be patient and listen. Something would come.

About twenty minutes later, a memory punched through: Carolina. This was specific to her.

Another fifteen minutes. He and Carolina had been in bed together. But when? He felt impatient, but knew impatience drove memory away. Getting off the swing, he walked the rows of the garden, fisting and unfisting his hands. He adjusted his breathing, calmed himself. After taking every pathway, admiring the beds, he went back to the swing and ran his hand over his stubble.

Ah. The *first* time they were in bed together. They hadn't made love yet. Up on Bender's Ridge, she'd clarified there was something she needed to tell him, but the wide 360-degree vista made her feel too vulnerable. They'd come back to the ranch house, dropped their clothes. He'd snuggled around her, providing support while she gathered courage. She explained him about the rape, and disclosed she hadn't told anyone—ever—not even Rafe, whom she married a couple of years later.

Oh my God. Moss knuckled his forehead. She must have never told anyone about getting pregnant, either. Her obstetrician knew, of course, but likely no one else. Now, finally, she'd found the courage to tell him this—after four years of marriage—and what did he frigging do? Yelled at her, accused her of not being honest. Walked out and left. *Holy moly.* He dropped his face into his hands. How could he make this right?

It took Jazz's bumps and licks to pull him out of the agony of his thoughts and discover moisture coursing down his cheeks. He invited his dog onto the swing, and held her, crying. "Jazz, I've blown it. What am I going to do? Will she be able to forgive me?"

She swiped her tongue across his face.

"Come on, girl. We've got to go back. Right now. Let's talk to Dakota. I have to postpone planning the spring gardens again."

Her hands protectively patting her son's butt in the front pack, Carolina walked back inside and checked the clock. It had been almost two days since their misunderstanding, but it felt like a week. A month. Damn, it felt like forever. Moss had only sent two texts.

Maybe he'd called while she tidied the yurt. Where had she left her phone? She checked their bedroom, her desk, purse, pockets. Nothing. "Teal," she called, "have you seen my cell?"

"On the kitchen counter." Teal walked into the living room and handed it to her. "I've got dinner prepped. Let me take Graham now." He handed her the phone. "We'll go for a walk down the road—I need to stretch my legs."

Carolina lifted the baby and set him in the corner of the sofa. She undid the front pack, handed it to Teal, and helped him fish Graham's feet through the holes.

"Could you tighten the strap in the back? I want him to ride a bit higher," he said.

"Maybe we need a second one of these so we don't have to keep adjusting the fit," she suggested. "Yes?"

"Please." He smiled at her. "Thanks. This feels right. Get the same kind—I like everything about this pack. Maybe a different color, so we know which is which. You look beat, Carolina. Take a nap while I'm gone."

"I will. I didn't sleep last night. After your walk, I want more snuggle time with Graham."

"Of course. Do you think Moss'll be back for dinner?"

Carolina shook her head. "Nope." She turned so Teal wouldn't see her fear. "Have a nice outing."

Rowan watched her mother pick at the meal, a delicious lasagna Teal had made. She seemed crushed. Row reached a hand out and patted her arm. "You got to eat, Mama, keep your milk up for Graham." Her little brother was busy pounding on his high chair, singing to his peas.

"No appetite. I'll have a non-alcoholic beer, instead. It's good for milk production. Sorry, Teal, it smells great. Maybe I can eat some for lunch tomorrow."

Zephyr went on alert. She trotted to the front window, sat, and stared out.

"Yay, Mossy's coming home," Row squealed. "Twenty minutes, you'll see."

"More likely deer in the front field," her mom said.

"Nope. It's Da. Zeph pensed me."

Sure enough, twenty minutes later, Moss's 4Runner pulled up. "I'll hug him, and give you two space to talk," Rowan said.

"We'll go out to the yurt," Carolina said. "I hope there's no yelling involved." Her voice was so low it could barely be heard. She wrapped her arms around herself.

As she waited by the door, Carolina's heart thundered so fast she was afraid she might faint. When Moss walked in, Jazz by his side, her knees buckled. He caught her.

"Oh my God, I'm sorry," he whispered. His strong arms clasped her. She tried to not to cry, but it was no use. He held her for a minute. "Let me greet the rest of the family, then let's go to the yurt. Okay by you?"

She pulled away and nodded.

He went to Rowan and hugged her. "I've missed you. And Zephy, too."

Jazz danced around Zephyr, who bumped her nose into Moss's hip. He stroked the huge dog. "Now, where are the men of the household?"

"In here, doing dishes," Teal called.

Carolina watched Moss go to the kitchen, Jazz at his heels. He picked Graham up and hugged him close before laying a hand on Teal's shoulder. "I'm glad to be home."

"Are you hungry?" Teal asked.

"I am. Could you leave a plate on the counter? Actually, fix a package for both Carolina and me. I'll come get it later." He grimaced. "I have fences to mend." He handed Graham back to Teal and went to the living room, taking Carolina's hand. "Come with me?"

They crossed the yard to the yurt and went to sit on the couch.

"I thought you were gone for good," she said. "At first I was shocked, then pissed, then frightened."

"I bet. Sweetheart, I have lots of regrets. You know how I get warning symptoms when a buried memory's going to surface?"

"It happened one other time since we've been together. A couple of years ago."

"Yes. And again this afternoon. It took more than an hour for it to work its way up."

"Memory of what?" Carolina looked at him intently.

"When you told me about the rape. I'd been so enraged by what those creeps did, I forgot you added you'd never told anyone before."

"You were the first. It took me sixteen years to find someone I could trust."

Moss stared down at his hands, worked his fingers in and out. When he looked at her, his eyes flooded. "You didn't share with anyone—other than your doctor—about being pregnant until you told me two days ago. Correct?"

"Well, I'll be. You figured it out."

"Damn. I can't say I'm sorry enough. How can I make amends?"

She pursed her lips. "Promise not to stomp out without talking. Ever again. Pull the stunt a second time? I'll walk out on you."

"I was terrified what I might say couldn't be taken back. I got flooded with … Sophie aborted our baby before I even knew she was carrying." His hands shook.

Carolina whistled. "I knew I'd triggered something."

"She didn't understand why I was crazy-mad, either. It made me nuts. She spat out, 'My body. I had the right to choose.' A day later, 9/11 happened and we lost Cousin Andrea. The next day, I left for basic training. I mean, she had the right, of course, but not without telling me. Without discussing it."

"Absolutely. Was that the watershed moment?"

He sighed. "Yeah, although I didn't realize at that time." He paced the room before coming to stand in front of her. "I won't march out again. Ever. You have my word. But if I whirl toward the wall, give me a minute. I'll be trying to control my mouth. I might even say, 'I need to take ten' and walk out the door. But I'll come back."

"Fair enough. The same goes for me. And you know what? I should have told you about losing the baby before we ever got pregnant. I'm sorry."

"Thank you," he whispered.

Carolina leaned into him, relieved. It felt like they'd made it over a huge chasm.

After a moment, he said, "I have a proposal."

"Proposal?"

"We have some healing work to do. Alone. I'm asking for five days with you at the ranch. Only the two of us. Dakota mentioned he wants some vacation."

She frowned. "Without Graham? I don't know if I can—or should—leave him all those days. I've gotten very close with him since the antidepressants kicked in."

"Sweetheart, we need this. Look—we made him. And we must be the very best parents we can be. Sometimes it means taking time for us. Besides, you now have a solid bond with him."

"Yes, that's true. He's the sweetest. What would it look like?"

"I plan to woo you. Start at the beginning." He tweaked an eyebrow and gave her a look.

She opened her eyes wide. "Oh. My." Her body tingled.

"I have conditions," he went on.

"Conditions? Exactly what kind?"

"For the five days, I want to run the show. Of course, you can always say no."

She gawped at him. "W-what? Why?"

He threaded his fingers through hers. "I want to guide the pacing." His thumb traced down her palm. "Trust me?"

"Holy shit, Moss. This is a big ask after bloody stalking out the door."

"Yes, I know." He held her gaze.

She saw the love in his eyes and his confidence he could make this right. She couldn't look away. Quivers started. "I'm scared. Why am I frightened?"

"Control makes you feel safe. Correct? Like when you called and came to visit me at Bender's Ridge the first time. You steered the timing."

He knows me. She ducked her head, embarrassed. "Yeah. Well."

"My turn."

She jerked up to stare at him.

He was smiling at her in the sweetest way. "No awful surprises, love. You *like* my timing."

He was right. "O-okay," she stuttered. "When?"

"Now."

"Now? Leave now, at night? Lordy, I'm repeating myself."

"Teal's on board. I called him this afternoon. You have plenty of breast milk frozen. All you need to do is nurse our son, hug our daughter, and we're on our way. I'm going to grab the lasagna Teal saved for me and eat while you're with Graham."

"Please ask him to pack me some."

"He already has."

"What about Jazz? Isn't she coming?"

"I'm leaving her with Rowan and Zephyr."

"But what if you have a nightmare? She won't be there to help you."

"No, but you will. Only the two of us. No other considerations." He smoothed her cheek. "Now you go nurse our sweet boy."

Chapter Thirty-two

On the drive, steel bands constricted Carolina's belly. Ever since the night of the rape, she couldn't bear anyone other than herself controlling events. It was a testament to how much she trusted Moss that she was even in his SUV right now. She watched herself wanting to create her own set of rules, or "conditions," as Moss called them. But that wasn't what she'd agreed to. This time. Trying to reduce her stress, she blew out a breath.

As they crowned the pass and headed down the other side, he patted her leg. "I heard you. It's okay, love. No nasty surprises."

"Better not be. I'm pretty freaked."

"Pretty?"

She heard the light humor in his tone.

"Okay, okay. Very freaked out."

"Want to talk about it? I'm listening."

"It's hard for me. I've stuffed this down too long." She stared out the window. The woods by the side of the road were an impenetrable wall. Nauseated and claustrophobic, she pressed her hands together to stop trembling. *We'll be at the ranch soon enough.*

But it wasn't soon enough. She needed out, now. "Pull over. I've got to breathe fresh air."

"Open the window. I'll look for a safe place to stop."

"Going to throw up." She got the window down before retching, and felt horrible because she knew she'd coated the outside of the door.

"Oh boy." He saw a pullout and stopped. Fishing behind the seat, he found an old, torn towel. Carolina had pushed open the door and was heaving in the bushes. He went to her and supported her clammy forehead.

After a minute, she said, "Awful sorry about your vehicle."

He patted her shoulder. "I'll wipe it down. I have a ratty towel. Sweetie, this could happen to anyone."

"Right, but it happened to me. Got water? I need to rinse my mouth."

"Hold on." He found an unopened half-gallon in the back and brought it to her.

She swished and spit three times. "Thanks. Any mint gum?"

He swung the water bottle and flooded the side of the car. "Maybe in the glove compartment. Can you face the ride again? I'd like to get us to the ranch."

"Yeah, I think I'm okay. Let's go." She slipped back in the SUV, and fished for gum. There was one blessed piece left, which she unwrapped and popped into her mouth, grateful for the strong mint flavor.

Forty-five minutes later, they parked in front of the ranch house. Dakota's van was gone. He'd switched on the pathway lights to the house.

Moss slung his arm over her. "Want a glass of wine before bed? Or maybe a hot toddy? It's chilly here."

"Oooh, hot toddy. Do we still have creamed lemon honey?"

"We do."

"Perfect."

"Yes, ma'am. Coming up. But first, I'll light the fire and change into my slumpies."

Carolina giggled. He always called his comfy clothes—sweat pants and top—slumpies. "I'll take a three-minute shower and change, too."

Fifteen minutes later, they met in the living room. "Feeling better?" he asked, handing her the toddy-filled mug.

She sniffed it, and glanced at him with a smile. "I'm not throwing up. A big improvement. I'm waiting for you to drop some plan on me. I know you have stuff up your sleeve."

He sat on the couch and patted the place next to him. "I was thinking we'd sleep in different rooms tonight—you in our room, and me in Teal's.

We can meet—like for the first time—in the kitchen, tomorrow morning, and go from there. Eight-thirty? Okay by you?"

She stared at him, horrified. "No. Oh, no. Not alone tonight. I'm already flipped out. I need to feel your familiar warmth so I can remember I like your pacing."

He glanced up. Her face had blanched, and she was quivering again. Without intending to, he'd put her on edge. "Well, okay," he said, reconsidering his plan. "We can sleep together, but no sex, not even kissing. I'll spoon you, if you'd like."

"Please," she said, her voice ragged.

In the morning, Moss made mochas for them. They sipped from their mugs in front of the fireplace.

"I miss Graham. He's become my best buddy. And the dogs," Carolina said. "A lot."

"Me, too."

She faced him. "Are you open to another dog? I think I want one of my very own."

"The more the merrier. Great cliché, eh? What are you thinking of?"

"A rescue. A sighthound rescue. She—hopefully, a she—could be a mix, but has to have sighthound nature."

"Fallen for them, have you?" He grinned. "I'm not surprised. I sure did." He put down his cup. "Ready for a walk?"

Her eyes widened. "Okay. Where are we going?"

"You'll see when we get there." He reached out his hand to her.

She punched him lightly on the arm before intertwining her fingers with his. "Dickens."

He winked at her. "I am. So, right here, the first weekend we spent together, I talked about losing my leg." He stood and helped her up. They walked in silence to the garden. He sat on the bench swing, and encouraged her to sit with him. "Here, I told you about some of my painful war losses. Frank...." His voice got rough and he trailed off, before picking up again. "But we got cold and went back inside." He walked her back to the living room and they sat on the couch. "And here, I told you about the awful raid and the boys." He teared up but didn't turn from her. "The next morning, we hiked to the ridge. Remember? Let's go there now."

They put on hiking shoes and jackets. A half hour later, they stood on the high point, staring at the mountains lit with morning glow. "It was afternoon, though. You intimated something you needed to tell me—you felt too exposed up here."

She nodded. "I sure did." Now she picked up the thread, took his hand again, and they started down the hill. "So, we went to your bedroom, shucked our clothes, and you held me until I was able to tell you about the gang rape."

"Right. *Your* terrible losses. We shared life-changing calamities. We had to in order to open the door to being together."

When they got back to the ranch house, they sat on the bed in silence for a while.

"It was surprising you were able to talk about it that early in our relationship. Thank you for trusting me," Moss said. "Now, come with me again." This time, he led her to the graveyard. Her feet dragged. They stood in front of Andrea's little mound.

"And here, we put our baby girl to rest and faced our first huge loss as a couple. But we've never truly talked about it, have we?"

Carolina leaned into him.

"We need to," he said.

Rowan walked a fussing Graham around the room, jiggling him. Zephyr followed at her heels. "Usually this works," she said to Teal. "I've seen you do it, too."

"I think he misses his mom, but let me check. Maybe he's teething; he's been drooling a lot." Teal washed his hands and ran a finger over the baby's gums. "Yup—it's swollen right here, center bottom. Let me get the icy teether ring for him. He might even be able to hold it."

"Isn't this awfully young?" Rowan asked, when he got back.

"Yeah, but not uncommon. The tooth may not come through for six weeks or two months." He crouched in front of Graham. "Poor guy. Teething is painful."

"I'm always startled how much you know about babies."

"Remember? Oldest of six." He rubbed the frozen key on the swollen spot. Graham's eyes got big and he stopped mewling.

"Mama and Da are extra lucky to have you."

He tipped his head at her. "I'm at least as lucky, and you know it. I've told you about my family."

Rowan put Graham in the rocker and wrapped his fingers around the ring. He promptly tried to stuff it in his mouth, and on the third try, gnawed on it.

"Let's use a bib to keep him from soaking his onesie with drool. I'll get it," Teal said.

Rowan fingered it when Teal got back. It had Winnie-the-Pooh bears all over it. "This was mine," she said, in a thoughtful tone. "I wonder why Mom kept it."

"Because it reminded her of you as an infant," Teal said, snapping the bib in place. "We need a picture of this to send your folks. Maybe we can set him against Zephyr. Got your phone?"

They propped Graham leaning on Zeph. Sensing the responsibility, the dog lay very still. Rowan rested Graham's arm on Zephy's back. Teal made a face and a squeaky sound; the baby chuckled for him, and Rowan clicked the picture. "Cute!" She showed it to Teal and texted it to her parents. "I hope they're doing all right," she said. "They scared me."

After eating omelets for lunch, Moss and Carolina sat on the front deck. He poured chamomile tea. She seemed coiled inside herself.

She spoke with a shaking voice. "I'd been so dang freaked ever since Andrea got diagnosed in utero. The birth was crazy, what with her almost landing on the floor, and then things got worse. I obsessed every moment—don't know what I would have done without you, Zephyr, Rowan, and Teal. And Jazz." She stood up and paced. "When she actually … died," her voice broke, and she swallowed hard, "the first thing I felt was relief. Such a sick thought. I'm so ashamed. After that, I got slammed by grief." She wouldn't look at him.

He went to her and cupped her face. "Lina, me, too. The grief didn't come until later. I thought, oh my God, we don't have to worry about her any more. She's at peace."

Her face shot up to peer into his. "You're not humoring me? I'm not the only one?"

He shook his head. "Scout's honor."

"Holy crap. These long weeks, thinking I was weird and twisted—I couldn't tell anyone." She shook and her nose ran. He held her until her sobs eased.

She spun away from him. "I could've had comfort during those days, but instead, I held myself separate because I didn't know how to voice the truth. What a fool I am."

He grabbed her shoulders again, but harder this time.

"Ouch!" She tried to wrest out of his grip.

"Stop. Don't do this. Grief takes up residence differently in each of us. Don't shame or blame yourself. We're here now, sharing. It's what matters." He let her go.

Frowning, she shrugged her shoulders up and down. "Too hard."

"Sorry. I was making a point. I wanted you to hear me."

"I did."

He stepped close to her and, very gently, lifted her chin. Her eyes opened wide. Just as gently, he kissed her—tentative, like a first kiss, tasting, checking her out. Then he wrapped his arms around her. "Your openness is the deepest gift you give me," he whispered. "I missed it terribly after Andrea died."

"Why didn't I think I could open up?" She relaxed into him and rested her head against his chest. "I've missed home," she said. "*This* home. Can we make love now?"

He threw back his head and guffawed. "Nope. We're not there yet. Not even close."

"Huh." She squinted at him. "Maybe I don't like your timing after all."

"Too bad, my sweet. You agreed to this. Want to go back to the ridge?"

"I want a nap first. Join me?" she asked.

"Tempting, but no. I've got to stretch my legs, take a hike, and find you later. I need another vista fix."

Moss stared out at the mountainscape in front of him. He sighed out a long breath and rubbed his thigh above the prosthesis. It seemed they were making progress toward healing. He felt a boulder of responsibility pressing on him. A wrong move might shut her down again, but it wasn't clear what the next step should be. This was delicate territory to navigate. *My turn to speak up, I guess.*

He lay belly down on the ground and splashed his face at the spring, savoring the bright chill, before rolling over and watched the clouds oh-so-slowly mist apart—where did they go?—and re-meld into soft, billowy shapes. He didn't bother trying to identify known objects, although he had as a boy. He loved how they moved at a nonhuman crawl. How many hours of his life had he spent in cloud reverie? Hundreds, he figured. Their lazy pace grounded him; he could locate breath in his animal body again. He gave a nod to Mary Oliver for her poem, "Wild Geese."

Carolina vaguely heard the door open. She felt the bed dip as Moss sat down. He rested a hand on her cheek. "Wow, I conked out," she said, and cracked her eyes open. "How long was I asleep?"

"I'm not sure, but I was gone an hour and a half. Want something to drink?"

"I'd love a decaf mocha. Are you making it?"

"Sure. Are you getting up?"

Carolina yawned and stretched. "You bet. Otherwise I won't sleep tonight." Swinging her legs out of bed, she pulled on jeans, long-sleeved tee, and fleece vest. One look in the mirror, running her fingers through her short bob, and she was ready for whatever came next. She went to the kitchen.

Moss stood holding the mochas. "Let's sit in the living room. More comfortable for talking." He handed her a mug and they settled on the couch, sitting quietly, sipping for a few moments. Carolina savored the natural coffee bitterness countered by sweet chocolate.

"I want to tell you more about my war experiences," Moss said. "It's part of being fully open with you." He leaned over and rested his elbows on his knees. He worked one hand over the fist of the other. "There were other night raids." He went into detail about them, and an earlier roadside bomb incident where he had barely missed getting hit, but lost a couple of buddies. Then he shared more about losing Frank. "I keep thinking if I hadn't called to tell him I was enlisting, maybe he wouldn't have. He might be alive today."

He swiveled away, and Carolina realized he'd teared up. "Hey, are you hiding your feelings? That's my game. Certainly you know self-blame's a mind attack."

"You're right on both counts." He met her gaze, blinking fast. "I was hiding. We were taught to, as kids, weren't we? To buck up, and keep our deepest feelings private. Some weeks are still hard to bear without him." He wiped his eyes. "I haven't found another truly close male friend." Moss scratched his chin. "It was more than just growing up together. Sharing grad school and our writing struggles deepened the friendship we carried from childhood." He ran a hand through his hair. "God. He was such a fine writer—died before he got published. Any interest in reading him? They're memoir, not fiction." He paused and frowned. "No, that's not true. He had a couple of short pieces accepted by literary journals during grad school. I bet I can find them. I have a couple of things he presented in class, too."

"Yeah. By reading his work, I can know him a little bit."

"Readers don't realize how much of the writer is in the work—memoir, of course—but even fiction," Moss said.

"I learned it, reading your books. I had no idea before, because I'd never had an author friend." She leaned over and kissed him, much the way he'd kissed her—exploring, familiarizing herself. Although she wanted more, she pulled away, honoring his plan. They hadn't made love in so long, before the twins were born, when Sierra gave them the "prescription" to invite labor to start.

"Yum. Your lips are velvety."

She watched him lay a fire to light after dark, as he often did. He had a precision and economy of motion she loved.

He brushed the wood dust off his hands and came to sit with her again. "Lina..." he paused. "I want you to tell me exactly what happened during the rape."

"Why? Why now?"

"My sense is it needs air. Exposing it allows even deeper healing. My therapist taught me and, in my experience, it's true. Can you share?"

"I don't know. It's violent and ugly." She bit her lip. "What if it changes how you see me forever?"

"Change is all we have in life—but it won't alter how I feel about you. It couldn't."

Carolina stood and walked to the window, staring toward the garden. The lump in her chest was back. "I'm afraid," she said. "But I'll try." She sat down next to him. Without mincing words, she described how the three men had savaged her twenty-two years before.

By the end, she was shivering.

Moss held his blanched face in his hands. Finally, he took her in his arms. "Oh, my love," he said, softly. "I'd kill them if I knew who they were. What a testament to the human spirit you were willing to gamble on men after what they did."

"I couldn't live frozen forever. I had to thaw or commit suicide. In general, I don't trust men. Rafe, and you—Rafe was familiar, my childhood friend. You're especially trustworthy. Kind. Gentle."

"Thank you. I know it took a lot of courage to divulge the worst details."

"I never did before. When the doctor examined me, she discovered and repaired the internal damage, but I never talked about it, other than to say I was raped. At the time, I couldn't bear to." She put a hand on his arm. "It's such a relief, though, to have spoken it—like I've taken some power back."

"There you go." They finished their coffees in silence. Moss said, "Remember our first morning together here? Can we talk about it now?"

"The hours we spent kissing? We touched some, too. One of my sweetest memories."

He raised an eyebrow. "Ready for more? In a similar vein?"

Unable to speak, and flushing with shyness, she nodded.

"Let's go lie down for an hour before we rustle up dinner." He took her hand.

On the short walk to the bedroom, a rush of anticipation flooded her.

He scooped her up and deposited her lightly on the bed. "I'll take off my leg and put on slumpies. No nakedness yet."

She yearned to feel his nest of chest hairs and long, firm leg muscles. When he lay beside her and grazed her lips with his, she fell into delighted, present-moment surrender.

Chapter Thirty-three

"Teal," Rowan called, "come check this out."

He walked into the living room, Graham tucked against his chest, and peered over Rowan at her laptop. "Read it to me, would you? I can't bend low holding him. He's put on weight—I think he's caught up with his age group."

"Look at this site. This is the retreat I want to attend. It starts the day after Christmas, when school's out." She read him the lead paragraph—about a retreat center west of Portland and the activities Colin James held each day.

"Oh man, I'd love to go," Teal said. "Only six weeks away. Enough time to plan, but not long to wait."

"Let's go together. I'm sure Mama and Da would be more likely to let me attend if you came, too. It'd be perfect. And you can drive us." She glanced up at him.

"Lordy, girl, your face is ablaze with joy. Let's try to make this happen."

She heard the flap-flap of the dog door, and paws skittering across the kitchen floor. Zephyr and Jazz flew into the room, tongues lolling. "Where have you girls been?" She set the laptop aside to pat and greet both dogs. "You've been in the woods. Look at the detritus you dragged in." She picked bits of fir tree out of Zeph's coat. "Jazzy, nothing sticks to you. Such an easy-care girl."

"Nice word, detritus," Teal said.

"My new one of the week."

"I'm due vacation time," Teal said. "I was planning to write, but I bet I can take my laptop and work there. The retreat folks might frown on it, but I don't care." He patted Graham's butt and hummed to him.

"We've got a plan. Now to get this past Mama. When do they come back?"

"Two days," he said. "Give or take."

"I want to sign us up, put down a deposit."

"Carolina would kill us. Ground us. Grumpf a lot. Why don't you wait?"

"Cool word. She can grumpf, for sure, but won't ground you—you're her hotshot, oh-so-reliable nanny, and an adult, besides. Me, on the other hand, I'm the annoying, teenage mystic."

Moss and Carolina nestled on the couch in front of the fire. The wind had whipped up; shutters banged. Even the flames grew wild from gusts puffing down the chimney. "The sound makes me chilly," he said. "We may get harsh rain. How about a hot shower?"

She pulled back and stared at him. "Naked? Together?"

"Yes ma'am. Next step. We can take this a bit further tonight."

She stood up and reached a hand to him. "Let's go."

"Well, aren't you the eager one." He smiled, and rising, cupped her butt.

She startled and laughed. "My boobs are overfull. I need to pump first."

They luxuriated in the shower longer than usual in water-thirsty central Oregon. He washed her back, then turned her around and drew soapy circles around her breasts.

She lathered his chest and trailed a hand down his abdomen. Meeting his gaze, she slid farther and cupped his balls.

"Oh my," he breathed. "Wonderful."

She glanced down. "You're standing up hard and tall. Are we going to make use of it tonight?"

"If you're asking, 'Am I going to enter you?' the answer is no, not yet. But we can be naked together, touch, fool around."

She pinched one of his nipples lightly. "I'll take what I can get. You sure are a tough sell."

"Are you seriously minding this?"

Carolina considered his question. "Nope. It's a real turn on. And we know each other better for it. At last, I'm at ease in my body and heart."

"Thank God," he replied.

She soaped his hair, and then he washed hers. "You go ahead and get out first," he said. "I turned the heated floors up—it should be toasty in the bedroom."

Carolina toweled her hair and considered her post-baby body in the long mirror. Not too bad. Different, though. She'd done isometrics while bedridden and after she gave birth until her doc gave her permission to exercise. She ran a finger down a stretch mark on her belly. *The price I paid for twins. I sure miss my baby boy.*

After drying off, she wrapped up in a big beach towel, lit two fat beeswax candles, and set them on the bedside tables. They provided a soft flickering glow, the perfect amount of light. She sat on the side of the bed and texted Teal.

A couple of minutes later, the response came. "Graham's doing great. Check out the photo Rowan sent you." She smiled when she gazed at it.

Moss crutched into the room, a towel knotted at his waist.

"Look at what Teal sent."

"Graham looks happy." He set the phone aside, took the bed's remote and buzzed it lower. "You're where I imagined you," he said. He opened her towel, but left it draped over her. Then he slowly spread her legs, and sitting on the floor, touched his lips to the inside of her knee. Delicious sensations rolled up her body.

"I want to pleasure you," he said, his voice smoky. "Okay by you?"

"Oooh, yes." Her words came out elongated and dreamy. "I wasn't expecting this."

His slow kiss warmed skin above her knee. Shivering with anticipation and delight, she opened her legs wider in welcome.

Moss cracked an eye open. Almost dawn. He pulled the covers snug over them and cuddled her close.

She sighed deeply against his naked chest, and entwined her legs with his. "Thank you," she whispered. "Last night was yummy. *You're* yummy." She kissed him. "And the sexiest man I know."

He blushed. "Thank you. Is there more we need to share with each other?" He pulled far enough away to look her in the eyes. "Anything else we've held back?"

Carolina rolled on her back and was quiet for a while. "Yes, there's more about the rape. I can't say it out loud. Let me whisper." She pulled him close and mouthed another part of the horror.

"If I could only get my hands on them. They didn't stop at anything. I kinda figured, though; part of the M.O. of psychopaths."

"At least they didn't murder me. I'm grateful for my life."

He pulled her close. "Me, too. More than I can say."

"I can't promise I've told you absolutely everything. Clearly, I've blocked memories that are too painful—they could surface later."

"It's true for both of us," Moss said. "But I feel we have solid grounding now. Do you?"

She nodded. "You were right. I miss Graham horribly, but we needed private time. I didn't realize how badly." She stroked his face. "You're a wise man."

Rowan knocked on Teal's door.

"Whaz-up?" he called. "Enter."

She walked in. "I did it. I signed us both up for the post-Christmas retreat."

"Holy moly, girl. You're going to be in a world of trouble."

She flung her head back and jutted her chin. "I don't care. This is *my* life. I have different interests from my parents, and I have a right to pursue them."

"Yeah, of course. But spending their money without asking, I don't know. It may not get you what you want."

"We'll see," she snarled. "I thought you'd be more supportive." She closed the door a little too hard and walked down the hall, suddenly aware her hands were clenched in tight fists. *Damn. I'm pissed.*

She went to find Zephyr, snapped her fingers, and ran toward the front field.

My girl's angry, Zephyr pensed, sprinting by her side.

So angry, she responded.

Angry at Zephyr?

Oh my God, no. Tearing up, she dropped to the ground and looked her dog in the eyes. *Not at you. Sorry. I'm mad at—.* She stopped. What was she pissed about? Not being seen as adult. Having to ask permission. How to tell this to Zephyr? *I'm mad at being treated like a puppy.*

The dog swiped her with her tongue. *Rowan and Zephyr play find Rowan game and my girl feels happy again.*

"What's your pleasure?" Moss asked.

"Wait a minute—this has been all about my gratification. How about you? It's your turn."

"I want to come inside you; it's been months." He snugged his body against hers.

"Good Lord, you're huge this morning," she said, eyes big. "After all this time, are you sure I can accommodate you?"

Moss roared with laughter. "Woman, two babies made their way through your channel. They were a hell of a lot bigger than I am, even when I'm good and randy."

She blushed. "You're right, of course. Go extra slow, though, okay?"

He looked at her thoughtfully. "Sweetheart, I would never be anything but cautious. I don't want to trigger you."

She squinted at him. "*That's* why you take such a long time with me?"

"I never forget what you've been through at the hands of men. As I see it, there's no room for error."

"Wow." She played with her thumbnail. "I have mixed feelings. Have I ruined your spontaneity?"

He chuckled. "Other than I can't slap your butt or snap you with a dishtowel, not really. It seems a small price to pay for what we have."

Her eyes filled. "Once something like a rape happens, a person can't ever forget or get away from it. It's not so different from a physical scar." She grazed her finger over a shrapnel crater on his side.

He touched the thin ridge on her scalp. "We've all got 'em, love. It's a matter of gradation. Some are harder than others. War and rape are prime examples of the worst kind."

Carolina considered his comment and nodded. She cupped his face in her hands and kissed him. "I'm ready."

He let out a whoosh of breath as he entered her. The familiarity after so long away, the moist, womanly warmth of her, broke open tears. Weeping, he went soft and slipped out. "Damn," he whispered between sobs. "Apparently, I can't stay hard and cry at the same time. Sorry."

She didn't speak, but held him, and crooned soft sounds.

They dozed in each other's arms. Carolina awakened first. She reached under the covers and took him in her hand. He hardened before he was even fully awake.

"Ummm, nice."

"Come inside," she said. "I can't wait any longer."

"Happy to oblige," he murmured.

He moved slowly, basking in the rich sensation. Once he was buried in the heat of her, they found their familiar rhythm.

"Home," she whispered. "We've made it home. Good on us."

Chapter Thirty-four

The next evening, Zephyr bumped Rowan and pensed her. *Kibble Man is close.*

Thanks for warning me, Rowan responded. "Teal, twenty minutes."

They rushed to get a fresh diaper for Graham and put some clutter away. Rowan gave a critical eye to the kitchen. "Looking good," she called to Teal. "You keep it nice."

"Like your mom and dad. I've learned a lot from them."

She frowned at Teal. "I hope Mama and Da are okay and they've made up."

"Yeah, me, too. Graham needs them together."

"So do I," Rowan said. "I don't know how I'd handle it if they split."

Five minutes later, Carolina opened the door, wearing a wide smile. Moss followed, also grinning. He slung an arm around his wife. "We're good, you guys. We found our way."

Rowan hugged her mom. "Thank God. You two scared me badly."

Jazz bounded into the room, and launched herself at Moss, who rubbed her all over. "I missed you, girl." Zephyr wormed her way in for Moss's touch.

"We scared us, too. But your da is a wise man. He knew what we needed." Carolina hugged Rowan, and said to Teal, who was holding Graham. "Thank you so much. I know five days was a lot on your own. I've missed him more than I can say."

"He's a good boy," Teal said. "Easy to distract. He's starting to teethe—he gets fussy and rubs his mouth. The icy chew works wonders."

"It's great you knew what to do for him. Row teethed early. You're right on time, aren't you, little one?" she said to Graham, taking him in her arms. "I swear he's bigger. Hey, baby boy, Mama's home."

Moss squeezed Rowan, hugged Teal, and waited until Carolina finished greeting Graham. "My turn now," he said. He lifted his son above his head, cooed to him, and flew him around. Graham giggled.

"I'm leaking," Carolina said. "I need to nurse him. Rowan, could you start tea water for four? I'll be about twenty minutes."

When Graham was asleep, she came out of the nursery and they all sat in the living room. Teal poured chamomile tea, and passed around chocolate chip cookies he'd made.

"So," Rowan said, and stopped, not quite knowing how to move forward. She glanced at Teal, but he gave a slight shrug. This one was on her. "I signed Teal and me up for a post-Christmas retreat, during vacation. The same teacher you spent time researching, Da—you know, the book you gave me?"

"You what?" Moss and Carolina spoke in unison, their tones shocked. Carolina went on, "Without asking us?" She stared at Rowan, then frowned at Teal. "Did you know about this?"

Rowan broke in so Teal didn't have to speak. "It's me. We were looking at the website, and he expressed interest, too. Anyway, I filled out the form and paid the deposit." She swallowed hard. "He didn't have any idea I was going to register us. He was aghast when I told him."

Mossy was tapping his thumbs together between his knees. Never a good sign, Rowan thought, shuddering inside. Teal was right. I'm in big trouble.

Her dad glanced at Carolina, and Rowan saw the thing they do where they communicate without words.

"You knew how I feel about this stuff. And spending a chunk of money without asking us first," Carolina said, sounding testy. "Row, what were you thinking?"

Teal shifted his gaze from one family member to another. He looked tense, too.

Rowan pressed her lips together. Snapping or yelling would make things worse. She took a big breath. "The nondual teaching the retreat is based on—it's how I've seen life ever since the coma. I woke up with a completely different and deeper understanding. I've been lonely. Finally, I've found a group who gets it. I can't wait."

She watched her parents. The thing *again*. How could her mother not understand pensing when she and Moss were clearly doing some version of it?

Apparently, the baton got passed back to Moss. Rowan waited, squirrelly anxiety building. What would they do to her? Forbid her from going? Ground her? Fire Teal? It wasn't his fault.

Her dad pulled a chair to sit directly in front of her, making her feel not only anxious, but frightened.

He held her gaze, and spoke quietly. "On the upside, planning to go with Teal was sensible; you assigned yourself a chaperone." Moss nodded to Teal. "We trust him, obviously—we left you and our infant son with him for five days. On the downside, this exposes a lack of trust in us—you don't have confidence in our willingness to hear what's important to you."

Rowan opened her mouth to disagree, but Moss raised one brow and shook his head. His expression stilled her into silence.

"It also shows a flagrant willingness to spend behind our backs. It's not the money, it's the 'behind our backs' which seriously concerns me." He cleared his throat. "You're maturing; we're both aware of it, but you don't have free rein to make big decisions on your own. Not yet." He dipped his head down and tapped his thumbs together again. "Knowing how important this retreat is to you, I'm inclined to let you go, but your mom may prefer grounding you. It's her call. One way or the other, there will be consequences. She and I will talk about it in private." More thumb tapping. When he raised his gaze again, his eyes had filled. "I didn't think I'd ever say this to a child of mine, but damn, Row, I'm angry and disappointed. We trusted you with the credit card for emergencies."

Her lower lip quivered. She pressed her mouth together to hide it, but her chin trembled, too. She used her fist to still it and looked at the floor. "I'm sorry." Her voice choked. "You're right, I knew Mama wouldn't let me go to a retreat. She hates the part of me attracted to spiritual stuff."

Carolina sputtered, and Moss reached out a hand to still her. "I'm not done yet. Hate's a powerful word," he said, "Knowing your mother as well as I do, there is *nothing* she hates about you. I agree, she doesn't quite understand this part of you. I'm not one-hundred percent sure I do either, but I trust your instincts. Okay, Lina, your turn."

Carolina switched places with him. "All I've tried to do is keep you safe, sweetheart. At your age, if you're too different, teens will turn on you. We've talked about this. Attending a retreat would mark you as very different. And signing up without asking…."

Rowan frowned. "But I'm not *like* other kids. My interests are more grown up, and the awakening experience changed my life forever. I can't be forced to wait until I leave home to learn more about what I love—it doesn't seem fair." She chewed on her thumbnail. "Like, fashion and makeup don't interest me, and boys my age act childish."

"Seth—"

"Seth's my childhood buddy. He's immature. Aren't you glad I'm after something meaningful and not pushing to date? Most parents would be thrilled." She shook her head to clear it. "Anyway, I screwed up bad. I was reaching for what matters to *me*. My desire isn't wrong, but I was out of line. You've made it clear. Can I go study now? Please? I'll be more prepared to hear my fate tomorrow."

Her parents exchanged looks, Moss nodded, and Rowan bolted from the room.

"I don't know whether to laugh or cry," Carolina muttered.

"You two are special," Teal said. "If only my parents had talked to me this way. Row's one lucky kid."

"Thanks. We try. Are you truly willing to chaperone her for a week? I'd want you to have her back, you know. Older-brother-lion stuff."

"I'll take care of her like she's my own little sister. Man, I miss her." He sighed. "FYI, I went to a similar retreat right before I began work here. I think it'd be good for Row."

"That's good to know. Carolina and I need to talk about consequences. Want to look in on Graham before taking some writing time? Keep an ear out for him, though, until we get back in the house."

Carolina fixed more tea, and they sat in the yurt away from prying ears. "The hard part is finding a punishment which fits the transgression," she said. "Do you think we should let her go to the retreat? The easiest consequence would be taking it away."

"Easy, maybe. But taking away a positive activity she yearns for doesn't feel right to me. I did a lot of research on this guy before I bought her that book. Everything I found is positive." Moss paced across the room and back. He stared out the window for a while. "I've got it—how about this? She's been looking forward to getting her learner's permit. We could make her wait another year. Driving takes maturity. I don't think spending our money without asking was a mature decision."

Carolina considered his idea. "You don't think that's awfully harsh? When I was her age, I wanted to drive more than anything in the world. How about six months, instead?"

"It's probably enough to get our point across."

"Will you deliver the news tomorrow?" Carolina asked.

"I've got a broad back. I only hope it's broad enough for teenage indignation."

She stood. "Let's go back inside where we can hear Graham."

Rowan huddled on her bed, wailing. Zephyr shoved her muzzle against her repeatedly. Finally, Row calmed enough to blow her nose and mop her eyes. Zeph jumped on the bed, and she wrapped her arms around the dog. *I was bad*, she pensed, *and Kibble Man and Pack Mama are going to punish me. I'm ashamed—like when you put your tail between your legs and hang your head. Remember when you were a pup and stole the roast? In a way, I stole, too.*

Is my girl hungry?

Not for food—for a retreat. Quiet time with people who understand me more than Pack Mama. People who know the big field.

Zephyr knows big field. Zephyr comes, too?

No, they don't allow dogs but, if I'm allowed to go, I can pense you many times a day.

In the morning, Rowan pulled on jeans and a tee and hesitated, looking to Zephyr for consolation. She had to go out and face her parents. When she thought about what she'd done, waves of guilt and shame rolled through her. She knew, just knew, they wouldn't let her go to a retreat until she was eighteen; then, at least, they could no longer forbid her. It seemed important, though, to accept her punishment with some amount of grace or, at the very least, stoicism. Arguing would only prove she wasn't grown up enough.

Zephyr whined with increasing insistence. When Row opened the door, her dog raced up the stairs toward the garage to get out. *She must have to pee badly.* Rowan climbed the staircase, feeling like a prisoner facing sentencing. In the kitchen, Mossy was just finishing his mocha.

"Morning," she said, not quite meeting his eyes. "I'd like to make my coffee first. I assume you'd like to sit down with me?"

"Where's my good morning hug?" he asked.

She whirled into his arms. "I'm really sorry," she whispered.

"We all make mistakes," he said. "It's an old adage, but true—it's how we learn. Come on now, it's not the end of the world."

"Sure feels like it."

"Make your mocha and come to the yurt."

"Where's Mama?"

"Nursing Graham. He was up a couple of times during the night cranky from teething, so she may nap for a while. See you out there."

"Just you and me?"

"Yes." He faced her. "Does that make it more or less scary?"

"Less."

He smiled and left for his writing space.

Teal walked in while she had the machine fired up. "Mornin'," he said, over the noise.

She flushed the machine and tightened the knob. "Did you have the night off? I guess Graham was awake quite a bit."

"Yeah. I needed sleep, too, after five days with him. Do you know what they've decided?"

"Not yet. He hugged me, though."

"Girl, they love you. You'll come out of this in one piece."

Her eyes filled again. "I get it, but what if I can't go to a retreat until I'm eighteen?"

"You'll take your punishment and wait. You can handle it." He turned to go. "I'm going to get Graham and let Carolina rest."

"Laters," she said, picking up her mocha. "Wish me luck."

Rowan was sure her heart would explode out of her chest as she dragged her way to the yurt. She had to grab breath in tiny sips. Her dad was concentrating at the computer when she knocked and entered.

"Sit on down," he said. "Let me finish this thought."

The thought became a ten-minute paragraph. While she swiveled in one of the recliners, she tried to talk her heart into quieting; it didn't seem interested in cooperating. Waiting was the worst.

Finally, he closed the computer, pushed away from the desk, and came to sit in the other chair. "Your mom and I talked for quite a while last night trying to decide the best course of action." He twiddled his thumbs.

Is he aware of how often he fiddles? It's a dead giveaway.

"I'd like to hear," he went on, "what you would do in our shoes. Think about it for a minute."

"Huh. I don't know. I sure didn't expect this question."

"Talk it through out loud," he said. "Different possibilities."

"But you've decided, right?"

"Yes, we have."

She planted her hands on her hips. "Why put me through this?"

"So you know what it's like for us."

"Oh. Well," She opened and closed her fists, stalling for time. Mossy wasn't going to let her squirm out of this. "I guess the easiest solution is to forbid the retreat. Any retreat, until I'm eighteen."

"How would it make you feel?" He pursed his lips, waiting.

"Horrible. Angry. Resentful. Most of all, misunderstood."

"Do you think that's what we want to elicit in you?"

"No. But most parents would forbid their kid."

"Are we 'most parents?'" He tipped his head, waiting.

She considered this. "No."

"So, try again. Think about what you did, and try to make the consequence fit."

She frowned. "This is awful hard."

"Parenting is. We love our kids more than anything, but they need to learn from poor decisions, too."

Rowan sat and sipped her mocha, considering. "Okay. I guess what I did was impulsive."

"Good start."

"If I look through your eyes, I'd see impulsive as irresponsible."

He smiled. "You're on the right track."

She took a breath. "Irresponsible—another description might be not very mature."

"Okay, keep going."

"So, if my kid wanted to go to a retreat more than anything in the world, and a retreat is a positive thing—not scary, like drugs or alcohol...." She paused, stuck for a moment. "Well, I'd want to support the positive goal, but not the way my child went about it." She walked to the window again and watched Zephyr and Jazz chasing each other.

"Bingo. And?"

"I'd let her go to the retreat and make the punishment about something else."

"What else? And let me be clear, it's not punishment, it's finding the appropriate consequence. A parent who spanks or straps their child? That's punishment. Consequence is the natural repercussion of immaturity." He rubbed his thigh.

"Does your leg hurt?"

"It's achy today. Don't know why. Keep going. You're doing great."

"I'm stuck, Da. I don't know where to go from here."

"Fair enough. Parents are trying to prepare their kids to launch into the world, right?"

"Yeah, I guess."

"No guessing about it. Our main job is to help you learn the tools which will best support you out there." He flung his arms open. "Where there's a medley of wonderful, awful, and everything in between."

She gaped at him. "Is that how you see life?"

He shook his head. "Pretty much. I gave you a clue, now back to it."

She chewed on it for a while. "I'm still baffled."

"Okay. As kids grow up, parents give them more and more—what?"

She brightened. "Oh—responsibility."

"Exactly. What big responsibilities are coming up for you?"

"College, dating, a job," she chewed her lip. "And driving. Maybe it's the biggest one."

"Because?"

"Because other peoples' lives are at stake."

"So true. Which of these responsibilities is coming up for you?"

Rowan giggled. "It should be dating, but I'm not interested or ready."

"Wise response."

"I guess driving is coming right up, and I can't wait." Suddenly, her heart tumbled. She stared at her father. "No!"

"Yes. We want you to wait six more months before getting your learner's permit."

Rowan, filled with horrible disappointment, recognized the guttural, wounded-dog sound she made. She hid her face for a long time, then finally pulled her hands down and clasped them in her lap. "Right," she said, "makes sense." She swiped at her face, trying to control her torrent of emotion.

"In addition, I want the credit card back, and you'll have to earn the money you took without asking. We'll return the card at the end of the six months. You may attend the retreat," Moss added, softly. "With Teal. And, if you like this Colin James, I might decide to go to one with you."

Rowan snapped her head up to see if Mossy was joking, but he looked serious and sincere.

"Sweetheart, the six months will be over before you know it."

"Easy for you to say. I need to be alone now." And, for the second time in two days, she bolted for her room.

Chapter Thirty-five

Rowan lay on her bed pounding her pillow, angry at what she'd brought upon herself. *I need to stop and think before taking action.* She glanced at the calendar where she'd been marking off the days until she could get her learner's permit. It made her want to cry. She went to her wolfhound calendar and took it down. "Damn. This ends December 31st, of course. I can't even mark six months from now 'til I get my new calendar for Christmas."

She pensed Zephyr, who zoomed in from outside.

Her dog's tongue was lolling. *My girl's sad?*

Remember when I told you I'd been bad? Now I can't learn to drive a car for seven moon cycles. I was supposed to start next month. Rowan wrapped her arms around her dog. *I wanted to be able to take you places—the park, the big land at Bender's Ridge. Go to the library and the bookstore, too. A writing class without Pack Mama or Teal or Kibble Man having to ferry me.*

What about big field people?

She stroked her dog and milked her ears. *They're allowing Teal and me to go to the retreat. I'll meet people who understand the big field.*

Zephyr stays with Kibble Man and Pack Mama?

Yep. And Jazz, too.

She heard a soft knock at the door. "Come in," she called.

Her mom walked in. "Are you doing all right? I know your consequence is huge."

Rowan looked at the floor. "Yeah, it's awful hard." She sighed. "I feel terrible. I'm sorry."

"I know. May I give you a hug?"

As her mom wrapped her arms around her, it dawned on her—for the first time—she felt bigger. "Mama, I think I'm taller than you."

"No, not possible." Carolina slipped her shoes off, and met Rowan in front of the full-length mirror. "Good Lord," she said. "Almost an inch. Makes me feel strange."

"Why?"

"You've passed me. I always thought you'd be shorter, like Grammie. I'm going to end up the smallest in the family."

Rowan giggled. "Not for about twelve or thirteen years, until Graham shoots by. You've got lots of time to get used to it."

"True. Come sit with me in the family room. I want your help on something."

"Me? Why me?"

"You'll understand when I show you. Bring your coffee."

Rowan followed.

Her mom sat at the window, watching Zephyr and Jazz play in the field. "They're so beautiful."

"They sure are. What's up?"

Carolina picked up her iPad. "When we were at the ranch, I told Moss I'd like a dog of my own. I'm envious of the bond you two have with your four-legged friends. I'm second or third best with both of them. I've been missing Stormy—it's been five years since the accident."

"What're you thinking of?"

"A rescue, for sure. And a sighthound. I've fallen in love with them. I applied at this place. Here's who Moss found." She pulled up a page. "Check out this lovely face."

"It's a Saluki. She's gorgeous."

"She's from Dubai." Carolina showed her another picture.

"Where's Dubai?"

"It's part of the United Arab Emirates. In the Middle East, on the Persian Gulf coast. She was found near a McDonald's, lying in the dirt and panting from the heat. A street dog."

Eyes wide, Rowan stared at the picture and traced her finger over the dog's patrician nose. "It's a world away. A purebred street dog—weird. McDonald's in the Middle East, even weirder. Geez, does she understand English?"

"I hadn't thought of it. Probably not. Her name is Salaam; it's Arabic. Moss told me it means 'peace.'"

"How old is she?"

Carolina slipped on her reading glasses and read further. "One-and-a-half to two years."

"Kinda perfect."

"Why?"

Rowan was nonplussed her mother was—seriously—asking her questions and interested in the answers. "Well, because puppyhood is over, but you'd have Salaam's companionship for almost her full adult life. She might know how to walk on a leash, maybe she's house-trained. You know, best of both worlds."

"I remember how crazy Stormy was as a pup. It would be great to miss wild puppyhood."

"I like the quality of Salaam's gaze," Rowan said, thinking, I wonder if this dog might be able to pense. If so, such a pity to waste it on Mama.

"What about it?"

"Notice how she's focused on the person taking the picture. See how she's open and present?"

"Huh. You're right."

"Has she been brought over yet? I suppose dogs get jetlag," Rowan said.

"Yes, to Portland, after a eighteen-hour flight. She's been here for two weeks—they needed to spay her. If dogs do suffer from jetlag, she's over it. Will you and Zephyr go with us tomorrow? I definitely want your take." Carolina rested a hand on Rowan. "It's important to me."

Rowan tipped her head. *Who is this person, and where has my normal mom gone?* "You couldn't keep me away. But check with the rescue people to make sure they're okay with Zephy coming."

"Good thought. I'll call."

Teal walked into the family room. His eyes were swollen and red.

"What happened?" she asked.

"This. I picked up mail from my P.O. box." He handed the paper to her. It looked like a legal document. "My parents—they've legally disowned me." Rivulets flowed down his face. "I'm no longer their child."

"My God, no." Carolina exclaimed. "May I see the paper?"

Rowan passed it on. Her mom perused it carefully. "How could they do this? It's unconscionable."

"Welcome to what used to be my family," he growled, wiping the wet from his face. "I didn't think they'd go this far—disown me for being who I am. It makes me feel like I'm dirty or something, even though it's a statement about their own transphobia. It hurts so bad. Cuts deep."

"How could it not? You're an upstanding, kind, intelligent man," Carolina said. "We're lucky to know and love you." She walked over and hugged him. "This is going to make Moss crazy. May I show him? Right now?"

Teal nodded. "There's nothing he can do, though. It's the final ruling."

Carolina took off. A few minutes later, they heard Moss roar, then he tore into the room and enfolded Teal in his arms. The young man wept in earnest.

Later that afternoon, Carolina walked to the front field to look for Rowan. She saw Zephyr and waved her arms. The dog came flying toward her. "Go find Rowan," she said.

Zephyr tore off and, two minutes later, girl and dog appeared at the edge of the woods.

"The whole crowd's going. 8 a.m. Want me to wake you?" Carolina asked.

"No need. Zephy wakes me when I want her to."

Surprised, Carolina only said, "I'll have breakfast ready."

After they enjoyed coffee cake and eggs, Moss pulled the van in front of the house. He was relieved they'd picked the Dodge Grand version to replace his old Caravan. With this family, they needed the additional space. Today, they'd still be crammed: five people—one of them in a car seat—and two not-small dogs. Who knew, maybe a third on the way home.

Five years ago, he hadn't known he could love this much, or had any idea he'd have a teenager and an infant. In addition, it was like Teal was his son. He wanted to adopt him, but it was too soon to bring it up, even with Carolina. He suspected she knew, though; her intuition unnerved him. In his innermost heart, he wanted to be able to give Teal both love and the stability of not having to worry about money. He could get additional gender reassignment surgeries if he chose. More important, he'd have a legal, loving family again.

Warmth bathed him as they poured out of the house toward the car, Zephyr and Jazz loping alongside. He wrapped his arms around himself and smiled.

"Go find your spots," Rowan called to the dogs, who pricked their ears and galloped to the field for a quick pit stop.

Teal fastened Graham into his car seat.

"You look very happy," Carolina said, after they got on the road.

"I am," Moss said, and squeezed her leg. "Happier than I've ever been."

Her name is Salaam, Rowan pensed to Zephyr after they got on the highway. *Mama wants her own dog. Tell me if Salaam is good for the pack. She has to like Graham.*

The Portland facility for Sighthound Friends was situated near the freeway. Cars and trucks vroomed by, the vibration rocketing through Rowan. She thought it was a strange environment for rescue dogs—some coming from faraway countries—nothing serene about this location to help them adjust. On the other hand, the rent was probably much lower because it *was* near an interstate. She leashed both dogs and, stretching her stiff muscles after the two-hour drive, got out so Teal had space to unstrap Graham from his car seat.

"I'll take him," Teal said. "Carolina, you need all of your attention on this dog."

"Thanks." She helped him get the baby into his front pack and gave Graham a kiss.

The family trooped inside. Rowan was struck by the smell of the place—earthy, but clean. What she could see was tidy, too. She heard an occasional bark. A large bulletin board sported more than a hundred photos of rescues who had been placed. She walked over to check them out. Lots of smiling families.

Moss limped to the front desk where he spoke to a twenty-something woman with tats and piercings. "Hi, we're here to meet Salaam. We've been through the approval process and Deborah is expecting us."

"The whole family came? Dope! I'm not sure about your dogs, though."

"Deborah gave us the okay. She just wants to assess them first. We've come from Eugene."

She snapped her gum. "I'll go find her. Y'all hang out here."

Ten minutes later, a woman around fifty came out, dressed in jeans, flannel shirt, and rubber boots. "Hello, Westburys." She introduced herself, then greeted the dogs. "Well, you're clearly Zephyr. Such a big, beautiful girl." She let Zeph sniff her hand. "And this is?" she looked at Jazz.

"This's Jazz," Rowan said. "Moss's girl."

"She seems more tentative."

"Her first owner was harsh," Moss said. "She's come a long way."

Deborah looked at Carolina. "I understand you're considering Salaam for yourself?"

"I am. I lost my dog Stormy in a rollover car accident five years ago. It took me a long while to get over it."

"And who's this cutie?" She reached out to Graham, who was trying to bounce in the front pack.

Moss clarified the relationships.

"So, this is the complete household?"

They all nodded.

"Follow me. We're going to an exercise yard—there are some chairs, though. I'll have Salaam brought out."

Once they got outside, Carolina said, "I'd like to greet her first, have a minute or two with her before she meets the whole crowd. Okay?"

Smart, Rowan thought.

When Deborah walked Salaam toward them, Rowan noticed how bone thin she was. Every rib poked out. Then she saw the Saluki hadn't tucked her tail. She looked unafraid, but not pushy, either. *Nice qualities.*

Zephyr immediately lay down. Jazz, as she always did when anxious, followed Zeph's lead and lay beside her, mirroring her position. Paws out front, they weren't rolling over and being submissive, but rather waited in a non-confrontive position. *Good girls.*

Teal jiggled Graham and watched with interest.

Carolina knelt in front of the slip of a dog. She didn't look at Salaam, but turned to the side. Rowan could hear her speaking soft words. Wow, Rowan thought, Mama has good instincts. I haven't given her credit.

Carolina reached out to stroke the rescue, but not on top of her head. She scratched the side of the dog's face, instead. She looked up at Deborah. "Why's she so darn skinny? She looks too thin, even for a sighthound."

"All the changes, I think. She's eating well now. She seems calm and doesn't show stress, but it apparently affected her appetite. We've put her on a high-calorie diet, and it would be good if she stayed on the same food. Later, when she's put on weight, you can switch her to what you feed your other dogs."

Carolina nodded. After a couple of minutes, she stood up. "I like her a lot. Okay, you guys can greet her now. And I have to see how she is with Graham."

"Row," Moss said, "you go first, and introduce her to Zeph and Jazz."

Rowan moved in closer, and like her mother, knelt. Salaam looked right at her—interested, with no sign of fear. Row talked to the dog, telling her how lucky she'd be to join this family. "Be cool with the baby," she whispered. She took the leash from the attendant and walked her over to Zephy, who didn't get up, but lifted her nose in greeting and wagged her tail. Salaam sniffed her, and did a play bow. Jazz whined and wriggled.

"May we let them off lead?" Rowan asked. "They're going to be fine. They should run around and spin off some energy before Salaam meets baby Graham."

Deborah stepped forward. "All right, they seem relaxed and curious. And you both greeted her in the best way possible."

Neither Jazz nor Salaam could match Zephyr's long strides, but they made tight corners, whereas Zeph had a wide turning radius. Within five minutes, all three were panting. Moss whistled and the dogs headed for him. He squatted and patted each one: Jazz, then Zephyr, Salaam third. "Zeph's the overall pack leader, but Jazz is my dog," he said to Deborah. "I always greet her first. Salaam's a pretty little thing. It looks like she'll fit in fine. Let's see how she does when she sniffs Graham."

Rowan pensed Zephy. *Can she join the pack?*

Zephyr lay down. *She fits in.*

Teal sat in one of the plastic lawn chairs. Carolina clipped the lead on Salaam and took her near the baby. Graham screeched with delight. The dog, surprised, arched her head back, but then her tail made slow, wide wags. Teal talked softly to her. She snuffled Graham for a solid minute and, seeming satisfied, went back to Carolina, who sat on the ground and hugged the dog. "My friend," she whispered, "I've found my four-legged friend."

"And Zephy likes her, too," Rowan said.

"Ah, good news, thanks," her mother said, "and what I wanted to hear."

Carolina filled out the extensive paperwork, signed the contract promising, should she ever have to give Salaam up, she would be returned to Sighthound Friends. She made out the check for the adoption fee and added an equal amount as a donation.

"Thank you." Deborah handed her a manila envelope. "Her health records, instructions about her diet," she said. "Please call with any questions. Send pictures, and we'll post them on the board up front." She leaned over and patted Salaam. "Bye, little one. I'm going to miss you, but it looks like you have a special home. Lucky girl."

Rowan got Zephyr and Jazz settled in the van before Carolina invited Salaam. The dog looked discombobulated, but jumped in and, with a soft groan, settled with the other two on the floor. Zeph carefully washed her available ear.

What a nice welcome, Rowan pensed.

Part of the pack, Zephyr sent back.

Carolina kept craning her head. As Moss started the car, Rowan said, "Mama, I'll trade seats with you. Come back here with your girl."

"That would be great." She got out of the front seat, opened the slider, and carefully stepped between the dogs to sit in the middle. Reaching down, she stroked Salaam. After a moment, the dog gave a wide yawn and fell asleep.

As Deborah waved from the door, Rowan saw her wipe her eyes.

Chapter Thirty-six

"Let's stop at the feed store on the way home," Carolina said. "I'll only be a few minutes. I need Salaam's kind of food, a bed, and a dog coat. I'll take her in to find the right size."

"May I come, too?" Rowan asked. "I love the place."

"Sure. Join me."

Rowan jumped out as Carolina leashed her girl and, softly talking to her, entered the store. Salaam was shivering. Carolina walked her to the coats first. She found a thick black fleece and slipped it on her. "Nope, you need a smaller one. Let's try a size down." She pulled it on. "Better. Cozy, huh? Gorgeous basic black." She left it with the tag intact and looked for the display of beds. One caught her eye immediately. It was like a big red fleece pocket. When she checked the label, it was called a "cave bed." "Great name. I bet you'll love this."

Rowan fingered it. "This is fabulous. You need to get one for Jazz, too. She doesn't have an undercoat, either."

"Right!" Carolina said. "Will you pick out a color for her?"

"You bet." Rowan sorted through the beds, picking royal purple with a gray lining.

"Perfect," Carolina said.

"I'll carry them to the counter—you have Salaam." She swung one over each shoulder.

"New dog?" The saleswoman asked.

Carolina nodded.

"She's a beauty." The woman looked at the sheet. "Yes, we carry this brand." She pointed. "Back right corner. Leave the beds here. Wait, I'll go with you. Let's take a cart."

Rowan set the caves down. "I'll be looking at bulk biscuits," she said.

Carolina was pleased when Salaam seemed unconcerned by the clatter of the wheels. She picked out a dozen cans of the high-calorie food and the largest bag of kibble. "Remember to ring up the coat, too," she said to the clerk, pointing to Salaam.

As they pulled into the driveway, Zephyr pensed Rowan, *Tell Pack Mama. Zeph teaches Salaam.*

Be gentle. She's little, Rowan responded.

Pack-leader Stormy teaches Zephyr, Zephyr teaches Salaam.

Mama will understand when I explain.

Carolina was excited to show Moss, Salaam, and Jazz the cave beds. When they got inside, she took Salaam's new coat off and hung it next to Jazz's in the utility room. Zephyr never needed extra warmth; she came with wiry fur and thick undercoat. With Salaam following, she put the sleeping caves in the master bedroom. She encouraged Salaam toward the red one, but the Saluki had other ideas. She whined and peered at Carolina.

"Do you need to go out? Are you hungry? Probably both. Come on, I'll show you the front field."

When they went outside, the other two dogs followed. Salaam seemed to stare at the big open space. Carolina realized she'd been in crates, cages, and small exercise yards for weeks. Once outside, Salaam sniffed the air. When she stepped on the grass, she lifted her paws high as though the turf tickled. Coming from Dubai, she's probably never seen a green field, Carolina thought. She was used to sand, not grass and weeds. As soon as Jazz and Zeph took off running, Salaam forgot the texture and flew after them. She marveled at their athletic play: dodging, feinting, leaping over one another.

When they'd tired out and done their business, she took them inside. "No dinner yet," she told them. Salaam shot down the hallway, and

Carolina followed behind, curious. The dog snuffled the cave thoroughly, and after stepping on it and off again—testing—she finally crawled in, curled up in the pocket, and closed her eyes. *She's a smart one.* Carolina smiled.

"Hey, sweet pea," Carolina called, hearing Rowan's footfall. "Check this out."

"That's the cutest thing ever! Look how at home she is, with her nose poking out. Has Jazz seen her pocket yet? Where's Da?"

"Around here somewhere. I was so addled with my new friend, I didn't see where they went. Dogs get under our skin—in a good way—so fast."

"They do. Mama, I want to remind you. Zephy's pack leader, and she may need to put Salaam in her place until she learns the routine around here."

Carolina frowned. "But my girl's so little. Insubstantial. Skinny. Zephyr's huge."

"Zeph'll be gentle. But she may growl or show her teeth. It's how dogs train the pack. Did you see Salaam running in the field today? She held her own, no problem." Rowan thought for a moment.

"What is it?"

"I'd limit how much she runs with the other dogs until she gains a few pounds so she doesn't sprint off all the calories you're stuffing her with. What'd it say in the records?"

"Thirty-nine pounds."

"Whoa, low. I figure she should be about forty-five. Wait until Dr. Francine meets her. She can advise you on her best weight." Rowan reached down and smoothed Salaam's nose.

"You know an amazing amount about dogs," Carolina said. "I'm always startled."

"It's what I love," Rowan said. "I research and read all the time, you know that."

Carolina sat down with her new friend and stroked her paws.

Fifteen minutes later, Moss walked in with Jazz. "Look at that," he said. "What a great invention." Jazz poked with interest at her new bed. Seeing Salaam curled up, Jazz shimmied into hers.

Lina smiled up at Moss. "Dinner time for the girls," she said. "I guess we need to stand by while they eat to make sure no one steals Salaam's food."

"She might eat better with them around," Rowan said. "The threat of competition can encourage appetite."

After Carolina set the dishes down in the laundry room, they stood back to watch. Jazz sniffed at Salaam's bowl. The new girl's lip went up, and Rowan heard a low-throated growl. Lina grabbed Rowan's arm. "Do something."

"Wait," Rowan whispered. "Give them time. They need to work this out."

When Jazz persisted, Salaam flashed a full toothy grimace, and the growl intensified. Jazz snarled back. Zephyr shouldered between them and gave a throaty, powerful rumble. Both dogs stepped back and dropped their tails.

"See? No problem," Rowan said. "Salaam can take care of herself. Small but mighty. I wouldn't mess with her. Zephyr, being pack leader, moderates everything."

"Salaam's street-dog training shows," Carolina said. "Having seen this, I'm a lot less worried about her joining our pack."

"Don't you wonder what she's been through?" Rowan asked.

"I think about it a lot," her mom answered. "I'm glad she's surrounded by love now."

The house settled for the evening. Moss finished up the dishes. Carolina nursed Graham and put him down for the night, Teal retired to his room to write, and Rowan and Zephyr went downstairs. Jazz and Salaam followed Moss and Carolina into the family room.

"The two of us," Moss said. "And the girls. Let's talk about the book-awards trip. Only ten days away."

Carolina tapped her cheek.

"What?" he asked.

She wrapped her arms around him and whispered, "I can't leave Salaam. Not for a couple of months. I'm sorry, I wanted to share the event with you. You've been working toward this for so long."

He pulled back. "You're not coming? Geez, I hadn't imagined." He walked across the room. "We've been planning this for a long time. You'd favor your dog over me?"

Lina frowned at him. "Wait a minute. Not fair. *You* found her; *you* brought me your iPad and pointed out she looked special."

"I did, but I never imagined you'd blow off going to New York. I want you by my side. This is a big deal, being a finalist for a well-known national award."

Carolina pulled a remorseful face and shrugged. "I know. It is. But life unexpectedly intervened. I'll stay here with Graham and the pack, and you, Rowan, and Teal can have a real writers' long weekend." She rubbed her fingers across her forehead. "Sue wouldn't stay here; she always wants the dogs at her place. Imagine how confusing it would be for Salaam. She'd think I'd abandoned her, sent her to yet another home. I'm *not* putting her through that. For God's sake, in my shoes, you wouldn't either."

Moss tapped his thumbnail on his teeth. "No," he grumbled. "You're right. I guess I wouldn't. We could get a paid dog sitter to stay here. Okay?"

Carolina shook her head. "I'm sorry, I'm not willing to leave her with a stranger."

"Well, damn," he said, and walked out of the room.

Guilt knotted her solar plexus. Her head heated up. She wanted to pound the wall. *He did it again. Up and left.*

Moss stuck his head back in the doorway. "I gotta take ten and clear my head."

"Okay," she said. *Well, at least he remembered his promise.* The lump in her chest softened. *I guess he's teachable.*

Chapter Thirty-seven

Fifteen minutes later, Moss walked back into the family room. "I'm calmer," he said, "and I have a plan for your consideration. What about this: Rowan, Teal, and I will go for the full four days. You and Graham fly in Saturday for cocktails, dinner, and awards ceremony. Work the room and schmooze with me, and we'll all head home the next morning." He tilted his head, eyebrows raised.

She swallowed and, glancing down at Salaam, smoothed her fingers over the dog's head, lingering on her soft ears. "Quite a trip for two days, but it's a fair compromise. You're on. But we still need a dog sitter to stay with the girls for those thirty-six hours. And will you get my tickets?"

"On it. I'll find a dog sitter, too, and have him or her come over three or four times beforehand, so Salaam gets familiar."

"Someone good who knows dogs. Please. Let's not skimp. Get Zephyr involved."

"You bet," he said. "Can we make up now? It takes a big toll when we get out of rhythm. Freaks me out."

"You're not kidding," she muttered, folding into his arms. "Me, too. I don't value my dog more than you, but she's brand new to us. And she's been through so much."

He pulled her close. "I know, sweetheart; it's awful timing. Thanks for accommodating me. I can't imagine facing an event like this without you—I'm such an introvert. I want you by my side."

"Thank you. Do you think you might win?"

"A war memoir?" He reared back and squinted at her. "Nope. Not people's favorite read. Some of us veterans have to write them, though; it's how we deal with what we've been through." He kissed her forehead. "If they think it's well-written and compelling, they make us a finalist—that's our prize. Then they give first place to a happier story."

She hugged him tight. "It's a huge honor to be a finalist. Stand proud."

Salaam slipped between them, stuck her head up, and nosed Carolina.

"She wants to be included." Carolina looked up at Moss and gave a happy sigh.

Moss leaned down to stroke Salaam. "Such a good sign; you've only had her a few hours. It was the same with Jazz, too—she fit in immediately."

Jazz heard her name and came to join the party. Any dinnertime animosity had vanished. Moss and Carolina sat on the floor and ruffled their dogs until it seemed like they were smiling.

Does Salaam fit into the pack? Rowan pensed Zephyr.

She listens to pack-leader. She can stay.

Rowan was curious. *Do you like her?* Zephyr looked up. Rowan could swear Zeph was trying to figure out what to communicate.

Salaam's friendly. She runs with us. Pack Mama needs her. She belongs to Pack Mama.

Salaam needs Mama, too. Maybe more. Can Salaam pense? I don't want to try—she's Mama's dog, not mine.

Can Pack Mama? Zephyr asked.

Good question. I doubt it. Come up on the bed. Rowan reached to turn off the light. *Kibble Man, Teal, Pack Mama, Graham, and I are traveling on an airplane. I guess you dogs will stay with Sue.*

Pack Mama leaves Salaam? Too fast.

You're right. I wonder what will happen. Rowan snuggled close.

Moss spent a busy morning calling dog sitters. He found a guy named Jason who was available. "Can you come over this afternoon?" he asked. "We'd like you to visit three or four times before my wife, Carolina, leaves a week from Saturday, early in the morning."

"Okay. Five o'clock?"

"Sure. I'll text the address."

Then, he set about getting Lina her flights and, once those were pinned down, he went to find her.

Carolina was in the kitchen chopping celery. Salaam lay nearby.

"What are you up to?" he asked, giving her a kiss and bending down to greet the Saluki.

"I'm making venison this-and-that soup—a variation of the chicken version. I'll ask Teal to pick up some seeded French bread." She began cutting up meat.

"Sounds yummy. A dog sitter, a guy named Jason, is coming today at five." He sat on a kitchen stool. "I got your tickets. Here's the itinerary. Sorry, it's a 6 a.m. flight out of Eugene. I had to route you through Denver—nothing direct."

"Ugh. I can leave the car parked at the airport, though."

"It has to be early to get you to New York in time for the festivities. You know, three hours later there."

Rowan and Zephyr answered a knock at the door. Zephyr greeted him, then backed off.

"Hi there," Jason said. "A little shy, are we?"

"Um, she's not shy at all," Rowan said, frowning.

"Oh, not to worry. I'll win her over." He snapped his fingers and made squeaky noises.

"Well, come into the living room."

Zephyr lay down, facing away from him.

What's wrong? Rowan pensed.

He bites.

Carolina and Moss walked in with Salaam, who ran over to meet the young man.

"She's a friendly one," Jason said.

"We've only had her a couple of days," Carolina patted her. "I hate to leave her for even twenty-four hours."

"She won't notice you're gone. Dogs love me."

My dog doesn't, Rowan thought. She said to Jason, "I'd like to know about your training methods. If one of our dogs did something wrong, like put her feet on the kitchen counter, what would you do?"

"Smack her paws and push them off."

Carolina, who'd leaned over to pat Salaam, jerked her head up. "What about a quiet 'no' instead?"

"I have a lot of experience. Dogs need stronger action than you'd think."

"Ours don't," Rowan said. She and her mom exchanged glances.

"We're done here," Carolina said. "This isn't a good fit."

"Wait, you misunderstood me. I have to be pack leader."

"There was no misunderstanding," Moss pushed up to his full height. "Did you not hear what my wife said to you? The interview is over. I'll see you out."

Rowan said, "Wait a minute. Jason, have you ever sat for sighthounds before?"

He stopped. "What are sighthounds?"

"Dogs who run like lightning and hunt with their eyes. And," she went on, "they are different from other dogs—far more sensitive. I knew one wolfhound who lay in the kitchen, a spot which blocked the route to the living room, the bathroom, and the bedrooms. The father snapped at the dog one day—'get out' in a raised voice. For the rest of her life, the wolfhound never lay there again."

Jason looked surprised. "Whoa. Well, good luck finding someone better than me."

"Morgan—a woman, I guess it's an androgynous name—is coming at 4 p.m. today," Moss said, five days later.

"It's a relief you found someone else. You're all leaving in two days," Carolina responded. "If we don't find anyone, I can't go."

"Mama, I could stay home. I'm the dog girl, after all. You need to be there, by Da's side."

"It's a sweet offer, but let's wait before making such a big decision," Moss said. "We'll see how this unfolds. If we like her, she can come the day before and sleep in the yurt. Her references checked out. I called three of them. They were all enthusiastic."

Rowan and Zeph were waiting when the doorbell rang.

The woman's hands flew to her face. "I'm Morgan. I didn't realize you had a wolfhound. I lost my wolfie five months ago." She was already on her knees with her arms wrapped around Zephyr's neck.

"I'm sorry. It's hard to lose our buddies. Zephy is actually a mix of deerhound and wolfhound."

"She's gorgeous." Morgan got to her feet and wiped her eyes.

Rowan invited her inside. The other two dogs trotted into the room. "This is Jazz, Moss's dog, and here's Salaam, the newest member of our family. My mom's only had her for a week—she's a rescue from Dubai. Come into the living room. My parents'll be here in a sec." She pointed to a comfortable chair.

Morgan sat, but her hands were busy patting all the dogs, smiling and talking to them. "Are they getting along all right? Accepting Salaam?"

"So far. Protecting her food, she got a bit uppity with Jazz, but Zephy shouldered her way between them. Problem solved."

"Zephyr is your pack leader."

"Yes. Jazz is a little older, but came into the family second. Here are my mom and dad, Carolina and Moss. This is Morgan."

Carolina shook her hand. "The rest of the family will be gone for four days, but I pared my participation down to a day and a half. I hate the thought of being away from Salaam any time in these first months, but it can't be helped." She sat on the couch. Salaam jumped up and lay beside Carolina, head in her lap.

"You're bonded already," Morgan said.

"It happens fast when the fit is right," Moss said. "Carolina has to leave around 4 a.m. so, if this works out, we thought you could come the night before and stay in our yurt." Moss pointed out the window. "There's a comfortable Murphy bed and a bathroom. If you want to stay the second night out there, the dogs are welcome in the space. They'll need to be with you."

They asked about her experience, and Rowan queried her about training methods. Zephyr jumped on the couch too, and pensed Rowan. *Girl doesn't bite.*

"Also," Moss said, "we have a huge field—no dog walking necessary. They run like crazy out there."

"If dog walking isn't required, I'd consider dropping my price."

"Please don't," Carolina said. "If you like the girls, we want you to be happy enough to come again."

Teal walked in with Graham nestled in the crook of his elbow, patting him on the butt with his other hand. "Sorry to interrupt, but he needs to nurse."

"Thanks." She took Graham, pulled a shawl from the couch back, and after draping herself, put him to her breast.

Carolina introduced Teal and Graham. "Now you've met the whole family."

"Where are you going?" Morgan asked.

"I'm a finalist for the American Literary Society awards. Everyone—except Carolina and Graham—is going to New York City for the writing conference associated with the organization. Rowan, Teal, and I all write. Lina didn't want to leave her new dog, but I talked her into coming for the awards dinner part."

"How exciting," Morgan exclaimed, her eyes wide. "You don't find out what you've won until dinner?"

"Exactly—*if* I've won. Being a finalist is all the honor I need. By the way, I called your references, and got excellent reports. Carolina? Rowan?"

Carolina glanced at her daughter, who gave her a little nod. "Morgan, we'd like to hire you. But can you come a couple of times so the girls get to know you before I actually leave?"

"Sure," Morgan said. "It'll be a pleasure to care for your sighthounds."

A collective sigh of relief passed through the room.

Chapter Thirty-eight

Rowan craned her neck as the plane approached New York but couldn't spot the skyscrapers. She slumped in her seat and turned to her dad. "I wanted to see the city from above. I'm disappointed."

"You're right, the plane doesn't give a view of the skyline. Wait 'til we drive into Manhattan."

"Why is the drive special? You're not above it like in an airplane."

"You'll see."

"Row, switch seats with me? I want to look out the window while we land," Teal said. "I've only ever been in the Lear, never in a plane this gigantic."

She squinched her mouth. "Okay, sure, fair enough. Come on, before they won't let us anymore."

Once they moved, Rowan asked Moss, "Where're we staying?"

"The Plaza Hotel. It's iconic, and I thought it'd be the most fun. Besides, it overlooks Central Park, and is only a five-minute walk to the conference venue."

"The Plaza—cool. Even I've heard of it," she said.

Teal went white at the thumps and rumbles in preparation for landing. "What the hell?"

"Landing gear," Moss said. "Completely normal."

The plane lurched and dropped hard. Some of the bins above them flew open and coats, laptop cases, even a couple of small carry-ons tumbled out. The woman in the seat in front of Moss got bonked by a suitcase and screamed.

Teal grabbed Rowan. She squealed.

"Not normal," Moss cried. "Are you two all right?"

A moment later, the pilot came on the intercom. "Sorry folks, bad air pocket. Call the attendants if you have injuries. I'll get us down as quickly and safely as possible."

Moss reached across Rowan to pat Teal's arm. "You can let go now. It's over."

"My heart's out of control." His voice shook. "It scared the crap out of me."

"Me, too. The woman's hurt," Rowan said, and stabbed at her call button. "Da, can you reach it? She's bleeding."

Moss raised his voice. "Wounded passenger at 56F. We need a doctor." He got out his handkerchief and held it against the stranger's forehead.

Emergency teams met the plane. Passengers disembarked, the staff asking each one: "Are you all right? Do you want to be seen by a doctor?"

Thirty minutes later, after answering questions, they trudged to the baggage claim. When they got there, Teal's eyes went wide. "This is ginormous. How do we know where to find our gear?"

Moss pointed to the airline and flight number on each carousel. "See the conveyor belt? Our suitcases will arrive through the little flappy door."

Forty minutes later, delayed by the flight incident and, after loud horn sounds, the bags finally lumbered along the conveyor belt. Teal and Moss grabbed them.

Once outside, Moss, giving a shrill two-fingered whistle, hailed a cab. The bulked-up cabby with missing teeth slung the bags into the trunk.

"Plaza Hotel. Take the Brooklyn Bridge, would you please?" Moss asked. "I know it's not the most direct, but I want them to catch a glimpse of Lady Liberty."

"Cost ya' a bit more." He glanced at Moss.

"Of course."

The cabby swiveled around. "First time in the ciddy for yew guys?" he asked, in a thick Jersey accent.

Both Teal and Rowan nodded.

"'Kay. I'll give yew a show of my town. I'm a proud New Yorka. Din't grow up here, though."

"I never would have guessed," Moss smiled at him.

"Yeah, damn accent gives me away every time. I don't even hear it. Oh well."

Rowan gasped when they entered the bridge span. "How beautiful this is!" She had her head out the window staring upward at the arches—they seemed like they belonged in a cathedral—and suspension cables.

"Man, check out the skyline," Teal whispered. "This city is huge."

"Approaching eight million souls," Moss said.

"There's the Lady," the cabby called out, pointing.

Both Rowan and Teal gawked at the statue.

"She's regal," Rowan said.

"Yes, she's supposed to be an inspiration for all people, but particularly immigrants who came through Ellis Island, which is closeby. She was dedicated in 1886—a gift from the people of France to the people of the United States. Please take us up Sixth Avenue," he said to the cabby. "They'll be able to catch a glimpse of the Empire State Building and the Museum of Modern Art. Sadly, we're not sightseeing—we're here for a conference."

"Will do, boss."

Traffic was thick. A half hour later, they pulled up in front of The Plaza.

"What a stately old building." Now, Teal had his head out the window gazing upward.

"Yes, it is. The furnishings are old-fashioned but elegant, if I remember correctly."

The bellhop led them to their rooms on the eleventh floor. He unlocked Rowan's first, carried her suitcase in from the cart, and placed it on the luggage rack. "I hope you're very comfortable, Miss. Call the front desk if there is anything you want or need. Enjoy your stay with us."

After he left, Rowan stared, her gaze landing first on the king bed with its ornate cream and gold headboard. She counted *six* pillows. A writing desk with Queen Anne legs sat at the window. She only knew the style because Ma had an antique table like this one in their Connecticut home. *What is Teal feeling?* She was sure he'd never been in a place like this before. She walked to the window and took in the view of Central Park. What a relief to see a large expanse of green in this stone-building and taxi-filled city. Horns blared. *Do they stop at night?* She unzipped her suitcase, but decided to find Teal, and knocked softly on his door. "It's me, Row."

"Come on in."

She tried the handle, but it was locked. She knocked again.

"Oh, sorry." Teal opened the door and bowed her in with a sweep of his arm. "Enter, my lady. Can you *believe* this place?"

"Nope. Very fancy. Did you check out the view?"

"Not yet."

They went to the window.

"Central Park," she said. "Isn't it gorgeous?"

"It's wonderful they saved the green space. Can you imagine what each square yard is worth?"

"I didn't think about the value. I was wondering if bunnies and deer live there."

"I kind of doubt it. More likely squirrels and birds." Teal leaned forward to squint out the window. "Probably raptors, too. I don't have a clue."

"Look, Teal. You have a writing table."

"The thing looks like it might break if I set my laptop on it."

"Go ahead. It's sturdier than you think—after all, it lives in a hotel."

"Good point. Maybe I can write about almost dying this afternoon." He blew out a loud breath. "Do I have to get back on a plane again to get home? How do I make myself go through the door?"

"We'll hang on to each other. It scared me, too."

"Are we going to walk over and register for the conference? Let's get Moss. Wait, I need to use the head, first." Teal trotted to the bathroom.

A couple of minutes later, he walked back into the room, eyes wide. "Did you see all the little bits in the bathroom? Soap, shampoo, body cream, conditioner, even. Do we have to pay for those?"

"Nope," Rowan said. "They're free. But anything in the fridge here—even water—costs. Big. Okay, let's go find Moss."

They walked the five blocks to the conference. The place was abuzz with people. "They're *all* writers," Moss said. "Let's pick up our packets. There's a keynote speaker tonight at dinner. Someone said the original person had to cancel due to a family emergency."

Teal tore open his envelope the moment he got it. "Moss—it's Tim O'Brien."

Moss's face lit up. "*The* Tim O'Brien? Let me see." He scanned the sheet Teal handed him. "I'll be darned. He was a finalist for the 1991 Pulitzer. I've looked up to him for decades. He wrote *The Things They Carried* as fiction rather than memoir. I think they call it 'semi-autobiographical.'"

They found some seats in the reception area and sat down. "What workshops did you two sign up for?" he asked.

"I chose mostly the nonfiction track, since I want to write about animal communication," said Rowan. "But I gave myself one fiction class. What about you, Teal?"

"Fiction and poetry. Moss?"

"Fiction and one workshop on memoir. It's on the difference between backstory and flashback."

"I wish I could take every workshop. Let's try to take useful notes and share them, okay?" Rowan suggested.

"Smart idea. It'll be a full four days." Moss pored over the rest of the packet.

"How's Mama getting here? Will you pick her up?"

"No. She'll take a cab to The Plaza and I'll meet her there at 3 p.m. Saturday." He tapped one sheet. "Look, there's an orientation in fifteen minutes. Let's go."

Rowan stretched out in the vast expanse of her bed, stuffed pillows behind her until the shape was cozy, and closed her eyes. It had been a long travel day, and the conference bustled with animated people. Used to a quiet, dog-filled life, she was worn from the commotion. She'd met a lot of wonderful writers, and was pleased that—though she was only sixteen—this crowd treated her as an equal. It felt great. She hadn't spotted any other teens. There were some college-age kids, though. She pensed Zeph.

How was your day?

Zephyr naps, but wakes for her girl. The pack is calm.

Is Salaam a good pack member?

Zephyr lip lifts and Salaam behaves at food time.

How's Jazz?

Jazz misses Kibble Man. Follows Pack Mama around.

We'll be home after four dark times. I miss you, Zephy.

Zephyr and Rowan together.

Yes, we are, always.

Chapter Thirty-nine

Carolina sat at her computer and added to the informational list about their dogs Rowan had started for Morgan: who eats what and when, where they each sleep, what words they know. Frowning, she focused on Jazz's vocabulary, which was different from Zephyr's. Salaam, of course, didn't know many English words yet, although she did respond to "dinner" tonight.

After her awful attitude over the past four years, she couldn't imagine telling Rowan, but she secretly wished she could communicate with Salaam. As her wacky mother's daughter, perhaps she could develop the ability. It felt scary to even consider opening that door with her own daughter. How could she possibly backtrack from her staunch, unbending, critical position? It would make her look like a fool. Wouldn't it? Did it matter?

She pushed away from her computer desk and paced the room, chewing on this dilemma. Graham let out a wail. She saved Morgan's dog list and went into her son's room. "Hey, baby," she soothed, picking him up. "I bet you're hungry and need changing. Let's get you a fresh diaper first. It's no fun sitting in a wet wad."

Graham gave her a gummy smile and reached for her face. She set him on the changing table and, keeping one hand on him, grabbed a diaper and fresh change of clothes. She unsnapped his footed sleeper and slipped it off. He cooed as she eased up his feet and slipped off the weighty diaper.

Teal surely made raising a baby much easier. Whenever she was beaten down by Graham's teething irritability, she could hand him over and collapse for a nap. They took night shifts, too—the three of them in rotation: Carolina, Teal, Moss. Rowan offered, but she had to be fresh for school. They'd nixed the idea.

As she settled in the rocker with a dry and hungry baby and put him to the breast, Salaam came to lie at her feet. Carolina was grateful to have a dog of her own again, and such a sweet one. Morgan had come by today—her third visit—and the Saluki seemed at ease with her.

She could tell Graham had gained weight. *He has a healthy pudgy feel.* For a moment, pictures of Andrea surfaced, and her throat clogged. Her chest felt full and tight. She allowed the feelings, and sent her little girl, forever gone, blessings.

While Graham suckled, she thought about the rest of her family in New York. What fun they must be having, all word mavens immersed in what they loved most. Neither Rowan nor Teal had been to a writing conference before. She was sure Moss delighted in introducing them to this part of the writing world. And to stay at The Plaza—so special.

She'd just heard from Ma and Pa in Connecticut. They're planning to surprise Moss at the awards dinner. He'd love that.

By the end of the third day, Rowan felt awash in fascinating, new writing information. She'd taken pages and pages of notes on her laptop. The three of them got together and debriefed each evening, sharing what they loved, what was most startling, and what they hadn't understood. They tried to puzzle through their confusions together.

"I'm excited about Mama getting here tomorrow," Rowan said.

"I've missed her," Moss added, "and my son."

Teal stretched to his full 5'7" height with his hands interlaced over his head. "And I'm anxious to see Graham. He's such a big part of my life; it's been weird to be away from him. Probably Carolina needs a nighttime break, and I'll be happy to get up with him."

"I wonder if she's stressed out leaving Salaam. I would be." Rowan pulled an earring out and rubbed her lobe.

"What's Zeph's report on the state of the pack?" Moss poured himself a glass of wine and offered one to Teal, who smiled and took it.

"Salaam pays attention to Zephy's lead, which is most important. It's all good. No fights. Da, are you nervous about tomorrow night?"

"What about?"

"Good grief. The *awards.*"

"No, sweet girl. The prize was getting to come to New York with the two of you and immerse ourselves in craft for four days. And to stay at this gorgeous old hotel."

"Well, I'm nervous for you," Teal said. "You deserve more. Your writing's fantastic."

"Named finalist in a national contest of this stature is huge. It's plenty, and could change the trajectory of my writing career." Moss scratched his chin. "Don't forget, tomorrow we have to dress for dinner."

"I get to wear my jacket for the first time." Teal moved from the window to a chair. "I hung it in the closet the moment we got here."

"Grab your dinner clothes, bring them here, and let's see if anything needs attention. If so, I'll call room service."

They laid their outfits on Moss's bed. "Row, we'll get your dress pressed. My shirt needs it, too. And your jacket, Teal. Did you bring a tie?"

"I forgot. Not used to them."

"There's time during the break to walk over to Fifth Avenue and buy one." He surveyed the clothes on the bed. "We're going to look smart tomorrow night."

Carolina and Morgan went over the specifics during dinner. "Here are our cell numbers," Carolina said. "Call with any questions. As you can see, Jazz's vocabulary is different from the others."

"Because?"

"Our vet in Sisters rehomed her with Moss after his owner died. The guy was very strict. She has phobias, and won't vary from the vocabulary she was taught—like she won't eat unless you say 'free chow.'"

"After four years, still she won't relearn some words?"

"Nope. She looks up with a worried expression."

"The guy never should have had a dog," Morgan muttered.

"My thoughts exactly. She's such a sweetie, too."

"We'll be fine. My, it's nine already. You need to get to bed early. What time are you getting up?"

"Four a.m. The flight's at six, but it's only a twenty-minute drive to the airport. I'm packed except for one thing—will you help me choose what to wear to the awards dinner tomorrow night?"

Morgan laughed. "I hardly know you. How can I help?"

"I've laid out three outfits; I have to pick one."

"Tell me about the dinner."

"It's at a fancy hotel. They expect more than four hundred people for the awards presentation—you know, lots of family supporting their writer. Come look."

Carolina had her clothes and accessories on the bed. One black dress, one red, one teal.

"I'm going to have to see them on you," Morgan said.

"Happy to." Lina grabbed the red outfit and slipped into the bathroom.

"Smart. Sassy, even," Morgan said, when Carolina came back into the bedroom. "Which is Moss's favorite? Wouldn't you want to wear it?"

"I'll tell you after you pick."

After Lina tried on all three outfits, Morgan pointed. "The teal. It's stunning, and complements your lovely red highlights. Now, which does Moss like?"

"The one you picked. I thought maybe I should do basic black. You know, New York City and all."

"Nope. Stand out. Be different. What's Moss wearing?"

"A navy suit. He's smashing in it."

"You'll be such a handsome couple. Does he have a teal tie? Take it with you if he does. Then you'll be coordinated."

"What a cool thought. I bought it for him. I'll go fish it out right now."

Carolina dragged herself out of bed in the dark when the alarm blared. The hardest part was saying goodbye to Salaam. Would she feel abandoned? Carolina knelt down and looked the Saluki right in the eyes. "I'll be back, girl, tomorrow late. We'll all be back. You be good for Morgan." She swiped her face and stood to leave. Salaam whined, a low disturbed sound. Carrying Graham, Carolina walked her to the yurt. She tried to open the door quietly, but Morgan woke up. "Salaam is upset I'm leaving. She seems to know."

"I'll bet she feels your anxiety. She'll likely be fine once you go. I'll keep a close watch on her. Where are Zephyr and Jazz?"

"In the house."

"We'll go in and all be together. Normal routine is best. Now you skedaddle and catch your plane."

Moss waited anxiously at The Plaza. Lina texted him when she and Graham were on the ground, but her flight was late and time was short. He checked his watch again. They still had ten minutes until the festivities started. He was dressed and ready. And nervous.

Fifteen minutes later, he heard the text ping. "Awful traffic. Finally on the Manhattan side. I'll make a quick change at the hotel. Go on to the party; we'll meet you there."

"Damn," he muttered, and punched the buttons for Rowan. "Mama's caught in heavy traffic. She said they'll meet us there. Are you dressed yet?"

"Five minutes and I'll be good to go," she said.

"Great. I'll call Teal."

"He texted me—he's waiting to hear from you."

"I'll collect him first. We'll come to your room."

Moss knocked on Teal's door. He stepped back when he saw the young man. "You certainly look handsome. The young guys will be checking you out."

Teal blushed. "You've never seen me dressed up. Thanks."

"Let's get Rowan and head over to the party. Carolina and Graham are going to be late—heavy traffic."

The three of them walked to the venue. They handed in their tickets at the registration table and received name tags. The room was huge, and

Moss's heart skipped beats seeing all the people. He badly wanted Lina by his side. Readings were easy—small groups. He'd been at large events before, but few since Afghanistan, and none where he was one of the guests of honor. PTSD made him warier of crowds, and he instinctively glanced around, noting the exits.

The bar took up the left side with plenty of space for the milling crowd. It looked at least sixty feet long with bartenders every seven feet or so. The rest was filled with round tables, neatly appointed with white tablecloths, handsome table settings, and place cards. Painted murals covered the high, vaulted ceiling. A large, well-appointed dais adorned the front.

Rowan showed up at his side. "Mossy, will you please get me a Shirley Temple and yourself a glass of merlot? You're tense."

"Terrified, more like it," he said. "Too many people. Sure. Teal, will you come with me? I can't carry three at once."

Teal hesitated, and Moss saw right through him. "The whole trip's on me. Have anything you want, son. Neither of us can get drunk, though." He laughed. "That's what I'd like to do right about now."

"I'd love to try something new. I've never had sangria; do you think they'd have it?"

"Let's ask the bartender."

Moss turned to his daughter. "Could you find our table so we know where to go when they call dinner?"

"Our table number's in the corner of our name tags. We're sitting"—she glanced at each person's badge—"at two. I'm assuming it's near the front, most likely for the finalists and their families." She pointed. "Near the platform."

"Here's a new word for you: dais. Raised platform."

"Dais. Cool. Thanks, Da. I'll go find the table."

Moss ordered drinks. Teal carried his sangria and Rowan's Shirley Temple; Moss picked up his merlot and took a deep sip.

A svelte gray-haired woman came up to him. "Moss Westbury?"

"Yes. How'd you know?"

She smiled. "You do have a name tag on, but I recognized you from your author photo. My name's Cara Stewart. I sit on the board. You wrote one powerful memoir."

"Thanks. It didn't come easily. Do you write?"

"I don't. But I'm an inveterate reader."

"What's your role on the board?"

"Fundraiser. I have a lot of experience, and organizations like this always need contributions."

"I'd be terrible at your job."

"And I'd rather be an author. But I believe we gravitate toward what we're good at, yes? Do you have family here with you? I'd love to meet them."

"My daughter's here, and a young writing friend. My wife and baby son are caught in traffic, but I expect them any minute." He waved at Rowan and Teal, signaled them to come over, and made introductions.

"We loved the conference," Teal said.

"They were even respectful of me, and inclusive, too," Rowan said.

"Well, they'd better be. What made you think they might treat you otherwise?"

"I'm only sixteen."

"They'd never say it, but I bet they're in awe of you, getting a start this young. I am. Wonderful."

"There's your mom and Graham," Moss said, waving.

"Go," Cara said, "but I'd love to meet them later."

Teal was holding and talking to the baby by the time Moss threaded his way across the crowded room. People had discovered Graham and were clustered around Teal. Moss had to get through them to reach Carolina, who was hugging Rowan. Frustrated, he gave a soft version of his shrill whistle. The group came to attention. "I want to greet my wife," he said, smiling. "May I slide through, please?"

The way parted and, when he got to Carolina, his first words were, "You look gorgeous."

Chapter Forty

Carolina blushed at his compliment, then let out a surprised "whoop" as he dipped her back, like a ballroom dancer, into a hungry kiss. "I've missed you so," he whispered. "Thank you, thank you for coming. Having you by my side means everything." He eased her up to standing again. "How about a glass of wine?"

"Please. I got anxious in traffic, sure we would never get here. After all this—leaving Salaam, the long trip with Graham—I didn't want a jam at the end to cause me to miss anything."

"You can afford to lose half an hour of a cocktail party. Perfect timing," he said. "But first, I need to say hi to my son." He went to Teal, who immediately handed him off. "Hey, baby boy."

Delighted, Carolina watched Moss lean over and breathe in Graham's scent. The baby grabbed his dad's ear.

"Whoa, what a grip. Okay son, let me go now."

Carolina reached over and peeled his baby fingers back. "Ouch."

"It smarted, all right. A new trick, I see."

"Every day something new."

"Is it a dad thing to assume it means he's especially bright?"

"Nah. Moms do it, too. Can you please give him back to Teal and get my wine before we sit for dinner?"

Moss, looking reluctant, handed him into Teal's outstretched arms. He heard a familiar voice, and glanced up. Smiling widely, Pa and Ma waved. He did a double take, not believing his eyes.

"They wanted to surprise you," Carolina said. "It's been really hard keeping it a secret."

His mom, tears in her eyes, gave him a hug. "We're so proud of you!"

"We wouldn't miss this," his dad said.

"Wow. I'm thrilled you're both here!" Moss replied. "Please get a drink at the bar, put it on my tab, and we'll meet you at the table. It's number two up front."

On the way, Carolina said, "You're looking very handsome. I brought you a different tie—it's only so it'll match my dress. Here." She fished in her purse and handed it to him.

"Do I have to?" He scrunched his forehead.

"It's a girl thing. Humor me."

"Okay, then. I love us to be seen as connected. You go to the bar with my folks, order your wine, and I'll make a brief pit stop to switch this out. Meet you here?"

They reconnected a few minutes later. "Like this tie better?" he asked Carolina.

She smoothed his suit jacket. "Perfect, thanks. You look dapper."

"Come with me, sweetheart." Moss looked around and spotted Cara. "The Society's fundraiser person wants to meet you. I talked to her before you got here."

"Why, I know you," Cara said, when they walked up to her. "We attended the same high school, remember? My last name was Bartholomew. I should have realized, with your less common first name, it was most likely the same person. How did you meet your husband?"

"Of course. We took Spanish together senior year—you were very good at languages." Carolina relayed the brief outline of how they met. "After we married, he adopted my daughter, Rowan. And now we have an infant son together, Graham." She teared up and looked down at the floor, blinking hard.

The ceiling lights flashed. "It's dinnertime," Cara said. "Do you need help finding your table?"

"Thanks, but our daughter already scoped it out," Moss said. "And my parents surprised me. They showed up about ten minutes ago."

"That's delightful," Cara said. "Good luck."

"Being a finalist was my good luck," Moss replied.

After dessert was served—dark-chocolate bread pudding—Cara rose to make an announcement. "When the dishes are cleared, you'll have fifteen minutes to use the facilities, refresh your drinks, and sit back down for the awards presentation. We'll ring a bell and flash the lights. Please be prompt."

Rowan savored the depth of the rich, scrumptious flavor. She nudged Teal. "This is even better than Maggie's fudge pie. Do you think they might give me the recipe if I beg?"

"I doubt it," Teal answered. "It's one of the hotel's specialties. I saw it listed on a menu posted near the door."

"I'm getting quivery. It's weird Da doesn't seem to be."

"He's told himself for months, this is it—no further award. I think it's how he's managed his expectations."

After the bell rang, and everyone settled in their chairs, Cara introduced the Society's president, Stephanie Greystone, an elegant, willowy, white-haired woman. She took the microphone. "I'll be presenting the awards this evening—until my voice gives out. I've had a touch of laryngitis. When I can't talk any longer, Tim O'Brien, who gave our keynote speech the first night, will take over. There are six finalists in each category: poetry, fiction, and memoir. I'll announce the three awards in reverse order, starting with third place. If your name is called, please come up to receive your plaque and monetary gift. The first-place winners in each genre will be asked to speak briefly or, if they choose, read a short segment from their work. In poetry—"

Fascinated, Rowan watched the faces of the authors. On some, she saw subtle disappointment they tried to cover when they hadn't placed higher. On others, joy they'd received an additional prize lit them up. She felt her own envy, and understood, for the first time, that she wanted her writing recognized someday. The conference had ignited new desire.

When the first-place fiction author finished speaking, she sensed a change in Moss. It was like he steeled himself. He wasn't completely immune after all.

At the start of the memoir presentations, the president apologized, and handed over the microphone to Tim O'Brien. Memoir's third place: not Mossy. Second place: not Mossy. Rowan's hopes skyrocketed. Eyes wide, she turned to her dad. First place: some woman from India.

He covered her hand. "It's fine," he mouthed. "Be glad for her. I'm sure she deserved it."

"We're not quite done," O'Brien said, after the winning memoirist completed her speech. "This year, for the first time since 1966, the Society has a grand prize to be awarded for outstanding excellence." He fumbled with the envelope. "I don't even know what category it's in."

Carolina knew—knew for sure—what was coming, and suppressed her desire to shove it down, like she'd had all other intuitions over the last twenty-five years. She needed to practice allowing the knowing if she ever wanted to learn to communicate with Salaam.

Tim O'Brien opened the envelope. Moss lifted his chin, clearly preparing for the final blow of the evening as he watched the card being pulled from the envelope. "The decision to offer the grand prize after forty-three years was not made lightly. The committee knew this book demanded special acknowledgment. Will Moss Westbury, author of *Daymares*, please come up?"

Carolina almost choked. His parents clapped. Rowan squealed. Teal fist-pumped.

Moss didn't move. His face seemed frozen, lost in disbelief. She put a hand on his arm and said, "Mossy, they're calling you."

He shook as he stood. Then he took a deep breath, squared his shoulders, and limped toward the dais.

O'Brien shook his hand, presented him with a plaque and an envelope, and handed him the microphone. "I read *Daymares*. It's outstanding. You deserve this."

Moss stared at the microphone. Silent, he rolled it between his hands, then gave a little nod as though he'd made a decision. He thanked the Society, and acknowledged the conference they'd put on. "Now," he said, "A two-minute rant. My book is a testament to the disgusting nature of war.

"How can we glorify the worst of humanity in video games, movies, television shows, music, even the news?" He paced a few steps. "The countries where conflicts are fought are decimated. Civil societies torn apart, towns and homes obliterated. In modern warfare, where we can murder from a distance, the civilians—mainly mothers and children—take the brunt of this faceless violence, and many of them, if they survive, never recover. At the very least, their innocence is ripped away. Innocence cannot be reclaimed." He moved back and leaned on the lectern. "And what of our boys who, raised in this culture, think combat is somehow cool, or inevitable? All of us"—he swept the microphone, like a flashlight, over the crowd, then pointed it at his chest, too— "are responsible. We need to bear witness to this carnage and grow up."

He raised the envelope. "This money will go into a foundation to benefit those who have served. We need all the help we can muster." He thought for a moment. "I lost a precious friend in the towers and, because of that, enlisted the day after September eleventh. My one tour in Afghanistan was cut short because my leg was blown off. I'll never be the same, physically or emotionally.

"For memoir writers out there, know this: writing about our most painful or devastating moments helps us face those times. I suggest going there in your writing for many short visits rather than long ones, less often. It's easier to bear. Then, when you leave your desk, do something fun, healthy, social, or all three—activities that don't include overeating, alcohol, or drugs. Take a walk in nature. And get to know other writers. Share writing with each other. Give kind feedback. Celebrate craft." He smiled and surveyed the audience. "Thank you for this astonishing honor."

The room exploded with applause. Like a wave, the audience rose for a standing ovation. Moss threaded his way back to the table, nodding, smiling, and shaking hands along the way, and saw Carolina and his parents waiting to throw their arms around him.

Chapter Forty-one

Carolina passed by Rowan's wolfhound calendar and paused, frowning. Salaam, by her side, halted too. This was Monday? She'd lost Sunday. December 14th, already? Moss was getting home after dinner today! Finally, the book-signing trip was over. He'd been to Boston and Seattle. He'd argued with his publisher until they agreed: no trips longer than seven days, and a week at home in between to reconnect with his family. She knew he'd be relieved to get back to routines and writing.

Even though Moss invited her to bring Graham and travel with him, she'd stayed home to keep the family rhythm. The flights with Graham to and from the New York awards ceremony hadn't been easy. She'd missed Moss in her bones, but having Teal share the household load made the days slide by. Every afternoon at 1:30, she lay down for an hour nap. Once she was up and functional, Teal took two hours to write. They traded off meal-prep days—Teal had paid close attention when Moss cooked, and now made different, but equally tasty, dinners. Lately, he was on a Thai kick. She couldn't imagine life without him.

She fit into her pants again. It had taken stiff karate workouts four days a week. She tucked her blouse in, turning around to look at her post-twins figure, dabbed on lipstick—her only nod to makeup—and stuffed her phone in her pocket.

Graham gave a happy screech, and she looked to see what he'd gotten into. He was sitting up for the first time, rocking with joy, kicking his legs out in front of him. "Look at you. Oh my God, your da missed it."

She grabbed her phone, but the moment she got the camera up, Graham tumbled over and, startled, pooched his lip out. She scooped him up before he cried. "Darn, baby, I didn't get a picture. How'd you manage all by yourself, anyway?" After soothing him, she set him back down.

Patting Salaam absentmindedly, she went to the calendar. Rowan's Christmas vacation started Friday; they'd head to Bender's Ridge the next day. She counted—they'd have eight days together before Teal and Rowan left for their retreat with Colin James on December 26th. At the thought, threads of anxiety shredded her belly. Oh for God's sake, she thought. I've got to get over this. Moss researched the guy, and I did, too. She'd watched YouTube videos—what was not to like? The man seemed straightforward, kind, and clear. She didn't admit it aloud, but she responded to what he said. *Like it or not, I am my mother's daughter.* She was going to have to get straight with Rowan about her interest in pensing, and wondered how, where, or when to begin the conversation. Maybe she could start with a card stashed in with presents on Christmas. Carolina wondered how her daughter would respond—mad, sad, glad? and she smiled at the memory of the chunky flashcards she'd used to teach her child about identifying emotions when she was a toddler.

Graham made urgent sounds. "Okay, baby boy, let's go nurse." When she picked him up, she could hardly believe how heavy he felt. They settled in the rocking chair.

Zephyr trots around the house looking for her girl. Her nose scents the air, and catching a whiff, she follows the smell and finds her in the food room. *Zephyr hears Pack Mama,* she penses.

Rowan whirls to look at her. *What? What do you mean, you hear her?*

Like Rowan. Pictures.

She's pensing you? No, not possible.

Pictures happen. What is "not possible"?

You know how Pack Mama feels about pensing. It scares her and makes her angry. And, if she is *sending pictures, it should be to Salaam, not Zephy.*

My girl is upset. Zephyr tongue-swipes her face. It's salty-wet.

You're right. I'm mad. Jealous, actually.

Zephyr sits and contemplates her girl. *Mad? What is "jealous"?*

Rowan dropped to the floor and sat cross-legged. Shame rolled through her. I'm jealous because Mama isn't communicating with her own dog, but with mine, she thought. How small-minded of me. Hadn't she always wanted her mother to understand human-animal communication? Now, maybe there was a chance she might be able to learn.

How could she explain jealousy to Zephyr? *Picture there are two male dogs and one female,* Rowan pensed. *The female is ready to breed. The two male dogs get jealous of each other and might fight for the chance to mate. They both want to be chosen.*

Zephyr had the oddest expression on her face, one Rowan had never seen. Her brow was wrinkled. It looked like incredulity. Clearly, her dog was trying to understand.

Never mind. Humans are silly. I need to talk to Pack Mama. How am I going to bring up pensing?

Moss pulled into the driveway, deeply tired, but ecstatic to be home. He checked his phone: 8:10 p.m.

Book signings required too much talking. Readers had lots of questions, comments, even opinions. Sometimes fans brought all three of his books to sign which made the lines longer. He responded with patience and kindness, but paid a price later. He'd need a chunk of alone time after reconnecting with his family. What he yearned for was a writing retreat, a long one. As a family man—he loved the role—he missed and longed for how it used to be before he met Carolina: uninterrupted days and nights of contemplation, where he could follow a train of thought for hours.

What he wanted now was to kiss his wife; hug his daughter, son, and Teal; hear about the seven days he'd lost of home life; tell them about his trip; and sip a substantial glass of merlot. Still stiff from the flight, he parked in front of the house and lumbered from the car. Unlegging was first on his list. His thigh hurt. Had he rubbed a blister? Thank God, no more trips for a couple of months.

All three dogs poured out of the dog door. Jazz came running for him, whining—complaining—at how long he'd been gone. The other two trailed her, tails high and happy. While he patted and talked to his girl, he checked out the others. Salaam had gained some weight; her back three ribs no longer stuck out. Zephyr looked satisfied and healthy.

Carolina had opened the door, and leaned against the frame, grinning at him, thumbs in her waistband of her jeans. Her pre-pregnancy 501 button-fly jeans again. God, she looked gorgeous. He couldn't wait to unbutton them.

Chapter Forty-two

The dogs woke Rowan early on Christmas morning. She let them out to speed toward the ruckus near the chicken coop; they'd take care of it. Bender's Ridge was chill and clear. The only thing missing was snow. She stretched tall on the porch, reaching her fingertips toward the lapis dawn sky.

The dogs settled the dispute, peed, and galloped toward her looking for breakfast. She shivered in the penetrating cold and sped back inside to light the fire. It would be nice for everyone to wake up to the crackling sound and delicious scent. Moss had already stacked the logs. She put a match to it, watched it catch, and then snugged the grate. Now, the utility room to feed the beasties.

While the dogs chowed down—peaceably, all together—she puttered in the kitchen making morning mochas. She made Teal's first and delivered it with Merry Christmas wishes. He thanked her with a grateful smile. Before she made drinks for her parents, she returned to her room to gather presents and put them under the tree.

Now she focused on Mama and Da's espressos, first readying a tray with cloth napkins and a blossom from the blooming orchid, before steaming the milk. Last Christmas had been difficult, and she wanted to launch this year's holiday on a positive note. After dusting chocolate on the top of the mugs, she carried the tray to their room, followed by the tick-tack of forty-eight dog nails on the hardwood floor. Time to clip their nails, she thought, and knocked softly.

"Come in," her mom called out. "Oh my. How special! Moss, Merry Christmas, you laggard. Look what your daughter brought us."

Tail whipping, Jazz jumped on the bed to greet him. Salaam ran to Carolina. Zephyr lay down, watching.

Moss rolled over, rubbing his eyes. "Why, it's the whole fam-damily. What a treat. Hey Jazzy, careful there, don't step on Graham." He shielded the baby as Jazz settled on the bed, then pushed up to lean against pillows. "Mochas—thank you."

"I wanted you guys to wake up happy," she said.

"Sweet," Carolina and Moss said in unison. They looked at each other and laughed. "Does this mean we've been married too long?" Lina asked.

"Not possible," Moss retorted. He took a long swig. "I need to shake awake and rustle up breakfast."

"Did you remember the croissants?" Rowan planted her hands on her hips and glanced at him sideways.

"You bet. I hid 'em from hungry teenagers and male youth in their twenties." Moss swung his leg over the side of the bed and reached for his crutches. "Two secs in the shower, then I'm on it. Row, could you whisk ten eggs? I'm afraid you'll need to collect them first." He stood and fitted the sticks under his armpits. "Please take the kitchen scraps for the birds. I forgot last night."

"Okay. Come on, Zephy."

Rowan snagged her coat off the hook in the hallway and slung it on, then dressed Jazz and Salaam in their coats. She nabbed the compost bin from the kitchen. All three dogs followed her outside, jigging in the frosty air. She dumped the bucket with vegetable ends she'd set near the gate, and, chattering and squawking, the birds came running to peck through the offering. Entering the chicken house, she slid her hands into the boxes and gathered seventeen eggs, an extra-fine haul. Zeph, Jazz, and Salaam sat in a line outside the pen, ears pricked, attending the proceedings. They gamboled around her feet on the way back to the house.

She washed the eggs carefully, putting the extras in the wire basket on the counter. Now, to see if she'd mastered cracking and dumping the eggs out one-handed like she'd seen chefs do on TV. The first was a disaster, and it took her a few minutes to fish all the shell bits out. The second went better. By the fifth, she had success. While whisking, she mentally listened for the rhythm her mom used. A few minutes later, the eggs frothed light with air and were ready for Mossy.

Teal showed up in the kitchen right after Mama, Da, and Graham, and reached for the baby. Rowan's breath caught when she remembered envisioning all of them here at Christmas, including Andrea. Not to be. She swallowed hard and carried dishes and silverware to the table.

After breakfast, they made their way to the Christmas room. Jazz and Zephyr sat, looking expectant. Salaam looked from one to the other, then Carolina, with an inquiring expression. "Sit, sweet pea," she said softly. "You'll get a present, too."

Moss reached out to Teal for Graham. "Would you give up that baby long enough to play us a couple of Christmas carols? We'd love to be serenaded. Do you know 'O Holy Night?' It's our favorite. We have the sheet music."

Teal nodded, blushed, and handed Graham over. After he pulled out the bench at the baby grand, he flexed his fingers open and closed. "I don't play much for other people," he said. "But your family has given me so much, you get serenaded whenever you want."

Rowan gasped when, with tender inflection, he filled the room with the music's sacred quality. The family gathered around and sang, Moss turning the pages. Graham's eyes went wide, staring from one person to another. Teal moved on to "The First Noel," "Joy to the World," and "O Come, All Ye Faithful." He ended by repeating "O Holy Night."

"Row," Carolina said, "why don't you introduce Teal to our Christmas tradition?"

"Okay. We open presents one at a time, so we can see and enjoy the process. Each year, we rotate who hands the gifts out. Last year, I presided." She glanced at her parents. "This year, Teal, you're up."

"Great," Moss said.

"Also, the dogs get their presents interspersed among the others."

"You don't worry about pack order? Zeph doesn't get hers first?"

"Not on Christmas. But Zephy will deliver people presents if you ask her—the ones she can manage." She frowned, thinking. "When you find one with your name, you get to open it. And one last thing: Mama or Da can say a present has to wait. Like if it's the main gift, they may want to save it 'til the end."

Teal smiled. "It's a nice tradition." He fished under the tree, pulled out a small box about the size of a deck of cards and looked at the name. "Zeph, this is for Pack Mama." The giant dog gravely accepted the package, took it to Carolina, and dropped it in her lap.

Lina patted Zephyr before reading the card. "Mossy, what have you done?"

"You'll see." He smiled at her. "I hope it's okay. I had to."

She tore off the paper, lifted the lid, and took out a gold necklace with a heart locket, a small diamond set in the front. "It's beautiful."

"Open it before you respond," he said. "I had it made. There's something special about it."

"I know what's inside, because I know you," she said, and using her thumbnail, parted the two halves. Rowan smiled at her from the left, Graham from the right. She gave a little love chuckle.

"But there's more—each half has two places for photos. Let me show you." He opened the second layer and handed it back.

Carolina gasped. Behind Rowan's image, a picture of Andrea peeked out, the photo they'd taken a few days before her death. On the other side, behind Graham, lay a space, waiting. "Perfect," she whispered.

"I don't want us to forget, ever," he said.

"It's perfect." She passed it around. "This way, you're all with me."

Rowan stared at the miniature picture, then closed the layers to look at the top images. "You gotta see this, Teal," and handed it to him.

He squinted, focusing on the locket. "Awww," he said.

"Teal," Moss said. "We're hoping you might want to join this family in a more formal way." He held the locket and pointed to the empty space that waited for Teal's picture.

The young man looked at him quizzically. "More formal? What do you mean, exactly?"

"We'd like to adopt you."

"I'm over eighteen, and it feels like you have already. You've made me so welcome."

"Legally. People can be adopted at any age. We're inviting you to become a Westbury."

"What?" Teal flew out of his seat. "Why?"

"Because we love you," Carolina said. "When the three of us talked about it, there was zero hesitation."

"I can't let you."

"Why not?" Rowan asked. "You deserve a family who loves you."

Teal looked at a loss for words. "I-I don't know. It-it feels like too much."

"It's something we all want. The question is, do you?" Moss asked.

"But what about my job? I love being Graham's nanny."

"Who said anything about losing your job?" Lina asked. "I'd be devastated if you didn't want to be with him."

"A true family member? Like you'd be my parents, and Row and Graham my sister and brother?"

"Yes," Moss said.

"But surely you'd want me to sign a pre-nup or something?"

"No, absolutely not." Moss spoke forcefully. "An equal family member, to inherit equally, too."

"Your picture would go behind Graham's in the locket," Rowan added.

Teal stood and looked out the window, hands clasped behind his back. Tears slid down his face. "I want it more than anything," he whispered, "but I don't know how to say yes." He glanced at them. "This is a hell of a Christmas present. May I think about it?"

"Take all the time you need," Moss said. "The offer stands. Would you open this present next?" He pointed.

Teal picked up a box the size of a briefcase. He shook it, but it didn't make a sound. When he opened it, his eyes got big. "A new laptop? Fantastic. I've been having problems with mine." He got to work unpacking it.

"A little birdie told us so," Moss said. "It's got Word and Scrivener installed for writing."

"This is great." He slid his hands over the top. "It's so thin."

"And light," Carolina said. "We hope it serves you well."

"Oh yeah, it will. I've been saving my files every other second to Dropbox because I'm so afraid my computer's going to croak. Sometimes it won't even start up. Perfect timing."

"Teal," Carolina said, "see the card in the tree? Can you give it to Rowan, please?"

Rowan opened it and worked the card out of the envelope. She grinned and showed it around. An Irish wolfhound, Scottish deerhound, greyhound, Saluki, Afghan, Borzoi, and whippet graced the front. She opened and read it. "Oh my God," she said. "Oh no, I need a minute." Rowan leapt up and ran from the room.

Lina stared at Moss. "Is she mad? It's the opposite of what I expected."

"What does the card say?" Teal asked.

"If she'd be willing to try to teach me to pense with Salaam. Isn't this what she's always wanted? For me to believe her? What did I do wrong? Shit. I can't ever get it right with my daughter."

"She's a teen," Teal said. "You can't have any idea what's going on inside her."

Wailing floated down the hallway, and Carolina jumped up.

"Sweetheart, don't," Moss said, reaching out a hand to her. "Give her time."

Carolina, Moss, and Teal took a break from opening presents, and Moss made more coffees, including one for Rowan. He kept reassuring Lina; whatever it was upsetting their daughter, they'd figure it out. They went back to the Christmas room to wait.

Twenty minutes later, swollen-faced, Rowan returned. "I feel horrible," she said. "Mommo, I wanted this so much, I'd given up hoping. I'd lost faith in us, and when I opened your card with your wonderful request, guilt and shame swamped me. I'm sorry." She wrapped her arms around her mom. "I'd be honored to work with you and Salaam. Maggie and Bender are having success now, so I'm excited to try with you. Zephy says you send pictures sometimes. But you have to be patient and not jump to 'I can't do this.' It took them a year."

Carolina sat by Rowan and took her hands. "No wonder you lost faith. I've been mean—dismissive, even—about your skills, and it's been going on for years."

Lina heard a sound, and both she and Rowan looked up. "Thank God," Moss said, his voice hoarse. "What a relief. To be stuck in the middle has been awfully hard. I love you both so much."

Teal swiveled from one family member to another. "Astonishing," he whispered.

Chapter Forty-three

The following day, Rowan and Teal packed the van for the Still Mountain retreat, then went to say goodbye.

"I don't need to ask you to drive safely," Moss said. "Remember, you two are precious cargo. We'll see you in Eugene on Saturday."

"Have fun," Carolina said. "I hope you find what you're looking for."

Rowan considered what her mom said. She actually meant it. "Thanks, Mama. I'll text you when we get there."

"I'd appreciate it."

They got lost west of Portland, so it took an extra half hour to find the retreat center. As they turned off the road at the Still Mountain sign, Teal glanced at the mileage. "Let's see how long the driveway is." They passed through a fir forest, broken now and again with a lush green glade. Ferns abounded. The road wound up and up. When they pulled in front of the lodge, he looked again. "A mile. This place is really private."

Teal dropped off Rowan and their gear. After he parked, they made their way to registration in the lobby. "Teal Landis, and my sister, Rowan Graham," he said to the gray-haired woman sitting at the table. Rowan's eyes went wide. "I'm trying it on for size," he whispered, grinning.

"I'm Sarah. Welcome." She pointed to a staircase. "Rowan, you're up in room seventeen, and Teal, you're her neighbor in sixteen. Dinner's in forty-five minutes, over there." She waved to the right.

"How many people are registered?" Rowan asked.

Sarah perused the ledger. "Thirty-seven. Oh, and one more is coming tomorrow."

Teal hefted the bags. "Small group. Nice."

"Colin prefers intimacy. See you at dinner. After, we'll gather for the first time this evening at 7:15. The meeting room is in the smaller of the two yurts outside." She indicated the direction.

Rowan climbed the stairs and opened her door, excited and curious to see where she'd spend the week. It was a monk's cell—single bed, small desk and chair, sink and mirror, armchair for reading, and a narrow closet cupboard. Opening it, she discovered a few shelves and five hangers. *My own space—at a retreat. I've wanted this for years.* She unpacked her suitcase and set her laptop, with reverence, on the desk. Maybe she could get some writing done. She sat down, and signed on to Wi-Fi. Then she grabbed her phone and texted her mom they'd arrived safely.

Startled by a knock, she opened the door. Teal stood there, smiling.

"Here's mine." She swept her arm wide. "Can I see your room?"

"You've already set up to write. Good girl. Come look." When he threw open his door, she laughed. His new laptop adorned his desk, too. "Did you find the internet password?" He pointed to a sign on the door.

"Yep. Ready to head to dinner?"

He nodded.

She grabbed his hand. "I'm so excited to be here."

"Me, too. I watched a YouTube vid of Colin last night. I'm always struck by how clear he is."

They capered down the hall, practically skipping, but slowed at the entrance. Rowan looked around. She'd figured she'd be the youngest person here. There were quite a few people of her grandparents' generation, and at least one person near Teal's age, too. If they didn't readily accept her, at least she'd have him.

They took plates and cutlery, serving themselves as they walked down the cafeteria-style line of cold and hot plates. The salad fixings looked as fresh as homegrown summer fare at the ranch, but there were many side offerings: varieties of olives, colorful grated beets, garbanzo beans, and more. She scooped a square of lasagna before glancing at the dessert table, which held homemade lemon bars and brownies. She'd come back for one of those later.

Rowan hesitated, not sure where to sit. Teal stabbed his fork toward a round table where two people sat. She nodded. While they emptied their trays, Rowan introduced Teal as her brother. It felt great.

"Welcome. I'm Sam," the slim gray-haired man said. "This is my wife, Evelyn. Is this your first retreat?" he asked Rowan.

She nodded.

"I've sat with Adya," Teal said, "but it's my first time with Colin."

"This is our tenth week-long with him. He's terrific. If you have questions or need anything, ask. He has a wonderful, heartful community of people around him."

"Are all the retreats here at Still Mountain?" Teal asked.

"Ours, yes, although he teaches on the East Coast, too. We love this place, and the food's fantastic."

Two thirty-something women slid into the last two spaces at the table. The blonde one looked curiously at Rowan. "How old are you?"

Rowan giggled. "You're awfully blunt. I'm sixteen. What's your name?"

Her eyes widened. "Oh, sorry. Gretchen. How did you come to be here? You must have a story. I'd love to hear it."

"I'm Rowan. I woke up one day different, and went looking for people like me. This is my first nondual retreat, although I'm familiar with the teaching."

"Someone handed me *The Power of Now* by Tolle. I've never been the same," Gretchen said. She turned to Teal. "How about you? You seem closer to my age."

"Twenty-four. You?" He took a bite of lasagna.

"Thirty-one. What brought you here?"

Rowan could see Teal considering how much he wanted to expose about himself—he always fingered his goatee when caught off guard. She dug into her salad while she waited for him to answer.

"I've had big questions about my life, so I started searching. I found Adyashanti first—he was a huge help. Rowan introduced me to Colin's videos. He's present in a way I haven't experienced before."

"Yes," Evelyn said. "He speaks clearly."

"We'd better eat up and get to the first meeting," Rowan said. "I don't want to miss anything." She glanced around the table. "Thanks for welcoming us. It means a lot."

"We're a growing family here," Sam said. "And we love having young people like you. I believe this understanding could change the world."

Colin opened the first gathering with an announcement. "Good evening, friends. I've decided to make a change in the retreats now and going forward. They're no longer going to be silent. I want you to get to know one another, develop connections, have deep conversations, remain in contact after the retreat is over. After morning meetings, we'll keep silence until we're in the lunchroom, but otherwise, enjoy each other."

Rowan watched a wave of surprise run through the group—no sound, but people looked at each other and smiled.

After the room settled down, he said, "Ask yourself the question, 'Am I aware?'" For half a minute, he remained quiet. "Notice, you 'went' inward. You fell still and checked inside, yes? And, because all six billion of us are conscious, and we can't deny we're conscious, you returned with the answer 'yes, I'm aware.' Consider how or where you looked when you confirmed this."

What an interesting way to start, Rowan thought.

"Notice," Colin went on, "you looked prior to thought."

Rowan considered her experience. *Right. He's talking about the big field.*

Rowan woke early in the morning. She dressed, took her warmest coat, and went for a walk in the chill, dark air on a path heading uphill. She loved being the only one up and about. After a twenty-minute hike, she came to a vista with a bench. The view extended for miles, and she soaked it in. Light glowed on the horizon.

What would happen today? she wondered. Her sense was it would be extraordinary but, in what way, she had no idea. She sat cross-legged on the bench and allowed thoughts to slide into the background.

When she came out of meditation and looked at her watch, she was stunned. Over an hour? Her stomach was rumbling; she'd have to rush to make breakfast. Refreshed, calm, and happy, she sped down the path, flew into the main building, and crashed into someone who gave an oomph, dropped his suitcase, and staggered a few steps. "I'm sorry," she sputtered, and offered a hand to help him regain balance. "Are you all right?" He seemed close to her age.

He stared down at her. Rowan felt profound shock. This young man had the clearest gaze; she could see right into his depth. What was it about his eyes?

"Well," he said, not looking away. "This is an auspicious meeting. And yes, I only got the wind knocked out of me. You're in a hurry."

"Breakfast is about to close, and I'm ready to devour a bear. Want to eat with me?" she asked, breathless. She couldn't pull her eyes away from his, and a tiny curling sensation fluttered in her belly.

He set his suitcase by the wall. "Sure—let's go." They took off for dining room, slipping in at the last minute.

After they dished up breakfast and found an empty table, she felt tongue-tied, but managed to say, "I didn't see you yesterday. I'm Rowan. Graham."

"I'm Ben. Ben Singleton," he said. "I just arrived—my family had a funeral yesterday."

"Sarah mentioned someone was coming late. I'm so sorry."

"My uncle Terence. Mom's brother. He served as my proxy dad." His eyes filled. "We're … damn. We *were* very close. I never met my bio-dad."

"That's so hard. I lost my father when I was seven. I felt—unmoored, I guess is the best description, although I didn't know the word. The feeling went on for a long time. Why didn't you cancel?"

"I need to be here. This is my tribe—there's no better place for me to begin recovery from the loss."

Rowan studied him. Ben was handsome, but in an unusual way. She guessed he was part African-American—he had gorgeous skin a shade darker than her own, and his hair sported short corkscrews. His luminous blue eyes were startling and wouldn't let her go. She felt like she knew him.

"You and I," he went on, "need to find a way to have conversations this week. The retreats are silent after the second day."

"Not this one. Colin said last night he wants us to build community and get to know one another. But why do we need to talk?"

"Because we're both awake," he said softly. "I knew the moment our eyes connected. Almost no people our age are."

Rowan, shocked into silence, stared at him. She choked out, "How old are you?"

"Eighteen," he said. "You?"

She looked down at the table. *Shit. He'll lose interest.* "Sixteen," she whispered.

Chapter Forty-four

Rowan pensed Zephyr after dinner. *I met someone you're going to like a lot. His name is Ben. He knows the big field.*

My girl likes this human?

Yes. He's special—kind, and thoughtful. Maybe he can even pense. He's in school to be a dog doctor like Francine. Zephy, if I touch him, and pense you, could you feel him?

Zephyr doesn't know.

We'll try, okay?

We try. My girl is happy.

Very happy.

In the morning, Rowan sat with Teal at breakfast. "How's it going for you?" she asked, stirring her oatmeal before scooping a bite. She smelled the sweet waft of honey.

"I'm gathering my courage to ask a question. I don't know if I'll get there this retreat, though." He munched a piece of toast slathered with peanut butter.

She blew on her spoon. "Me, too. I'm trying to figure out how to word what to ask—don't want to sound totally dumb."

Teal frowned at her. "I don't think you could ask a dumb question—and surely you've noticed how kind and attentive Colin is."

"Yes, I have," she admitted. "So, why do you need courage?"

"It's not Colin. It's asking something this personal in front of thirty-seven people."

"I get it." Rowan touched his hand. "It feels safe to me, though. Don't you think?"

"Yeah, but won't they look at me differently? Forever?"

"But you *are* different. And there's nothing remotely wrong with you. You're having an uncommon experience."

"Out of the mouth of my uhh … little sister. You're right, of course. It helps. Thanks." He tilted his head. "You had a late breakfast with someone yesterday. Who was he? I saw you walk into the meeting with him." He took a sip of coffee.

"I about knocked him off his feet, tearing in late from an early meditation on the mountain. His name's Ben."

"He's beautiful."

Rowan pursed her lips and decided she'd better tell Teal right now. "Hands off, okay? I think I met my soul mate yesterday."

"Whoa, no way. You're only sixteen and haven't even dated. How can you say such a thing?"

"My heart knows what it knows." She quirked an eyebrow. "You'll see. We share the most important understanding of all."

"I'm your older brother and your chaperone. Your—*our* parents—will wring my neck. You be very, very careful, okay?"

Rowan laughed out loud. "We're not going to have sex if that's what you're worried about. There's a big difference between sixteen and eighteen. Besides, I'm not ready."

"Thank God." Teal looked up. "Oh Lordy, here he comes, heading straight for you."

"Are you sure?" She was afraid to look.

"Hey." Ben approached Rowan with a smile. "Mornin'." He turned to Teal. "I'm Ben Singleton."

"Teal Landis." He caught his breath, and broke into a grin. "I'm Rowan's brother."

Ben glanced from one to the other. "Much older, I'd guess?"

"Eight-and-a-half years."

Rowan piped up. "I've been adopted since my mom married again, and Teal's about to be."

"Married, or adopted? Married, I suppose."

Teal jumped in. "Oh no. Adopted."

Ben sat down. "Now there's a story. How come?"

"Well," Teal began, but fell silent, his forehead furrowed.

"Because he completes us," Rowan said, softly.

Teal jerked, looking first startled, then pleased.

"We have a little brother, too, Graham, who's only six months," Rowan said. "Ben, you'd better get breakfast before they close the kitchen."

"Already did. I was up early."

"Why'd you come back to the dining room?"

"Looking for you, of course."

"O-oh." She felt a flush start at her neck and flood her face. Her hands rose to block the scarlet from view.

Ben caught her wrists. "No need to ever hide." His voice dropped. "Not from me. Please don't."

The color in her cheeks eased. "Right," she whispered. "Thank you."

Their eyes locked for a long moment.

When Rowan glanced away, Teal was staring at them. She caught his minuscule tic of recognition.

After grabbing a chair pillow and sweater from her room, Rowan made her way to the meeting room. She noticed Ben but, not wanting any distraction, moved away from him. His energy rattled her. She felt her body wanting to move closer—hungry. She'd never experienced this sensation before. Hungry for contact, for connection. What a weird feeling, she thought. I'm becoming a woman at this very moment.

Colin began a talk, clear and compelling in its directness, which pulled Rowan's attention away from her new friend. She felt her heart cast itself open to his words for the first time. A few minutes later, she glanced at Ben. He was looking at her. Acknowledgment passed between them. *He fully understands Colin. And he knows I know.* She shivered. *What now? How do I do this?* The shivering continued. *There's my question.*

As soon as Colin's talk was over, he asked, as he had each time, "Is there anything you'd like to discuss?" Her hand flew up. She watched the motion and thought, how'd that happen?

"Rowan. Do I have your name right?"

She nodded, trying to figure out how to word what she wanted to ask. Well, she thought, I guess I have to give a tiny bit of history. "A few years ago, my mom and I had a rollover car accident. I came to four days later from a coma, blind. A few days later, I woke up with a different understanding," she said. "It altered every aspect of my life. I got my physical sight back a couple of months later, but the inner sight has remained. Longing to share, I began looking for people like me. I didn't find any nearby, but I discovered nonduality and you." She took a deep breath. Realizing she'd offered a statement, not a question, she stumbled before asking, "Now, how do I live?" Not knowing what else to say, she fell quiet.

He shut his eyes for a while. When he opened them, he said, "I will answer your question, but first, tell me more about your 'different understanding,' as you call it."

Rowan opened her hands palm up, and held them out.

"Perfect," he said.

Two beats of silence passed, and Rowan thought, oh good. Maybe it's all he needs.

"Now," Colin went on, "use words to describe your experience."

She tried, faltered, and said, "Words don't work."

"True. Words always fail. Yet I spend week-long retreats using them, correct? We need to learn to speak about nothing. No thing. Take a minute and try again."

She cleared her throat. Paused. Cleared it again. *If I'm not safe here, I'm not safe anywhere. I have to try.* She took a deep breath. "I think of it as the 'big field,' although it's neither a field nor big. It isn't anything. Everyone seems to have it backwards. They think: first come amoebas, plants and animals, humanoids, then consciousness in humans. Consciousness in our tiny brains. But that's not my experience at all. It *starts* with consciousness. Which seems"—she hesitated, looking again for the right words—"infinite and eternal. Consciousness first, followed by"—she waved her hand to include everything—"all this. Manifestation comes out of it, not the other way around."

He took a quiet moment before looking up. "Yes. Thank you. Very clear. Now I have a better sense of how to respond." He closed his eyes.

The room went still—no coughs, no shuffling. Anticipation, she thought. Me, too. I can hardly wait.

A couple of minutes later, he opened his eyes and focused on her. "Here's my suggestion about how to live. Regardless of the situation confronting you, whether it be a close moment with a loved one or a person in your school wielding a gun, come from your deepest love and understanding. Don't misunderstand me: your response may be—in either situation—tender or powerfully fierce. But when you move from inner knowing, what you're called to do will meet what's happening." He fell silent again before asking, "Rowan, how old are you?"

Suddenly shy, she almost whispered, "Sixteen."

He nodded, and remained quiet. It was at least a minute before he spoke again. "You're the youngest person to attend one of my retreats. But I've been your age, and in a similar situation. I understood the world around me in a way other people did not."

Another long silence.

"These next few years may not be easy. I'm not assuming they'll be hard; we can't know what's in store. But if you look around this room, you'll notice almost no one under twenty, only a couple of young adults, and mostly people with gray hair." He smiled at the assemblage. "It can take a lifetime to open to the depth of recognition you've already expressed." He paused to sip water. "To thrive during these years, you'll need to build like-hearted community such as we have here. It doesn't have to be this group, but it could be. And do meet Ben Singleton—he's closest to your age, and in a similar situation."

Ben piped up. "We have, Colin."

Colin broke into a wide smile. "Good. I suspect you can be tremendous support for each other."

He sat, silent for a minute, but his eyes remained open. "In addition," he said, "I suggest you not try to explain your apperception to anyone unless they ask you a direct, specific question. Even your parents. *Especially* your parents. If they do ask, answer in the plainest language you can. Stay close to their specific query, rather than making an assumption and striking out into bolder territory. Let them lead the conversation." He looked directly at her. "Model your understanding instead. Do you have a feel for why?"

Rowan nodded, trembling. No one had ever grokked what she meant. She paused. She sensed Ben did, but they hadn't talked about it yet. Colin got her—saw right into her, grasped her more deeply than anyone. Even Mossy, and he was pretty cool. She felt both ripped open—no, shattered—and put back together, and knew she'd met her teacher. Her teacher! She had a teacher.

And a precious, precious friend in Ben.

Chapter Forty-five

Leaving the yurt, Rowan felt Ben fall in step beside her.

"Hey. Do you want to grab sandwiches and go up the mountain? It's time we get to know each other."

The quivering in her belly began again. "Sounds good." Her voice came out squiggly, so she cleared her throat and began again. "I'm nervous."

"Awww," he said. "I don't bite. I'm grateful to meet someone close to my age who gets it. Besides, Colin suggested we get to know each other. You trust him, right?"

"After this morning, I sure do. He knew exactly what to ask in order to answer my question. I've found my teacher."

"Of course you have. He's very skillful and clear. Deeply kind, too."

They beat the crowd to the lunchroom. Ben asked the bald man behind the counter, "May we have sandwiches in a bag? We want to hike."

"Stay on the paths. Remember Lyme—it's good to be careful even in December."

Ben nodded and took the paper bag. "I'll grab my backpack and water bottle from my room," he said to Rowan. "Get your coat; it'll be cold up there."

They headed for the staircase. "I'm in the garret," he said. "Number twenty-five."

"I'm in seventeen on the second floor. Meet me there?"

She trotted to the bathroom, snagged her coat, and knotted her hiking boots. She opened the door at his knock. There Ben stood, real and present, wanting her company. *Wow.*

The path he chose was steep and rocky, but he offered a hand over the hard and occasionally soggy parts. The hill was capped with a long, flat sitting rock on wood piers overlooking a small lake.

"Five Buddhist monks reside on the property—in a building over there." He pointed. "They rent the place to like-hearted groups. One of the monks, Simon, constructed this." He patted the seat. "It's his favorite meditation place. He got the guys together, and they dug the lake over a decade ago. It took a few summers." He sat, crossed his leg and grabbed his hiking boot. He pointed to the yellow mud stuck in the ridges. "Good clay here on the western edge of the Tualatin Mountains. The lake filled and stayed full. A spring feeds it in summer." He pointed at a ripple in the water. "They stocked it with trout, too. We may have dinner from here. Usually, one meal of the retreat week they serve fish."

Rowan felt tongue tied and unsure what to do. *Where to start to build a friendship?*

"Sit with me," he said. "You seem like a deer or a bunny—watchful, about to flee."

She relaxed and slid onto the bench. *Better.*

"You asked a good question," he said. "I like how Colin responded, too—with another question to make sure he knew what you meant. He's careful. Did his answer help?"

She nodded. "It felt like an invitation not to hold back anymore. He clarified I can live—quietly—from what I know to be true."

"Exactly."

"I've been lonely," she said. "I didn't realize how much until I got here."

"Me, too. I've got great friends in this group, but I've needed someone close to my age."

Something eased in Rowan. She smiled. "Here I am. Can I annoy you with questions?"

"Annoy me? Are you kidding?"

She giggled.

He punched her lightly on the shoulder. "Dickens."

"Moss—my adoptive dad—uses the same expression."

"Terence did too." He stared at the ground and dashed a tear from his cheek. More slid down.

"Moss taught me to smooth tears in instead of swiping them away. It honors them more, somehow. He spent time in Afghanistan and learned about it over there. It's a Qawwali tradition. Try it."

Ben rubbed his cheeks with tentative fingers. "Nicer," he said. "Thank you." He leaned over and planted his lips on Rowan's forehead.

She reared back and touched her fingertips to the spot. It tingled, alive with his energy. "No, too much. It was … impulsive."

"Sorry, I should've checked. I didn't mean to offend you."

"You didn't. It startled me, though. Kind of scared me. I haven't ever kissed a boy."

His eyebrows flew up. "Quite a disclosure. It's brave of you to share. Do you want to? Kiss?"

"No. I mean yes, someday, of course, but not now." She didn't look away. "Most kids move way faster, which I think is backwards and twisted. I'm not ready. Not sure how I know, but it's true for me. I'm not going to rush it. Is it something you need?"

"Want, sure. I'm a guy, after all. Need? Nope. But hey, we hardly know each other. Let's focus on changing that. Deal?"

She sighed with relief. "Deal." They shook hands. She watched the movement in the pond for a moment. "Are you in college? I forgot to ask you at breakfast."

"I started in September—pre-med at UC Davis. I'm headed for veterinary medicine."

"Darn. That's far. I've thought about vet school, but my work is with animals in a different way." She considered him, wondering if she dared share about pensing. Instead, she pulled her phone out. "Too bad. No signal. I wanted to show you a pic, but it's in Dropbox. My dog's name is Zephyr." Rowan stood and tapped her hip. "She comes up to here."

"Really. Great Dane? Borzoi? Wolfhound?"

"Wolfhound/deerhound mix. A rescue. She's five."

"Tell me about sighthounds; I've never known one. I hear we get them at the school clinic, though. Sobering problems. And I've learned there are some different protocols, like with anesthetic."

"True. I figure you know they're prone to osteosarcoma, torsion, bloat—like all the large, deep-chested breeds. But they're unique and special; it's worth it to me. I had Zephyr's stomach tacked as a precaution. And I'm hoping a mix might have stronger genetics."

"Tacking—they suture the stomach to the abdominal wall?"

"Exactly. So it can't flip over."

"How do you see sighthounds as different from other breeds?"

"Mellow and, most of all, intuitive." Rowan considered leaving it there.

"I can tell there's more."

"Let's save it, okay?"

He gave a thoughtful nod. "When you're ready. But damn, I'm curious."

Changing the subject, she asked, "Do you have brothers or sisters?"

"Only me and my mom. And Uncle Terence, until he died. He lived next door to us."

"Where?"

"In Portland."

"We live in Eugene. And at a ranch called Bender's Ridge outside of Sisters. Our family spends a lot of time there. Besides Zephy, we have a greyhound mix—my dad's rehomed dog—her name is Jazz. And Mom recently got a rescue Saluki from Dubai she calls Salaam. Do you have a dog?"

"Dubai? Didn't realize dogs across the world got placed in the U.S. I lost Buck last summer. A standard Schnauzer—very smart and sweet. He was eleven. Liver cancer. And now that I'm in college out of town, I have to wait before I have another four-legged friend."

"Ouch. I'm sorry. But beyond dogs"—she paused to frame her question—"when did you know you saw life differently from most people?"

"Age seven. Luckily, I have the coolest mom in the world. My statements and questions stumped and frightened her, I think. She eventually found Colin and brought me to meet him when I was nine. She adores him, but I'm not sure she groks the teaching."

"He must be like a wise father to you?"

"No. He's always treated me as a friend. He sent me home to Terence for fatherly advice."

"You have one smart mom. Mine resisted—until recently. She almost lost me because of it." She stood and stretched. "I have another, more personal question. You're such a gorgeous color. What's your background?"

"Mom's part black, part Scottish." He looked at her with brows furrowed. "Is it a problem for you?"

"Problem?" She laughed. "I love it."

"I hope your parents feel the same way," he said. "People react different ways, some hurtful. I think I was the product of a brief affair, but Mom clams up. I got my mother's 'fro, but apparently my bio father's blue eyes. I suppose they could've come from the Scottish part. My coloring's unusual, I know."

"I think you're handsome," she said in a whisper. "And the people who've hurt you are mean. And uneducated."

He smiled. "Thanks. I'm very careful around policemen, for sure. Portland has serious racial divides."

"Geez." Suddenly, she was afraid for him.

"Before I got big enough to defend myself, the older kids beat me up. Often. No longer, though." He straightened his back. "Terence sent me to karate at eight. I'm a black belt."

"So's my mom." She hesitated. "I'm getting ready to take my brown belt test."

"Good for her. And you. At least she and I have one thing to talk about. And you—you'll have your black belt in no time."

"I'm working hard. Mom's my teacher, but she sends me to her sensei for the tests." Rowan glanced at the pond and beyond. "When's afternoon group?"

Ben looked at his phone. "Fifteen minutes. We have to go back so we don't miss anything." He stood up and gave her a hand. "I'd like to hug you," he said.

Thoughtful, she stared up at him. *He must be six-three.* His statement felt more like a question. "Thanks for asking. If we can keep it there—I do love physical contact."

"Me, too. And we can." He enfolded her in his arms.

Rowan leaned into his chest, felt the warmth of him, overcome by the powerful sense of home.

Every day, after breakfast and lunch, Rowan and Ben went for a walk except during the two days of drenching rain. They holed up—by unspoken agreement—not in Ben's bedroom, but in the unoccupied space on the same floor. Unfailingly, Teal came to check on her. She waved him in. "Want to join us?" One day, he sat on the floor, arms around his knees, and talked with them for hours. He asked a lot of questions about Colin's teaching.

Finally, he said to Ben, "I guess it's time to tell you the truth. What with you and Row getting close, it's going to get dicey if you don't know. I didn't want her to have to lie while waiting for me to disclose. I'm trans. I was born with a girl's body."

"I didn't have any idea," Ben said. "Good on you for living your truth; it can't be easy. We both have life complications, don't we? Mine are more visible, that's all."

"Yeah, and mine have long-term health implications. I'm not trying to one-up what you face. More visible may well be harder."

Ben chuckled. "Maybe, but when you get to know someone, *you* have significantly more explaining to do."

Teal roared with laughter. "You got that right."

"Will you help us navigate your parents?" Ben asked. "They're going to make assumptions different from what's happening."

"That could change quickly," Teal responded, grinning.

"Stop that, right now," Rowan snapped, frowning. "Not for a long time. No teasing, please. Ben and I talked. I'm way too young, and he's facing years of schooling. Besides, either of us could meet someone else. It happens all the time."

"But the attraction's there, right?"

"For me," Ben said. "Rowan?"

"Yep."

"Just checking," Teal said. "The bond you two have is remarkable. The age difference, which is nothing later—but kind of big right now—doesn't seem to matter."

"Right," they said in unison.

"Look at how much we have in common," Rowan said.

"You haven't asked a question," Rowan said to Teal at dinner.

"Next retreat, for sure," he responded. "But I've learned a lot from this one. And made some friends, too. Look up the dates?"

"On it." She fiddled with her phone. "July. Thank God, school will be out. Mama and Da won't have a reason to keep me from going."

"You don't think Ben may be the excuse they come up with? I'm sure he'll visit before summer."

"I'll toe the line," she responded. "No more impulsive behavior. Everything's changed for me."

"Understatement."

Her head jerked up. "Wait. Da said he wants to come. Remember? Now there's a complication."

"You'll figure it out. On a different topic"—Teal reached for her hand—"I've made my decision. I want the adoption to go through. I miss my family something awful, but they've rejected me for good. I'm very grateful to become part of yours."

"Thank God." She threw her arms around him. "My bro. Forever. I wanted a brother, and now I have two. One much younger and one much older."

After breakfast the final morning, Rowan and Ben hiked up the mountain, taking the path she'd found the first day. The weather had cleared. White cumulus clouds piled like giant puppies in the distance. They found a smooth rock to lean against, and sat side by side facing west.

"I have something to share. It's very important to me," Rowan said. "I've been shy about it."

He shifted his position to focus on her.

She had to take a deep breath in order to continue. "Zephy and I communicate. Mind to mind. It started the day I met her. First, I got fleeting images. I knew they weren't mine, but it was confusing—and shocking." She stretched her foot out and worked her ankle up and down.

"How'd you figure out what was going on?"

"I developed simple tests. Like, I left her in the garage near the dog door, and told her to wait. I hid in the woods. I'd picked a position where I could see the last hundred feet or so. Then, with my mind, I asked her to find me, and showed her the location. I call it 'pensing.'"

He took her hand and intertwined his fingers, smoothing his thumb against the mound at the base of hers.

Her breath caught at his touch. She remembered to pense Zephy. *Can you feel him?*

"She trotted fast, nose up, coming directly to my location," she said, continuing the thread with Ben.

"Good Lord," he breathed.

Gentle human, her dog pensed back.

Yes. You can feel him.

"We play with it a lot," she said. "After the car accident when Zeph was lost, she sent me images of the mountain lion that attacked her, along with loneliness and fear. Those were the first feelings she ever communicated. I pressured Mama to search—she was only focused on getting me oriented to blind reality. But I lost it, had a full-on temper tantrum. I knew Zephy was in life-threatening trouble. We left for Sisters the next morning."

"Did Zephyr show you where she was?"

"No, she didn't have context—that kinda takes a map. I directed Mom, though, and I could sense when we were getting closer. Like"—she stared toward the vista—"true North pulling me. We got within a quarter mile, but Mom wanted to go back to the motel. She was cranky and I was disappointed. I knew we were very close. When we got to our room, there was a message from some guy named Moss. Zephy's chipped, of course, and the vet had scanned her."

Ben's eyebrows flitted up. "You all met because of the chip."

She giggled. "Yup. The first phone call was rough. They didn't like each other." She glanced at her watch and stood up. "Darn, it's time to go to the last meeting." Her lip trembled.

"We have Skype or Facetime." He looped her in for a hug. "Thank God for technology."

"Right." But her shoulders shook.

"Rowan."

It wasn't a question.

"I'm going to kiss you. Really kiss you. This once. Okay?"

"Yes." She tilted her face back.

He put a knuckle under her chin and grazed her lips. His were trembling.

He pulled her in close. As his mouth explored hers, shock coursed through her, but she held steady, soaking in the tender warmth. *My dear Ben. Life as I've known it is gone. Reborn. Completely new.*

She sobbed against him. "How are we going to—negotiate this?"

"You mean wait, don't you? Because that's the only way this has a chance of working," he whispered. "I apologize for crossing the line. I had to know."

"Know what?"

"Our chemistry. You know, how we respond to touching."

She leaned back in his arms. "Well, no question about that."

Chapter Forty-six

"Let me take the lead with your folks," Teal suggested to Rowan when they arrived home in Eugene.

"Why?" She undid her seatbelt and swiveled to face him.

"You'll see. I have a plan."

"You were pretty quiet on the way. Plotting?"

"I guess so," he said. "Now, remember—don't offer too much information. Wait for their questions, and rest in what you know you are. Right?"

"Right. Why is it I forget when I'm with them?"

"Because they're your parents." He set the brake. "Oh my God, *our* parents. I need to respond to their offer."

"It's going to be different for you getting adopted, because you're an adult. I was only eleven when Mossy adopted me. They won't try to instruct you. You're already formed, and they love you the way you are."

He unclipped his seatbelt. "Well, I hope they'll counsel me when I want their opinion."

"They will. They're both great about it."

"Ready to head inside?" he asked.

"Here we go," she said. "I'm a bit nervous, but in your capable hands. Hey, we get to see Graham."

"Sure have missed the little bugger."

The door opened. Moss walked out holding Graham and grinning widely. Carolina followed, also with a big smile. The dogs tore out the door and bounded past the humans. Zephyr headed straight for her girl.

Rowan knelt and buried her face in Zephyr's fur. *Missed you.*

With my girl. No distance.

How wise you are. Rowan stroked her ears, before standing back up and hugging her parents.

Teal, laughing, flew Graham in the air. "My brother," he said. "And my parents." He handed Graham to Rowan and stepped in to first hug Moss, then Carolina. "I'm grateful—no, thrilled—to be part of your family."

Carolina leaned back, resting her hands on his arms. "You're saying you accept? We're so pleased."

"At the retreat, Teal introduced me as his sister," Rowan said. "When I looked surprised, he said he was trying it on. It felt great to both of us."

"It looks like you two had a good time. Come, tell us about it." Carolina linked her elbow through Moss's arm. "Dinner's about ready."

Teal took Graham from Rowan and nuzzled his neck. "I'm happy to see you, little bro. Need any help?" he called after Carolina.

She went back to him. "We're good tonight. I'll carry Graham if you both want to wash up."

Teal handed the baby over.

The dogs gamboled after them, Zephyr bumping Rowan's hand up in the air until she rested it on her dog's head.

Fifteen minutes later, they sat down to dinner. After the plates were served, Teal said, "We made a good friend at the retreat. His name's Ben—he falls between me and Rowan, but he's closer to her age."

"What do you like about him?" Carolina asked.

Cool, Rowan thought. Smart of Teal to bring him up. Better than me.

"He's wise beyond his years and a great listener," Teal said. "His mom took him to meet Colin when he was only nine and he's been attending retreats ever since. A good-looking guy. Bi-racial."

"He's thoughtful and kind," Rowan said. "Ben's uncle, who served as his father figure, died last month. It's a hard loss for him."

"His dad's not in the picture?" Moss asked.

"No. But his mom has a PhD in economics. She's a professor at Lewis and Clark," Teal said.

"When did you find that out?" Rowan asked.

"He and I stayed up late one night yacking." Teal dished out more sautéed vegetables. "Who made this? It's delicious."

"Thanks, I did," Moss said. "Fresh ginger."

Graham banged his high chair, frowned, and pushed his lip out. Teal set down his fork. "I'll mash some banana for him."

"Parenting takes six hands," Moss said. "I'm surprised humans don't have three each. We need them. Ben sounds like a nice fellow."

"Way more than nice. No matter where I go or who I marry—if I do—Ben will be a precious friend until my last breath," Rowan said.

"What a statement," Moss said.

"We share the same understanding."

"Of the teaching?"

She nodded. "Finally, a friend who does. Oh, and he's going to be a veterinarian."

"Very special," Carolina said.

"He's extraordinary," Rowan added.

Moss's brows went up, and he focused on Rowan. "Do you plan to see more of him?"

"I hope so."

Later, Carolina knocked on Rowan's door.

"Enter," Row sang out.

"You're cheerful. I love it."

"Zephy, shove over." The dog moved to the other side of the bed and plopped her head in Rowan's lap. "Good dog." She patted the newly cleared space. "I've been a terrible grump. Something's cracked open and I feel much better."

"I imagine there's relief at feeling understood."

Her daughter nodded. Her eyes filled up.

"I'm terribly sad I couldn't provide what you needed, sweetie."

"You did in some ways. I've always known you love me." She took her mother's hand.

"It wasn't enough, though."

"Not completely. I need a community like the one at the retreat."

"You want to go back, I suppose."

"Yes. There's a retreat in July."

"I think you should. Clearly, it feeds you." Her mom interlaced her fingers with her daughter's. "Now, tell me more about this young man. I sense he's important?"

Rowan's eyes narrowed. Carolina felt like her daughter was considering whether she could be trusted. *Humbling.*

"I almost knocked him down, tearing around a corner toward breakfast before the dining room closed." Rowan looked out the window for a long moment. "You may not remember, but five years ago, I was there with you in the Sisters' library when Mossy walked in and limped over to introduce himself. I heard the sound of his gait. Of course, I was blind at the time, but the whole atmosphere changed. It's like it got electric between you two. I never forgot." Rowan looked directly at her. "When Ben's and my eyes met, life shifted."

Whoa. Carolina stared at her daughter. *This is serious.*

Her mother's expression startled Rowan. What was it? Then, it dawned on her—Mama had figured out she cared for Ben. Was terror on her face? No, more complex, surprise mixed with fear, she guessed.

Carolina started to speak, sputtered, and tried again. "A-are you two physical?"

Rowan smothered a giggle before she got annoyed. "No. We're *friends.* We hold hands and hug, though." *I won't tell her about our kiss. It's too private, too special to be shared.*

Her mom coughed. "Uh—do you need birth control?"

"Nope. I'm not interested in more. Not now. I'm not ready. Not for a long time."

Her mom gave a tremulous sigh.

She's relieved, Rowan thought. And no wonder. I've never even dated. She must feel blindsided.

After her mother went upstairs to bed, Rowan heard Skype ping on her computer. She leapt up, startling Zephyr. *It's okay,* she pensed. *Either*

Ben or Maggie is calling. She jiggled the mouse. Maggie. Her heart fell a little. She answered the video call, trying to buoy up her voice. "Hi, couz, how goes it?"

"Great! Cool stuff's happening with Bender."

"Tell me." Drawn into Maggie's delight and the clear improvement in communication her cousin was having with her dog, Rowan's spirits lifted. "You're getting the hang of it," she said. "Your confidence is way better. What else is new?"

They talked for half an hour, but Rowan never mentioned Ben. She glanced at the computer. 10:30 p.m. Was it possible he'd try to reach her this late? Probably not. Maybe he wouldn't. Ever. Her insides crumpled.

Nope, she thought, that's just my crazy mind. He'll call. Eventually. It might take a week or two. She wanted to invite him to the ranch. *I could Skype him. If he doesn't reach out by tomorrow evening, I will. I'll text him the invite.* She glanced around the bed, feeling under the laptop and books for her phone. It wasn't there. Frowning, she got up and searched the whole room, moving books and papers. "Huh. Where the heck is it?" She thought of her coat in the utility room. "Probably there. I'll get it tomorrow."

The following morning, Rowan took the stairs two at a time, Zephyr in fast pursuit. Her phone was not in her coat. Now worried, she rechecked her purse, suitcase, everywhere she could think of. No cell. Frowning, she dashed through the freezing rain to the van, slipping her hands into seat crevices and feeling around on the floor. Coming up empty, she loped back to the house and asked Teal if he'd seen it.

"Nope, sorry," he said, patting Graham's back.

She scoured the house. *I must have left it at the retreat. Damn. Time to call Still Mountain.*

The phone rang at the center, but the message machine came on. She explained the problem.

Three hours later, Brother Simon called her back. "Hello, Rowan. Ben found the phone sitting on your chair in the retreat yurt and took it with him. He'll bring it to you tomorrow on his way to school—Eugene's on his way."

"Great." Her heart thudded so hard she wondered if her chest could contain it.

"He emailed you, but it bounced. He figured you'd call us when you found it missing."

"Thanks, Simon. Good news." Her breath came fast with excitement and fear. *Ben was coming here*? *Tomorrow*? To figure out when he might arrive, she raced for her computer and Google maps to see how long the trip from his home to college took. Oh my God, her parents were going to meet him soon! Hands trembling, she typed in the start and end of his complete trip from Portland to Davis. Nine-plus hours. "I bet he leaves around seven so he can get here by 9:30 or so. We can spend a chunk of time together before he has to get back on the road."

Zephy, she pensed. *Ben's coming.* She went upstairs to find Teal and her parents.

Chapter Forty-seven

Rowan woke up Sunday feeling jittery, not clear if it was fear, excitement, or both. Her stomach roiled and she had no appetite. She glanced at the clock. 6:10 a.m. Getting up, she peered out the window. The deluge was flying sideways, and she was worried at the thought of Ben driving in it.

Zephyr, lying snug against her, pensed, *My girl is upset?*

I suppose I am. It's excitement—like when you're expecting us to come home—but I'm worried about Ben in this bad weather.

The dog raised her head and pondered Rowan. *Excitement because Ben comes?*

Yes. No more sleeping for me. Let's go to the feeding room. Rowan threw on her clothes and went to make a mocha, Zephyr tagging her heels.

A half hour later, Moss showed up. "You're an early riser." He squinted at her. "Why, I think you can't sleep because Ben is coming."

She blushed. "I like him, Da."

"Quite obvious." He slipped an arm around her. "It's precious. I'm happy for you."

"Don't scare him off, okay?"

"Me? Scary?" He laughed out loud. "I suppose to a young man with eyes for my daughter, I might be. The big, overbearing father. I do want to get to know him a bit." Rowan stepped away with her mocha, and he slipped in to make his.

"You'll like him. He's different from other boys his age."

"That's probably a good thing, yes?"

"Oh yeah." She peered out the kitchen window. "Now it's sleeting and not letting up. I hope he's okay."

"What does he drive?" her dad asked.

"Subaru Forester."

"They're great bad-weather cars with all-wheel drive. He'll be fine. Maybe delayed, though, if low visibility slows him down."

"Darn. We'll hardly have any time together. He has to get to Davis tonight. The quarter starts tomorrow, and he mentioned he likes early-morning classes."

Nine o'clock came and went. Ten. Rowan wanted to whimper and wail. *Where is he? Did the monk get the day wrong? Unlikely.*

When the clock passed eleven, she fled to find her dad in the yurt, Zephyr at her heels.

He looked up when she knocked and walked in. "Oh, sweetie," he said, "come here." He wrapped his arms around her. "No news is good news, remember? Don't worry until there's something actual to worry about."

"My mind's run away with me. Caring is painful. I hadn't realized." She collapsed in the recliner near his computer. With a groan, Zephyr lay near Jazz.

"It's more than painful, though," Moss went on. "On the upside, there's joy and ecstasy. But you're right, caring means we open ourselves to being vulnerable. It can be tough and seems to come in waves. Stay with me a while. Teal or Carolina will find you when he arrives."

Carolina saw her daughter head out to the yurt. Her heart contracted, and she wrapped both arms tight around herself. *Why won't Rowan look for me instead of her da? I'm her mother.* "Because I blew it with her for years," she mumbled. "My own damn fault."

Salaam nosed her hand and pressed against her. "Yes, sweet one, I am upset. Thanks for comforting me." Carolina smoothed her velvety ears.

At 1:45, Rowan saw Teal heading for the yurt. She jumped to her feet and rushed to open the door. "Is he here?"

"He is," he said, "and okay. When we're all together, he'll tell us what's gone on."

They tramped through the icy rain, Zephyr trotting ahead. Jazz remained glued to Moss's side. Rowan had to rein herself in to prevent charging across the yard. She stumbled over her feet and realized she was quivering. And then, there Ben stood, Salaam by his side—framed in the living room window—talking with her mom. Her heart skipped a couple of beats before thudding hard. He had a sling on his arm. *Oh my God, what happened?*

Teal opened the door for her. Zephyr flew in first, and went right up to their visitor.

"Wowee," Ben said, "you're a beauty. You must be Zeph." He knelt down to greet her eye to eye. The dog offered him a paw, which he took. He glanced up and saw Rowan. A smile spread across his haggard face. He patted Zephyr and said to her, "I need to greet your girl."

He stood and opened his one good arm to Rowan who, with a guttural sound, carefully leaned into him.

"Oh, Ben!"

"I'm all right. Shaky. But my car's totaled," he said. "For a few seconds there, I wondered if I'd make it."

She looked up at him. "Thank God you're all right. Ben, this is my father, Moss. You met Mom and Salaam already. Of course, you and Teal are already friends. And here's Jazz, Moss's dog. When you can, tell us what happened."

"You two sit on the couch," Moss said. "Ben needs you close."

Carolina frowned. *What is he thinking?*

"I know trauma when I see it. It'll help him come to himself and heal," he said softly to her.

She nodded. "Okay. I'll go make chamomile tea. It'll soothe all our nerves. I'm rattled, too."

"Ben, I doubt you're in any shape to drive tonight, and the weather's still terrible. Stay with us," Moss said.

"Tea would be good. You're right, I probably shouldn't drive, and I'd love to spend the night. The shaking's getting worse, not better." He held out his hand, which trembled badly. "I'll email my professors I'm a wreck. I'll need to rent a car in the morning."

Rowan nestled close to him, and he slipped his good arm around her. Teal took a chair nearby. Her mom came back holding a tray filled with tea pot, mugs, cheese and crackers.

Once everyone was served, Carolina sliced cheese, spread the Brie on crackers, and passed them around. She made Ben a couple of cracker sandwiches.

He munched them down. "Thank you, food helps. Visibility got worse and worse as I approached Eugene. The temperature must have dropped, because sleet clung to the roadbed. Slick as hell." He picked up the mug but, still shaking, set it back on the table.

Rowan noticed, and helped him with it.

"I was in the slow lane, of course. All of a sudden, out of the corner of my eye, I see a car skidding straight into my driver's door. Ka-bam!

"Later, the police told me the guy hydroplaned and lost control. He creamed me. My car spun two or three times and ended up on the side of the freeway pinned against an abutment." He drew a harsh breath. "The side airbag went off and nailed my shoulder—at least that's what the fireman said later. *Something* sure did." A little tea sloshed on his jeans as he tried to take a sip.

"A few seconds later, another car barreled into the guy who hit me. Oh God, he was going fast. Madness in sleety weather. Fire broke out. I tried to help, but they both … were fatalities." His face blanched again. "I couldn't get to them." Now his legs beat a rhythm and he tried to still them with his hand. "We were somewhere not very far north of Eugene—near Coburg, I think the policeman said? They insisted I take the ambulance to Riverbend. Emergency checked me out and gave me the sling. Nothing's broken, but I'm sore. I caught a cab here." He shuddered. "Nothing to drive, and I couldn't have, anyway."

"I'm so sorry," Moss said. "Here's advice from my war experience. Find someone you can talk to, and speak about the accident in detail.

Sooner is better. Talking about everything you can remember—no matter how awful—will help flush the memories. They won't completely go away, but may at least not haunt you as badly. I'm sure Davis has a counseling center. Ask if they have a trauma specialist." He reached across and touched the young man on the knee. "I waited way too long. Please, don't make the same mistake. PTSD is ugly to live with."

"I can't imagine talking about it more deeply than I have here. I need to sit with Colin, but it'll have to wait until I get back up north."

"If you can't face taking care of yourself, do it for your friend," Moss said, his voice firm, nodding toward Rowan and squinting at the young man.

For a moment, Ben put his face in his hands before meeting Moss's eyes. "Yes, of course."

Moss nodded.

"Row," Ben said, "I guess I jotted down your email wrong. Teal, I need yours, too. It was frustrating not to be able to call or email. I looked up Moss Graham, but couldn't find anyone."

Moss's grim face softened. "It's because my last name is different. Row decided to keep hers to honor her bio dad. I supported her. Did you phone your mom?"

"Yeah, from the hospital. A nurse reminded me, kind soul. I wouldn't have remembered, at least not right away." He fumbled in his pocket. "Row, here's your cell."

"Thanks. I feel awful you had this accident getting it to me."

"I had to come through Eugene, anyway. I would have been in the same spot at the same time."

Graham let out a cry, and Teal rose to get him.

"Thanks, Teal. What are you going to do about a car?" Carolina asked Ben.

"Mom's replacing the Subaru, but we need to buy it in Oregon—no sales tax. Saves over $1,500. I'll fly to Portland some weekend to pick it up."

"Come to Bender's Ridge for Presidents' Day weekend," Rowan said. "Maybe you can combine the two."

"That could work." He glanced at Carolina and Moss. "If you're okay with a visit, I'll plan on it. I hope I'll be comfortable driving again."

Carolina glanced over at Moss. He gave an imperceptible nod. "We'd love to have you visit Bender's Ridge," she said.

Rowan's eyes widened. "But don't you *dare* come if the weather's bad."

"Trust me, I won't," Ben said. "I don't ever want a repeat of this experience."

"I'm going to start dinner," Carolina said. "Moss, will you help?"

"Yes. Ben, anything you don't eat?" Moss asked.

"I'm an omnivore. If someone's willing to cook, I'll happily eat it. I can help. Chop? Peel onions?"

Moss grinned. "How are you going to work with a sling? When you come to the ranch, I'll tap you for assistance. Not today. You two, have a nice visit."

Rowan cleared her throat. "Normally, I'd suggest we go for a walk, but the weather stinks. May we talk in the yurt for a while?"

"That'd be all right. We're fine here," Moss said.

Teal came back with Graham, and Ben lit up. "May I play with him? I love babies." He reached his arm out, before realizing he needed two. He sat on the couch and Teal handed the youngster over. Ben put Graham on his knee, and bounced him. Soon, the little guy was giggling.

"You're great with him," Rowan said, feeling a twinge of jealousy. She wanted time with Ben alone.

He glanced up. "Five minutes more, okay? Then we'll head out back. I need a cuddle fix with this guy."

Frowning, Carolina followed Moss into the kitchen. "Are you so comfortable with them alone out there? Good lord, there's a bed."

"It's tucked into the wall, his arm's in a sling, and these are smart kids. I like Ben—he's sensible. And they deeply care for each other. It's obvious, isn't it?"

Carolina nodded. "They're twenty years younger, but they remind me of us."

"Me, too. Weird, isn't it? I wish I'd met you at their age." He took Carolina's hand and spun her—a dance move—into his arms.

She snuggled against his heart. "All those years, lost to us. But then we wouldn't have our Rowan."

"She's very special, and you seem to have made peace with her spiritual nature."

"It's about time. Long overdue, in fact."

He leaned back and laughed. "True."

After Ben reluctantly let Teal take Graham back, they slipped on their hooded coats—Rowan helped Ben—before heading to the yurt. He shifted sides and interlaced the fingers of his good hand with hers, a signature habit of his, she realized. They swung arms, sleet pinging their backs. Upon entering the many-sided structure, Ben whistled. "Tasty," he said. "Look at the wonderful writing desk."

"Moss has a feel for quality. What with his missing leg, he needs to regularly switch between sitting and standing. The desk is electric. The yurt's mainly used as his writing space, although there's a Murphy bed in here." She stroked the oak cabinetry. "And a bathroom." She pointed. "When Mom was coughing badly from a cold, she slept out here, and Teal handled Graham so she could get a full night's rest."

"Is there a view? I can't tell in this weather."

"A gorgeous one. It overlooks a wide valley."

He hooked Rowan close with his good arm. "I'd like a real hug. Maybe you weren't comfortable in front of your parents?"

"You're right. I think they'll need a bit of time to get used to us." Being careful of his injured shoulder, she slipped into his embrace. "Oh!" She eased back, her eyes wide.

"Sorry, guys have no control over erections. They show up at the *least* convenient, most embarrassing, times. Pay it no mind; it'll subside." He laughed. "And most likely, rise up again the next time we hug. It's only a sign of how attracted I am to you."

She blushed. "I-It startled me. I don't know much other than teen gossip. Mom always said we'd talk when I got interested in dating."

"Please don't be flustered. We'll figure this out together, over time."

"Are you sure we can, you know, weather this? Be honest."

"Think about everything we share, and how deep our conversations went at the retreat. I'll lay bets on it."

"I hope so," she whispered. "I care."

"I care, too. Big time. In addition, we have our understanding of the teaching. Now, let's hang out in these recliners and, like Colin says, talk about nothing, okay?"

"First, I need to talk about something."

"What about?"

"You're wonderful with Graham."

He frowned in puzzlement. "Yeah, I adore kids."

"I know my work is with animals, and I see how children usurp all of a mother's time."

He stood and paced the length of the room and back before sitting again. "I feel a responsibility, as an awake man, to offer our level of consciousness to parenting. Imagine the gift of being raised by Colin."

"Quite a thought. But does Colin raise his daughter, or does most of the responsibility fall on his wife?"

"Huh. A good question—I don't know. Let's ask him when we're together. He'll give us an honest answer."

Carolina and Moss decided Ben should sleep in the guest room rather than the yurt. They'd hear comings and goings on the same floor as their bedroom, but the temptation of Rowan slipping out and visiting Ben in Moss's writing space loomed—even though they trusted her.

At 9 p.m., Ben yawned and glanced at his watch. "I'm fried. I need sleep. Thanks again for the invitation."

After Rowan settled in her room, Carolina went to see her. She knocked quietly and, invited in, sat on the bed. "I was proud of you today," she said.

Rowan looked startled. "Why?"

"When Ben arrived, you didn't swamp him with questions. You gave him the space to tell us what happened in his own time. It showed real maturity."

Her daughter blushed. "Wow—how unexpected."

"He's a special young man, and clearly cares for you."

Rowan ducked her head and fingered the duvet cover. "We may have a big challenge."

"What?"

"You saw how sweet he was with Graham. I'm afraid he'll want kids."

Carolina thought before answering. "You're not having children any time soon. Either one of you could change your minds."

Her daughter looked up, agony in her eyes. "But what if we don't?"

"You're smart, caring people. You'll work it out. Whatever happens, you'll have a deep, lifelong friend, and a special relationship."

Rowan twisted her mouth. "Yeah. Right, but..."

"But at this moment, it's not what you want to hear."

Swallowing hard, she nodded.

"Over the years, you've advised me about remaining in the present. Sweetheart, it's your task now. No future-tripping. Isn't it what you call 'the mind train'?"

"You *were* listening when I told you and Mossy."

"You bet. Resistant, but I listened."

Rowan stared at her. "Thanks. I misjudged you."

"No, you didn't. You know firsthand how I've been. But I'm capable of change, apparently." Carolina gave an embarrassed giggle, and found herself enveloped in her sixteen-year-old's arms. "Aww, thanks, sweetie. I love you, too. Now, follow your own good advice. I'm not saying it's easy, but you can do it. Isn't it lucky school doesn't start until Tuesday? You'll get to see Ben off."

"Yes."

Carolina kissed Rowan on the top of her head and went upstairs to bed.

Chapter Forty-eight

In the morning, Ben walked into the kitchen and leaned against the counter, stabilizing himself so he could rub his eyes one at a time.

"Good morning," Moss said.

Carolina echoed him.

Ben jumped. "You startled me; I didn't see you. Good morning."

"Want a mocha?" Moss asked.

"Please. I'll watch, then I can make one for Row another time. It's clearly a two-handed job."

"It is." Moss twisted knobs on the latte machine. Five minutes later, the racket was over and he set the drink near Ben. "Sometime after breakfast, I'll drive you to the car rental office."

"Thanks."

Rowan walked in, covering a wide yawn. "I wanted to make sure I got to say goodbye."

"Hey you, good morning. I hardly slept. Haunted by yesterday's memories." Ben went to pick up his coffee and, to still his quivering hand, pressed it against the counter.

Rowan flicked her wide eyes toward her father. "He shouldn't drive. Can't you stop him?" she mouthed.

Moss moved to stand in front of Ben. "Okay, here's how this is going down. We'll head out to the rental place, and both be on the contract. But I'm driving you to Davis"—he waved his hand to dismiss Ben's refusal.

"You're not ready to be behind the wheel. Admit it. My time is my own, and I'm happy to do this." He watched Ben struggle to accept the offer.

Rowan moved over and touched Ben's good arm. "Da always tells his truth. If he says he's happy to drive you, he is. Please take him up on it."

Moss went on, "I'll leave the car with you and pick up another one to drive back. Then, you'll have wheels until you come north to get your new car."

"No sir," Ben forced the words out. "I can't accept."

Moss frowned. "This is not a negotiation. Either I drive you, or you're not leaving."

Ben looked startled. "You can't—"

"I can. I'm pulling rank, and looking for your good common sense here. Don't disappoint."

Carolina interjected, "I'll be right back. I need to check on something."

The young man frowned. "I *have* to get to school. Today."

"Exactly. That's why I'll ferry you."

"I need a moment." Ben whirled and stepped outside.

Moss watched him repeatedly flex his fists and blow out breaths. *He handles frustration pretty well for someone his age.*

Five minutes later, Ben returned. He closed the door with care as though afraid he might slam it. "Okay," he said. "I accept." A longer-than-comfortable pause. "Thank you."

"You're welcome." Moss felt the tension slide out of Rowan. He smiled at Ben. "Good choice. It's a chance for me to get to know you better. If you're developing a deep friendship with my daughter—"

"Speaking of which," Rowan said, "I'd like fifteen minutes alone with Ben to say goodbye. Now, Da, take your coffee and please skedaddle. Keep Mama busy, too."

Carolina walked back in. "Since *I* have common sense, I checked the updated weather report. *Neither* of you is driving today. Although it has cleared here, the conditions are icy through the mountains. This weather will break this afternoon; you can go tomorrow." She folded her arms in front of her chest and lifted her chin. "Pack Mama has spoken. Any questions?"

"Pack Mama?" Ben asked, confused.

"Zephy's name for her," Rowan said. "Moss is 'Kibble Man' because, when she was lost, he lured her with nuggets he dropped on the ground."

"Really." Ben looked from Carolina to Moss and back. "Your last word?"

"The last word." Moss and Carolina spoke in unison.

"I'll call school," Ben said, looking defeated.

"We have a whole day," Rowan crowed.

After Ben made his call, Rowan said, "Let's bundle up and go for a walk." She put on her parka and helped Ben with his. They pulled on gloves and boots and headed out. Zephyr trotted alongside.

"Where're Jazz and Salaam?" Ben asked.

"Jazz keeps Moss company in the yurt while he writes. Salaam shadows Mama. I think she's grateful to have been rescued; she's only been with us for six weeks."

"What fortunate dogs," he said, "to have ended up in a family where they're treated as equal."

"They are. Very lucky. Let me show you where I play with Zephy most often." She struck out across the front field. The giant dog bounded in front of them, stretching her long legs with delight. Snow flew in the air, crystals catching the light.

"Look at her." Ben whistled. " No one could keep up." He squatted to watch. "Her strides must be nine or ten feet long. Stunning."

"And why sighthounds must only be let loose in fully fenced areas. If they see a bunny, deer, or raccoon, they're off, flying across roads and not looking out for cars. *No* one can catch them. They get killed or maimed. It's sad, and unconscionable for an owner to let them run free."

Ben took her hand. "I love how much you care."

"It's who I am. You care, too. You're studying to be a vet."

"Exactly. It's been my lifelong dream."

They entered the quiet of the woods and walked for ten minutes. "Here's the creek Zephy had to cross to find me when we began pensing," Rowan said. "And here's where I hid—under these salal bushes. Look how big they get in the shade. She found me immediately. No hesitation."

"Where is she?"

"Probably chasing bunnies. We have ten acres fenced. She can feel free here."

"Ten acres? That's a lot of posts."

Rowan sat on a flat boulder and patted the space beside her. "Originally, we used the invisible stuff but, two years ago, Moss decided we needed traditional barriers to keep the deer out. Deer versus sighthound isn't pretty. We had to put one doe down; she broke her leg trying to get away. Of course, Moss took the meat and we ate her all winter."

Ben eased down by her. "He shot her?"

"With his bow, yes. Moss won't keep a gun. Since the war, he doesn't touch firearms."

"A bow hunter? I understand that takes real skill."

"The Army discovered he excelled with guns. Good enough to be a sniper."

"I suspect it didn't appeal to him?"

"You're right. He enlisted the day after 9/11. He isn't attracted to violence like some guys. He's not testosterone-driven. His favorite cousin, Andrea, died in the towers. He felt compelled to do something."

"Clearly the war took its toll on him—beyond his missing leg."

"Yeah. He has awful PTSD and terrible nightmares. Jazz jumps on the bed and wakes him the moment he starts moaning and thrashing." Rowan saw Zeph loping toward them, tongue lolling. "There you are. The bunny got away, huh?" She grabbed her dog's jowls and kissed her between the eyes. "Moss has lots of tools for during the daytime, but the nightmares were harder to figure out. Jazz spontaneously woke him the first time he had one after she came to live with him."

"What a gift."

"It is. He hates traveling without her."

"Do you think it'd be possible to have a sighthound specialty practice? I've fallen for these girls."

She frowned. "You could, but you'd have to live in a big city; otherwise you wouldn't have the clientele pool. Portland might be large enough. Eugene isn't."

"I'd need to see other breeds, too."

"It might work. Ask your profs what they think. I'd be thrilled if you decide on it."

They sat quietly. The silence engulfed Rowan. Zephyr plopped at their feet and gave a cleansing groan. Both started talking at once, laughed, glanced shyly at each other. "You go first," Ben said.

"I was thinking about you spending almost eight hours in the car with Moss tomorrow. Are you comfortable with him?"

"Any reason I shouldn't be?"

Rowan giggled. "Other than you're the boy his daughter's crazy about? No, no worries at all."

He stared at her. "You're crazy about me?"

She cuffed him lightly. "How could you not know?"

"Because it's everything I hoped to hear and was terrified I wouldn't."

"Silly boy. Trust your instincts."

"I feel the same way." His expression was serious.

"I know. But it's extra-special to hear."

"We got that out of the way. It's a bit early, but oh well. Do you think your dad will grill me?"

"Not exactly, but he'll be direct and say what he feels he needs to. Nothing falls through the cracks with him." Rowan described how Moss handled her credit card infraction when she'd booked the retreat without asking.

Ben's eyes went wide. "Colin might say the same thing in a similar situation. Cool."

"Cool, right," Rowan snapped. "Except it's delayed getting my license by six months."

"You're only a sophomore. There must be lots of other kids who can't drive."

"No, I'm a junior. I skipped a grade a while back."

"Fantastic—you'll be going to college in a year and a half! But, you broke the unspoken rules. Surely you knew there'd be consequences?"

"I didn't think," Rowan answered. "I wanted to go to the retreat so badly, I lost the bigger picture."

Ben pulled off his glove, eased hers off too, and interlaced their fingers. His touch was electrifying, and she gasped.

"Got ya," he whispered. "Our connection startles me, too." He pulled her close.

Her face muffled against his chest, she said, "Be forthright with Moss. He'll know for sure if you're not."

He rested his chin on the top of her head. "I don't know how to be anything else."

"I know you are with me; I love it. I wasn't so sure about with him. He can be intimidating, but he doesn't mean to be."

He let her go and faced forward again. "Row?"

"Yeah?"

"You could apply to Davis. Have you thought about it?"

"I looked at their website, but they don't have an undergrad writing program. The classes are prep for academic stuff, not creative writing. Not what I want at all."

He frowned. "What's your latest plan?"

"Lewis and Clark in Portland. They have a full-on program, and Kim Stafford teaches there. Eventually, I want to study with him at his Northwest Writing Institute."

"I sure would love it if you attended UCD and lived in town. Even the thought gives me chills. Good chills."

Rowan sighed. "They don't have what I need. Maybe it's best, anyway—you need to concentrate on pre-med. How could you with me around?" She saw his look of disappointment. "I bet I can come down every month or two, weekends we aren't studying. And you could come see me?"

Ben brightened a little. "Please think more about this, okay? Lewis and Clark is expensive. Besides, you could go there for graduate work."

"I'll think about it. Money isn't an issue, but not being with you is. It's lunchtime soon; let's head back." She whistled for Zephyr, and they made their way toward home.

Carolina raced up the stairs and out the door to find Moss working in the yurt. "Rowan is considering going to Davis," she said, trying to catch her breath. "The website is up on her computer. We have to get her to change her mind."

"You checked her laptop? Without her knowing?"

"Every now and again. The high school advised me to."

"Huh. Of course she's thinking about UCD. Wouldn't you, at her age, looked at the school where your first love was enrolled?"

"But she's too young—way younger than most kids who go to college. She needs to explore, date a variety of people—not hone in on her first boyfriend and limit herself."

Moss sighed. "We haven't given her a chance to share her thinking with us. I trust her to make the best decision."

"I don't. You need to convince her."

He frowned. "Me? Why not you? It's your agenda."

"Because she'd hate me forever. We've only recently found our way with each other. You need to be the one."

"I'm not willing to until she comes to us—not the other way around—and expresses her wishes in the matter."

"What?" Carolina fisted her hands on her hips. "You're not being helpful. I need you on my side."

"Sweetheart...." He moved toward her, but she backed away. He lifted his hands, palms out. "I'm not taking sides. Neither yours nor hers. I want information first. We can talk and decide how to proceed when we know more."

Frustrated, she teared up. "It could be too late. We need to step in before she's formed a strong opinion."

"It'd be a big mistake. If she's old enough to go to college—to live on her own—we need to respect her enough to hear what she has to say."

"Damn you. I need your backing." Carolina whirled and fled the room, slamming the door on the way out.

Moss glanced at his watch. *Will she come back within ten minutes, meet the same deadline she gives me when we have a spat?*

Nine minutes later, with a sheepish expression, she sidled back into the room. "I almost forgot and pulled the same crazy stunt you used to."

He nodded, smiling. "Yeah, I was clocking it. You made it back right under the line."

She grimaced. "Just like you to keep track."

"Fair's fair. What's good for the gander's good for the goose. And every other appropriate cliché."

"I'm still blue-blazes mad."

He gave a soft smile and shrugged. "Sorry, but I'm not changing my position because you're bent out of shape. I'm her dad now. My opinion counts, too."

Carolina frowned. "Right." She walked to the window and stared toward the house. "They're back from their walk. Time to put a smile on my face and fix something to eat. You coming?"

He nodded.

Chapter Forty-nine

After lunch, Moss took Ben to pick up a rental car. Walking through light snow, they stomped their feet before entering the small, flat-roofed building.

"We requested an all-wheel drive vehicle," Moss said to the attendant. "We have to drive into California."

"Will you both be on the contract?"

"Yes," Moss replied.

"Are you the other driver?" The twenty-something balding guy squinted at Ben. "How old are you?"

"I'm eighteen."

"You have to be twenty-five to rent an SUV. And anyway, we don't rent to anyone under twenty-one."

Moss looked at Ben. "Sorry, I didn't realize, or I never would have made the suggestion. Let's rethink this. We'll take my 4Runner—it's four-wheel drive—to Davis, and leave it with you until you pick up your new car." He paced for a moment. "I'll get a rental to drive home."

Ben looked relieved. "Sounds good."

"Thanks," Moss said to the attendant. "We won't be renting after all."

The man shrugged, snapping his gum. "Whatever," he said, and turned away.

"He was rude," Ben said, as they approached the 4Runner.

"Yes, he was. They won't get my business anymore. Maybe I should call the manager."

"And pray that guy's not the manager." Ben chuckled.

When they got back, Rowan greeted them. "Ben, would you like some quiet time in the yurt? Da, may we use your space?"

Carolina looked nervously at Moss. "The bed's up, right?"

Rowan snarled, "You think we're going to jump in the sack, or something?"

Her parents glanced at each other.

"Enough," Rowan snapped. "Family meeting. Right now. Here, in the living room. I'm running it. My agenda."

Her mom blanched.

"Is this a family tradition?" Ben asked.

"Yes. Anyone can demand it, and the request has to be honored." Rowan went to find Teal.

When everyone sat and the dogs had settled on the couch, Rowan called the meeting to order. "I'm pissed at all of you right now, everyone except Ben, and Graham, of course."

Zephyr threw her head up and peered at Rowan.

"Not you, Zephy, nor any of the dogs. Teal, you teased us at the retreat. Mama and Da, you act like we're about to have sex at any moment. Listen up." She strode to the window to gather her thoughts before facing them again. "I'm not having intercourse—I hate the word—with anyone until I'm ready to face the reality of parenting. If ever. It's too damn easy to get pregnant." She turned to Ben. "Get used to the idea. I want to hug and kiss you, and I want to be able to do it in front of my family without," she focused on her parents, "you getting tense and weird." She faced Teal. "And no damn teasing. It's not funny, and it makes me uncomfortable."

"Got it," Teal said, "I'm sorry. I guess your interest in the opposite sex came on so fast, I didn't know how to handle it."

Ben threw his hands up, palms out. "I don't want to have sex, either. I've got too much at stake with my education and getting into vet school. I'm into kissing and hugging, though." He smiled.

"Okay. At least you and I are in agreement. Wonderful. Mama, Da—you need to back off. We teens have raging hormones, but it's only bodily sensations. Ben and I can deal with it." She put her hands on her hips and calmed down enough to glare at her parents.

They stared at her, mouths open.

"Well? I'm waiting for you to say something."

Moss cleared his throat. "Okay. I get it. And yes, you may use the yurt."

"Mama?" Rowan wasn't going to let this go until she had everyone's agreement.

Her mom looked at the floor. "I'm feeling strange. We got a lecture from our sixteen-year-old, and we deserved it. We've been making assumptions when neither of you is anywhere near ready, it appears."

Rowan saw her catch Moss's eye, and watched the little whiffle of communication, so easy to miss if you weren't looking for it.

Her mother gulped. "I was out of line. I'm remembering how I was as a teenager, but you're not me. I apologize to both of you."

"I jumped to conclusions, too," Moss said.

"Thank you. When Ben comes to the ranch over Presidents' Day, I'd like to invite his mom, and Colin and his wife. It's time everyone gets on board," Rowan said. "Okay? Mama and Da? Ben?"

Ben smiled and shrugged. "If you can accommodate a crowd, why not? I'd love to see all my favorite people together."

"All right. Any other business?" Rowan asked.

"Yes," Carolina said. "You'll let me know when you do want to talk about birth control?"

"Deal," Rowan said.

"One other thing," Moss said. "There's another word for intercourse. Congress."

"Much better word," Rowan said. "It goes on my list."

"Who's going to call Ben's mom and Colin?" Carolina asked.

Ben glanced at her, and Rowan realized they were doing what her mom and dad did in private communication. "Ben can let them know the invitation is coming, but then Mama, you can call them. All right, everyone?"

Moss and Carolina nodded.

"Perfect." Ben was still grinning.

"Meeting adjourned. We're going to the yurt. No weird faces. Zephy, come."

When they closed the yurt door, Ben burst out laughing. "Girl, you're a force."

"Did you expect anything else?"

"No, but to see you in action is splendid. You did great—strong but respectful."

"Sorry I didn't forewarn you. In the moment, I was too upset."

"I can't wait to tell my mother about your tradition of calling meetings. It's fair to everyone—rare in families."

"It is. What I love is anyone can request one. The first time I used the power I was six."

"This goes back to life with your bio-dad?"

She nodded. "May we kiss in peace now?"

"Come here." Ben held her face in his hands and kissed her, long and strong—less hesitant than before.

After an entwined moment, they felt a nudge. Zephyr pushed her nose gently between them, joining in. Ben stroked her ears. "What a sweetheart. She doesn't seem jealous at all. I feel welcomed by her."

"We're happy together and she senses it."

After dinner, Ben suggested a game of Scrabble. Moss took Graham so Teal could play. He bounced the baby on his knee and watched the board and participants with interest. He knew Rowan was a killer player—he'd been beaten by her 80 percent of the time, but had no idea if Ben was aware of what a wordsmith she was. Two hours later, Rowan beat them by over 150 points.

"Man," Ben said. "You'd better not have much of an ego if you're going to play with this girl." He ruffled Rowan's hair. "You're dynamite."

She blushed. "Words are sport for me. I collect and play with them."

"We've got to get to bed," Moss said. "Ben and I are leaving early—no later than 7 a.m."

"I'll be up by 5:45 anyway," Rowan said. "It's a school day, and I want a chance to say goodbye. I have a school meeting at 7:15. Ma, I guess you're taking me?"

"I'll drive you," Teal said.

ꟹ

Rowan invited Zeph onto her bed and cuddled with her. *Ben leaves tomorrow. I'll miss him a lot.*

Doctor Man is my girl's mate. Packmate to Zephyr.

Yes, right. Do you think he can pense?

Zephyr teaches Rowan. Doctor Man knows big field. Zephyr teaches Doctor Man?

Please try.

ꟹ

Rowan bolted up when the alarm rang. Foggy-headed, she rubbed her eyes and rested in the big field where thoughts didn't live. While waking up, she patted Zephy, dreading this morning, having to say goodbye to Ben for almost six weeks. Six long weeks. Time to get used to being apart; they faced years like this. Rowan figured they'd Skype or Facetime when they weren't too busy studying. She preferred the new Apple technology out this year; it seemed more stable than Skyping—it didn't freeze up all the time. She thought Ben had an iPhone. Best to check.

She slipped into school clothes—cords instead of jeans, flannel shirt instead of her usual pullover, long-sleeved tee. She slung her backpack on, stumbled upstairs and into the kitchen. Da and Ben had beaten her to the latte machine.

"I'm making you one," Ben said to her. "I need to hone my skills. Moss's giving me pointers."

She hugged him from behind. "Mornin'," she said. "I can't call it good, exactly." She cocked her head. "You took off your sling."

"It's feeling better. I'll put it back on when I'm done here."

She looked at her dad. "You drive carefully, transporting my two favorite men in the whole wide world."

Moss tilted his head. "Aha. Pa's been bumped by this young fella?"

"Afraid so. He's slipped to third place. Pa and Ma are my grandparents on Moss's side," she explained to Ben. "They live in Connecticut."

A half hour later, the moment to say goodbye came. In the chill air by the 4Runner, Rowan put her hands on Ben's arms, stood on her toes, and kissed him. "Please text me along the way and when you get there, okay? I hope it goes okay with Da."

"Of course. I love you," he said, leaning in to kiss her more firmly.

Chapter Fifty

"Do you want to drive?" Moss asked when they loaded into the 4Runner.

"Nope. I hope you don't mind; I'm still shaky," Ben replied.

"It's okay. I prefer your honesty."

Wistful, Rowan watched the SUV pull out of the driveway, carrying her men toward Davis. She sighed and, after one last wave, went back inside. Now to put on a decent face to start the winter term. How could she concentrate? Her fingers touched her lips, still feeling Ben's kiss.

As Moss drove, they fell into companionable silence. For two hours, they made progress south on Highway 5, although slowed by an accident near Canyonville. Snow still clumped on the trees, but the main highway lanes had been plowed clear.

When they approached Exit 76, Ben spoke up. "How about we stop at Wolf Creek Park, take a pee break at the campground, and stroll for a bit, stretch our legs? It's right off the interstate."

"Fine. Show me."

Ben directed him off the freeway.

Moss parked by the only other vehicle and they stepped into the frigid air. After stopping at the men's room, they walked down near the creek.

"I need to sit for a few minutes and take my leg off," Moss said. "If it doesn't make you uncomfortable."

Ben nodded. "I'd like to watch."

"Okay. We can go over there."

They went to the closest picnic table. "I love these convertible pants." Moss unzipped the lower leg section and eased off his prosthesis. "I'm lucky to have this"—he pointed at his fake leg—"but it's a relief to remove it. Want to check it out?"

Ben took the prosthesis and examined it. "A suction fit?"

"Yep."

"What remarkable technology. Better than a wooden peg."

Moss laughed out loud. "Yes."

They sat quietly, enjoying the rushing creek.

"I want to talk to you about Rowan," Ben said.

Moss swiveled and focused on him.

"Our connection astonished us both from the moment we met. Even though she's underage, I'd like your blessing to court her." He paused. "I know she's my life partner," he added. "You could choose not to offer your good wishes, of course, but I suspect life will pull us together anyway. Our bond is strong."

Fraught with emotion, Moss stared out over the river before answering Ben. "I appreciate your request. Thank you. But before I respond, tell me what you like about her."

Ben nodded and absently scratched his cheek. "First, she's so wise. I don't mean wise for her age, I mean wise compared to most people on the planet. I love her kind heart, too. And she's shockingly smart—it's wonderful to see how unafraid she is to let her brightness shine." He got up and strode back and forth. "She's attractive, too, but that's the less important part." He interlaced his fingers and stretched his arms out. "Of course, she's two-and-a-half years younger than I am. It makes a difference. I want you to understand she'll run the show regarding intimacy, unless she wants to move faster than I do. I'll slow us down."

"It sounded yesterday like you two were in agreement," Moss said.

"We are. I want you to know I'll respect her, always. She's like my very own self."

Moss nodded. "Good. I have two requests. If you agree to those, I'll give my blessing."

"You must have been thinking about this. Since when?"

"Since Rowan came back from the retreat and made it clear how important you are to her."

"Okay. Hit me."

"When I was an undergrad, a prof of mine, a striking woman about twenty years my senior, mentored me—she taught me what women love."

"Really?" Ben's expression was both quizzical and astonished.

"Yes. Authorities would lock her up today, but I'm grateful for her training. If you have questions and feel comfortable asking me, I'm available."

Ben took a deep breath. "Thank you. I don't have a dad to go to."

Moss cleared his throat. "Second: please don't ask for this conversation until you've been together a year. The way I see it, your sexuality is not my business—I can't order you—but these things have a natural rhythm, and all I can do is ask. Forbidding wouldn't stop you anyway, would it?"

"Okay. You're probably right. I agree to both."

"Do I need to mention the words 'birth control'?"

"You heard Rowan on the subject of pregnancy," Ben said.

"Then I offer my blessing. I like what I've learned of you so far, and I see how connected you are. It's touching." He put his hand on Ben's arm. "I'll slip my leg back on. Want to walk a little before we jump back on the road?"

"I'd like to. And Moss, thank you. I never could have imagined a conversation like this with my girl's dad."

Before arriving in Davis, Moss said, "I did some research on trauma counselors because they don't have one who met my standards at your university medical center. I've found you someone skilled, who has other modalities beyond talking. I've paid for ten appointments, and your first is this afternoon." He glanced at his watch. "In an hour. Before you say anything, I know I've overstepped. I'm not going to apologize, but I want you to know I understand boundaries and, I think, in general, I hold them well. This felt like a special case."

"Overstepped is an understatement. How am I supposed to accept this from you?" Ben's voice cracked.

"Can't you receive a gift from a wounded warrior?" He gave Ben a crooked grin. "Please. Take it. For Row's sake."

Ben blew out a loud sigh. "Damn. I'm terrified to share the horror I saw. To have to relive those poor people dying. I guess you understand."

"I do. I've been there. But the only way out is through, and a true trauma specialist can point the way. I talked to this woman on the phone for quite a while. She knows her stuff. Her name's Clara Bertoli."

"Okay, I'll go, but I have to pay you back."

"There's no need," Moss said.

"I have to," Ben repeated.

"Got it. Do we need to stop at your place first?"

"If we pause at the dorm, I'll drop off my backpack before we go to the rental car place."

Moss handed him a sticky note. "Here's her information."

Ben examined it. "She's close to campus. You can head out or, better yet, to a motel. I hope you aren't planning to drive back tonight?"

"I've got common sense," Moss said. "I'm bushed, and have a reservation nearby."

"Here's the street," Ben said. "It's the big building down on the left."

Moss pulled in front and stopped. "I'll wait."

A few minutes later, Ben trotted down the dorm steps, and they drove to the rental car office.

"Wait a moment," Moss said. "I'm getting out to say goodbye to you. We're a hugging family. Are you open to that?"

Ben seemed surprised. "I'd like it."

Moss wrapped his arms around the young man and gave him a solid, loving squeeze.

Ben returned it. "When you get home to Eugene tomorrow, hug that girl of ours for me, please," he said.

"I will. Take good care. I hope the counselor works out." He handed Ben the keys to the 4Runner.

Rowan knew she'd finished last semester a girl. This term, would she look as different as she felt? Although she couldn't yet call herself a woman, certainly her adult life's path had opened before her. Opened wide.

Teal slung his arm over her. "I know how hard this was, watching Ben leave. Presidents' Day weekend will be here before you know it. Come on, let's get you to school. Your day will improve after you get there. Distraction always helps. Go grab your pack?"

She swiped away a tear, nodded, and traipsed inside to collect it.

Her mom hovered by the door. "The weeks will pass quickly. I promise."

"I'm awfully sad," she said, tears brimming. "Classes will be good. Anyway, I have to get used to this. Separations are going to be part of our lives for years to come." *Those words are becoming a mantra I'm not fond of.* She straightened, hugged her mom, and swung her backpack over one shoulder. "See you on the other end."

Once at Eugene High, she realized she was comparing the boys she passed in the hallway to Ben. None of them matched up. Most seemed gawky, hadn't grown into their noses yet, and acted goofy.

She trudged to the meeting with her adviser, Jeffrey Long. In previous meetings, he'd listened well enough. A professional basketball player before completing graduate studies at Brown University, he had to duck entering any room.

"Where are you thinking of applying?" Jeffrey asked.

"There's only one school I want to attend: Lewis and Clark. I'm interested in their writing program."

"I wouldn't apply to less than three," he said. "Any others catch your eye?"

"No. Most are in the East or deep in the Midwest. I have important reasons to remain on the West Coast."

"I hear you, but how about you at least apply to the University of Iowa? And maybe Colorado College in Colorado Springs? They both have strong writing programs and aren't on the East Coast. Iowa's may be the best in the country." He thumbed through her records. "Your grades and test scores are so high, you'll likely get in to all three. It could be nice to have your pick. A lot can change in a year."

He must think I want to stay on the West Coast because of a boyfriend. How'd he figure it out? Do I look different? "A lot won't change," she said firmly. "But I can apply to those other two as well."

"Good. You'll want to think of people to write recommendations for you. Do you have connections with any well-known authors?"

Rowan giggled. "My dad won grand prize at the American Literary Awards last fall. I guess he can't recommend me even though our last names are different?"

Jeffrey smiled. "Nope, sorry, he's out. Anyone else?"

"Once, at a reading three years ago, I made a nice connection with Dani Shapiro—probably because I was the only thirteen-year-old in the room. We occasionally email. Shall I ask her? She has six or seven published books, and a new one coming out this month called *Slow Motion*. I've already ordered it."

"Sounds good. I'm not familiar with her, but I bet the writing programs will be."

Rowan checked her cell during lunch break. Her heart skittered when she saw the text from Ben.

We stopped at Wolf Creek Park for a bit, a couple of hours south of Eugene. Your dad and I talked. He's a cool guy. On the road again. ♥

Smiling, she hugged the phone close. *Yikes—what did Ben and Da talk about? Will he tell me?* She texted back, *Thanks for the update!*

After hearing from Ben, she concentrated more on her afternoon classes. Later, during English, she wanted to pull her phone out and check messages, but she'd promised her parents to leave her cell alone except at lunch. *I've got to keep them on my side.*

She fished out her phone in the car while Teal drove. A brief text greeted her:

We're nearly there. How about we Skype tonight? 9?

Her thumbs got busy. *I'd* ♥ *to.*

The evening dragged. She was working on her final math problem when Skype pinged. She leapt up, went to her desk and, hand quivering, clicked to accept the video call.

"Hey," Ben said.

"You're there safely. Thank heavens."

He looked serious. "Moss found me a counselor. I had my first appointment—it was rough, but a good start. He was right; this woman knows her way around trauma. If one kind of therapy doesn't seem to work well, she has others up her sleeve."

Rowan sighed with relief. Da was smart to speak up about what he knew Ben needed. After all, Da should know. "Is this someone at the school's health center?"

He shook his head. "Moss called ahead yesterday. They don't have a trauma person he thought was good enough. He did a bunch of research, and found Clara Bertoli. She's suffered trauma herself, so knows what she's talking about. She doesn't rely only on her education."

"Can you share with me what happened?"

His tone got sharper. "I saw two people burn to death. Clara says I have to get desensitized. I wonder how we'll do that."

"Oh Ben. Awful."

"Let's drop it. I'm way too emotional."

"You could ask Moss to talk sometime."

"He made it clear he's happy to sit down with me when I need it. You were right about him. He speaks his mind. And heart."

"And?"

"Let's say we had a man-to-man talk. I'd like to leave it there."

Rowan knew her disappointment showed.

"I'll tell you this much: I asked for his blessing to court his under-age daughter."

She blushed. "You did?"

"It's the respectful thing to do."

"Did he give it?"

"After asking me some questions, yes, he did."

Rowan's hand jumped to cover her mouth. "Oh, thank God."

"My thoughts exactly."

Chapter Fifty-one

Over the six weeks, Rowan and Ben Skyped or Facetimed every day—not necessarily a long call, sometimes only ten minutes, but enough to connect and get to know each other more deeply.

Both Ben's mom and Colin accepted the invitation to the ranch.

"My wife isn't able to come," Colin told Carolina. "She's visiting an aunt in Chicago—it's her ninetieth birthday celebration—and taking our daughter for perhaps their last visit. I know Tiana, Ben's mom, of course. We're good friends. We've been in each other's lives for almost ten years now. I'd like to spend time with her; we don't get to very often."

The Friday came. Everyone was loaded in the van ready to head to the ranch when Rowan realized she'd forgotten her laptop. "Be right back," she hollered, and ran for the house.

Zephyr raised her head, ears pricked, and watched her go.

Minutes later, Row was back, computer in hand.

"All in?" Carolina called from the front.

"Present, and speaking for Graham, too," Teal answered. He tickled the baby, who joy-squealed in response.

"Three dogs present, tails safely in," Rowan said. "I'm here, too."

"I'm here and drivin'," Moss said. "And we're taking off now." He started the engine and pulled out of the driveway. "We packed the food, right?"

"Behind the back seat," Carolina said.

The family routine always feels so comforting, Rowan thought. We know where we are in relationship to each other.

Today didn't feel routine at all. They'd arrive in time for lunch. Ben was due midafternoon. Her heart fluttered at the thought of being together in person and introducing him to the ranch. She couldn't wait to hike to the top of the ridge together—probably for sunrise tomorrow. Sunset was out tonight because his mom and Colin were arriving later in the afternoon.

Seeing Colin in the same room with her parents would be exciting, and daunting. She wasn't concerned about her dad. After all, he'd expressed interest in attending a retreat. But her mom? A larger unknown. She'd made big changes, but Rowan didn't know how deeply to trust those yet.

She dozed, waking as the tires crunched on the gravel drive. The dogs were up on their feet, tails wagging, sniffing frosty air through window cracks. The moment she opened the slider, they took off, a pack of friendly racers jostling each other.

Graham came to, drooling and cranky, so Rowan grabbed him and flew him high like a little zooming airplane as she made her way toward the house. It always shifted his mood, and soon he was babbling again. She plopped him on the rug in the living room, signaled to her mom she was leaving him, and went back to get luggage, laptop, and dog supplies. Teal passed her, carrying a new forty-pound bag of kibble.

Moss and Carolina checked the rooms and the guest cottage, pulled out towel sets, and wiped down the bathrooms until they sparkled. Moss went to put a sign at the end of the driveway so, with his instructions and some luck, their guests could find the place.

At 3:10, Moss's 4Runner pulled in the driveway. Heart pounding, Rowan flew outside, the dogs trailing close behind. Her head buzzed and she couldn't control her wide smile. "You made it. Welcome to Bender's Ridge."

Ben slid out of the car.

She watched him tense and release his shoulders, stiff from the long drive. Then, beaming, he opened his arms. She flew into them and melted against him. *Home. I'm home.* "It's hard being apart this long," she whispered.

"It is. But maybe, just maybe, it makes the homecoming that much sweeter?" He nuzzled her neck, then lifted her chin and kissed her. "Is Mom here yet with my new car? Colin's driving separately so he can take Mom home."

The dogs were milling around him, vying for attention, their breath white in the cold air. He scratched their ears in turn, starting with Zephyr.

"They're coming around five. Your mom texted when she left Portland. Let me look at you." She cocked her head at him. "I think you seem better. Less stressed, maybe."

"Counseling helps. Clara's brilliant. I want to thank Moss first thing."

"Come in and say hi to the whole fam-damily."

He smiled. "Teal here?"

"Yeah. He's waiting for you, too. These three girls are happy to see you."

"It's mutual." He grabbed his bag, slung his other arm around her, and they went inside.

Moss and Carolina were busy in the kitchen, but wiped their hands to greet him.

"It looks like your arm's healed," Carolina said, holding her arms open.

"It has."

After embraces all around, Carolina pulled out a stool for him.

"Moss, Clara's fantastic. Thank you. I've made some headway."

"Great news. I'm happy for you."

"I have a check in my wallet for the sessions. And, let me help here, please," Ben said. "After all, it's my clan who's descending. Are we making what I requested?"

"Yep," Moss said. "Venison stew. Our go-to comfort food." He put him to work chopping vegetables.

Rowan fed the dogs, then pitched in alongside Ben.

A little over an hour later, Rowan heard gravel crackling. "Someone's here," she said. *Oh my God, I'm about to meet Ben's mom. What if she doesn't like me, or thinks I'm not right for her son?*

"It'll be fine," he said. "She's going to love you."

"Can you read my mind?" She stared up at him.

"Maybe. Come, take my hand. Walk proud."

Two cars had arrived. Rowan opened the front door and welcomed them in. *She's stunning.*

Ben gave his mother a warm hug first, then Colin. "Mom, this is Rowan."

Row found herself enveloped in a hug so similar to Ben's, it made her smile.

"Call me Tiana, please." Her voice was cultured and deep. Her skin glowed the same beautiful shade as Ben's. She was dressed for ranch life: jeans, flannel shirt, low boots.

When Moss walked into the room, Tiana glanced up. Rowan saw something go on behind her eyes, but she seemed to gather herself.

Row looked at Ben, and he was wide-eyed. He'd seen it, too. She could have sworn he'd said, "Something's up," but no words came out of his mouth. Did he pense her?

Mossy greeted Tiana and Colin warmly before introducing Carolina. "Dinner's almost ready. Would you like to wash up? Let me grab your bags and show you to your rooms. You'll be staying in the guest cottage next door."

"I've got to run out and see my new Subaru. I've named her 'Gracie,'" Ben said.

When Tiana and Colin came back to the living room, Carolina introduced Teal and Graham.

Ten minutes later, they sat down to an early dinner. The dogs lay in a row on the margin of the dining room, heads on paws.

"They're very well-behaved," Colin remarked.

"We only have a few rules," Rowan said. "Staying out of here while we eat is one of them. We feed them beforehand—it helps, too."

Moss served the stew; Carolina passed the steamed leeks and the bread.

"This is delicious," Tiana said. "A perfect winter meal."

They made small talk as they ate.

After stashing leftovers in the fridge, Carolina invited them into the living room.

Tiana cleared her throat. "Ben shared your tradition of family meetings," she said. "I'd like to call one." Her voice cracked at the end.

Carolina coughed. Ben sputtered. Everyone gawked.

Moss found his voice. "Of course," he said. "Let me make tea first." He went to the kitchen.

"Should I step out?" Colin asked. "I'm not family."

Tiana hesitated. "Please stay. We may need your skill."

Ben took Rowan's hand and they pressed close together on the couch. Teal played with Graham on the carpet.

They sat in uncomfortable silence waiting for Moss to come back. Only Colin seemed at ease.

After a few minutes, Moss brought in the tea tray with cookies on the side. He poured and passed the cups. "The floor is yours, Tiana."

She went to the window and peered into the dark. Carolina watched her opening and closing her hands, and could hear her blow out a slow breath. *She's awfully nervous. Could this be some kind of bombshell? She doesn't even know us.*

Graham began babbling, his tone getting louder and louder as though trying to fill the silence. Teal stood and jiggled him until he quieted.

Then Tiana sat down in the circle of chairs. Her face had gone a little gray. "First," she said, "I'd like to apologize. I had no idea until I got here that I'd need to request a family meeting. This is a bit of a show stopper. For me, too." She turned to Moss. "I assumed your last name was Graham. But is Ash Westbury your father? You look exactly like him, only younger."

"That's Rowan's last name. He's my dad, yes. You know him?"

"I did." She paused before speaking to her son. Her face took on the tenderest expression. Finally, she managed, "Ben." The word sounded almost apologetic. She reached out and cupped his cheek. "Moss is your half-brother."

Rowan choked and gripped Ben's fingers hard. "Oh no!"

Carolina put a hand on her daughter. Teal took Graham from her other arm.

Ben took a huge, surprised inhale. "What? How is it even possible?"

"Nineteen years ago, I had an affair with Ash during a one-week financial seminar in Phoenix. We were presenters. We agreed to not ask about the other's family, nor have any contact after. Six weeks later, I found out I was pregnant—at age forty-two, mind you. Lord knows how it happened; we used birth control." She squeezed Ben's hand. "You were meant to be here." She got up and paced. "I wasn't going to barge into Ash's life and ruin his family. I reinvented myself: closed my business, legally changed my first and last names—I'd always wanted to—and moved from the East Coast to Oregon." She sat again. "I completed a PhD in Economics while Ben was small. Lewis and Clark hired me and I've been there ever since. Ash knows me as Samantha Carruthers, not Tiana Singleton." She fell silent.

"How can you be sure Ben is Ash's son?" Carolina asked, frowning.

"Do you think I *wouldn't* know?" The firmness underlying Tiana's question felt like a challenge.

Rowan pensed Zephyr. *Is she hiding a bone?*

No bones, Zephyr pensed back. *Good human.*

"Let's take a collective breath together," Colin said. "Breathe in and out kindness. Our most important job here is to be open-hearted and truthful with each other." He waited until the assembled group followed his instruction before he went on. "Tiana, what can you share about Ash only someone who's been close to him could know?"

"It was nineteen years ago. Give me a minute." She walked to the window again before facing them. "Ash had appendicitis, but his scar's an unusual shape. They had to enlarge the incision because his appendix was swollen and about to explode, and they wanted to remove it intact."

"True," said Moss.

She hesitated, flushing a little. "And he has an Ohio-shaped birthmark on his left buttock."

"Bingo. Correct again." Moss said.

"Well." Carolina said. "I still think a DNA test is appropriate."

"Pa might want it," Moss responded. "Let's leave it up to him."

"Whoa," Ben said, his voice filled with emotion. "The truth has surfaced, and it's way stranger than fiction." He looked toward Moss who was already eyeballing him.

Rowan sobbed.

Carolina crouched in front of her. "Sweetheart," she said. "I know what you're thinking. Moss adopted you. You're not genetically related to Ben. There's no problem."

Her daughter raised her head. Moisture still clung to her lashes. "Even though they're b-brothers, we can be boy- and girlfriend?"

Carolina nodded. "Right."

"But it's weird."

"It is," her mom said, "but life is peppered with strange left turns."

Ben frowned at Colin. "Did you know this? Did you keep it from me?"

"Oh no. I'm as smoked as everyone else. I imagine Carolina's right; Ash might want proof. Tiana, are you ready to provide it?"

"Of course. We'll get it done whether Ash wants proof or not." She touched her son on the arm. "Your full name is Benjamin Westbury Singleton. I thought a nine-syllable name was a bit much, and I didn't want Westbury to be public, anyway. It's why there's an initial W for your middle name on the birth certificate."

"What the hell was Pa doing having an affair? It's not like him," Moss said, slowly. "It's shocking. I wonder if Ma knows."

"He promised me he'd tell her," Tiana said. "It was part of our agreement when we parted."

"I hope this doesn't tear our family apart. My God, I dread phoning him," Moss said.

"Not your job," Tiana said. "It's my responsibility to break the news." Her hands shook. "I'll need his contact information."

"Of course." He checked his watch. "They stay up late; you can call. But first," Moss turned to Carolina. "Hon, do we have a hand mirror?"

"I'll go get it."

Her mom came back quickly and handed it to Moss, who signaled for Ben to sit next to him. Colin moved over to make space. They peered in the glass together.

"I'll be damned," Moss said.

"Kinda hard to miss," Ben said. He traced a finger along Moss's chin line in the mirror, then his.

Eyes wide, they stared at each other.

"Oh my God, like another brother." Teal giggled. "Fantastic."

Rowan began to laugh. It took her a minute to control herself. "Ben's my uncle," she said, mopping her face. "Look at them. I knew his eyes were familiar the moment I met him. Other than the difference in skin color and hair texture, his features are a lot like Da and Pa. Look at their eyes—both the brilliant blue, and notice the shape. The truth was right in front of me, and I couldn't see it."

Moss threw an arm around Ben and gently knuckled his head. "Rowan told me you come from a small family. Welcome to this big crowd. You have two more half-siblings—Theo and Heather—plus cousins, nephews, and nieces. Ma's name is Alice; she'll love you. Tiana, welcome to you as well."

Chapter Fifty-two

Just before 7 p.m., Moss took Tiana into his office where she could have privacy for her phone call.

"Please stay," she said. "I'd like to put it on speaker and have you listen. Four ears are better than two. I have to make sure I've heard him correctly." She walked back and forth, fisting and unfisting her hands. "Okay. I have to do this." She unfolded the piece of paper Moss had given her with his father's mobile number, sat at the desk and tapped the buttons, then put her cell on speaker. When Ash picked up, she nearly dropped the phone. "Ash? This is Samantha Carruthers, from the Phoenix seminar nineteen years ago."

"Sam? It's you?"

Moss could hear both the astonishment and the uplift in his tone.

"It's me. But I changed my name to Tiana Singleton. I'm at Bender's Ridge with Moss, Carolina, and Rowan. Moss is here with me now. He's on speaker."

"What are you doing at Bender's Ridge? Moss, what's going on?"

"Hey, Pa."

"Wait … Singleton? There was a long pause before Ash spoke again. "Isn't that Rowan's boyfriend's last name? "

"Yes, Ben's my son."

Silence hung in the room. The wall clock tick-tick-ticked.

"How old is he?"

"Eighteen." She let the information sink in.

"Eighteen?" Another longer silence. "Sam—sorry, Tiana—he's our son? You never told me? What the hell?"

"We had an agreement, remember? I wasn't going to ruin your family. I *never* planned on telling you, but today, when I walked into Bender's Ridge to meet Rowan's family, and saw Moss … it's weird, the cliché that burst into my head was 'Houston, we have a problem.' Ben looks a lot like him. And you. He got the best of both of us."

"My God, what do I tell Alice? I have to meet him. You'll be there through the weekend?"

"Yes, we will."

"I'll call you back after I talk with her." The phone went dead.

Ash phoned a half hour later. Moss and Tiana went to the office where she put Ash on speaker again.

"As you can imagine, this is quite a shock for Alice. We're coming in the Lear, leaving at the crack of dawn. I was planning to come alone, but she insisted on traveling with me. We'll get there around 5 p.m. Moss, could you pick us up?"

"Of course."

"How'd it go with your wife?" Tiana asked. Her voice was apprehensive.

"Very, very hard. But she's strong. She'll be okay. It'll take time."

"I can trust you'll both be kind to Ben? I'm a protective mama lion."

"This is not Ben's fault. It's yours and mine. Of course we'll be thoughtful. Besides, Rowan apparently loves this young man; he must be special."

She scratched at a dried coffee drip on Moss's desk. "He's precious, and I don't think just because I'm his mom."

Moss stepped closer to the phone. "He's wonderful. A great addition to the family. You'll see. I'll pick you up tomorrow."

"Son, I suppose you're pretty upset with me. Do you have space for us? Otherwise, get a room in Sisters."

"You can have the guest house. I'm completely pissed, yes. Running around on Ma? How could you?"

"You have every right to be angry. We'll talk."

Rowan, Ben, and Colin sat by the fire after the others went to bed. Zephyr lay at Rowan's feet.

Ben leaned over, tapping his thumbs together between his knees.

"Mossy does the exact same thing." Rowan said.

"What thing?" Ben asked, glancing up.

"With his thumbs." She pointed to his hands. "When he's deep in thought."

"What are you thinking?" Colin asked Ben.

"It's weird to suddenly have an older brother," Ben said. "I miss Terence something awful. Moss can't replace him, but he is a mentor—he proved that when he drove me back to school last month." He stopped. "Row, I'm still hungry. I need a snack. Can you tell me where to look?"

"Cookies? Cheese and crackers? Tea? Come into the kitchen and I'll show you. It's time you learn where stuff is. Colin? Come with us."

"I'd like tea and a cookie, please," their teacher said.

"How about a bowl of the stew we had for dinner. And some toast," Ben said.

Zephyr followed them.

They talked while the stew heated. Rowan set a dish of cookies on the table by the window and heated tea water, and got a biscuit for Zeph, who held it between her front paws and crunched it.

"I don't know what having a brother is like since I don't have siblings," Ben said to Colin. "But more than a brother, I need Moss to be Rowan's dad, and a father figure for me as well."

"Will you tell him?" Colin asked.

Ben nodded. "At some point." He buttered the toast, took the stew from the microwave, and sat at the table. "I'm always hungry."

"You're tall, slender, and eighteen," Colin said.

"Of course you're ravenous. You have hollow legs," Rowan added.

"What a great expression," he said, spoon suspended in mid-air. "Where'd you hear it?"

"From Pa. My grandfather. Your bio-dad. I adore him."

"Oh." He gulped. "I'll be meeting him, won't I."

"Yes," Colin said. "Remember, he didn't know about you. If he had, I bet he'd have been in your life. Ash raised Moss, and you've experienced how special *he* is. I hope you'll give your father a chance."

"I can't believe Mom never told me. She should have. It' took a lot of courage to call him."

"Her consequences," Colin said, softly, "for the choices she made. No judgment, simply a fact."

"You're right. Okay, then. I'll be curious to see how this unfolds."

"Exactly." Colin smiled.

"I have a question," Rowan said. "Different topic. It stems from a conversation Ben and I had."

"Tell me," Colin said.

"Your daughter. Who mainly raised her? You or your wife?"

"It was pretty equal. Obviously, when I held a retreat, Alexandra took care of Skylar. Outside of the four retreats a year, I was with her more of the time. Before she was born, we talked about this."

"Huh." Rowan sat back down and took a bite of cookie.

"Do you want to tell me why you asked?"

She flushed. "I saw Ben playing with my baby brother. He clearly loves kids. In most families, parenting falls to the mom. He suggested we ask you about your experience." She shot Ben a glance.

Colin watched them both carefully. "I suggest you remain wholly in the present on this one. Let the future unfold as it will. Either of you might switch positions more than once."

"My mom said the same thing," Rowan said.

"Don't underestimate her. She's smart."

"I know, but for years, she's been negative about my interest in the unseen. Resistant, dismissive, even. Recently, she seems to be changing. I don't know if I can trust it."

Colin asked more questions and Rowan told him about her mom's painful teasing in high school.

"I bet," he said, "your mother is much more like your grandmother and you than she lets on. Hold true to your understanding. Keep the channels open. She'll come around. Maybe, one day, we can get her to a retreat." He stood up. "I'm headed to bed. Tomorrow's going to be a big day."

Later the next afternoon, leaving for the airport, Moss bid family and guests goodbye. "I should be back in under an hour and a half," he said.

He had plenty of time to think on the way, and tried every possible scenario. He put himself in his dad's shoes, wondering if he could ever cheat on Carolina. He didn't think so. Besides, she'd boot him out on his butt. But, by the time Pa had the affair with Tiana, his mom and dad had three children and twenty-five years together. A lengthy marriage would be hard to throw away. We kids were out of the house; we hadn't been privy to the fallout.

Was everyone allowed a transgression of this magnitude? Boy, he'd have loved to be a bug on the wall when Pa told Ma what happened in Phoenix. Did she rail? Scream? Stalk out in a chilly fit? Kick him out of the bedroom?

Limping into the Redmond airport, his gut got tight. Shit, I'm nervous, he thought. But why? I didn't do anything wrong. Maybe I'm anticipating Pa's nerves.

When he saw them walk through the lobby doors, he went directly to his mom and hugged her. "Are you coping all right?" he asked.

She hugged him back. "It wasn't as hard as your pa telling me he'd had the affair. This did bring it all back, though."

He gave her a kiss on the cheek. "It's a form of PTSD, Ma. It returns during stressful times." He turned to his father. "Well. Hi, Pa. Here we are."

"Please don't lay it on too hard, Moss. Trust me, I'm paying for this in myriad ways."

"As you should."

"Harsh," Alice said. "What's done is done. This isn't anything new—Ben's been around a long time. We just didn't know."

"You're wonderfully practical. Pa shouldn't have run around on you." Moss grabbed his mom's carry-on, and they made their way to the van. "Mom, sit up front with me?"

"Stop it," Alice snapped. "We're not forming a camp against your father. This is hard enough. Please don't make it tougher. Ash, sit up front with Moss."

They barely exchanged words driving back to Bender's Ridge. Moss stared at the road and considered his actions. "Sorry, Pa," he said, when he parked on the circle.

"Ash," Alice said. Her voice quivered. "Please go in and greet Tiana without me. You can hug her or whatever you choose after nineteen years. I'd like to meet her before the kids join us. I want to be with you when you meet Ben, though. Moss, can you go in and orchestrate moving people around?"

"I will, but I'm coming back out to sit with you. You won't be alone more than a minute."

"Thanks."

Moss unloaded the suitcases. Ash rolled one and he took the other. "Wait outside for a minute, Pa. Let me make sure the kids aren't in the family areas."

His father nodded and stopped before the deck stairs.

Moss took both bags, went in, and told everyone Alice's wishes. Exchanging glances, Ben, Rowan, Teal, and Colin retreated to the library with the dogs.

Carolina took Graham to the kitchen to work on dinner, closing the glass door behind her. She wouldn't be able to hear, but she might be able to catch a glimpse of Ash and Tiana meeting after all this time. She knew it was nosy, but couldn't shut down her desire. She set the baby in his high chair and gave him frozen peas to gum.

Tiana, trembling, stood in the living room.

Through the window, Carolina watched Moss limp out, give his father a curt nod, and head to the car to sit with his mother. She saw Moss say something to Ash, couldn't hear it, but did catch Ash's reply when he called out, "I'll come get her."

Squaring his shoulders, Ash strode into the house. Once he was inside, she saw him reach his hands out to take Tiana's. He didn't hug her, but they stood holding each other's hands for a long moment. Tiana was crying. She saw Ash shake, too. Their mouths were moving, but she'd been right, she couldn't hear a thing. Probably best.

They sat on the couch for a couple of minutes. She could only see the backs of their heads. Suddenly, they stood, and Ash rested a hand on Tiana's cheek. His face held a question—maybe, "Are you ready?" before he moved toward the door. They'd had all of three minutes of privacy.

When Ash went back outside, Carolina slipped into the living room and opened her arms to Tiana.

"Oh my gosh, thank you. I need a hug. I know I won't get one from Alice. I don't deserve it."

"Maybe not, but don't underestimate her. She's a powerful woman."

Moss watched his father approach the car. Ash helped Alice out, then he wrapped his arms around her. "You're my dearest love, sweetheart. I'm so sorry I've put you through this. Come on, Moss, let's go in and support Alice meeting Tiana. Your ma's one courageous woman." The three walked to the house together.

Carolina stepped back as the door opened. She started for the kitchen, but Moss signaled for her to stay.

"Sweetheart," Ash said, "I'd like you to meet Tiana Singleton, Ben's mom. Tiana, this is Alice."

Alice shrugged off Ash's touch and stepped forward, holding out her hands. "Tiana."

Tiana took them. "I'm very sorry for how I've hurt you. I assumed we'd never cross paths, but I'm grateful for the opportunity to apologize, and for you to meet my son."

"I appreciate it. Thank you. Now, where's this young man Rowan's so crazy about?"

"Shall I get the rest of the crew?" Moss asked.

Alice and Ash nodded.

"Please make sure Colin comes as well," Tiana said. "He's insightful."

Graham wailed.

"Oh my, I left him in the high chair." Carolina dashed into the kitchen, lifted him, and hugged him close. Not wanting to miss seeing Pa and Ma's first reaction to Ben, she slipped back into the living room with Graham on her hip.

Moss came back with the rest of the family. Ben walked to his mother's side, casting curious glances at the new elders in the room.

"Ash and Alice," Tiana said, "this is Ben. Ben, your father and his wife."

Alice's hands jumped to her mouth. "My God, Ash. Ben looks a lot like you. He's a Westbury, through and through."

"My past comes to greet me," Ash said, softly. "Hi, Ben. If I'd known you existed, I'd have been in your life from the start."

"I'm glad to meet now," Ben said. "What do I call you?"

"You have a choice. Ash or Pa, like all my kids and grandkids."

Rowan stood at the side, where she could see Ben and Ash clearly. He met his father's gaze with the same clarity Rowan recalled the moment after they collided at the retreat—a penetrating glance which took in character.

Ash's eyes widened in response.

"I guess I should call you Ash until the DNA tests are complete. Given the results we anticipate, I'll call you 'Pa' then. And you, 'Ma,' if you don't mind," Ben said to Alice, "and if my mom doesn't object."

"It's fine," Tiana said.

"I'd love it," Alice responded.

"Do you hug?" Ben asked his father. "I hope so, because I do, a lot."

"You bet."

The young man walked into his father's embrace. Rowan saw how Ben melted into the hug. He shook a little.

Zephyr moaned softly.

What is it? Rowan pensed.

Zephyr feels love. Sad, too.

Wow, Rowan thought. Her communication has gotten much subtler over the last six months. *Yes, sweet dog, they're feeling both.*

Ash put his hands on Ben's shoulders. "I'm so grateful I lived long enough to meet you."

"Me, too," Ben whispered. He turned to Alice.

She opened her arms to him. After they hugged, she cupped his face. "Welcome to the family, Ben. We're an affectionate crowd. You have two other siblings, Theo and Heather. You'll meet them soon enough. I hope you'll grow to love us all."

After letting Ben go, Alice said, "Now. I'd like one of those famous family meetings. I need to clear the air. Before dinner. Everyone."

Exchanging covert glances, and responding to the grit in her tone, they settled in the living room. Zephyr, Jazz, and Salaam found spaces on the floor since the couches and chairs were filled.

"Ash, I'm outraged with you and Tiana," she said. "Not because of my pain—sure, I've been hurt and jealous—but because of the real injury to Ben. Your little agreement to never be in contact neglected to take into account that any time people are sexually intimate, a child can be conceived. Ben was denied a relationship with his father from birth because of it."

"I did okay." Ben shrugged. "I had Mom, Uncle Terence, and Colin."

Alice said, "Can you honestly say you never wondered why your biological father wasn't in the picture? Didn't step up? Did you not feel unseen, left out, or rejected?"

Ben knit his forehead, considering her question. "You're right. I did. In fact, I've talked to Colin about it more than once. Uncle Terence, too."

Colin cleared his throat. "He was quite upset. The worst came around age eleven, when he started middle school. He needed his dad."

"There's the hurt and harm," Alice said. "I hope Ash and Tiana will take the time to apologize to you." She huffed out a breath. "Okay. Enough said. Now, let's eat dinner and open our hearts to this new maxi-family. I want to hold Graham again. He's changed so much since I saw him." She smiled, and reached for the baby. "In the morning, let's walk out to the graveyard so we can introduce our guests to Andrea. I still feel her little presence."

The next morning, Zephyr meanders alongside her girl and Colin, who talk while they stroll along the path. The rest of the pack follows. She knows where they are going—to where Andrea Pup stays. When they get to the place of stones, she moves forward, finds Andrea Pup's small mound, and lies down, curling around the dome of it, head between paws.

Zephyr misses Andrea Pup, she penses her girl.

I know. The whole pack does. Look, someone put a pot of blooming crocuses on her headstone. I wonder who planted them. Pack Mama?

No, Kibble Man. Zephyr and Jazz come when he brings flowers.

Moss stood alongside Rowan.

"Da, you brought the crocuses?"

"I did. The bulbs we all planted won't bloom for a couple of months, and I didn't want her to be without beauty. How did you know it was me?"

"Zephy told me she came with you."

"Zephyr told you?" Colin's eyebrows shot up. "Sorry, I overheard."

"We communicate. I discovered we both rest in the big field, and we meet there."

"Och! Amazing."

"What's 'och'?"

"Surprise. Tell me more sometime, okay?"

She nodded. Ben hooked his arm through Rowan's. "Sometimes his accent gets broader and Scottish expressions slip in."

"I love it," Rowan said. "How are you doing? It's been quite the time."

"It's strange, but I'm good. I like my father and step-mom. I appreciate having a decent-sized family—it felt pretty thin growing up. It'll take a while to get to know them."

"You and Teal are kind of in the same situation, gaining new family members. His adoption is final this spring. It's different because his family of origin was huge. He's the oldest of six kids."

Ben seemed puzzled. "If he has a family, why is he being adopted by your parents?"

"They legally disowned him."

"Because he's trans?"

She nodded. "They're very conservative."

He smacked his forehead. "Unbelievable. Unconscionable."

"Exactly what my mom said."

Everyone had made their way to the graveyard and stood around Zephyr and the mound. Moss and Carolina glanced at each other. She gave a little nod.

"For Colin, Tiana, and Ben, Andrea was Graham's twin," Moss said. "She was born with a severe heart defect and had other complications. We lost her in August at age two months."

"I'm deeply sorry." Colin knelt by the grave and rested a hand on Zephyr. "She misses Andrea."

"Yes," Rowan said. "Zephy was very connected to her—slept every night right by the crib. Dogs grieve, too."

"We all do," Teal said, patting Graham's butt in the front pack. "It's been five months, but it feels like yesterday."

Colin rose. "I think there's enough of us. We can surround the grave." He waited until the circle formed. Zephyr remained on the mound.

Ben took his father's hand. Rowan grabbed Ben's other one. Tiana held Colin's. Moss and Carolina stood on either side of Teal, Alice next to Carolina. Graham babbled.

"I'd like to offer a blessing. May I?" Colin looked first at Carolina, then Moss.

"Please," they said in unison.

"I know you find your daughter Andrea in your hearts where she's very alive, but remains two months old. Let's bless her lively presence and send her our love by blowing kisses. They'll help Zephyr, too."

Zeph lifted her head, attentive, as everyone followed Colin's request.

"Now let's bless her twin, Graham, in the same way. He doesn't have words yet, but he feels the loss, too."

Rather than blowing, Teal leaned over and kissed the top of his head.

"I want to add," Colin went on, "you have a remarkable family. You've been through a real shock this weekend, but each one of you showed the others gentleness and love. It's rare in this kind of situation."

They broke into little clumps and talked softly for a few minutes before heading back to the house. Alice walked with Colin; Carolina looped her arm through Tiana's. Ben said to Rowan, "I have so little time with my father. I'll catch you later."

She squeezed his arm. "Of course."

He caught up with Ash and fell in step.

Moss reached out for Graham and levered him up on his shoulders.

Rowan slipped her hand into Teal's.

"Sis," Teal said, love in his voice. "I'm so, so happy to have you as my sibling."

She smiled. "Me too, having two brothers. I know how Ben felt growing up an only child. We're all lonely no longer."

They swung their hands until they reached the ranch house.

Westbury Favorite Recipes

Brown Betty

Preheat oven to 350 degrees F.

Ingredients:
1 pack graham crackers, crushed
⅓ cup melted butter
5 cups peeled diced or sliced apples
½ cup packed brown sugar
1 teaspoon cinnamon
¼ teaspoon each nutmeg and cloves
¼ teaspoon salt
1 teaspoon grated lemon rind
1 teaspoon vanilla
1 tablespoon lemon juice
2 tablespoons water

2 tablespoons lemon juice
2 tablespoons water
¼ cup raisins (optional)

Instructions:
- Combine graham cracker crumbs and melted butter. Line the bottom of a baking dish with one-third of crumb mixture. This has enough butter so that no greasing is necessary.
- Sift together: brown sugar, cinnamon, nutmeg, cloves, salt.
- Add grated lemon rind and vanilla.
- Place half of the apples in the dish. Cover the layer with half the sugar mixture. Sprinkle with 1 tablespoon lemon juice. Add 2 tablespoons water.
- Cover the apples with ⅓ of the crumb mixture, and add raisins if you are including them. Add the remaining apples and sprinkle them as before with sugar mixture, remaining 2 tablespoons lemon juice, and 2 tablespoons water.
- Place the last third of crumb mixture on top.
- Cover, bake 40 minutes until apples are nearly tender.
- Uncover, increase heat to 400 degrees and let pudding brown for about 15 minutes.
- Serve hot with whipped cream or lemon sauce.

Kimchi

Ingredients:

1 medium head green cabbage, chopped coarsely
1-2 inch knob of ginger, peeled
6-8 cloves garlic, minced
1-2 fresh hot peppers, minced
1-2 carrots, finely chopped
1 medium daikon radish, finely chopped
½ large leek or ½ white onion, thinly sliced
1-2 tablespoons dried red chili powder or sambal oelek (purchase at an Asian store)
3 tablespoons unrefined sea salt

Instructions:

- In a large bowl, toss cabbage with two tablespoons of sea salt. This can sit up to six hours.
- In a small bowl, stir together ginger, garlic, peppers, and one tablespoon salt.
- In a larger bowl, stir together carrots, radish, and onions or leeks.
- Wearing gloves, toss the ginger/garlic/pepper mixture and sambal oelek into the vegetables.
- Pack into glass or ceramic fermentation jars and apply weight. (Plastic bag filled with water, smaller glass jars, boiled stones all can be used as weight.) DO NOT SEAL WITH LID. Put plate or tray under jars in case of overflow.
- Check after 6–12 hours to ensure brine has covered vegetables. If not, you may add non-chlorinated water to cover vegetables. (Chlorinated water can wreck fermentation process.)

Suggestions:

- The longer you allow the cabbage to sit with salt, the more liquid will be drawn from the cabbage. This way you don't damage the cabbage leaves by squishing.
- Traditional recipes use fish sauce or shrimp paste. If you add this, be sure there are no preservatives or dye.
- The longer the fermentation goes on, the more developed the sour taste will be.
- The peppers will be the spiciest in the first weeks but mellow over time. Allow 2-4 week fermentation between 60-70 degrees before packaging for the fridge for up to six months.
- Use organic ingredients to make sure the fermentation works properly.

This-and-That Chicken Soup

Preparation time: 30 minutes
Cooking time: 45 minutes
8 servings

Ingredients:
1 large onion, chopped
2 celery stalks, chopped
2 carrots, chopped
2 lbs naturally-raised skinless chicken thighs, cut up and fat removed
1 Delicata squash, deseeded and chopped, with skin left on
(or substitute sweet potato)
1 large or three small yellow beets, scrubbed and chopped
1 quart organic chicken stock, boxed is fine
2 cups water
½ red bell pepper, chopped
3 large cloves garlic, chopped
1½-2 inches fresh ginger, chopped
3 broad shakes of Mrs. Dash, any of the flavors
1 glug of inexpensive sherry
1 bunch kale or chard, coarsely chopped

Instructions:

- Sauté onion first until softened, add celery and carrots and sauté for 5 minutes.
- Add chicken, squash, and beets. Sauté for 10 minutes.
- Add the stock and rest of the ingredients except kale or chard.
- Bring to boil and turn down, simmer for about 30 minutes. Then add kale or chard to the soup. Simmer another 15 minutes.
- Top with grated Parmesan cheese, if that's a treat for you, and serve with seeded French bread.

Note: the sweetness of this soup comes from using winter squash and beet, *not* potato.

Venison Stew

A hearty stew you can make on your stove top. If venison seems too gamy, soak the meat in milk for two days in your refrigerator. Discard the milk.

Cooking time: 2 hours 30 minutes
8 servings

Ingredients:

1 (3 pounds) venison roast cut into 1½ inch cubes
Mrs. Dash, any flavor, to taste
3 tablespoons olive oil, divided
2 onions diced
2 stalks celery, finely chopped
2 cloves garlic, minced
3 tablespoons all-purpose flour
1 tablespoon tomato paste
1 cup dry red wine
2 cups chicken broth
5 sprigs fresh thyme or 1 teaspoon dried
2 bay leaves
1½ pounds potatoes, scrubbed and quartered
4 carrots, peeled and sliced
1 cup frozen peas

Instructions:

- Dry venison pieces with paper towel; season with salt and pepper.
- Heat 1 tablespoon oil in a large stockpot or Dutch oven over medium-high heat. Add half the meat in a single layer and cook until browned on one side, about 5 minutes. Flip each piece of venison and continue cooking until browned on the second side.
- Remove the first batch and set aside in a bowl. Adding more oil, repeat with remaining venison until browned. Transfer to bowl.
- Heat last tablespoon of oil. Add onion and celery and cook until softened, about 5 minutes. Stir in garlic until fragrant, about 30 seconds.
- Stir in flour and cook until lightly browned, about 2 minutes. Add tomato paste, wine, chicken broth, thyme, bay leaves, and browned venison, scraping up any browned bits on the bottom of the pan.
- Bring to a boil. Reduce heat, cover, and simmer for 1 hour.
- Stir in potatoes and carrots. Return to a boil, reduce heat, cover, and simmer 1 hour longer, until venison is tender. Remove bay leaves. Stir in peas and cover for 5 minutes. Season to taste.

Dark-Chocolate Bread Pudding

Total time: about 1 hour 40 minutes
Preheat oven to 325 degrees F.

Ingredients:
1 (1-pound) loaf French or Italian bread, cubed
3 cups milk
¼ cup heavy cream
1 cup sugar
1 cup packed light brown sugar
¼ cup natural cocoa powder
1 tablespoon vanilla extract
2 teaspoons almond extract
½ teaspoon cinnamon
6 eggs, lightly beaten
8 ounces semisweet chocolate, grated (or use melted dark chocolate drops)
whipped cream (optional)

Instructions:

- Lightly grease a 13 by 9-inch baking dish and place bread in the dish. In a large bowl, whisk together milk and cream.
- Using another bowl, combine sugar, brown sugar, and cocoa powder and mix well.
- Add sugar mixture to milk mixture and mix well.
- Add vanilla, almond extract, and cinnamon to the beaten eggs.
- Combine the egg mixture with milk mixture and mix well.
- Stir grated chocolate into the mixture and pour over cubed bread in pan.
- Let stand, stirring occasionally for approximately 20 minutes or until bread absorbs most of the milk mixture.
- Bake 1 hour or until set. Check pudding by inserting a knife through the middle: it should come out clean.
- Serve the pudding warm, or refrigerate and serve chilled with whipped cream if desired.

About the Author

Skye Blaine writes short essays, memoir, fiction, and poetry, developing themes of aging, coming of age, disability, and awakening. In 2003, she received an MFA in Creative Writing from Antioch University.

Bound to Love: a memoir of grit and gratitude, was published in 2015, and has won two first prizes and an IndieBRAG medallion. *Unleashed,* the first novel in the series, came out in 2017. It won an IndieBRAG medallion.

Skye has had memoir, fiction, and poetry published in eleven anthologies, and personal essays in national magazines: *In Context* (now known as *Yes!* magazine) and *Catalyst*. Other essays have been published in the *Register-Guard* newspaper, and the *Eugene Weekly*. She also presented radio essays on KRML 1410 AM in Carmel, CA.

Skye recently retired from teaching fiction and memoir in the Older Adults Program at Santa Rosa Junior College.

She can be reached at skye@skyeblaine.com, and welcomes comments.

Thank you for taking time to read *Must Like Dogs.* If you enjoyed it, please consider telling your friends and posting a review on Amazon and/or Goodreads. Word-of-mouth referrals are an author's best friend, and I appreciate them deeply.

Work on the third in the series is ongoing.

Colophon

This book is set in Minion Pro, 11.5 point.

Minion is a serif typeface designed by Robert Slimbach in 1990 for Adobe Systems and inspired by late Renaissance-era type.

...

As the name suggests, it is particularly intended as a font for body text in a classical style, neutral and practical while also slightly condensed to save space. Slimbach described the design as having "a simplified structure and moderate proportions." (Wikipedia)

Made in the USA
Middletown, DE
21 September 2020